USA Today bests[...] [...]e of romance was firs[...] [...]ora Roberts years a[...] [...]nly eighteen...ish. Pu[...] [...] her days writing sizzling romances with heart, a touch of humour and snark. She is wife to Superman – or his non-Kryptonian equivalent – and mother to the most awesome kids ever. They live in perfect, sometimes domestically-challenged bliss in the southern US.

Reese Ryan writes sexy, contemporary romance featuring a diverse cast of complex characters. She presents her characters with family and career drama, challenging love interests and life-changing secrets while treating readers to emotional love stories with unexpected twists. Past president of her local RWA chapter and a panelist at the 2017 Los Angeles Times Festival of Books, Reese is an advocate of the romance genre and diversity in fiction. Visit her online at ReeseRyan.com

Andrea Laurence is an award-winning contemporary author who has been a lover of books and writing stories since she learned to read. A dedicated West Coast girl transplanted into the Deep South, she's constantly trying to develop a taste for sweet tea and grits while caring for her boyfriend and her old bulldog. You can contact Andrea at her website: www.andrealaurence.com

Secrets and Seduction

Secrets and Seduction:
A Dangerous Bargain

NAIMA SIMONE

REESE RYAN

ANDREA LAURENCE

MILLS & BOON

First Published in Great Britain 2022
By Mills & Boon, an imprint of HarperCollins*Publishers,* Ltd
1 London Bridge Street, London, SE1 9GF

www.harpercollins.co.uk

HarperCollins*Publishers*
1st Floor, Watermarque Building,
Ringsend Road, Dublin 4, Ireland

SECRETS AND SEDUCTION: A DANGEROUS BARGAIN © 2022
Harlequin Books S.A.

The Billionaire's Bargain © 2019 Naima Simone
Savannah's Secrets © 2018 Roxanne Ravenel
From Seduction to Secrets © 2020 Andrea Laurence

ISBN: 978-0-263-30424-4

THE BILLIONAIRE'S BARGAIN

NAIMA SIMONE

To Gary. 143.

One

Delilah. Jezebel. Yoko. Monica.

According to past and recent history, they were all women who'd supposedly brought down a powerful man. Isobel Hughes silently snorted. Many of the people inside this North Shore mansion would include her name on that tarnished list.

Swallowing a sigh, she started up the stairs of the pillared mansion that wouldn't be out of place in the French countryside. Sitting on acres of meticulously landscaped grounds, the structure screamed decadence and obscene wealth. And though only a couple of hours' travel separated it from her tiny South Deering apartment, those minutes and miles might as well be years and states.

I can do this. I have no choice *but to do this.*

Quietly dragging in another deep breath, she paused as the tall, wide stained-glass doors opened to reveal an imposing gentleman dressed in black formal wear. His tuxedo might fit him perfectly, but Isobel didn't mistake him for who, or what, he was: security.

Security to protect the rarefied elite of Chicago high society and keep the riffraff out of the Du Sable City Gala.

Nerves tumbled and jostled inside her stomach like exes battling it out. Because she was a member of the riffraff who would be booted out on her common ass if she were discovered.

Fixing a polite but aloof mask on her face, she placed the expected invitation into the guard's outstretched hand as if it were a Golden Ticket. As he inspected the thick ivory paper with its gold engraved wording, she held her breath and resisted the urge to swipe her damp palms down the floor-length black gown she'd found at a consignment shop. Once upon a time, that invitation would've been authentic. But that had been when she'd been married to Gage Wells, golden child of the Wells family, one of Chicago's oldest and wealthiest lineages. When she'd believed Gage had been her handsome prince, the man who loved her as much as she'd adored him. Before she'd realized her prince was worse than a frog—he was a snake with a forked tongue.

She briefly closed her eyes. The present needed all of her focus. And with Gage dead these past two years and her exiled from the social circle she'd never belonged in, the present required that she resort to deception. Her brother's highly illegal skills were usually employed for forged IDs such as driver's licenses, birth certificates and passports for the city's more criminal element, not counterfeit invites to Chicago's balls. But he'd come through, and as the security guard scanned the invitation and waved a hand in front of him, she whispered a thanks to her brother.

The music that had sounded subdued outside seemed to fill the space here. Whimsical notes of flutes and powerful, bright chords of violins reverberated off the white marble walls. Gold tiles graced the floor, ebbing out in the shape

of a flowering lotus, and a huge crystal-and-gold chandelier suspended from the glass ceiling seemed to be a delicate waterfall over that bloom. Two sets of staircases with
gilded, intricate railings curved away from the walls and
ascended to the next level of the home.

And she was stalling. Ogling her surroundings only de-
layed the inevitable.

And the inevitable awaited her down the hall, where
music and chatter and laughter drifted. All too soon, she
approached the wide entrance to the ballroom, and the glass
doors opened wide in invitation.

But instead of feeling welcomed, nausea roiled and shuddered in her belly.

You can still turn around and leave. It's not too late.

The tiny whisper inside her head offered a lifeline she
desperately wanted to grasp.

But then an image of her son wavered across her mind's
eye, invoking an overwhelming swell of love. The thought
of Aiden never failed to grasp her heart and squeeze it. He
was a gift—*her* gift. And she would do anything—suffer
anything—for him.

Including seeking out her dead husband's family and
throwing her pride at the feet of the people who despised
her. She'd committed the cardinal sins of being poor and
falling for their golden child.

Well, she'd paid for that transgression. In spades.

Over the last couple of years, she'd reached out to her
husband's family through email and old-fashioned snail
mail, sending them pictures of Aiden, offering updates. But
every email bounced back, and every letter was returned to
the sender. They hadn't wanted anything to do with her or
with the beautiful boy they considered her bastard.

She wanted nothing more than to forget their existence,
just as they'd wiped hers out of their minds. But to keep a
roof over Aiden's head, to ensure he didn't have to shiver in

the increasingly chilly October nights or go to sleep hungry as she debated which overdue bill to pay, she would risk the wrath and derision of the Wells family.

The mental picture of her baby when she'd left him tonight—safe and happy with her mom—extinguished her flare of panic. Because it wouldn't do to enter these doors scared. The guests in this home would sense that weakness. And like sharks with bloody chum, they would circle and attack. Devour.

Inhaling yet another deep breath, she moved forward. Armored herself with pride. Ready to do battle.

Because she could never forget. This was indeed a battle. One she couldn't afford to lose.

Hell no. It can't be.

Darius King tightened his fingers on the champagne flute in his hand, the fragile stem in danger of snapping.

Shock and disbelief blasted him like the frigid winds of a Chicago winter storm, freezing him in place. Motionless, he stared at the petite brunette across the ballroom as she smiled at a waiter and accepted her own glass of wine. Though he'd only met her a couple of times, he recognized that smile. Remembered the shyness in it. Remembered the lush, sensual curve of the mouth that belied that hint of coy innocence.

Isobel fucking Hughes.

Not Wells. He refused to honor her with the last name she'd schemed and lied to win, then defiled for the two years she'd been married to his best friend. She didn't deserve to wear that name. Never had.

Rage roared through him, incinerating the astonishment that had paralyzed him. Only fury remained. Fury at her gall. Fury at the bold audacity it required to walk into this mansion as if she belonged here. As if she hadn't destroyed a man and dragged his grieving, ravaged family to the very brink of destruction.

"Oh, my God." Beside him, Gabriella Wells gasped, her fingers curling around his biceps and digging deep. "Is that…"

"Yes," Darius growled, unable to soften his tone for Gage's sister, whom he cared for as if she were his own sibling. "It's her."

"What is she doing here?" Gabriella snarled, the same anger that had gripped him darkening her lovely features. "How did she even manage to get in?"

"I have no idea."

But he'd find out. And asses would be kicked when he did. The security here was supposed to be tighter than that of the goddamn royal family's, considering the people in attendance: politicians, philanthropists, celebrities, the country's wealthiest business people. Yet evidence that the security team wasn't worth shit stood in this very room, sipping champagne.

"How could she dare show her face here? Hell, *in Chicago*?" Gabriella snapped. "I thought we were rid of her when she left for California. No doubt whatever sucker she attached herself to finally got tired of her and kicked the gold-digging bitch out. And she's probably here to suck Dad and Mother dry. I swear to God…" She didn't finish the thought, but charged forward, her intentions clear.

"No." He encircled her arm, his hold gentle but firm. Gabriella halted, shooting him a let-me-go-now-dammit glance over her shoulder. Fire lit the emerald gaze that reminded him so much of Gage's. At twenty-four, she was six years younger than her older brother, and had adored him. And though she'd been in college, studying abroad for most of her brother's marriage, tales of her sister-in-law had reached her all the way in England, and Gabriella despised the woman who'd hurt Gage so badly.

Darius shook his head in reply to her unspoken demand of freedom. "No," he repeated. "We're not causing a scene. And running over there and confronting her will do just that. Think of your parents, Gabriella," he murmured.

The anger didn't bleed from her expression at the reminder, but concern banked the flames in her eyes to a simmer, and the thin, grim line of her mouth softened. Neither of them needed to voice the worry that Darius harbored. Gabriella and Gage's father, Baron Wells, had suffered a heart attack the previous year. Nothing could convince Darius that it hadn't been grief over his son's death in a sudden car accident that had precipitated the attack, added to long work hours, poor eating habits and a lax exercise regimen.

The last several months had finally seen the return of the imposing, dignified man Darius had known and admired all of his life. Still, a sense of fragility stubbornly clung to Baron. A fragility Darius feared could escalate into something more threatening if Baron glimpsed his dead son's widow.

"I'll go and find security so they can escort her out," he said, the calm in his voice a mockery of the rage damn near consuming him. "You can locate your parents to make sure they don't realize what's going on."

Yes, he'd have Isobel Hughes thrown out, but not before he had a few words with her. The deceitful, traitorous woman should've counted herself lucky that he hadn't come after her when she'd skipped town years ago. But with the Wells family shattered over their son and brother's death, they'd been his first priority. And as long as Isobel had remained gone, they didn't have to suffer a daily reminder of the woman who'd destroyed Gage with her manipulations and faithlessness. In spite of the need to mete out his own brand of justice, Darius had allowed her to disappear with the baby the Wells family doubted was their grandson and nephew. But now...

Now she'd reappeared, and all bets were off.

She'd thrown down the gauntlet, and fuck if he wouldn't enjoy snatching it up.

"Okay," Gabriella agreed, enclosing his hand in hers and squeezing. "Darius," she whispered. He tore his attention away from Isobel and transferred it to Gabriella. "Thank you for…" She swallowed. "Thank you," she breathed.

"No need for any of that," he replied, brushing a kiss over the top of her black curls. "Family. We always take care of one another."

She nodded, then turned and disappeared into the throng of people.

Anticipation hummed beneath his skin as he moved forward. Several people slowed his progress for meaningless chatter, but he didn't deter from his path. He tracked her, noting that she'd moved from just inside the entrance to one of the floor-to-ceiling glass doors that led to a balcony. Good. The only exit led out onto that balcony, and the temperature of the October night had probably dropped even more since he'd arrived. She wouldn't venture through those doors and into the cold. He had a location to give security.

It was unfair that a woman who possessed zero morals and conscience should exhibit none of it on her face or her body. But then, if her smooth, golden skin or slender-but-curvaceous body did reveal any of her true self, she wouldn't be able to snare men in her silken web.

Long, thick, dark brown hair that gleamed with hints of auburn fire under the chandelier's light flowed over one slim shoulder and a just-less-than-a-handful breast. Dispassionately, he scanned her petite frame. The strapless, floor-length black gown clung to her, lifting her full curves so a hint of shadowed cleavage teased, promised. A waist that a man—not him—could span with his hands flowed into rounded hips and a tight, worship-worthy ass that he didn't need to see to remember. Even when he'd first met her—as the only witness and friend at her and Gage's quickie court-house marriage—it'd amazed him how such a small woman could possess curves so dangerous they should come with a blaring warning sign. Back then he'd appreciated her curves. Now he despised them for what they truly were—an enticing lure to trap unsuspecting game.

Dragging his inspection up the siren call of her body, he took in the delicate bones that provided the structure for an almost elfin face. One of his guilty pleasures was fantasy novels and movies. Tolkien, Martin, Rowling, King. And he could easily imagine Arwen, half-Elven daughter of King Elrond in *The Lord of the Rings*, resembling Isobel. Beautiful. Ethereal. Though he couldn't catch the color of her eyes from this distance, he clearly recalled their striking color. A vivid and startling blue-gray that only enhanced the impression of otherworldly fragility. But then there was her mouth. It splintered her air of innocence. The shade-too-wide lips with their full, plump curves called to mind ragged, hoarse groans in the darkest part of night. Yeah, those lips could cause a man's cock to throb.

He ground his teeth together, the minute flare of pain along his jaw grounding him. It didn't ease the stab of guilt over the sudden, unexpected clench of lust in his gut. He could hate himself for that gut-punch of desire. Didn't he, more than anyone, know that a pretty face could hide the black, empty hole where a heart should be? Could conceal the blackest of souls? His own ex-wife had taught him that lesson, and he'd received straight fucking A's. Yeah, his dick might be slow on the uptake, but his head—the one that ruled him, contrary to popular opinion about men—possessed full disclosure and was fully aware.

Isobel Hughes was one of those pretty faces.

As if she'd overheard her name in his head, Isobel lifted her chin and surveyed the crowded ballroom. Probably searching for Baron and Helena. If she thought he'd allow her within breathing space of Gage's parents, she'd obviously been smoking too much of that legalized California weed. He'd do anything to protect them; he'd failed to protect Gage, and that knowledge gnawed at him, an open wound that hadn't healed in two years. No way in hell would this woman have another shot at the people he loved. At his family.

The thought propelled him forward. Time to end this and escort her back to whatever hole she'd crawled out of.

Clenching his jaw, he worked his way to the ballroom entrance. Several minutes later, he waited in one of the side hallways for the head of security. Glancing down at his watch, he frowned. The man should've arrived already...

Darkness.

Utter darkness.

Dimly, Darius caught the sound of startled cries and shouts, but the deafening pounding of his heart muted most of the fearful noise.

He stumbled backward, and his spine smacked the wall behind him. Barely able to draw a breath into his constricted lungs, he frantically patted his jacket and then his pants pockets for his cell phone. Nothing. *Damn.* He must've left it in the car. He never left his phone. Never...

The thick blackness surrounded him. Squeezed him so that he jerked at his bow tie, clawing at material that seconds ago had been perfectly comfortable.

Air.

He needed air.

But all he inhaled, all he swallowed, was more of the obsidian viscosity that clogged his nostrils, throat and chest.

In the space of seconds, his worst, most brutal nightmare had come to life.

He was trapped in the dark.

Alone.

And he was drowning in it.

Two

*B*lackout.
  Malfunction. Doors locked.
  Remain calm.
  The words shouted in anything but calm voices outside the bathroom door bombarded Isobel. Perched on the settee in the outer room of the ladies' restroom, she hunched over her cell phone, which had only 2 percent battery life left.
  "C'mon," she ordered her fingers to cooperate as she fumbled over the text keyboard. In her nerves, she kept misspelling words, and *damn autocorrect*, it kept "fixing" the words that were actually right. Finally she finished her message and hit send.

Mom, is everything okay? How is Aiden?

  Fingers clutching the little burner phone, she—not for the first time—wished she could afford a regular cell. But with her other responsibilities, that bill had been one of the first things she'd cut. Constantly buying minutes and battling a battery that didn't hold a charge presented a hassle, but the prepaid phone did the job. After seconds that seemed like hours, a message popped up on the screen.

He's fine, honey. Sleeping. We're all good. Stay put. It's a blackout and we've been advised to remain inside. I love you and take care of yourself.

Relief washed over Isobel in a deluge. If she hadn't already been sitting down, she would've sunk to the floor. For the first time since the world had plunged into darkness, she could breathe.

After several moments, she located the flashlight app and aimed it in the direction of where she believed the door to be. The deep blackness seemed to swallow up the light, but she spied the handle and sighed. Without ventilation, the area was growing stuffy. The hallway had to be better. At the very least, she wouldn't feel like the walls were closing in on her. Claustrophobia had never been a problem for her, but this was enough to have anyone on edge.

She grabbed the handle and pulled the door open, the weak beam illuminating the floor only feet in front of her. As soon as she stepped out into the hall, the light winked, then disappeared.

"No, not yet," she muttered, flipping the phone over. But, nope, the cell had died. "Dammit."

Frustration and not-a-little fear scrabbled up her chest, lodging there. Inhaling a deep breath and holding it, she forced herself to calm down. Okay. One thing her two years in Los Angeles had granted her was a sense of direction. The ballroom lay to the left. Follow the wall until it gave way to the small alcove and the side entrance she'd exited.

No problem. She could do this.

Probably.

Maybe.

Releasing that same gulp of air, she shuffled forward, hands groping until they knocked against the wall. Step one down.

With halting steps, she slid along, palms flattened, skimming. The adjacent corridor shouldn't be too far...

Her chest bumped into a solid object seconds after her hands collided with it. A person. A big person, if the width of the shoulders and chest under her fingers were anything to go by.

"Oh, God. I'm sorry." She snatched her arms back. Heat soared up her neck and poured into her face. She'd just felt up a man in the dark.

Horrified, she shifted backward, but her heel caught on the hem of her dress, and she pitched forward. Slamming against that same hard expanse of muscles she'd just molested. *"Dammit.* I—"

The second apology drifted away as a hoarse, ragged sound penetrated the darkness and reached her ears. For a long moment, she froze, her hands splayed wide over the stranger's chest. It rapidly rose and fell, the pace unnatural. She jerked her head up, staring into the space where his face should've been. But she didn't need to glimpse his features to understand this man suffered some kind of distress. Because those rough, serrated, *wounded* sounds originated from him.

The urge to comfort, to stop those god-awful moans overrode all embarrassment at having touched him without his permission. At this moment, she needed to touch him. To ease his pain.

As she slid one palm over his jackhammering heart, she swept the other over his shoulder and down his arm until she enclosed his long fingers in hers. Then she murmured, "Hi. Talk about an awkward meet cute, right? Citywide blackout. Get felt up in the hallway. Sounds like the beginning of a rom-com starring Ryan Reynolds."

The man didn't reply, and his breathing continued to sough out of his lungs, but his fingers curled around hers, clutching them tight. As if she were his lifeline.

Relief and determination to tow him away from whatever tormented him swelled within her. It didn't require a PhD in psychology to figure out that this man was in the throes of a panic attack. But she had zero experience with how to handle that situation. Still, he'd responded to her voice, her presence. So she'd continue talking.

"Do you know who Ryan Reynolds is?" She didn't wait for his answer but kept babbling. "*The Green Lantern*? *Deadpool*? I'm leading with those movies, because if you're anything like my brother, if I'd have said *The Proposal*, you would've stared at me like I'd suddenly started speaking Mandarin. Well…that is, if you *could* stare at me right now." She snickered. "What I wouldn't give for Riddick's eyes right now. To be able to see in the dark? Although you could keep Slam City and, ya know, the murder. Have you ever seen *Pitch Black* or *The Chronicles of Riddick*?"

This time she received a squeeze of her fingers and a slight change in the coarseness of his breathing. A grin curved her lips. Good. That had to be a positive sign, right?

"*The Chronicles of Riddick*? I enjoyed watching Vin Diesel for two hours, but the movie? Meh. *Pitch Black*, though, was amazing. One of the best sci-fi movies ever. Only beat out by *Aliens* and *The Matrix*. Although I still maintain that *The Matrix Revolutions* never happened, just as *Dirty Dancing 2* is a dirty rumor. They're like Voldemort. Those Movies That Shall Not Be Named."

A soft, shaky chuckle drifted above her, but seemed to echo in the dark, empty hallway like a sonic boom. Probably because she'd been aching to hear it. Not that she'd been aware of that need until this moment.

An answering laugh bubbled up inside her, but she shoved it back down, opting to continue with what had been working so far. Talking. The irony that this was the longest conversation she'd indulged in with a person outside of her family in two years wasn't lost on her. Cruel experience had taught her to be wary of strangers, especially those with pretty faces wielding charm like a Highlander's claymore. The last time she'd trusted a beautiful appearance, she'd ended up in a loveless, controlling, soul-stealing sham of a marriage.

But in the dark...

In the dark lived a kind of freedom where she could lose her usual restrictions, step out of the protective box she'd created for her life. Because here, she couldn't see this man, and he couldn't see her. There was no judgment. If he were attending the Du Sable City Gala, then that meant he most likely came from wealth—the kind of wealth that had once trapped her in a gilded prison. Yet in this corridor in the middle of a blackout, money, status, lineage traced back to the Mayflower—none of that mattered. Here, they were only two people holding on to each other to make it through.

"My next favorite sci-fi is *Avatar*. Which is kind of funny, considering the famous line from the movie is 'I see you.'" She couldn't smother her laughter. And didn't regret the display of amusement when it garnered another squeeze of her hand. "Do you have a favorite?"

She held her breath, waiting. Part of her waited to see if his panic attack had finally passed. But the other part of her wanted—no, *needed*—to hear his voice. That part wondered if it would match his build.

Being tucked away in a mansion's dark hallway in a blackout...the insane circumstances had to be the cause of her desire. Because it'd been years since she'd been curious about anything regarding a man.

"The Terminator."

Oh. Wow. That voice. Darker than the obsidian blanket that draped the city. Deeper than the depths of the ocean she sorely missed. Sin wrapped in the velvet embrace of sweet promise.

A dangerous voice.

One that invited a person to commit acts that might shame them in the light of day, acts a person would revel in during the secretive, shadowed hours of night.

Her eyes fluttered closed, and her lips parted, as if she could breathe in that slightly abraded yet smooth tone. As if she could taste it.

As if she could taste him.

What the hell?

The inane thought rebounded against the walls of her skull, and she couldn't evict it. Her eyes flew open, and she stared wide into nothing. For the second time that evening, she thanked God. At this moment, she offered her gratitude because she couldn't be seen. That no one had witnessed her unprecedented, humiliating reaction to a man's *voice.*

"A classic." She struggled to recapture and keep hold of the light, teasing note she'd employed with him BTV. Before The Voice. "But I take your *Terminator* and one-up you with *Predator.*"

A scoff. "That wasn't sci-fi."

Isobel frowned even though he couldn't see her disapproval. "Are you kidding me?" She dropped her hand from his chest and jammed it on her hip. "Hello? There was a big-ass alien in it. How is that not sci-fi?"

A snort this time. "It's horror. Using your logic would mean *Avatar* was a romance."

Okay, so this guy might have the voice of a fallen angel tempting her to sin, but his movie knowledge sucked.

"I think I liked you better when you weren't talking," she grumbled.

She was rewarded with a loud bark of laughter that did the impossible. Made his voice even sexier. Desire slid through her veins in a slow, heady glide.

She stiffened. No. Impossible. It'd been years since she'd felt even the slightest flicker of this thing that heated her from the inside out.

If she harbored even the tiniest shred of common sense, she'd back away from this man now and blindman's bluff it until she placed some much needed distance between them. Desire had once fooled her into falling in love. And falling in love had led to a heartbreaking betrayal she was still recovering from.

No, she should make sure he was okay, then leave. With moving back to Chicago, raising her son as a single mother and working a full-time job, she didn't have the time or inclination for something as mercurial as desire.

You're sitting here in the dark with him, not dating him. One night. Just one night.

She sighed.

And stayed.

"Is something wrong?" A large hand settled on her shoulder and cupped it. She gritted her teeth, refusing to lean into that gentle but firm hold.

"Nothing. Just these shoes," she lied, bending and slipping off one and then the other to validate the fib. "They're beautiful, but hell on the feet."

He released another of those soft chuckles that sent her belly into a series of tumbles.

"What's your name?" His thumb stroked a lazy back-and-forth caress over her bare skin, and she sank her teeth into her bottom lip. Heat radiated from his touch. Until this moment, she hadn't known her shoulder was an erogenous zone. Funny the things she was finding out in the dark.

What had he asked? Right. Her name.

Alarm and dread filtered into her pleasure, tainting it.

Gage had done a damn good job of demonizing her to his family, and then his family had made sure everyone with a willing ear and flapping gums knew Isobel as a lying, greedy whore. It'd been two years since she'd left Chicago, but the insular ranks of high society never forgot names when it came to scandals.

Again, she squeezed her eyes shut as if she could block out the scorn and derision that had once flayed her soul. She still yearned to be known as more than the cheap little gold digger people believed her to be.

"Why do you want my name?" she finally replied.

A short, but weighty pause. "Because I need to know who to thank," he murmured. "And considering we've known each other all of ten minutes, 'sweetheart' seems a little forward."

"I don't mind 'sweetheart,'" she blurted out. His grasp on her shoulder tightened, and a swirl of need pooled low in her belly. "What I mean is we don't need names here. In the dark, we can be other people, different people, and I like the idea of that."

The bit of deception plucked at her conscience. Because she had no doubt that if he was familiar with her name, he would want nothing to do with her. And selfish though it might be, she'd rather him believe she was some coy debutante than the notorious Widow Wells.

That large hand slid over her shoulder, up her neck and cradled the back of her head. A sigh escaped her before she could contain it.

"Are you hiding, sweetheart?" he rumbled.

The question could have sounded inane since it seemed like the whole city was hunkered down, cloaked in darkness. But she understood what he asked. And the lack of light made it easier to be honest. At least in this.

"Yes," she breathed, and braced herself for his possible rejection.

"You're stiffening again." The hand surrounding hers squeezed lightly, a gesture of comfort. "Don't worry, your secrets are as safe with me as you are." He paused, his fingertips pressing into her scalp. "Just as I am with you."

Oh, God. That...vulnerable admission had no business burrowing beneath skin and bone to her heart. But it did.

"Keep your name, but, sweetheart—" he heaved a heavy sigh, and for an all-too-brief moment he pressed his forehead to hers "—thank you."

"I..." She swallowed, a shiver dancing down her spine. Whether in delight or warning, she couldn't tell. Probably both. "You're welcome. Anyone would've done the same," she whispered.

Something sharp edged through his low chuckle. "That's where you're wrong. Most people would've kept going, only concerned with themselves. Or they would've taken advantage."

She didn't answer; she wanted to refute him but couldn't. Because the sad fact was, he'd spoken the truth. Once she'd been a naïve twenty-year-old who'd believed in the good in people, in the happily-ever-after peddled by fairy tales. Gage had been her drug. And the withdrawal from him had nearly crushed her into the piece of nothing he'd constantly told her she was without him.

Shaking her head to get him out of her mind, she bent down and swept her hands along the floor, seeking the purse she'd dropped. Her fingertips bumped the beaded clutch, and with a small sound of victory, she popped it open and withdrew the snack bar she'd stashed there before leaving her apartment. With a two-year-old, keeping snacks on hand was a case of survival. And though her son hadn't joined her at the gala, she'd tossed the snack in out of habit. Now she patted herself on the back for her foresight.

Unbidden, a smile curved her lips. If Aiden could see

her, he would be holding out his chubby little hand, demanding his "eats."

She pinched the bridge of her nose, battling back the sting in her eyes. Obtaining help for her son had driven her to this mansion, and she'd failed. It would be easy to blame the blackout for her not locating and approaching the Wellses. But she couldn't deny the truth. She'd left the ballroom and headed to the restroom to convince herself not to leave. The plunge of the city into darkness had snatched the decision out of her hands, granting her a convenient reprieve from facing down the people who'd made it their lives' purpose to ensure she understood just how unworthy and hated she was.

But it was only that—a reprieve. Because when it came down to a choice between her pride and providing a stable environment for her son, there wasn't a choice.

When the blackout ended, she still had to face the Wellses.

"Did I lose you?" His softly rumbled question drew her from her desperate thoughts.

Clearing her throat, she settled on the floor, tucking her legs under her. She tugged on the hem of his pants, and he accepted her silent invitation, sinking down beside her. When the thick muscles of his leg brushed her knee, she reached out and skated a palm down his arm until she located his hand. She pressed half the cereal bar into it.

"What is this?" His low roll of rich laughter slid over her skin, and she involuntarily tightened her grip on her half.

"Dinner." Isobel bit into the snack and hummed. The oats, almonds and chocolate weren't caviar and toast points, but they did the job in a pinch. And this situation definitely qualified as a pinch.

"I have to say this is a first," he murmured, amusement still warming his voice.

God, she liked it. A lot. No matter how foolish that feeling might be.

"So, you don't want to share your name," he continued. "And I'll respect that. But since I'm sharing a cereal bar with you, I feel like I should know more about you besides your predilection for sci-fi movies. Tell me something about you."

She didn't immediately reply, instead nibbling on her snack while she figured out how to dodge his request. She didn't want to give him any details that might assist him in figuring out her identity. But another nebulous reason, one that she felt silly for even thinking, flitted through her head.

Giving him details about herself…pieces of herself… meant she couldn't get them back.

And she feared that. Had been taught to fear that.

Yet…

She bowed her head, silently cursing herself. What was it about this man? She'd never seen his face, didn't know his name. And still, he called to her in a way that electrified her. If she'd learned anything from the past, she would shield herself.

"I'm a grudge-holder," she said, the words escaping. *Damn it.* "I'll never let my brother off the hook for burning my Christmas Barbie's hair to the scalp when I was seven. I still give Elaine Lanier side-eye, whenever I see her, for making out with my boyfriend in the eleventh grade. And I will never, ever forgive Will Smith for *Wild, Wild West.*"

A loud bark of laughter echoed between them, and she grinned. The sound warmed her like the sun's beams.

She tapped his leg. A mistake on her part. As she settled her hand back in her lap, she could still feel the strength of his muscle against her fingertips. Good God. The man was *hard.* She rubbed her fingertips against her leg as if she could erase the sensation. "Now your turn," she said, forcing a teasing note into her voice. "Tell me something about yourself."

He hesitated, and for a moment, she didn't think he would answer, but then he shifted beside her, and his thigh pressed closer, harder against her knee. Her breath snagged in her throat. Heat pulsed through her from that point of contact, and she savored it. For the first time in years, she... embraced it.

"I love to fish," he finally murmured. "Not deep sea or competitive fishing. Just sitting on a dock with a rod, barefoot, sun beating down on you, surrounded by quiet. Interrupted only by the gently lapping water. We would vacation at our summer home in Hilton Head, and my father and I would spend hours at the lake and dock behind the house. We'd talk or just enjoy the silence and each other. We even caught fish sometimes."

His low chuckle contained humor, but also a hint of sadness. Her heart clenched at the possible reason why.

"Those were some of my best memories, and I still try to visit Hilton Head at least once a year, although I haven't been in the last two..."

His voice trailed off, and unable to resist, she reached out, found his hand and wrapped her fingers around his, squeezing. Her heart thumped against her chest when his fingers tightened in response.

"I have the hugest crush on Dr. Phil. He's so sexy."

He snorted. "I cook the best eggplant parmesan you'll ever taste in your life. It's an existential experience."

Isobel snickered. "I can write with my toes. I can also eat, brush my teeth and play 'Heart and Soul' on the piano with them."

A beat of silence passed between them. "You do know I recognize that's from *The Breakfast Club*, right?"

Laughter burst from her, and she fell back against the wall, clutching her stomach. Wow. She hadn't laughed this hard or this much in so long. It was…freeing. And felt so damn good. Until this moment, she hadn't realized how much she'd missed it.

At twenty, she'd met Gage, and within months, they'd married. She'd gone from being a college student who worked part-time to help pay her tuition to the wife of one of Chicago's wealthiest men. His family had disapproved of their marriage and threatened to cut him off. Initially, Gage hadn't seemed to care. They'd lived in a small one-bedroom apartment in the Ukrainian Village neighborhood of Chicago, and they'd been happy. Or at least she'd believed they had been.

Months into their marriage, the charming, affectionate man she'd wed had morphed into a spoiled, emotionally abusive man-child. Not until it'd been too late had she discovered that his fear of being without his family's money and acceptance had trumped any love he'd harbored for Isobel. Her life had become a living hell.

So the last time she'd laughed like this had been those first four months of her marriage.

A failed relationship, tarnished dreams, battered self-confidence and single motherhood had stolen the carefree from her life, but here, stuck in a mansion with a faceless man, she'd found it again. Even if only for an instant.

"Hey." Masculine fingers glanced over her knee. "You still with me?"

"Yes," she said, shaking her head. "I'm still here."

"Good." His hand dropped away, and she missed it. Insane, she knew. But she did. "It's your turn. Because you phoned it in with the last one."

"So, we're *really* not going to talk about how you know the dialogue to *The Breakfast Club*?" she drawled.

"Yes, we're going to ignore it. Your turn."

After chuckling at the emphatic reply, she continued, "Fine. Okay, I…"

Seconds, minutes or hours had passed—she couldn't tell in this slice of time that seemed to exist outside of reality. They could've been on another plane, where his delicious scent provided air, and his deep, melodic voice wrapped around her, a phantom embrace.

And his touch? His touch was gravity, anchoring him to her, and her to him. In some manner—fingers enclosing hers, a thigh pressed to hers, a palm cupping the nape of her neck—he never ceased touching her. Logic reasoned that he needed that lodestone in the blackness so he didn't surrender to another panic attack.

Yet the heated sweetness that slid through her veins belied reason. No, he wanted to touch her…and, God, did she want to be touched.

She'd convinced herself that she didn't need desire anymore. Didn't need the melting pleasure, the hot press of skin to skin, of limbs tangling, bodies straining together toward that perfect tumble over the edge into the abyss.

Yes, she missed all of it.

But in the end, those moments weren't worth the disillusionment and loneliness that inevitably followed.

Here, though, with this man she didn't know, she basked in the return of the need, of the sweet ache that sensitized and pebbled her skin, and teased places that had lain dormant for too long. Her nipples furled into tight points, pressing against her strapless bra and gown. Sinuous flames licked at her belly…and lower.

God, she was hungry.

"You've gone quiet on me again, sweetheart," he murmured, sweeping a caress over the back of her hand that he clasped in his. "Talk to me. I need to hear your beautiful voice."

Did he touch all women this easily? Was he always this affectionate? Or was it the darkness? Did he feel freer, too? Without the accountability of propriety?

Or is it me?

As soon as the traitorous and utterly foolish thought whispered through her head, she banished it. Yes, these were extraordinary circumstances, and she was grabbing this slice in time for herself, but never could she forget who she was. Because this man might not know her identity, but he still believed her to be someone she absolutely wasn't—wealthy, a socialite...a woman who belonged.

"Sweetheart?"

That endearment. She shivered. It ignited a curl of heat in her chest. It loosed a razor-tipped arrow at the same target. No one had ever called her "sweetheart." Or "baby" or any of those personal endearments. Gage used to call her Belle, shortening her name and because he'd met her in her regular haunt, the University of Illinois's library, like a modern-day version of the heroine from *Beauty and the Beast*. Later, the affectionate nickname had become a taunt, a criticism of her unsophisticated and naïve nature.

She hated that name now.

But every time this man called her sweetheart, she felt cherished, wanted. Even though it was also a stark reminder that he didn't know her name. That she was lying to him by omission.

"Can I ask you a question?" she blurted out.

"Isn't that kind of our MO?" he drawled. "Ask."

Now that she could satisfy the curiosity that had been gnawing at her since she'd first encountered him, she hesitated. She had no right—never mind it not being her business—to probe into his history and private pain. But as hypocritical as it made her, she sought a piece of him she sensed he wouldn't willingly offer someone else.

"Earlier, when I first bumped into you...you were having a panic attack," she began. He stiffened, tension turning his body into a replica of the marble statue adorning the fountain outside the mansion. Sitting so close to him, she swore she could feel icy waves emanate from him. Unease trickled through her. *Damn it*. She should've left it alone. "I'm sorry…" she rasped, tugging on her hand, trying to withdraw it from his hold. "I shouldn't have pried."

But he didn't release her. Her heart stuttered as his grip on her strengthened.

"Don't," he ordered.

Don't what? Ask him any more questions? Pull away? How pathetic did it make her that she hoped it was the latter?

"You're the only thing keeping me sane," he admitted in a voice so low that, even in the blackness that magnified every sound, she barely caught the admission.

A thread of pain throbbed through his confession, and she couldn't resist the draw of it. Scooting closer until her thigh pressed against his, she lifted the hand not clasped in his to his hard chest. The drum of his heart vibrated against her palm, running up her arm and echoing in her own chest.

She felt and heard his heavy inhale. And she parted her lips, ready to tell him to forget it. To apologize again for intruding, but his big hand covered hers, halting her words.

"My parents died when I was sixteen."

"God," she breathed. That hint of sadness she'd detected earlier when he'd talked about fishing with his father… She'd suspected, and now he'd confirmed it. "I'm so sorry."

"Plane crash on their way back from a business meeting in Paris. Ordinarily my mother wouldn't have been with my father, but they decided to treat it as an anniversary trip. They were my foundation. And I…" He paused, and Isobel waited.

She couldn't imagine… Her father had been a nonfactor in her life for most of her childhood, but her mom… Her mother had been her support system, her rock, even through the years with Isobel and Aiden's move to California and back. Losing her…she closed her eyes and leaned her head against his shoulder, offering whatever comfort he needed as he relayed the details of the tragedy that had scarred him.

"My best friend and his family took me in. I don't know what would've happened to me, where I would be now, without them. But at the time, I was lost. Adrift. In the months afterward, I'd skip school or leave my friend's house in the middle of the night to go to the building where we'd lived. The penthouse had been sold, so I no longer had access to my home, but I would sneak into the basement through a window. It had a loosened bar that I would remove and squeeze through. I'd sit there for hours, just content to be in the building, if not in the place where I'd lived with them. My best friend—he followed me one night when I sneaked out, so he knew about it. But he never told."

Another pause, and again she didn't disturb him. She wanted to hug that best friend for standing by the boy-now-man. She'd had girlfriends in the past, but none that would've—or could've, given their own family situations—taken her in as if she were family. This friend of his, he must've been special.

"About four months after my parents' death, I'd left school again and went to the basement. I'd had a rough night. Nightmares and no sleep. That's the only reason I can think of for me falling asleep in the basement that day. I don't know what woke me up. The noise? The heat?" His shoulder rose and fell in a shrug under her cheek. "Like I said, I don't know. But when I did, the room was pitch-black. I couldn't even see my hands in front of my face. I heard what sounded like twigs snapping. But underneath that, distant but growing louder, was this dull roar. Like engines revving in a closed garage. I'd never been in one before, but somehow I knew. The building was on fire, and I was trapped."

"No," she whispered, fingers curling against his chest.

"I couldn't move. Thick black smoke filled the basement, and I choked on it, couldn't breathe. I can't tell you how long I laid there, paralyzed by fear or weak from inhaling smoke, but I thought I was going to die. That room—it became my tomb. A dark, burning tomb. But then I heard someone shouting my name and saw the high beam of a flashlight. It was my friend. I found out later that he'd heard about the fire on the news, and when I hadn't shown up at his house after school, he'd guessed where I'd gone. The firemen had believed they'd cleared the entire building, but he'd forced them to go back in and search the basement. He should've stayed outside and let them come find me, but he'd barreled past them and entered with only his shirt over his face to battle the smoke, putting his life in danger. But if he hadn't... He saved my life that day."

"Oh, thank God." Sliding her hand from under his, she wrapped her arm around his waist, curving her body into his. She'd known him for mere hours, and yet the thought of him dying, of being consumed by flames? It bothered her in a way that made no sense. "He was a hero."

"Yes, he was," he said softly. "He was a good man."

Was a good man. No. It couldn't be... Horror and disbelief crowded up her throat. "He's gone, too?"

"A couple of years now, but sometimes it seems like yesterday."

"I'm so sorry." Isobel shifted until she knelt beside him. She stroked her hand up his torso, searching out his face. Once she brushed over his hard, faintly stubbled jaw, she cupped it and lowered her head, until her forehead met his temple.

His fingers drifted over her cheek, and after a moment's hesitation, tunneled into her hair. Her lungs seized, shock infiltrating every vein, organ and limb. Only her heart seemed capable of movement, and it threw itself against her sternum, like an animal desperate for freedom from its cage.

Blunt fingertips dragged over her scalp. A moan clawed its way up her throat at the scratch and tug of her hair, but she trapped the sound behind clenched teeth. She couldn't prevent the shudder that worked its way through her. Not when it'd been *so long* since she'd been touched. Since pleasure had even been a factor. So. Long.

"I need to hear that lovely voice, sweetheart," he rumbled, turning and bowing his head so his lips grazed the column of her throat as he spoke. Sparks snapped under her skin as if her nerve endings had transformed into firecrackers, and his mouth was the lighter. "There are things I want to do to your mouth that require your permission."

"Like what?" Had she really just asked that question? And in that breathy tone? What was he doing to her?

Giving you what you're craving. Be brave and find out, her subconscious replied.

"Find out if it's as sweet as you are. Taste you. Savor you. Learn you," he murmured, answering her question. He untangled their clasped fingers and with unerring accuracy, located her chin and pinched it. Cool but soft strands of hair tickled her jaw, and then her cheek, as he lifted his head. Then warm gusts of air bathed her lips. She could taste him, his breath. Something potent with faint hints of lemon, like the champagne from earlier. But also, underneath, lay a darker, enigmatic flavor. Him. She didn't need to pinpoint its origin to know it was all him. "Then I want to take your mouth. Want you to take mine."

"I..." Desperate, aching need robbed her of words. Of thought.

"Give me the words, sweetheart." He didn't breach that scant inch of space between them, waiting on her consent, her permission.

When so much had been ripped from her in the past, choices not even offered, that seeking of her agreement squeezed her heart even as his words caused a spasm to roll through her sex.

"Yes," she said. Then, as if confirming to herself that she was indeed breaking her self-imposed rules about caution and recklessness, she whispered again, "Yes."

With a growl, he claimed that distance.

She expected him to crush his mouth to hers, to conquer her like a wild storm leveling everything in its path. And she would've thrown herself into the whirlwind, been willingly swept up. But his tenderness was as thorough in its destruction as any tornado.

His lips, full, firm yet somehow soft, brushed over hers. Pressed, then withdrew. Rubbed, cajoled, gave her enough of him, but waited until she granted him more. On the tail end of a sigh she couldn't contain, she parted for him. Welcomed the penetration of his tongue. Slid into a sensual dance with him. It was she who sucked him, licking the roof of his mouth, sampling the dark, heady flavor of his groan. She who first brought teeth into play, nipping at the corner of his mouth, raking them down his chin, only to return to take just as he'd invited her to do.

She who crawled onto his lap, jerking her skirt up and straddling his powerful thighs.

But it was he who threw oil onto their fire, ratcheting their desire from a blaze into a consuming inferno.

With a snarl that vibrated through his chest and over her nipples, he tugged her head back and opened his mouth over her neck. She arched into the hot, wet caress of tongue and teeth, her hands shifting from his shoulders to his hair and holding on. Every flick and suck echoed low in her belly, between her thighs. Fleetingly, the thought that she should be embarrassed at how drenched her panties were flitted through her head. But the clamp of his hand on her hip and the roll of his hips, stroking the hard, thick length of his cock over her sex, obliterated every rationalization.

Think? All she could do was *feel*.

Pleasure, its claws tipped with greed, tore at her. She whimpered, clung to him.

"Again," she ordered. Begged. Didn't matter. As long as he did it *again*.

"That's it," he praised against her throat, licking a path to her ear, where he nipped the outer curve. Hell, when had *that* become an erogenous zone? "Tell me what you want, what you need from me. I'll give it to you, sweetheart. You just have to ask."

Keep turning me inside out. Keep holding me like I'm wanted, cherished. Keep making me forget who I am.

But those pleas veered too close to exposing that part of her she'd learned to protect with the zeal of a dragon guarding a treasure.

So instead she gave him what she could. What she'd be too embarrassed to admit in the light of day. "Here." With trembling, jerky movements, she yanked down the top of her dress, drew him to her bared breasts. "Kiss me. Mark me."

He followed through on his promise, giving her what she'd requested. His tongue circled her nipple, lapped at it, swirled before sucking so hard the corresponding ache twinged deep and high inside her. She tried to hold in her cry but couldn't. Not when lust arrowed through her, striking at the heart of her. He murmured against her flesh, switching breasts, and treating her other peak to the same erotic torture. Skillful fingers plucked and pinched the tip that was damp from his mouth.

"More," she gasped. "Oh, God, more."

"Tell me." The hand on her hip tightened, and he delivered another slow, luxurious stroke to her empty, wet sex. "Tell me once more. I want your voice, your words."

Frustration, the last stubborn remnants of shyness and passion warred within her. Her lips moved, but the de-

mand *make me come* that howled inside her head refused
to emerge. Finally she grabbed the hand at her waist and
slid it over her hiked-up dress, down her inner thigh and
between her legs. She pressed his palm to her, moaning at
the temporary relief of him cupping her.

"You're cheating," he teased, but the almost guttural
tone had her hips bucking against him. As did his, "You're
soaked. For me."

"Yes," she rasped. "For you. Only for you." Truth. That
piece of herself, she offered him. She'd never been this hungry, this desperate before. Not even for—*no!*

She flung herself away from the intrusive thought. Not
here. In this hall, there was only room for her and this
nameless, faceless man, who nonetheless handled her like
the most desirable, beautiful creature he'd ever held. Or at
least that's what she was convincing herself of for these
stolen moments.

"Touch me," she whispered, grinding down against his
hand. "Please touch me."

The fingers still sweeping caresses over her nipple abandoned her flesh to cradle her face. He tipped her head down
until their mouths met. "Don't beg me to touch you," he
said, his lips grazing hers with each word. "You'll never
have to beg me to do that."

He sealed the vow with a plunge of his finger inside her.

She cried out, tossing her head back on her shoulders as
pleasure rocked through her like an earthquake, cracking
her open, exposing her.

"Damn," he swore. "So damn tight. So damn..." He bit
off the rest of his litany, slowly pulling free of her, then
just as slowly, just as tenderly thrusting back inside. But
she didn't want slow, didn't want tender. And she told him
so with a hard, swift twist of her hips, taking him deeper.
"Sweetheart," he growled, warned.

"No," she panted. "I need to... Please." He'd said she

didn't need to plead with him, but if it would get her what she craved—release, oblivion—she wasn't above it.

With a snarl, he crushed his mouth to hers, tongue driving between her lips as he buried himself inside her. She moaned into his kiss, even as she spread her legs wider, granting him deeper access to her body. And he took it. He withdrew one finger and returned to her with two, working them into her flesh, working *her*.

Something snapped within her, and she rode his hand, rode the exquisite storm he whipped to a frenzy with every stroke, every brush of his thumb over her clit, every curl of his fingertips on that place high and deep in her sex. He played her, demanding her body sing for him. And God, did it.

With one last rub over that, before now, untouched place, she splintered, screaming into his mouth. And he swallowed it, clutching her to him, holding her tight as she crashed headlong into the abyss, a willing sacrifice to pleasure.

Isobel snuggled under her warm blanket, grabbing ahold of those last few moments of lazy sleepiness before Aiden cried out, demanding she come free him from his crib and feed him. She sighed, curling into her pillow...

Wait. Her pillow wasn't this firm. Frowning, she rolled over...or tried to roll over. Something prevented the movement...

Oh, hell.

Not something. Some*one*.

She stiffened as reality shoved the misty dredges of sleep away and dragged in all the memories of the night before. Gala. Blackout. Finding a mysterious man. Calming him. Laughing with him. Kissing him...

She jerked away, her lashes lifting.

Weak, hazy pink-and-orange light poured in through the large window at the end of the hall. Morning, but just barely. So maybe about six o'clock. Still, the dawn-tinged sky provided enough light to realize the warm blanket was really a suit jacket. Instead of a mattress, she perched on a strong pair of muscular thighs. And her pillow was a wide, solid chest covered in a snow-white dress shirt.

Heart pounding like a heavy metal-drum solo, she inched her gaze up to the patch of smooth golden skin exposed by the buttons undone at a powerful throat. Her belly clenched, knots twisting and pulling tight as she continued her wary, slow perusal.

A carved-from-a-slab-of-stone jaw dusted with dark stubble.

An equally hard chin with just the faintest hint of a cleft.

A beautiful, sensual mouth that promised all kinds of decadent, corrupting pleasures. Pleasures she had firsthand knowledge that he could deliver. She clearly remembered sinking her teeth into the bottom, slightly fuller curve.

Suppressing a shiver that he would surely feel, as they were pressed so closely together, she continued skimming her gaze upward past a regal, patrician nose and sharp, almost harsh cheekbones.

As she raised her scrutiny that last scant inch to his eyes, his dense, black, ridiculously long lashes lifted.

She sucked in a painful breath. And froze. Except for her frantic pulse, which reverberated in her head like crashing waves relentlessly striking the shore. Deafening her.

Not because of the striking, piercing amber eyes that could've belonged to a majestic eagle.

No. Because she recognized those eyes.

It'd been two years since they'd coldly stared at her over a yawning, freshly dug grave with a flower-strewn mahogany casket suspended above it. But she'd never forget them.

Darius King.

Gage's best friend.

The man who blamed her for Gage's death.

The man who hated her.

Hated her... Hated her... As the words—and the throbbing pain of them—sank into her brain, her paralysis shattered. She scrambled off him, uncaring of how clumsy her backward crab-walk appeared. She just needed to be away from him. From the shock that quickly bled from his gaze and blazed into rage and disgust.

God, no. How could she have kissed...touched... Let him...

You're fucking him, aren't you? Admit it, goddamn you. Admit it! You're fucking my best friend! You whore!

The memory of Gage's scream ricocheted off the walls of her skull, gaining volume and power by the second. Darius hadn't been the first man he'd thought she'd been cheating with—not even the third or fifth. But she'd never seen him as enraged, as out-of-control at the thought of her being with this man. Gage had never physically abused her during their marriage, but that night... That night she'd truly been afraid he would hit her.

Afterward she'd made a conscious effort to not look at Darius, not be alone in the same room with him if she couldn't avoid him altogether. Even after he'd married an iceberg of a woman, she'd maintained her distance.

And now, not only had she laughed and talked with him, but she had allowed him inside her body. She'd allowed him to bring her the most soul-shattering pleasure.

Meeting his stare, she could read the condemnation there. The confirmation that she was indeed the whore Gage had called her.

Humiliation, hurt and fury—at him and herself—barreled through her, propelling her to her feet. Snatching up her purse and shoes, she clutched them to her chest.

"Isobel." The voice that had caressed her ears with its deep, melodious tone, that had stirred desire with explicit words, now caused ice to coat her veins. Gage used to take great delight in telling her how much his friend disliked her. Though she now knew when her husband's lips were moving, he was lying, hearing Darius's frigid disdain directed at her, meeting his derisive gaze... She believed it now, just as she had then.

"I-I..." She dragged in a breath, shaking her head as she backpedaled. "I need to go. I'm sorry," she rasped.

Hating that she'd apologized, that she sounded scared and...broken, she whirled around and damn near sprinted down the thankfully empty hallway, not feeling the cold marble under her feet. Or the stone as she escaped the mansion. None of the valets from the night before appeared, but she'd glimpsed the direction in which they'd driven off and followed that path.

Twenty minutes later, with keys snatched from the valet stand and car successfully located, she exited onto the freeway. Though with every mile she steadily placed between her and the mansion—and Darius—she couldn't shake the feeling of being pursued.

Couldn't shake the sense that she could run, but couldn't hide.

But that damn sure wouldn't stop her from trying.

Three

Darius stood outside the weathered brick apartment building, the chill of the October morning not having evaporated yet.

At eight thirty, the overcast sky didn't add any cheer to this South Deering neighborhood. The four rows of identical windows facing the front sported different types of shades, and someone had set potted plants with fake flowers by the front entrance, but nothing could erase the air of poverty that clung to this poor, crime-stricken section of the city. Foam cups, paper and other bits of trash littered the patch of green on the left side of the apartment complex. Graffiti and gang tags desecrated the side of the neighboring building. It sickened him that only thirty minutes away, people lived in almost obscene wealth, a good many of them willingly choosing to pretend this kind of poverty didn't exist. He'd been born into those rarefied circles, but he wasn't blind to the problems of classism, prejudice and ignorance that Chicago faced.

Still… Gage's son was growing up here, in this place that hovered only steps above a tenement. And that ate at Darius like the most caustic acid.

Stalking up the sidewalk, he approached the front entrance. A lock sat above the handle, but on a whim, he tugged on it, and the door easily opened.

"You have to be kidding me," he growled. Anyone off the street could walk into the building, leaving all the residents here vulnerable where they should feel safest. Aiden being one of the most vulnerable.

Darius stepped into the dimly lit foyer, the door shutting behind him. Rectangular mailboxes mounted the wall to his right, and to his left, the steel doors to an elevator. In front of him, a flight of stairs stretched to the upper floors. With one last glance at the elevator doors, he headed for the stairs. He wasn't trusting the elevator in a building this damn old.

According to the information his investigator had provided, Isobel lived on the third floor. He climbed several flights of stairs and entered the door that led to her level. Like the lobby, the hallway was clean, even if the carpet was threadbare. Bulbs lit the area, and the paint, while not fresh, wasn't as desperately in need of a new coat as the downstairs. The broken lock on the front door notwithstanding, it appeared as if the landlord, or at least the residents, cared about their home.

Seconds later, he arrived in front of Isobel's apartment door, standing on a colorful welcome mat depicting a sleeping puppy. It should've seemed out of place, but oddly it didn't strike him that way. But it did serve to remind him that a young boy lived behind the closed door. A boy who deserved to live in a home where he and the puppy could run free and play. A place with a yard, a swing set.

A safe place.

Anger rekindled in his chest, and raising his fist, he

knocked on the door. Moments passed, and it remained shut. He rapped on the door again. And still no one answered.

Suppressing a growl, he tucked his hands into the pockets of his coat and narrowed his gaze on the floor.

"Isobel, I know you're home. I can see the shadow of your feet. So open the door," he ordered.

Several more seconds passed before the sound of locks twisting and disengaging reached him, and then she stood in the entrance.

He deliberately inhaled a calming breath. For the entire drive from his Lake Forest home, he'd tried to prepare himself for seeing her again. It'd been a week since the night of the blackout. A week since he'd suffered a panic attack, and she'd held his hand and dragged him back from the edge with her teasing, silly conversation and lilting laughter. A week since he'd feasted on her mouth, experienced the tight-as-hell grip of her body spasming around his fingers, and her greedy cries of pleasure splintering around his ears.

A week since he woke and the piercing anticipation of finally glimpsing the face of the mysterious woman he'd embraced faded into a bright, hot anger as he realized her true identity.

Yes, he'd tried to ready himself for the moment they'd face each other again. And staring down at her now, with all that long, thick hair tumbling over her shoulders, framing a beautiful face with fey eyes that should have existed only within the pages of a fantasy novel, his attempt at preparation had been for shit. Even in a faded pink tank top and cotton pajama pants, with what appeared to be fat leprechauns and rainbows, she knocked him on his ass.

And he resented her for it. Hated himself more.

Because no matter how he tried, he couldn't forget how she'd burned in his arms that night. Exploded. Never had a woman been that uninhibited and hot for him. She'd scorched him so that even now—even a week later—he still felt the marks on his fingers, his chest, his cock. He had an inkling why his best friend had been driven crazy because of her infidelities.

Because imagining Isobel aflame like that with another man had a green-tinted anger churning his own gut.

Which was completely ridiculous. Gage had tortured himself over this woman. It would be a breezy spring day in hell before Darius allowed himself to be her next victim.

"What do you want?" Isobel asked, crossing her arms under her breasts. Her obviously braless breasts.

"To talk," he said, trying and failing to completely keep the snap out of his voice. "And I'd rather not do it out in the hallway."

Her delicate chin kicked up, and even though she stood almost a foot shorter than his own six feet three inches, she continued defiantly standing there, a female Napoleon guarding her empire. "We don't have anything to talk about, so whatever you came here to say should be a very short conversation. The hallway is as good a place as any."

"Fine." He smiled, and it must have appeared as false as it felt because her eyes narrowed on him. "But the private investigator I hired to find you also spoke with your neighbors. Including a Mrs. Gregory, who lives across the hall. A lovely woman, from what he tells me. Seventy-three, lives alone, never misses an episode of the *Young and the Restless* and is a terrible gossip. At this very moment, she probably has her ear against the door, trying to eavesdrop on our conversation. So if you don't mind her finding out where you spent the night of the blackout—and *how* you spent it—I don't either."

Her head remained tilted at that stubborn angle, and the flat line of her mouth didn't soften. But she did slant a glance around him to peek at the closed door across the hall. Whatever she saw made her lips flatten even more.

"Come in." She stepped back, allowing him to pass by her. When he moved into the tiny foyer, she called out, "Good morning, Mrs. Gregory," and shut the door. "I swear that woman could tell the cops where Jimmy Hoffa is buried," she muttered under her breath.

Humor, unexpected and unwelcome, rippled through his chest. He remembered this about her from the night of the blackout. Funny, self-deprecating, charming. Given everything he knew of Isobel's character, the side she'd shown him in the darkness must've been a charade.

Her shock and horror the following morning had been real, though.

He gave his head a mental shake. He wasn't here to rehash the colossal mistake he'd committed in the dark. He had a purpose, an agenda. And before he left this morning, it would be accomplished.

Making resolve a clear, hard wall in his chest, he moved into the living room. Well, *moved* was generous. The change in location from foyer to the main room only required two steps.

Jesus, the whole apartment could fit into his great room—three times. The living room and dining room melded into one space, only broken up by a small counter that separated it from the equally small kitchen. A cramped tunnel of a hallway shot off to the left and led to what he knew from floorplans of the building to be a miniscule bedroom, bathroom and closet.

At least it was clean. The obviously secondhand couch, coffee table and round dining table wore signs of life— scratches, scuff marks and ragged edges in the upholstery. But everything was neat and shined, the scent of pine and lemon a pleasant fragrance under the aroma of brewing coffee. Even the colorful toys—blocks, a plastic easel, a colorful construction set and books—were stacked in chaotic order in one corner.

A hard tug wrenched his gut to the point of pain at the sight of those symbols of childhood. A tug that resonated with yearning. Aiden had been only six months old the last time Darius had seen him. That'd been at Gage's funeral. How much had the boy changed in the two years since? Had his light brown hair darkened to the nearly black of Gage's own color? As he'd matured, had he grown to resemble his mother, or had he inherited more of his father's features?

That had been the seed of Gage's and the family's doubts regarding the baby's parentage. The boy had possessed neither Gage's nor Isobel's features, except for her eyes. So they'd assumed he must look like his father—his true father. That Isobel had refused a paternity test had further solidified their suspicions that Gage hadn't been Aiden's father. And then, out of spite, she'd made Gage choose— his family or her. Of course, out of love and loyalty, and foolish blindness, he'd chosen her, isolating himself from his parents and friends. Till the end.

Selfish. Conniving. Cold.

Except maybe not so cold. Darius had a firsthand example of how hot she could burn…

Shit.

Focus.

Unbuttoning his jacket, he turned and watched Isobel stride toward him. She did another of those chin lifts as she entered the living room. Jesus, even with suspicion heavy in those blue-gray eyes, they were striking. Haunting. Beautiful.

Deceitful.

"You're not going to ask me to have a seat?" he drawled, the dark, twisted mix of bitterness and lust grinding relentlessly within him.

"Since you won't be staying long, no," she replied, crossing her arms over her chest again. "What do you want?"

"That's my question, Isobel." Without her invite, he lowered to the dark blue, worn armchair across from the couch. "What do you want? Why were you at the gala last week?"

"None of your business."

"See, that's where you're wrong. If you came there to pump the Wellses for money, then it is most definitely my business," he said. Studying her, he caught the flash of emotion in her eyes. Emotion, hell. Guilt. That flash had been guilt. Satisfaction, thick and bright, flared within him. "What happened, Isobel? Did whatever fool you sank your claws into out there in Los Angeles come to his senses and kick you out before you sucked him dry?"

She stared at him, slowly uncoiling her arms and sinking to a perch on her sofa. "The *poor fool* you're so concerned about was my Aunt Lila, who I stayed with to help her recover from a stroke," she continued, derision heavy in her voice. "She died a couple of months ago from another massive stroke, which is why I'm back here in Chicago. Any more insults or assumptions you want to throw out there before finally telling me why you're here?"

"I'm sorry for your loss," he murmured. And he was sorry. He, more than anyone, understood the pain of losing a loved one. But that's all he would apologize for. Protecting and defending his family from someone who sought to use them? No, he'd never regret that. "Now... What do you want with the Wells family? Although—" he deliberately turned his head and scanned the tight quarters of her apartment, lingering on the pile of envelopes on the breakfast bar before returning his attention to her "—I can probably guess if you don't want to admit it."

Her shoulders rolled back, her spine stiffening. Even with her just-rolled-out-of-bed hair and clothes, she appeared...regal. Pride. It was the pride that clung to her as closely as the tank top molding to her breasts.

"What. Do. You. Want. With. Them?" he ground out, when she didn't answer.

"Help," she snapped, leaning forward, a matching anger lighting her arctic eyes. "I need their help. Not for me. I'd rather hang pictures and lay a welcome mat out in a freshly dug hole than go to them for anything. But for the grandson they've rejected and refused to acknowledge, I need them."

"You would have the nerve to ask them for help—no, let's call it what it is—for *money* and use your son to do it? The son you've kept from them for two years? That's low even for you, Isobel." The agony and helplessness over Gage's death, the rage toward the woman who was supposed to have loved him, but who had instead mercilessly and callously broken him, surged within him. Tearing through him like a sword, damn near slicing him in half. But he submerged the roiling emotions beneath a thick sheet of ice. "The answer is no. You don't get to decide when they can and can't have a relationship with the grandson who is the only part they have left of the son they loved and lost. You might be his *mother*, and I use that term loosely—"

"Get out." The quiet, sharp words cut him off. She stood, the fine tremor shivering through her body visible in the finger she pointed toward the door. "Get the hell out and don't come back."

"Not until we discuss—"

"You're just like them," she snarled, continuing as if he hadn't even spoken. "Cut from the same golden but filthy cloth. You don't know shit about me as a mother, because you haven't been there. You, Baron or Helena. So you have zero right to have an opinion on how I'm raising my son. And for the record, I didn't try to keep them from Aiden. They didn't want him. Didn't want to know him. Didn't even believe he was their grandson. So don't you dare walk in here, look at this apartment and judge me—"

"Oh, no, Isobel," he contradicted her, slowly rising to his feet as well, tired of her lies. Especially about the people, the *family*, who'd taken him in when he'd lost his own.

Who'd accepted him as their own. "I judged you long before this. Your actions as a wife—" he spat the word out, distasteful on his tongue "—condemned you."

"Right." She nodded, a sneer matching his own, curling her mouth. "I was the money-grabbing, social-climbing whore who tricked Gage into marriage by getting knocked up. And he was the sacrificial lamb who cherished and adored me, who remained foolishly loyal to me right up until the moment of his death."

"Don't," he growled, the warning low, rough. He'd never called her a whore; he detested that word. Even when he'd discovered his ex-wife was fucking one of his vice presidents, Darius had never thrown that ugly name at her. Yet to hear Isobel talk about Gage in that dismissive manner when his biggest sin had been loving her... "You don't get to talk about him like that."

"Yes." Her harsh crack of laughter echoed in the room. "That's right, another rule I forgot from my time in my loving marriage. I don't get to speak until I'm spoken to. And even then, keep it short before I embarrass him and myself. Well, sorry to break it to you, but this isn't your home. It's mine, and I want you out—"

"Mommy." The small, childish voice dropped in the room like a hand grenade, cutting Isobel off. Both of them turned toward it. A toddler with dark, nearly black curls and round cheeks, and clad in Hulk pajamas, hovered in the entrance to the living room. Shuffling back and forth on his bare feet, he stuck his thumb into his mouth and glanced from Isobel to Darius before returning his attention to her.

Aiden.

An invisible fist bearing brass knuckles landed a haymaker against Darius's chest. The air in his lungs ejected on a hard, almost painful *whoosh*. He couldn't breathe, couldn't move. Not when his best friend's son dashed across the floor and threw his tiny but sturdy body at his mother, the action full of confidence that she would catch him. Which she did. Kneeling, Isobel gathered him in her arms, standing up and holding him close.

Over his mother's shoulder, Aiden stared at Darius with a gaze identical to Isobel's. A hand roughly the size of a toddler's reached into his chest and squeezed Darius's heart. Hard.

Christ.

He'd expected to be happy or satisfied at finally seeing Aiden. But he hadn't been prepared for this…this overwhelming joy or fierce protectiveness that swamped him, weakened his knees. Gage's son—and there was no mistaking he was indeed Gage's son. He might have Isobel's eyes, but the hair, the shape of his face, his brow, nose, the wide, smiling mouth… They were all his best friend.

The need to protect the boy intensified, swelled. Darius would do anything in his power to provide for him… raise him the way Gage didn't have the opportunity to do. Resolve shifting and solidifying in his chest, his paralysis broke, and he moved across the room, toward mother and son.

"Hello," he greeted Aiden, the gravel-roughened tone evidence of the emotional storm still whirling inside him.

Aiden grinned, and the tightening around Darius's ribcage increased.

"Aiden, this is Mr. King. Can you tell him hi?" Isobel shifted so she and Aiden faced Darius. Her voice might've been light and cheerful, but her eyes revealed that none of the anger from their interrupted conversation had abated. "Tell Mr. King, hi, baby," she encouraged.

"Hi, Mr. King," he mimicked. Though it actually sounded more like, *Hi, Mih Key.*

"Hi, Aiden," he returned, smiling. And unable to help himself, he rubbed the back of a finger down the boy's warm, chubby cheek.

A soft catch of breath reluctantly tugged his attention away from the child. He glanced at Isobel, and she stared at him, barely blinking. After a moment, she shook her head, turning her focus back to her son.

What had that been about? He studied her, trying to decipher the enigma that was Isobel Hughes.

There's no enigma, no big mystery. Only what she allows you to see.

As the reminder boomed in his head, he frowned. His ex-wife had been an expert at hiding her true self until she'd wanted him to glimpse it. And that had only happened toward the end of the relationship, when both of them had stopped pretending they shared anything resembling a marriage. Not with her screwing other men, and Darius refusing to play the fool or pay for the black American Express card any longer.

"Want milk," Aiden demanded as Isobel settled him on the floor again. "And 'nana."

She brushed a hand over his curls, but the hair just fell back into his face. "You want cereal with your milk and banana?" she asked. Aiden nodded, smiling, as if congratulating her for understanding him. "Okay, but can you go play in the room while I fix it?"

Aiden nodded again, agreeing. "Go play."

She took his hand in hers and led him back down the hall, talking to him the entire time until they disappeared. Several minutes later, she returned alone, the adoring, gentle expression she gave her son gone.

"I have things to do, so…" She waved toward the front door, but Darius didn't move. "Seriously, this is ridiculous," she snapped.

"He's Gage's son," he murmured.

Fire flared in her eyes as they narrowed. "Are you sure? You can tell that from just a glance at him? After all, I've been with so many men. Any of them could be his real father."

"Don't play the victim, Isobel. It doesn't fit," he snapped. "And I'm not leaving until we talk."

"I repeat," she ground out. "We have nothing to—"

"We're getting married."

She rocked back on her bare heels as if struck. Shock rounded her fairy eyes, parted her lips. She gaped at him, her fingers fluttering to circle her neck. He should feel regret at so bluntly announcing his intentions. Should. But he didn't.

He'd had a week to consider this idea. Yes, it seemed crazy, over-the-top, and he'd rejected it as soon as the thought had popped into his head. But it'd nagged at him, and the reasons why it would work eventually outweighed the ones why it wouldn't. Of all the words used to describe him, *impetuous* or *rash* weren't among them. He valued discipline and control, in business and in his personal life. His past had taught him both were important. It'd been an impromptu decision that had robbed him of both his parents, and an impulsive one that had led him to marry a woman he'd known for a matter of months. The same mistake Gage had made.

But this…proposition was neither. He'd carefully measured it, and though just the thought of tying himself to another manipulative woman sickened him, he was willing to make the sacrifice.

Whatever doubts might've lingered upon walking up to her building, they had disintegrated as soon as he'd laid eyes on Aiden.

"You're crazy," she finally breathed.

He smiled, and the tug to the corner of his mouth felt cynical, hard. "No. Just realistic." He slid his hands into the front pockets of his pants, cocking his head and studying her pale, damnably lovely features. "Regardless of what you believe, I'm not judging you on the neighborhood you live in or your home. But the fact is you aren't in the safest area of Chicago, and this building isn't a shining example of security. The lock on the front door doesn't work. Anyone could walk in here. The locks on your apartment door are for shit. There isn't an alarm system. What if someone followed you home and busted in here? You would have no protection—you or Aiden."

"So I have a security system installed and call the landlord about the locks on the building entrance and my door. Easy fixes, and none of them require marriage to a man I barely know who despises me."

"If they were easy fixes," he said, choosing to ignore her comment about his feelings toward her, "why haven't you done them?" He paused, because something flickered in her gaze, and a surge of both anger and satisfaction glimmered in his chest. "You have contacted your landlord," he stated, taking her silence as confirmation. "And he hasn't done a damn thing about it." He stepped forward, shrinking the space between them. "Pride, Isobel. You're going to let pride prevent you from protecting your son."

Lightning flashed in her gaze, and for a moment he found himself mesmerized by the display. Like a bolt of electricity across a morning sky.

"Let me enlighten you. Pride became a commodity I couldn't afford a long time ago. But in the last two years, I've managed to scrape mine back together again. And neither you nor the Wellses can have it. I'm not afraid to ask for help. That's why I was at the gala. Why I was willing to approach Baron and Helena again. *For my son.* But you're not here to offer me help. You're demanding I sell my soul to another devil, just with a different face and name. Well, sorry. I'm not going to play your game. Not when it won't only be me losing this time, but Aiden, as well."

"Selling your soul to the devil? Not playing the game?"

he drawled. "Come now, Isobel. A poor college student nabbing herself the heir to a fortune? Trapping him with a pregnancy, then isolating him from his family? Cry me a river, sweetheart. I was there, so don't try to revise history to suit your narrative."

"You're just like him," she whispered.

Darius stifled a flinch. Then cursed himself for recoiling in the first place. Gage had been a good man—good to her.

"You have two choices," he stated. "One, agree to marry me and we both raise Aiden. Or two, disagree, and I'll place the full weight of my name and finances behind Baron and Helena to help them gain custody of Aiden."

She gasped and wavered on her feet. On instinct, he shifted forward, lifting his arms to steady her. But she backpedaled away from him, pressing a hand against the wall and holding up the other in a gesture that screamed *stop right there*.

"You," she rasped, shaking her head. "You wouldn't do that."

"I would," he assured her. "And I will."

"Why?" She straightened, lowering both arms, but the shadows darkening her eyes gathered. "Why would you do that? Why would they? Baron and Helena...they don't even believe Aiden is Gage's. They've wanted nothing to do with him since he was born. Why would they seek custody now?"

"Because he *is* their grandson. I'll convince them of that. And he deserves to know them, love them. Deserves to learn about his father and come to know him through his parents. Aiden is all Baron and Helena have left of Gage. And you would deprive them of that relationship. I won't let you." The unfairness of Isobel's actions, of her selfishness, gnawed at him. She hadn't witnessed the devastation Gage's death had left behind, the wreckage. Baron had suffered a heart attack not long after, and yes, most of it could be attributed to lifestyle choices. But the loss of his only son, that had definitely been a contributing factor.

Yet if they'd had Aiden in their lives during these last two difficult years...he could've been a joy to them. But Isobel had skipped town, not even granting them the opportunity to bond. If she'd stayed long enough, Baron and Helena would've done just what Darius had—taken one look at the child and *known* he belonged to Gage.

"And I won't let you make Aiden a pawn. Or worse, a substitute for Gage. *He won't become Gage.* I refuse to allow you and the Wellses to turn him into his father. I'll fight that with every breath in my body."

"He would be lucky to become like the man his father was," Darius growled. "To be loved by his parents. They welcomed me into their home, raised me when I had no one."

She didn't get to smear the family that had become his own. Gage had been his best friend, his confidante, his brother. Helena had stepped in as his mother. And Baron had been his friend, his mentor, his guiding hand in the multimillion-dollar financial-investment company Darius's father had left behind for his young, inexperienced son.

So no, she didn't get to malign them.

"I'm his mother," she said.

As if that settled everything.

When it didn't.

"And they're his grandparents," he countered. "Grandparents who can afford to provide a stable, safe, secure and loving home for him to thrive and grow in. He'll never want for anything, will have the best education and opportunities. Aiden should have all of his family in his life. You, me, his grandparents and aunt. He should enjoy a fulfilled, happy childhood, with the security of two parents and without the weight of struggle. With you marrying me, he will."

And the Wellses would avoid a prolonged custody battle that could further tax Baron's health and possibly endanger his life. His recovery from the heart attack was going well, but Darius refused to add stress if he could avoid it.

Besides, as CEO and president of King Industries Unlimited, the conglomerate he'd inherited from his father, not only would Aiden be taken care of, but so would Isobel. She would want for nothing, have all the money available to satisfy her every materialistic need. He had experience with bearing the albatross of a greedy woman with Faith, his ex-wife, and though it galled him to have to repeat history, he'd rather take the financial hit than allow Isobel to extort more money from the Wellses. They'd protected him once, and he would gladly, willingly do the same for them.

"No." Isobel stared up at him, shoulders drawn back, hands curled into fists at her side. Though she still wore the evidence of her worry, she faced him like one general standing off against another. A glimmer of admiration slipped through his steely resolve. She'd reminded him of Napoleon earlier, and she did so again. But like that emperor, she would fail and eventually surrender. "I don't care how pretty you wrap it up, blackmail is still blackmail. And I'm not giving in to it. Now, for the last time, get out of my house."

"Call it what you want to help you sleep at night," he murmured. He reached inside his suit jacket and removed a silver business card holder. He withdrew one as he strode to the breakfast bar, and then set it on the counter. "Think carefully before you make a rash decision you'll regret. Here's where you can reach me."

She didn't reply, just stalked to the front door and yanked it open.

"This isn't anywhere near over, Isobel," he warned, exiting her apartment.

"Maybe it isn't for you. But for me, I'm going to forget all about you as soon as you get out." And with that parting shot, she closed the door shut behind him. Or more accurately, in his face.

He didn't immediately head down the hallway, instead pausing a moment to stare at the door. And smile.

He'd meant what he'd told her. This wasn't over.

And damn if he wasn't looking forward to the next skirmish.

Four

A week later, Isobel drove through the winding, tidy streets of Lake Forest. During the hour and fifteen minutes' drive from South Deering, the inner-city landscape gave way to the steel-and-glass metropolis of downtown, to the affluent suburb that made a person believe she'd stepped into a pretty New England town. The quaint ice cream shop, bookstore, gift shop and boutiques in the center of the town emanated charm and wealth. All of it practically shouted history, affluence and *keep the hell out, riffraff!*

She would be the aforementioned riffraff. Discomfort crawled down her neck. Her decade-old Honda Civic stuck out like a sore thumb among the Aston Martins, Bugattis and Mercedes Benzes like a poor American relation among its luxurious, foreign cousins. Her GPS announced her upcoming turn, and she returned her focus to locating Darius's home.

Minutes later, Siri informed her that she'd reached her destination.

Good. God.

She didn't know much about architecture other than what she retained from the shows on HGTV, but even she recognized the style of the three-story home as Georgian. Beautiful golden bricks—not the weathered, dull color of her own apartment building—formed the outside of the huge structure, with its sloped roof and attached garage. It curved in an arc, claiming the land not already seized by the towering maple trees surrounding the property. Black shutters framed the many windows that faced the front and bracketed the wide wine-red door.

"You are not in South Deering anymore," she murmured to herself.

No wonder Darius had scrutinized her tiny apartment with a slight curl to his lips. He called this beautiful, imposing mansion home. Her place must've appeared like a Hobbit hole to him. A Hobbit hole from the wrong side of the Shire tracks.

Sighing, she dragged her attention back to the reason she'd driven out here.

She had a marriage bargain to seal.

After climbing the three shallow steps that led to the front door, she rang the bell. Only seconds passed before it opened and—instead of a housekeeper or butler—Darius stood in the entryway.

It wasn't fair.

His masculine beauty. His affect on her.

She was well versed in the danger of handsome men. They used their appearance as a lure—a bright, sensual lure that entranced a woman, distracted her from the darkness behind the shiny exterior. And by the time a woman noticed, it was way too late…

Even though she was aware of the threat he presented, she still stared at him, fighting the carnal thrall he exuded like a pheromone. His dark brown hair waved away from his strong brow, emphasizing the slashing cheekbones, patrician nose, full lips and rock-hard jaw with the faint dent in the chin. And his eyes…vivid, golden and piercing. They unleashed a warm slide of heat in her veins, even as she fought the urge to duck her head and avoid that scalpel-sharp gaze.

With a quick glance, she took in the black turtleneck and slacks that draped over his powerful shoulders, wide chest and muscular thighs. It didn't require much effort to once again feel those thighs under hers or recall the solid strength of his chest under her hands. Her body tingled with the memory, as if he'd imprinted himself in her skin, in her senses, that night. And no matter how she tried, she couldn't evict him.

"Isobel." The way that low, cultured drawl wrapped around her name was indecent. "Come in."

She dipped her chin in acknowledgment and moved forward. Doing her best not to touch him, she still couldn't avoid breathing in his delicious scent—cedar and sun-warmed air, with a hint of musk that was all male. All him. She'd tried her best to forget the flavor of him from that night, too. Epic fail.

The heels of her boots clacked against the hardwood floor of the foyer, and she almost bent to remove them, not wanting to make scuff marks. She studied the house, not even attempting to hide her curiosity. Yes, the inside lived up to the splendor of the exterior. A wide staircase swept to an upper level, and two airy rooms extended from each side of the entryway. Huge fireplaces, furniture that belonged in magazines and rugs that could've taken up space in museums. And windows. So many windows, which offered views of acres of land.

But she examined her surroundings for hints into the man who owned the home. Framed photos lined the mantel in one of the living rooms, but she couldn't glimpse the images from this distance. Were they of the parents he'd told her about during the blackout? Were they of Gage, when they were teens? Around the time he'd saved Darius's life? Did the photographs contain images of the Wellses?

Her survey swept over the expected but beautiful portraits of landscapes and zeroed in on a glass-and-weathered-wood box. A step closer revealed a collection of antique pocket watches. She shifted her inspection to Darius, who watched her, his expression shuttered. Oh, there had to be a story there.

But she wasn't here to find it out.

"You know why I'm here," she said. "I'd like to get this over with."

"We can talk in the study." He turned, and after a moment of hesitation, she followed.

They entered the massive room, where two walls were floor-to-ceiling windows and the other two were filled with books. A large, glossy black desk dominated one end, and couches, armchairs and an immense fireplace claimed the rest. It invited a person to grab a book and settle in for a long read. She couldn't say how she knew, but she'd bet her last chocolate bar that Darius spent most of his time here.

"So, you've come to a decision." He perched on the edge of his desk and waved toward one of the armchairs. "Please, have a seat."

"No, thank you," Isobel murmured. "I—" She swallowed, for an instant unable to force the words past her suddenly constricted throat. A wave of doubt assailed her, but she broke through it. This was the right decision. "I'll agree to marry you."

She expected a gloating smile or a smirk. Something that boasted, *I win*.

Instead his amber gaze studied her, unwavering and intense. Once more she had the inane impression that he could see past her carefully guarded shields to the vulnerable, confused and scared woman beneath. Her head argued it was impossible, but her heart pounded in warning. His figuring out her fears and insecurities when it came to the situation and *him* would be disastrous.

"What made you change your mind?" he asked.

No way was she telling him about arriving home with Aiden after work one night last week to find the police staked out in front of her building because of a burglary and assault. It'd only nailed home Darius's warning about the unsafety of her environment—for her and for Aiden.

Instead she shrugged. "Does it matter?"

"This was a hard decision for you, wasn't it?" he murmured.

Anger flared inside her like a struck match. "Why would you say that? Maybe I just held out longer so you wouldn't guess how giddy I am to have a chance at all your money? Or maybe I was hoping you would just offer more. I'm a mercenary, after all, always searching for the next opportunity to fill my pockets." His mouth hardened into a firm line, but she didn't care. She was only stating what they both knew he thought of her character. Straightening from the chair, she crossed her arms over her chest and hiked her chin up. "Like I said, I'll agree to marry you, but I have a few conditions first. And they're deal breakers."

He nodded, but the slight narrowing of his eyes relayed his irritation. Over her sarcasm or her stipulations, she couldn't tell, but in the end, neither mattered. Just as long as he conceded.

"First, you must promise to place Aiden, his welfare and protection above anything else. Including the Wellses' needs and agenda."

Another nod, but this one was tighter. And the curves of his mouth remained flattened, grim. As if he forced himself to contain words he wanted to say. If that were the case, he controlled it, and she continued.

"Second, I'm Aiden's mother, and since he's never known a father, you'll fill that role for him. If you don't, I won't go through with this. If you can't love and accept him as if he's your own blood, your son, then we're done. I won't have him hurt or rejected. Or worse, feel like he doesn't belong." Like she had. The soul-deep pain of being unworthy had wounded her, and she still bore the scars. She wouldn't subject Aiden to that kind of hurt. Even if it meant going to court.

"He *is* my blood," Darius said, and she blinked, momentarily stunned by his fierceness. "Gage and I might not have shared the same parents, but in all other ways we were brothers. And his son will be mine, and I'll love Aiden how his father would have if he'd lived and had the chance."

Satisfaction rolled in, flooding her and sweeping away the last of her doubts surrounding that worry. Even if Darius knew next to nothing about the man he called his brother. She believed him when he said he'd love Aiden how Gage *should have*.

"Which brings me to my next concern. I'm Aiden's mother and have been making all decisions regarding him since he was born. I'm not going to lie and claim including you will be an easy adjustment, but I promise to try. But that said, we're his parents, and we will make those decisions together. Us. Without interference from the Wellses."

"Isobel," he growled, pushing off the desk. He stalked a step closer to her, but then drew to an abrupt halt. Shoving a hand through his hair, he turned his head to stare out the window, a tic pulsing along his clenched jaw.

Cursing herself for doing it, she regarded the rigid line. That night when they'd been two nameless, faceless people in the dark, she hadn't needed sight to tell how strong and hard his jaw had been. Her fingers and lips had relayed the information.

God, she needed to stop dwelling on that night. It was

gone, and for all intents and purposes, it didn't happen. It'd disappeared as soon as the morning light had dawned.

"Isobel." He returned his attention to her, and she braced herself for both the impact of his gaze and his words. "I agree with your conditions, but they are his grandparents. And you need to understand that I won't keep him away from them."

Like you have. The accusation remained unsaid, but it screamed silently in the room.

"I emailed Baron and Helena pictures of Aiden after I left for California. And when every one of those messages bounced back as if I'd been blocked, I mailed them, along with letters telling them how he was doing and growing. But they came back unopened, marked 'return to sender.' So I didn't keep him from them. They kept themselves out of his life."

Darius frowned. "Why would they lie about that?"

"Yes. Why would they lie about that?" She shook her head, holding up a hand when his lips parted to what would, no doubt, be another defense of his friend's family. "I have one last condition."

She paused, this one more difficult than the previous ones. Demanding things on Aiden's behalf proved easy for her. But this one… This one involved her and Darius. And it acknowledged that something had happened between them. That "something" being he'd made her body sing like an opera diva hitting notes high enough to shatter glass.

"What is it?" Darius asked when she didn't immediately state the added rule.

"No sex," she blurted out. Mentally rolling her eyes at herself, she inhaled a deep breath and tried it again. "This arrangement is in name only. No sex."

He stilled, his powerful body going motionless. Shadows gathered in his gaze, broiling like a storm building on a dark horizon.

"I guess I need to applaud your honesty," he drawled. "This time around, you're being up front about your plans to betray your husband with another man."

Fury scalded her, and as unwise as it was, she stalked forward, until only inches separated them. "You're so damn sure of yourself. It must be nice to know everything and have all the answers. To be so sure you have all the facts, when in truth you don't. Know. A. Damn. Thing," she bit out.

He lowered his head until their noses nearly bumped, and his breath coasted across her mouth. She could taste his kiss, the sinful, addictive flavor of it.

Memories bombarded her. Memories of his lips owning hers, taking, giving. Of his hands cupping her breasts, tweaking the tips that even now ached and taunted beneath her bra. Of his fingers burying themselves inside her over and over, stroking places inside her that had never been touched before.

Of his cock, so hard and demanding beneath her...

"So you don't care if I take another woman?" he pressed, shifting so another inch disappeared.

An image of him covering someone else, moving over her, straining against her...driving into her, filled her head. A hot wave of anger swamped her, green-tipped claws raking her chest. Her fingers curled into her palms, but she shook her head. Whether it was to rid herself of the mental pictures or in denial of the emotion that smacked of jealousy—a jealousy she had no business, no right, to feel—she didn't know.

"No," she lied, retreating. "Just respect my son and me."

The corner of his mouth tipped into a scornful half smile. "Of course," he said, the words containing more than a hint of a sneer. "Now I have a couple of conditions. The first, we marry in three months. That should give you plenty of time to become accustomed to the arrangement, me and condition number two. You and Aiden are going to move in with me."

Oh, hell no. "No, not happening."

He nodded. "Yes, you are," he contradicted, the flint in his voice echoed in his eyes. "That's my deal breaker. One of my reasons for this whole arrangement is for Aiden to be raised in a safe, secure environment. He'll have both here."

"Okay, fine. I understand that. But why do we need to live with you. We could find an apartment or home in Edison Park or Beverly—"

"No," he stated flatly, cutting her protest off at the knees. "You'll both live here, and Aiden will know a home with two parents. This isn't a point for discussion, Isobel."

Shit. Living under the same roof as Darius? That would be like Eve sleeping under the damn apple tree. Temptation. Trouble. But what option did she have? Sighing, she pinched the bridge of her nose. Okay, she could do it. Besides, this house was huge. She didn't even have to occupy the same side as Darius.

"Fine," she breathed. "Is there anything else?" She had the sudden need to get out of the house. Away from him. At least until she had no choice but to share his space.

"One last thing," he said, his tone deepening, sending an ominous tremor skipping up her spine. "Say my name."

She stared at him, not comprehending his request. No, his order.

"What?"

"Say my name, Isobel," he repeated.

Tilting her head to the side, she conceded warily. "Darius."

Heat flashed in his eyes, there and gone so fast, she questioned whether she imagined it. "That's the first time you've said my name since that morning."

He didn't need to specify to which morning he referred. But the first time… That couldn't be true. They'd had several conversations, or confrontations, since then... Then again, if it were true...

"Why does it matter?" she asked, something dark, complicated and hot twisting her stomach, pooling lower. "Why do you want to hear me say your name?"

He stared at her, the silence growing and pulsing until its deafening heartbeat filled the room. Her own heart thudded against her sternum, adding to the rhythm.

"Because I've wanted to know what it sounds like on your tongue," he said, his voice quiet.

But so loud it rang in her ears. *On your tongue*. The words, so charged with a velvet, sensual promise, or threat—she couldn't decide which—ricocheted against the walls of her head.

She shivered before she could check her telltale reaction. And those eagle eyes didn't miss it. They turned molten, and his nostrils flared, his lips somehow appearing fuller, more carnal.

Danger.

Every survival instinct she possessed blared the warning in bright, blinking red. And in spite of the warmth between her legs transforming to an aching pulse, she heeded it.

Without a goodbye, she whirled around and got the hell out of there.

Maybe one day she could discover the trick to outrunning herself.

But for now, escaping Darius would have to do.

Five

Darius passed through the iron gate surrounding the Wellses' Gold Coast mansion and climbed the steps to the front door. The limestone masterpiece had been in their family for 120 years, harkening back to a time when more than the small immediate family lived under its sloped-and-turreted slate roof. As he twisted his key in the lock and pushed the heavy front door open, he considered himself blessed to be counted among that family. Not by blood, but by choice and love.

After entering the home, he bypassed the formal living and dining areas, and moved toward the rear of the home, the multihued glow from the stained-glass skylight guiding his way. This time of day, a little after five o'clock, Baron should have arrived home from the office. Since his heart attack, he'd cut his work days shorter. Helena and Gabriella should also be home, since they served dinner at six o'clock sharp every evening. In the chaotic turns Darius's life had suffered, this routine and the surety of family tradition had been—and still was—a reassurance, one strong, steady stone in a battered foundation.

But tonight, with the news he had to deliver, he hated potentially being the one taking a hammer to them.

"Darius," Helena greeted, rising from the feminine couch that had been her domain as long as he could remember. The other members of the family could occupy the armchairs or the other sofa, but the small, antique couch was all hers, like a queen with her throne. "There you are."

She crossed the room, clasping his hands in hers and rising on her toes. Obediently, he lowered his head so she could press her lips to one cheek and then the other. Her floral perfume drifted to his nose and wrapped him in the familiarity of home. "I have to admit we've all been discussing you, wondering what it is you have to talk to us about. You're being so mysterious."

She smiled at him, and her expression only increased the unease sitting in his gut. He'd called to give them a heads-up without relaying the reason. This kind of information—about his impending marriage—required a face-to-face conversation.

"Hi, son." Baron came forward and patted him on the shoulder, enfolding Darius's hand in his. Warmth swirled in his chest, as it did every time the man he admired claimed him. "Sit and please tell us your news. Helena and Gabriella have been driving me crazy with their guessing. Do us all a favor and put them out of their gossipy misery."

"Oh, it's just been us, hmm?" Gabriella teased, arching an eyebrow at her father. She turned to Darius and handed him a glass of the Remy Martin cognac he preferred. "He wasn't exactly tuning out over the gossip about the blackout. It seems several people have leveled suits against Richard Dent, the tech billionaire who owns the mansion, for emotional distress. Apparently his apology for trapping people in overnight wasn't enough." She shook her head. "I didn't see him, but I even hear Gideon Knight was there. Can you imagine being caught in the dark with *him*?"

"I've met the man," Darius said, referring to the financial genius who'd launched a wildly successful start-up a couple of years ago. "He's reserved, but not as formidable as people claim."

He accepted the drink, bending to brush a kiss across Gabriella's cheek. She clasped his other hand in hers, squeezing it before releasing him to sit on a chair adjacent to her mother. He sank onto one across from her, while, with a sigh, Baron lowered to the largest armchair in the small circle.

Darius shot him a glance. "How're you feeling, Baron?"

"Fine, fine." He waved off the concerned question. "I'm just old," he grumbled.

After studying him for another few seconds, Darius finally nodded, but his worry over causing Baron more stress with his announcement doubled. Even so, he had to tell them, rather than have them discover the truth from another source.

"You already know Isobel Hughes has returned to Chicago."

All warmth disappeared from Helena's face, her gaze freezing into emerald chips of ice, her lips thinning. Gabriella wore a similar expression, but Baron's differed from the women in his family. Instead of furious, he appeared... tired.

"Yes," Helena hissed. "Gabriella told us Isobel showed up at the gala. How dare she?" she continued. "I would've had her arrested immediately."

"Attending a social event isn't a punishable offense, honey," Baron said, his tone weary.

His wife aimed a narrow-eyed glare in his direction, while Gabriella shook her head. "She's lucky the blackout occurred. Criminal or not, I would've had her escorted from the premises."

Leaning forward and propping his elbows on his spread knees, Darius sighed. "I have an announcement, and it concerns Isobel…and her son. I've asked her to marry me, and I'll become Aiden's stepfather."

A heavy silence plummeted into the room. They gaped at him, or at least Helena and Gabriella did. Again, Baron's reaction didn't coincide with his wife's or daughter's. He didn't glare at Darius, just studied him with a measured contemplation, his fingers templed beneath his chin.

"Are you insane?" Gabriella rasped. She jolted from the chair as if propelled from a cannon. Fury snapped in her eyes. But underneath, Darius caught the shivering note of hurt and betrayal. "Darius, what are you thinking?"

"You saw for yourself what she did to Gage, how she destroyed him. How could you even contemplate tying yourself to that woman?" Helena demanded, her voice trembling.

Pain radiated from his chest, pulsing and hot, with the knowledge that he was hurting the two women he loved most in the world. "I—"

"He's doing it for us," Baron declared, his low baritone quieting Helena's and Gabriella's agonized tirades. "He's marrying her so we can have a relationship with the boy."

"Is this true?" Helena demanded. Darius nodded, and she spread her bejeweled hands wide, shaking her head. "But why? He's not even our grandson."

"He is," Darius stated, his tone brooking no argument. "I've seen him," he added, softening his tone. "He's definitely Gage's son."

Gabriella snorted, crossing her arms over her chest. "You'll forgive us if we don't trust her lying, cheating words."

"Then trust mine."

He and Gabriella engaged in a visual standoff for several seconds before she spun on her heel and stalked across the room, toward the small bar.

"Gabriella's right," Helena said. "Sentimentality could be coloring your opinion, have you seeing a resemblance to Gage because you want there to be one." She paused, her pale fingers fluttering to her throat. "That she refused to have a DNA test done after his birth solidified that he wasn't Gage's son, for me. If he was, she wouldn't have been afraid to have one performed. No." She shook her head. "She's caused too much harm to this family," Helena continued. "I can't forget how she isolated Gage from us, so he had to sneak away just to see us. She destroyed him. I'll never forgive her. Ever."

"And no one asked you to be our sacrificial lamb," Gabriella interjected. "What about your life, marrying someone you love?" she rasped. Clearing her throat, she crossed the room and handed her mother a glass of wine before returning to the chair she'd vacated. "There's a very reasonable solution, and it doesn't require you shackling yourself to a woman who's proven she can't be trusted. If by some miracle the child is really Gage's, then we can fight for custody. We would probably be more fit guardians than *her* anyway."

"Take a small boy away from the only parent he's ever known? Regardless of our opinion concerning her moral values, I've seen her with him. She adores him, and she's his world. It would devastate Aiden to be removed from her." And it would kill Isobel. Of that, Darius had zero doubt. "Isobel wouldn't give up custody without a hard battle, which would be taxing on all of you, too. No, this is the best solution for everyone." He met each of their eyes. "And it's done."

Several minutes passed, and Darius didn't try to fill the silence, allowing them the time to accept what he understood was hard news. But they didn't have a choice. None of them did.

"Thank you, Darius," Baron murmured. "I know this wasn't an easy decision, and we appreciate it, support you in it. Bringing the boy into his family—it's what Gage would've wanted. And we will respect Isobel as his mother...and your wife."

Helena emitted a strangled sound, but she didn't contradict her husband. Gabriella didn't either. But she stood once more and rushed from the room.

"Just be careful, Darius. I've lost one son to Isobel Hughes. I don't think I could bear it if I lost another," Helena pleaded, the pain in her softly spoken words like jagged spikes stabbing his heart. Rising, she cradled his cheek before following Gabriella.

"They'll be fine, son," Baron assured him.

Darius nodded, but apprehension settled in his chest, an albatross he couldn't shake off. His intentions were to unite this family, return some of Helena and Baron's joy by reconciling them with their son's child.

But staring at the entrance where Helena and Gabriella had disappeared, he prayed all his efforts wouldn't end up destroying what he desired to build.

Six

Isobel leaned over Aiden, gently sweeping her hand down his dark curls. After the excitement of moving into a new home and new room jammed with new toys and a race car bed he adored, Aiden had finally exhausted himself. She'd managed to get him fed, bathed and settled in for the night, and all while avoiding Darius.

It'd been a week since she'd agreed to the devil's bargain, and now, fully ensconced in his house, she could no longer use Aiden as an excuse to hide away. With a sigh, she ensured the night-light was on and exited the bedroom, leaving the door cracked behind her. She quietly descended the staircase and headed toward the back of the home, where the kitchen was. She would've preferred not to come downstairs at all, but her stomach rumbled.

The room followed what appeared to be the theme of the home—huge, with windows. Top-of-the-line appliances gleamed under the bright light of a crystal chandelier, and a butcher block and marble island dominated the middle of the vast space. A breakfast nook with a round table and four chairs added a sense of warmth and intimacy to the room. Isobel shook her head as she approached one of the two double-door refrigerators.

She should be grateful. But even now, standing in a kitchen her mother would surrender one of her beloved children to have, she couldn't escape the phantom noose slowly tugging tighter, strangling her. Powerlessness. Purposelessness. Futile anger. The emotions eddied and churned within her like a storm-tossed sea, pitching her, drowning her.

She'd promised herself two years ago that she'd never be at the mercy of another man. Yet if she didn't find some way to protect herself, maintain the identity of the woman she'd come to be, she would end up in a prison worthy of *Architectural Digest*.

Minutes later, she had the makings of a ham-and-cheese sandwich on the island. Real ham—none of that convenience-store deli ham for Darius King—and some kind of gourmet cheese that she could barely pronounce but that tasted like heaven.

"Isobel."

She glanced up from layering lettuce and tomatoes onto her bread to find Darius in the entrance. Her fingers froze, as did the rest of her body. Would this deep, acute awareness occur every time she saw him? It zipped through her body like an electrical current, lighting every nerve ending.

"Darius," she replied, bowing her head back over her dinner.

Though she'd removed her gaze from him, the image of his powerful body seemed emblazoned on her mind's eye. Broad shoulders encased in a thin but soft wool sweater, the V-neck offering her a view of his strong, golden throat, collarbone and the barest hint of his upper chest. Jeans draped low on his hips and clung to the thick strength of his thighs. And his feet...bare.

This was the most relaxed she'd ever seen him, and that he'd allow her to glimpse him this way...it created an intimacy between them she resented and, God, foolishly craved. Because as silly as the presumption might be, she had a feeling he didn't unarm himself like this around many people.

Remember why you're here, her subconscious sniped. *Blackmail and coercion, not because you belong.*

"Did you want a sandwich?" she offered, the reminder shoring up any chinks in her guard.

"Thank you. It looks good." He moved farther into the room and withdrew one of the stools lining the island. Sitting down across from her, he nabbed the bread bin—because what else would one store freshly baked bread in?—and cut two thick slices while she returned to the refrigerator for more meat and cheese. "I'm sorry I had to leave earlier. I didn't want to miss Aiden's first night in the house. There was a bit of an emergency at the office."

"On a Saturday?" she asked, glancing at him.

He shook his head, the corner of his mouth quirking in a rueful smile. "When you're the CEO and president of the company, there's no such thing as a Saturday. Every day is a workday."

"If you let it be," she said. But then again, she understood the need to work when it called. As a single mom with more bills than funds, she hadn't been able to turn down a shift at the supermarket or tell her mom she would skip helping her clean a house.

"True," he agreed, accepting the ham she handed him. "But then I've never had a reason to dial back on the work. I do now," he murmured.

Aiden. He meant Aiden and being a stepfather. She silently repeated the words to herself. But they didn't prevent the warm fluttering in her belly or the hitch in her breath.

"How old are you?" she blurted out, desperate to distract herself from the completely inappropriate and stupid heat that pooled south of her belly button. "I don't mean to be rude, but you don't seem old enough to run a company."

"Thirty," he replied. She could feel his weighty gaze on her face like a physical touch as she finished preparing his meal. "My grandfather started the business as one corporation, and my father grew it into several corporations, eventually folding them all under one parent company. When he died, my father left King Industries Unlimited to me, and I started working there when I was seventeen, in the mail room. I went from there to retail sales associate to account manager and through the ranks, learning the business. By the time I stepped in as CEO and president at twenty-five, and with the guidance of Baron, I had been an employee for seven years."

"Wow," she breathed. "Many men would've just assumed that position as their due and wouldn't bother with starting from the bottom." She hesitated, but then whispered, "I can only imagine your father would've been proud of your work ethic."

With his amber eyes gleaming, Darius nodded. "I hope so. It's how he did it, and I followed in his footsteps."

Their gazes connected, and the breath stuttered in her lungs. Her pulse jammed out an erratic beat at her neck and in her head.

Clearing her throat, she dropped her attention to her sandwich, and with more effort than it required, sliced it in half and did the same to his. "Tell me more about your work?" she requested, cursing the slight waver in her voice. Her biggest mistake would be letting Darius know he affected her in any manner. *Get it together, woman*, she scolded herself. "Was it hard suddenly running such a huge company?"

Over ham-and-cheese sandwiches, they spoke about his job and all it required. Eventually the conversation curved into more personal topics. He shared that his home had been his parents', one they'd purchased only months before they'd died. And the pocket watch collection had been his father's, and like the family company, Darius had taken it over and continued to add to it. She told him about her family, leaving out the part about her brother's lucrative but illegal side business. Even her mother pretended it didn't exist and refused to accept any money earned from it. Isobel also added amusing stories about Aiden from the last two years.

"He took one look at Santa and let out the loudest, most terrified scream. I think the old guy damn near had a heart attack." She chuckled, remembering her baby's reaction to the mall Santa. "He started squirming and kicking his legs. His foot caught good ol' Saint Nick right in the boys, and they had to shut down Winter Wonderland for a half hour while, I'm sure, Santa iced himself in his workshop."

Darius laughed, the loud bark echoing in the room. He shook his head, shoulders shaking. His eyes, bright with humor, crinkled at the corners, and his smile lit up his normally serious expression.

An unsmiling Darius was devastatingly handsome.

A smiling Darius? Beyond description.

Slowly, as they continued to meet each other's gazes, the lightness in the room dimmed, converting into something weightier, darker. A thickness—congested with memories, things better left unspoken and desire—gathered between them. Even though her mind screamed caution, she didn't—couldn't—glance away. And if she were brutally honest? She didn't want to.

"You're different from how I remember you," he said, his gaze roaming over her face. Her lips prickled when that intense regard fell on her mouth and hovered for several heated moments. "Even though it was only a couple of times, you were quieter then, maybe even a little timid and withdrawn. At least around me. Gage said you were different around your family."

"I trusted them." She knew they wouldn't mock her just because she didn't use the proper fork or couldn't discuss politics. They accepted her, loved her. She'd never feared them.

Darius frowned, leaning forward on the crossed arms he'd propped on the marble island. "You didn't trust your husband?"

She paused, indecision about how much to share temporarily muting her. But, in the end, she refused to lie. "No," she admitted, the ghostly remnants of hurt from that time in her life rasping her voice. "I didn't."

How could she? Gage had been a liar, and he'd betrayed their short marriage. He'd promised her Harry and Meghan and had given her Henry VIII and wives one, two and five.

To gain his family's sympathy after marrying Isobel, he'd thrown her under the proverbial bus, accusing her of tricking him into marrying her by claiming she'd been pregnant. She hadn't been, though it'd happened shortly after their marriage. At first, they'd been happy—or at least she'd believed they'd been. True, they'd lived in a tiny apartment, living off her small paycheck from the grocery store while he looked for work since his family had cut him off, but they'd loved one another. After she'd refused to take a paternity test at the demand of his parents, things had changed. Subtly, at first, he'd isolated her from family and friends. He'd claimed that since his family had disowned him, it was just the two of them—soon to be the three of them—against the world. But that world had become smaller, darker, lonelier...scarier.

Gage had been a master gaslighter. Unknown to her, he'd thrown himself on his parents' mercies, spewing lies— that she'd demanded he abandon his family, that she was cheating on him. All to remain in the family fold as their golden child and maintain their compassion and empathy by making Isobel out to be a treacherous bitch he couldn't divorce and turn back out on the street. In truth, he'd been a spoiled, out-of-control child who hadn't wanted her but didn't want anyone else to have her either.

"He was your husband," Darius said, his tone as low as the shadows already accumulating in his eyes.

"He was my jailor," she snapped.

"Just like this is a prison?" he growled, sweeping a hand to encompass the kitchen, the beautiful home. "He gave you everything, while giving up his own family, his friends—hell, his world—for you. What more could he have possibly done to make you happy?"

Pain and anger clashed inside her, eating away any trace of the calm and enjoyment she'd found with Darius during the past hour. "Kindness. Compassion. Loyalty. Fidelity."

"It's convenient that he isn't here to defend himself, isn't it? Still, it's hard to play the victim now when we all know how you betrayed him, made a fool of him. In spite of all that, he wouldn't walk away from you." Fire flared in his eyes. The same fierce emotion incinerating her, hardened his full lips into a grim line. "I saw him just before he died. I begged him to walk away, to leave you. But he wouldn't. Even as it broke him that he couldn't even claim his son because of the men you'd fucked behind his back."

Trembling, Isobel stood, the scratch of the stool's legs across the tiled floor a discordant screech. Flattening her palms on the counter, she glared at him, in this moment, hating him.

"I broke him? He broke me! And destroyed whatever love I still had for him when he looked at our baby and called him a bastard. So don't you dare talk to me about being ungrateful. You don't know what the hell you're talking about."

Refusing to remain and accept any more accusations, she whipped around the island and stalked toward the kitchen entrance. Screw him. He didn't know her, had no clue—

"Damn it, Isobel," he snapped, seconds before his fingers wrapped around her upper arm.

"Don't touch—" She whirled back around and, misjudging how close he stood behind her, slammed into the solid wall of his chest. Her hands shot up in an instinctive attempt to prevent the tumble backward, but the hard band of his arms wrapped around her saved her from falling onto her ass.

The moment her body collided with his, the protest died on her tongue. Desire—unwanted, uncontrollable and greedy—swamped her. Her fingers curled into his sweater in an instinctive attempt to hold on to the only solid thing in a world that had constricted then yawned endlessly wide, leaving her dangling over a crumbling edge.

"Isobel." Her name, uttered in that sin-on-the-rocks voice, rumbled through her, and she shook her head, refusing to acknowledge it—or the eruption of electrical pulses that raced up and down her spine. "Look at me."

His long fingers slid up her back, over her nape and tunneled into her hair. She groaned, unable to trap the betraying sound. Not when his hand tangled in the strands, tugging her head backward, sending tiny prickles along her scalp. She sank her teeth into her bottom lip, locking down on another embarrassing sound of pleasure.

"No," he growled, pressing his thumb to the center of her abused lip and freeing it. With a low, carnal hum, he rubbed a caress over the flesh. "Don't hold back from me. Let me hear what I do to you."

Oh, God. If she could ease her grip on his shirt, she'd clap her palms over her ears to block out his words. She hadn't forgotten how his voice had aided and abetted his touch in unraveling every one of her inhibitions the night of the blackout. It was a velvet weapon, one that slipped beneath her skin, her steel-encased guards, to wreak sensual havoc.

"Look at me, sweetheart," he ordered again. This time she complied, lifting her lashes to meet his golden gaze. "Good," he murmured, giving her bottom lip one last sweep with his fingers before burying them in her hair so both hands cupped her head. "Keep those fairy eyes on me."

Fairy eyes.

The description, so unlike him and so reminiscent of the man in the dark hallway weeks ago, swept over her like a soft spring rain. And then she ceased to think.

Because he proceeded to devastate her.

If their first kiss in the dark weeks ago started as a gentle exploration, this one was fierce. His mouth claimed and conquered, his tongue demanding an entrance she willingly surrendered. Wild and raw, he devoured her like a starving man intent on satisfying a bottomless craving. Again and again, he sucked, lapped, dueled, demanding she enter into carnal battle with him.

Submit to him. Take him. Dominate him.

With a needy whimper that should probably have mortified her, she fisted his shirt harder and rose on her toes, granting him even more access and commanding more of him. Angling her head, she opened her mouth wider, savoring his unique flavor, getting drunk on it.

But it wasn't enough. Never enough.

"Jesus Christ," he swore against her lips, nipping the lower curve, then pressing stinging kisses along her jaw and down her throat.

Kisses that echoed in her breasts, sensitizing them, tightening the tips. Kisses that eddied and swirled low in her belly. Kisses that had her thighs squeezing to contain the ache between her legs. Already a nagging emptiness stretched wide in her sex, begging to be filled by his fingers, his cock. Didn't matter. Just as long as some part of him was inside her, branding her.

The thought snuck under the desire, and once it infiltrated, she couldn't eject it. Instead it rebounded against her skull, loud and aggressive. *Branding me. Branding me.*

And Darius would do it; he would imprint himself into her skin, her body until she couldn't erase him from her thoughts...her heart. Until he slowly took over, and she ceased to exist except for the sole purpose of pleasing him...of loving him.

No. No, damn it.

Never again would she allow that to happen.

With a muted cry, she shoved her palms against his chest, lunging out of his embrace, away from his kiss, his touch.

Their harsh, jagged breaths reverberated in the kitchen. His broad chest rose and fell, his piercing gaze narrowed on her like that of a bird of prey's, waiting for her to make the slightest move so he could swoop in and capture her.

Even as her brain yelled at her to get the hell out of there, her body urged her to let herself be caught and devoured.

"No," she whispered, but not to him, to her traitorous libido.

"Then you better go," Darius ground out as if she'd spoken to him. *"Now."*

Not waiting for another warning, she whipped around, raced down the hall and bounded up the stairs. Once she closed the bedroom door behind her, she stumbled across the floor and sank to the mattress.

Oh, God, what had she done?

The no-sex rule had been hers. And yet the first time he'd touched her, she'd burned faster than kindling in a campfire.

Desire and passion were the gateways to losing reason, control and, eventually, independence.

Those who forget the past are condemned to repeat it.

She'd heard the quote many times throughout her life. But never had it been so true as this moment.

She'd made this one mistake.

She couldn't afford another.

Seven

An ugly sense of déjà vu settled over Isobel as she stared at the ornate front door of the Wellses' home. It'd been a slightly brisk October evening just like this one four years ago when she'd arrived on this doorstep, arm tucked in Gage's, excited and nervous to meet his family. She'd been so painfully naïve then, at twenty, never imaging the disdain she would experience once she crossed the threshold.

The differences between then and now could fill a hoarder's house. One, she was no longer that young girl so innocently in love. Second, she fully expected to be scorned and derided. And perhaps the most glaring change.

She stood next to Darius, but with Gage's son riding her hip.

Her stomach clenched, pulling into knots so snarled and tight, they would need Houdini himself to unravel them.

"There's no need to be nervous," Darius murmured beside her, settling a hand at the small of her back. The warmth of his hand penetrated the layers of her coat and dress, and she steeled herself against it, wishing he'd remove it. When about to enter the lion's den, she couldn't allow her focus and wits to be compromised by his touch. "I've already talked to them about us, and I'll be right here with you."

Was that supposed to be a reassurance? A pep talk? Well, both were epic fails. She wore no blinders when it came to Gage's family. Nothing—no talk or his presence—would ever convince them to accept her. She'd robbed them of their most precious gift. There was no forgiveness for that.

"This night is about Aiden," she said more to herself than him. "All I care about is how they treat him."

The weight of his stare stroked her face like the last rays of the rapidly sinking sun. She kept her attention trained on the door. It'd been almost a week since she'd moved into his home—since the night they'd kissed. And in that time, she'd become a master of avoidance. With a house the size of a museum, it hadn't proven to be difficult. When he spent time with Aiden, she withdrew to her room. And when she couldn't evade him, she ensured Aiden remained a buffer between them. A little cowardly? Yes. But when engaged in a battle for her dignity and emotional sanity, the saying "by any means necessary" had become her motto.

"They'll love him," he replied, with certainty and determination ringing in his voice.

Before she could respond, the door opened and Gabriella, Gage's sister, stood in the entranceway. The beautiful, willowy brunette, who was a feminine version of her brother, smiled, stepping forward to press a kiss to Darius's cheek.

An unfamiliar and nasty emotion coiled and rattled in Isobel's chest. Her grip on Aiden tightened, while her vision sharpened on the other woman.

Whoa.

Isobel blinked. Sucked in a breath. What the hell was

going on? No way could she actually be...*jealous*. Not by any stretch of the imagination did Darius belong to her. And even if in some realm with unicorns and rainbows where he was hers to claim, Gabriella was like a sister to him.

Get a grip.

If this overreaction heralded the evening's future, it promised to be a long one. Long and painful.

"It's about time you arrived," Gabriella said, laying a hand on his chest. "Mother and Dad are climbing the walls."

"Now, that I'd pay money to see," he drawled.

So would Isobel.

"Gabriella, you remember Isobel." Darius's hand slid higher, to the middle of her back, and just this once, she was thankful for it.

The other woman switched her focus from Darius to Isobel. Jade eyes so like her brother's met hers, the warmth that had greeted Darius replaced with ice. Isobel fought not to shiver under the chill. *She can't hurt you. No one in this house can hurt you*, Isobel reminded herself, repeating the mantra. Hoping it was true.

"Of course," Gabriella said, her tone even, polite. "Hello, Isobel." She shifted her gaze to Aiden, who hugged Isobel's neck, his face buried against her coat. Unsurprisingly, he had a thumb stuck firmly in his mouth. Isobel didn't blame him or remove it. Hell, she suddenly wanted to do the same. "And this must be Aiden."

"Yes, it is." Darius removed his hand from Isobel's back and reached around to stroke a hand down her son's curls. Curls that were the same nearly black shade as Gabriella's. "Aiden, can you say hi?"

Shyly, Aiden lifted his head and whispered, "Hi," giving Gabriella a small wave.

The other woman stared at the toddler, her lips forming a small O-shape. Moisture brightened her gaze, and she blinked rapidly. "Hi, Aiden," she whispered back. Drawing in an audible breath, she looked at Darius. "He looks like Gage."

Anger flared to life in Isobel's chest. She wanted to snap, *Of course he does*, but she swallowed it down. Yet she could do nothing about the flames still flickering inside her.

Part of her wanted to say screw this and demand Darius drive them home. But the other half—the half that wanted the Wells family's derision toward her regarding Aiden's paternity laid to rest—convinced her to remain in place. She still resented their rejection of her son, but if they were willing to meet her halfway so Aiden could know them, then she could try to let it go.

Try.

"Come in." Gabriella stepped backwards, waving them inside, her regard still fixed on Aiden.

Minutes later, with their coats turned over to a waiting maid, they all strode toward the back of the house and entered a small parlor. Helena, lovely and regal, was perched upon the champagne-colored settee like a queen surveying her subjects from her throne. And Baron occupied the largest armchair, his salt-and-pepper hair—more salt now than the last time she'd seen him—gleaming under the light thrown by a chandelier.

Their conversation ended when Gabriella appeared with Darius, Aiden and Isobel in tow. Slowly, Baron stood, and Isobel just managed to refrain from frowning. Though still tall and handsome, his frame seemed thinner, even a little more…fragile. And perhaps the most shocking change was that the hard, condemning expression that had been his norm when forced to share the air with her was not in attendance. By no means was his gaze welcoming, but it definitely didn't carry the harshness it formerly had.

But the censure his demeanor lacked, Helena's more than made up for. She rose as well, her scrutiny as frigid and sharp as an icicle. Her mouth formed a flat, disapproving line, and for a moment Isobel almost believed she'd stumbled back in time. Gage's mother had disliked her on sight, and like a fine wine, the dislike had only aged. Into hatred.

Suddenly Isobel's arms tightened around Aiden, flooded with the need to shield him, protect him. And herself. He was her lodestone, reminding her that she was no longer that timid, impressionable girl from the past.

"Darius." Baron crossed the room, his hand extended. Darius clasped it, and they pulled each other close for a quick but loving embrace. Then the older man turned toward her, and even with his lack of animosity, she braced herself. "Isobel, welcome back to our home." He stretched his hand toward her, and after a brief hesitation, she accepted it, her heart pulsing in her throat. His grip squeezed around her fingers, rendering her speechless, the gesture the most warmth he'd ever shown her. "And this is Aiden."

Awe saturated his deep baritone, the same wonder that had filtered through his daughter's in the foyer. His nostrils flared, his fingers curling into his palms as if he fought the need to reach out and touch her son. Clearing his throat, Baron switched his gaze back to Isobel.

"He has your eyes, but his features... It's like looking at a baby picture of my son," he rasped. "May I...?" He held his arms out toward Aiden.

Nerves jingled in her belly, but the plea in the man's eyes trumped them. "Aiden? Do you want to go to Mr. Baron?" She loosened her grip on her son and tried to hand him, but the child clung harder to her as he shook his head. "I'm sorry," she murmured, feeling regret at the flash of disappointment and hurt in the man's gaze. "He's a little shy around new people."

"A shame," Gabriella murmured behind her.

Isobel stiffened, a stinging retort dancing on the tip of her tongue. But Darius interceded, tossing a quelling glance toward Gage's sister over his shoulder. With an arched eyebrow and open hands, he silently requested to take Aiden. Dipping her chin, she passed her son to Darius, who practically launched himself into the man's arms. Aiden popped his thumb back into his mouth, grinning at Darius around it.

"Well, how about that," Baron whispered. "He certainly seems to have taken to you."

Darius shrugged, sweeping a hand down Aiden's small back. "It doesn't take long for him to warm up. And once he does, he'll talk your ear off." He poked Aiden's rounded tummy, and the boy giggled.

The cheerful, innocent sound stole into Isobel's heart, as it'd had done from the very first time she'd heard it.

"I have to admit, he does resemble Gage," Helena said, appearing at her husband's side, studying Aiden. "Isobel." She nodded, before dismissing her and turning to Darius, an affectionate smile thawing her expression. "Darius." She tilted her head, and he brushed a kiss on her cheek. "I haven't seen you in days. But it seems you have time for everyone else." She tapped him playfully on the chest. "Beverly Sheldon told me how she saw you at the Livingstons' dinner party. And how Shelly Livingston couldn't seem to keep her hands to herself." Helena chuckled as if immensely amused by Shelly Livingston's grabby hands.

Isobel fought not to react to the first shot fired across the bow. It hadn't taken long at all. She thought Helena or Gabriella would've at least waited until after drinks before they got in the first dig, but apparently the "you're an interloper and don't belong, darling" portion of the evening had begun.

Yet her purpose—letting Isobel know that Darius had attended a social event without her on his arm, probably out of shame—had struck true. Which was as inane as that flash of jealousy with Gabriella. Pretending to be the newly engaged, loving couple hadn't been a part of their bargain.

He could do as he wanted, escort whom he wanted, flirt with whom he wanted...sleep with whom he wanted. It didn't matter to her.

Liar.

Flipping her once again intrusive, know-it-all subconscious the middle finger, she shored up the walls surrounding her heart.

"Beverly Sheldon gossips too much and needs to find a hobby," Darius replied, frowning. "It was an impromptu business dinner, not a party, and I'm sure Shelly's fiancé, who also attended with her father, would've had some objections if she 'couldn't seem to keep her hands to herself.'"

Helena waved his explanation off with a flick of her fingers and another laugh. "Well, you're a handsome man, Darius. It's not surprising women flock to you."

"Helena," Baron said, a warning heavy in her name.

"Now, don't 'Helena' me, Baron." She tsked, brushing her husband's arm before strolling off toward the bar across the room. "Would anyone like a drink?"

Good God. This was going to be a really long evening.

"Have you decided on whether or not you'll acquire SouthernCare Insurance?" Baron asked Darius, reclining in his chair as one of the servants placed an entrée plate in front of him.

Isobel let the business talk float over her, as she had most of the discussions around the dinner table. If the topics weren't about business, then it was Helena and Gabriella speaking about people and events Isobel didn't know anything about, and neither woman had made the attempt to draw her into the conversation. Not that she minded. The less they said to each other, the better the chance of Isobel making it through this dinner without emotional injuries from their sly innuendoes.

Still, right now she envied her son. By the time dinner

was ready to be served, Aiden had been nodding off in Darius's arms. He'd taken Aiden to one of the bedrooms and settled him in. Aiden had escaped this farce of a family dinner, but she hadn't been as lucky.

Mimicking Baron, Isobel shifted backward, granting the servant plenty of room to set down her plate of food. When she saw the food, she barely managed not to flinch. Prime rib, buttered asparagus and acorn squash.

Gage's favorite meal.

She lifted her head and met Helena's arctic gaze. So the choice hadn't been a coincidence. No, it'd been deliberate, and just another way to let Isobel know she hadn't been forgiven.

Nothing had been forgotten.

Message received.

Picking up her fork—the correct fork—and knife, Isobel prepared to eat the perfectly cooked meat that would undoubtedly taste like ash on her tongue.

"I was leaning toward yes before the trouble with their vice president leaked." Darius paused, murmuring a "thank you" as a plate was set in front of him. "One of their employees came forward about long-time, systematic sexual harassment within the company, and their senior vice president of operations is one of the key perpetrators. No," he said, shaking his head, tone grim. "I won't have King Industries Unlimited tainted with that kind of behavior."

Unlike the rest of the conversation surrounding business, Darius's comment snagged her attention, surprising her so much, she blurted out, "You would really base your decision on that?"

Silence crackled in the room. In the quiet, her question seemed to bounce off the walls. Everyone stared at her, but she refused to cringe.

It was Darius's scrutiny she resolutely met, ignoring

the others'. And in his eyes, she didn't spy irritation at her interruption. No, just the usual intensity that rendered her breathless.

"Of course. I don't condone it, and I won't be associated with any business or person who does. Every person under my employ or the umbrella of my company should have the expectation of safety and an environment free of intimidation."

"Your employees are lucky to work for you then," she murmured.

More and more companies were trying to change their policies and eliminate sexual harassment—or at least indulge in lip service about removing it. But the truth couldn't be denied—not everyone enjoyed that sense of fairness or security. Even at the supermarket, the supervisor didn't think anything of calling her honey or flirting with her, going so far as to occasionally say how "lucky" her man was. She'd never bothered to correct him, assuming if he knew she didn't have a "man" at home, the inappropriate behavior would only worsen.

That Darius would turn down what was most likely a multimillion-dollar deal because of his beliefs and out of consideration for those under him... It was admirable. Heroic.

"I like to hope so," he replied just as softly.

A sense of intimacy seemed to envelop them, and she couldn't tear her gaze away from his. Her breath stuttered in her lungs, her heart tap-dancing a quick tattoo at the heat in those golden depths.

"Of course his employees are fortunate," Gabriella interjected, shattering the illusion of connection. "Darius is a good man. He doesn't brag about it, but he's founded—and often single-handedly funded—several foundations that provide scholarships for foster children, housing for abused women coming out of shelters, and literacy and job-placement programs for under-privileged youth. And those are just some of his…projects."

The strategic pause before "projects" let Isobel know Gabriella considered *her* to be one of those charity cases. If passive-aggressiveness was a weapon, Gabriella and Helena would own codes and security clearances.

"It's wonderful to know Aiden will have an admirable role model in Darius," Isobel said, voice neutral. Silence once more descended in the room, but Isobel didn't shrink from it. The scared, quiet girl they had known no longer existed; the woman she was now wouldn't stand mutely like a living target for their verbal darts.

Darius glanced at her, and once more she found herself trapped in his gaze. Something flickered in the golden depths. Something that had her lifting her glass of wine to her lips for a deep sip.

"If Gage couldn't be here to raise him, he would've wanted family to do it," Darius finally said to the room, but his eyes… His eyes never wavered from her.

"Still," Helena pressed, not looking at Darius but keeping her attention firmly locked on Isobel. "A boy should know his father. Tell me, Isobel, since you claim Aiden is Gage's, have you showed him pictures? Does he know who his real father is?"

"Helena," Darius growled a warning.

"Darius, darling," Helena replied, tilting her head to the side. "We all commend you for your sacrifice in this difficult situation, but I think you'd agree that a child deserves to know who his true parents are, right?"

A muscle jumped along Darius's jaw, but Isobel set her glass down on the table, meeting Helena's scrutiny.

"I've always shown Aiden pictures of Gage, since he is Aiden's father, as well as talked to him about Gage. And he understands who his *real father* is, as much as a two-year-old can."

"Hmm," came Helena's noncommittal, *condescending* answer.

"Aiden looks so much like Gage when he was that age," Baron added from the head of the table, aiming a quelling glance at his wife.

But Helena didn't respond, instead turning to Gabriella and asking about a function she was supposed to attend that week.

Pain and humiliation slashed at Isobel, but she fought not to reveal it. Not only did she refuse to grant them that pleasure, but she didn't have anything to be ashamed of. They accused *her* of cheating, when the opposite had been true.

But what would be the point in trying to explain the truth to his family? They would never believe her. Not after they'd always accepted every utterance from Gage as the gospel.

And with him dead, he was even more of a saint.

And she would always be a sinner.

Eight

Darius poured himself another glass of bourbon. This would be his third. Or maybe fourth. Didn't matter. He wasn't drunk yet; he could still think. So whatever number he was on, it wouldn't be his last. He'd keep tossing it back until the unease and anger no longer crawled inside him like ants in a colony.

Tonight had been a clusterfuck. Oh, it'd been frigidly polite, but still… Clusterfuck.

After crossing the study, he sank down onto the couch and took a sip of the bourbon. Clasping the squat glass, he slid down, resting his head on the couch's back, his legs sprawled wide.

Jesus, when would the forgetful part of this begin?

He hated this sense of…betrayal that clung to him like a filthy film of dirt. And no matter how hard he tried to scrub it clean with excuses, it remained, stubborn and just as grimy.

When he'd asked Isobel to the Welles' house that night,

he'd promised her they would be civil, and she would be in a safe space, be welcomed. Baron had, but Helena and Gabriella, they'd made a liar of him. He understood their resentment—even now, when he thought of Gage, that mixture of anger and grief still churned in his chest, his gut. But tonight had been about Aiden, about them connecting with the boy, and that meant forging a fragile truce with his mother. Showing her respect, at least.

Hours later, the disappointment, the disquiet continued to pulse within him like a wound, one that refused to heal.

Isobel had definitely been enemy number one when she'd been married to Gage. All of them believed Gage had moved too fast, married too young. Darius had been equally confused when he'd cut them all off for almost a year. None of them could understand why Gage hadn't divorced her, especially when he started confiding in them about her infidelity. As far as Darius could tell, his friend had genuinely been in love with his wife, and her betrayals had destroyed him.

Still. Remembering the woman he'd shared a hallway with in the dark… The woman who loved her son so selflessly… The woman whose family rallied around her, supported her and her son unconditionally… That Isobel didn't really coincide with the one the Wellses detested.

But if he were brutally honest—and alcohol had a way of dragging that kind of truth forth—it hadn't only been this evening that had unnerved him.

She did.

Everything about her unsettled him.

From the thick dark hair with the hints of fire to the delectable, curvaceous body that tempted him like a red flag snapping in front of a bull.

Earlier, when she'd thrust her chin up in that defiant angle, he'd had to force himself to remain in his seat instead of marching around the table and shocking the hell out of everyone by tugging her head back and claiming that beautiful, created-for-sin mouth.

Another truth he could admit in the dark with only bourbon for company.

He wanted her.

Fuck, did he want her.

Maybe if the past had stayed in the past, he could have convinced himself their space of time in the hallway had been just that—a blip, an anomaly. But once he'd kissed her again, once he'd swallowed her moans, once he'd felt her slick, satiny flesh spasm around his fingers as she came... No, he craved this woman with a need that was usually reserved for oxygen and water.

Even knowing that she'd betrayed Gage just as Faith had cheated on Darius, he still couldn't expunge this insane, insatiable desire.

So, what did that say about him? About his dignity? His fucking intelligence?

He snorted, raising his glass to his lips for a deep sip.

It said that, as much as he'd claimed to the contrary, his dick had equal partnership with his brain.

Yet...he frowned into the golden depths of the bourbon. The more time he spent with Isobel, the more doubt crept into his head, infiltrating his long-held ideas about her, about the woman he'd believed her to be. But for him to accept that she was not the woman who'd betrayed her husband in the past, it would mean that Gage had consciously—and maliciously—lied to Darius's face. And to his family. And to all of their friends. It would mean Darius's best friend, the man who'd been closer to him than a brother, had intentionally destroyed Isobel's reputation.

And that he couldn't believe.

Could Gage have somehow misinterpreted her actions? Or maybe there was more to the story that Gage hadn't shared with his family before his death?

"Darius?"

He glanced in the direction of the study's entrance, where the sound of his name in *her* voice had originated.

And immediately wished he hadn't.

Now the image of her standing in the doorway, barefoot, her long, toned legs exposed by some kind of T-shirt that hit her midthigh, and hair a sexy tumble around her beautiful face would be permanently branded onto his retinas.

"What are you wearing?" he growled.

Hell, he hadn't intended to vocalize that question. And with his bourbon-weakened control, no way in hell could he prevent the lust careering through him.

She peeked down at herself, then returned her fairy eyes to him. "What?" she asked. "This is what I sleep in. Excuse me if it's not La Perla enough for you, but I didn't exactly expect to bump into anyone."

La Perla. Fox and Rose. Agent Provocateur.

His ex-wife had insisted on only purchasing the expensive, luxury lingerie for herself, and they'd shown up regularly on his credit card statements, which was the only reason he recognized the brands.

But damn. Now, staring at her body with those lethal curves, he would love to put that useless-until-now information to work. To drape her in the softest silk and the most delicate lace. To personally choose corsets, bras and panties to adorn a woman who didn't need anything to enhance her ethereal beauty and earthy sensuality. And still he wanted to give them to her. To see her in them.

To peel them from her.

Taking another sip, he wrenched his gaze from the temptation in cotton.

"What do you want, Isobel?" he rasped.

She stepped into the room, the movement hesitant. It should be. If she had any idea of the need grinding inside him like a relentlessly turning screw, she'd leave.

"I was headed toward the kitchen and saw the light on in here. I thought you'd gone to bed." A pause. "Are you okay?"

"I'm fine," he said automatically. *Lie.*

"I'm sorry for you," she said, gliding farther into the room and halting a small distance from him. As if unsure whether or not she should chance come any closer.

Smart woman.

The way the alcohol and lust coursed through him like rain-swollen rapids, he should warn her away, bark an order to get out of the study. Instead he watched her, a predator silently waiting for his prey to approach just near enough for him to pounce.

"Sorry for me," he repeated on a serrated huff of laughter. "Why?"

"Because I went there tonight knowing I wouldn't be welcome. I wasn't surprised by anything that happened. But you were shocked...and hurt. And for that, I'm sorry."

He lifted his head, stared at her, astonishment momentarily robbing him of speech.

Discomfort flickered across her features, and she shrugged a shoulder. "Anyway... Your relationship with them isn't my business..."

"You weren't hurt?" He ground his teeth around a curse. He hadn't intended to snap at her. Dragging in a deep breath, he held it, then exhaled. "You weren't hurt by what they said, how they acted?"

She studied him for a long second, then slowly shook her head. "No, Darius. For me, it was business as usual. For the two years I was married, I was never good enough. Smart enough. Sophisticated enough. Just never...enough."

"I can't believe that," he snapped, banging his glass on the table and surging to his feet. Tunneling his fingers through his hair, he paced away from her. He *couldn't*.

Because then what did that say about the past, about what he'd believed?

What would it say about the family he idolized?

"It's not that you can't believe it. You won't," she contradicted, her voice low, laced with an unmistakable thread of resignation. As if she hadn't expected much from him. Certainly not for him to accept her truth. "And you never will. You won't allow yourself to even consider that the brave man who saved you from a burning building, the honorable man who became your brother when you lost your parents could've changed. Or at the very least, had one side with you and another with his wife, who he grew to resent almost from the moment he said 'I do.'"

"No," Darius rasped, stalking closer and eliminating the small space between them. "He went against his family's wishes to have you, risking everything for you..."

"And he came to hate me for it," she whispered, tilting her head back to meet his gaze. "Just like you eventually will. You said you're going through with this engagement and marriage for Baron, Helena and Gabriella. What happens when they force you to choose between your pretend wife and them? Because it'll happen. They've earned your love, your loyalty, but you've given your word to me. Oh, yes." She nodded, shadows swirling in her lovely, haunted eyes. "In the end, you'll resent me, too."

He squeezed his eyes closed, his jaw so hardened, so tense, the muscles along it twinged. Emotion. So much emotion howled and whistled inside him, he feared one misstep, one wrong-placed touch, and he would shred under the power of it.

"I already resent you, Isobel," he ground out, forcing himself to meet her gaze. Her scent—delicate like newly opened rose petals and intoxicating like the bourbon he'd been drinking—wrapped around him with phantom arms. Heat emanated from her petite body, and he wanted to curl against it. "And it has nothing to do with tonight or a future emotional tug-of-war. I hate that I can't get you out of my head. Can't stop replaying a night that should've never happened. I can still *feel* you. Your lips parting for mine. Your skin under my hands. Your tight, soaking-wet flesh gripping my fingers so hard, it almost bruised me. You just won't get out of my goddamn head."

Lust churned his voice to the consistency of gravel. "I hate that I know who you are, and I still want to fuck you. I hate that I can't tell if you're the sweet, giving woman from that dark hallway or the conniving one who was married to my best friend." He shifted that scant inch forward and brought his chest to hers, his thighs to hers. His breath to hers. "I hate that I want to find out."

Her labored pants broke across his mouth, and he slicked his tongue across his lips, seeking to taste that hard puff of breath. Her scrutiny followed the movement, and like clouds moving in over a blue sky, lust darkened her gaze. God, why didn't she close those beautiful eyes? Shield both of them from the knowledge that she craved him as he did her? He placed the responsibility on her, because he was the weaker one. She had to be the strong one and save them both.

"Turn around and walk out of here, Isobel," he warned her, his voice so guttural, he almost winced. "I'll break your condition. I'll put my hands and mouth on you. I'll finish what we started in the dark if you don't."

A small, muted whimper escaped her. Almost as if she'd tried to trap the needy sound but hadn't been fast enough.

"You're not running, sweetheart." He lifted his hand, let it hover over her cheek for a weighty moment, granting her time to evade it. But she remained still, and he swept the pad of his thumb over her cheekbone, then lower, across the lush curve of her bottom lip.

"No," she whispered. "I'm not."

"Your rule," he whispered back.

"Break it... Break me."

The request, uttered on a trembling breath, snapped the already tattered ropes on his control, and with a groan, he crushed his mouth to hers. When her heady taste hit his tongue, that groan morphed into a growl. Delicious. Addictive. He drove his fingers into her hair, tipping her head back so he could gorge on her. Yeah, he was committing the sin of gluttony, and resigned himself to hell for it.

Her palms slid over his sides and up his back, curling into the backs of his shoulders. The bite of her nails sent pleasure sizzling through him like an electrical charge, arrowing straight for his cock. He shifted, pressing harder against her, giving her full, undeniable disclosure to what she did to him.

Abandoning her hair, he dropped his arms, molding his hands to her ass, cupping the curves. He bent his knees, then abruptly straightened, hiking her into his arms. A bolt of carnal satisfaction struck him when her legs wrapped around his waist and her arms encircled his neck, holding on to him. Her mouth clung to his, that wicked tongue twisting and tangling, dancing and dueling. Damn, he wanted that talented mouth on his skin, on every part of him.

After quickly striding back to the couch, he sank down to the cushions, arranging her so she straddled his thighs. He broke their kiss long enough to fist the hem of her shirt and yank it over her head. All that hair tumbled down around her shoulders, back and chest, transforming her into a seductive siren. He wanted to crash himself against her and drown in pleasure.

"You're going to take me under, aren't you?" he murmured, voicing his thoughts.

"Are you afraid?" she asked.

He shifted his enraptured gaze from her hair to her eyes. *Yes.*

The reply erupted inside him, ringing with certainty,

but he didn't vocalize it. Instead he cradled the nape of her neck and drew her forward until their lips brushed, pressed, mated.

Impatient, he stroked a caress over her shoulders, down her chest and finally reacquainted himself with the flesh he'd dreamed about before waking up, hard and hurting. He cupped her, squeezed...and it wasn't enough. Ripping his mouth free of hers, he bent his head, trailed his lips over the soft swell of her breast, then circled his tongue around the taut, dusky peak.

Her cry rebounded off the walls and windows, and her arms clasped him to her. Her scent, rich and deep, filled his nostrils, and he licked it off her skin. In response, her hips rolled, rocking her lace-covered folds over him. The pressure against his erection had him hauling in a breath and bracing himself against the stunning pleasure barreling through him. He shifted beneath her, sliding down a fraction so his length notched firmly against her. He dropped a hand to her hip, encouraging her to continue riding him. Continue stoking the fire between them until it consumed them.

"You're so sweet." He lapped at her nipple, then drew it into his mouth, suckling on her, tormenting her as she was doing to him. "Dangerous," he admitted.

Her only response was to buck those slim hips. It was the only response he needed. Switching to her neglected breast, he worshipped it, losing himself in the taste, texture and wonder of her.

"Let me," she panted, gripping his hair and tugging his head up. He resisted, but spying her flushed cheeks, swollen lips and glazed eyes, he relented. "I want to...need to..."

She didn't finish the thought, but with trembling fingers, plucked at his shirt buttons. Too impatient, he replaced her attempt with a hard yank. The buttons flew, scattered, and he tore off the offensive material.

"God," she breathed, flattening her palms to his chest. He shuddered, the sensation of being skin to skin almost too sharp. "You're beautiful. So...beautiful."

Another shiver rippled through him, just as intense, but it was the result of her words rather than her touch. Or rather the stark truth in her words. When they were clothed, minds and bodies not warped by passion, he didn't trust her. But here...with their bodies stripped...honesty existed between them. The honesty of lust and pleasure. She couldn't hide from him, couldn't lie to him. Not when the evidence of her desire soaked her underwear and his pants.

He loosened a hand from the soft ropes of her hair and slid it down her back, over her hip and between her legs. She stiffened a second, and he paused, imprisoning a groan as her wet heat singed him. But only when she melted against him, her whispered, "Please" granting him permission to continue, did he slip underneath the plain but sexy-as-hell underwear to the soft, plush flesh beneath.

She jerked, whimpered as he glided through the path created by her folds, ending his journey with a firm circle over her clit. The little bundle of nerves contracted and pulsed under his fingertip, and he teased it. She straightened, her hands clutching at his shoulders, her back arched, surrendering to his touch.

She was the most goddamn beautiful thing he'd ever seen.

"I love how wet you get for me," he rasped, stroking her hair away from her face, studying her pleasure-stricken expression. Dipping his hand lower, he rimmed her tiny, fluttering entrance. "You have more for me, sweetheart?"

He didn't wait for a reply but drove a finger inside her. Her cry caressed his ears even as her silken sex clutched at him, convulsed around him. He growled, loving her response to him. Hungry for more. Withdrawing, he slid in another finger, stretching her, preparing her to take him so he wouldn't inadvertently hurt her. And the selfish side of him reveled in the tight clasp of her body, in the soft undulations of her flesh that relayed her pleasure and impatience. Impatience for him, for what he was giving her. For what he was promising her.

"Can you take another?" he murmured, pulling free again.

"Yes." Her fingernails denting his skin. "Please, yes."

Leaning forward, he opened his mouth over the pulse throbbing like a snare drum at the base of her throat as he slowly buried three fingers inside her. She bucked her hips, twisting like a wild thing on his lap. Jesus, she was gorgeous in passion—sexy, uninhibited and burning like a blue flame. Her desire scorched him.

Grinding out a curse, he lifted her off his thighs and set her beside him. Ignoring her disappointed cry, he shed her of the underwear, leaving her bare before him. With his gaze fixed on her lovely nakedness, he removed his wallet from his pants. Then he snatched out a condom and shoved his pants down his legs, too desperate to be inside her to completely strip them off.

With hands he prayed were gentler than the maelstrom of greed tearing at him, he repositioned her over him. He couldn't prevent the shiver that worked its way through him as he fisted the base of his cock, notching the tip at the entrance to her body. Perspiration trickled down his skin as he slowly—so damn slowly—lowered her over him.

God. Every muscle in his body tightened, with the control it required not to plunge himself inside exacting its toll.

Hot.

Tight.

Ecstasy.

Fire raced up and down his spine, snapping and crackling. It rolled and thundered through his veins, transforming his blood to pure, undiluted pleasure. Already she consumed him, and he hadn't even seated himself fully inside her. And though razor-sharp need sliced at him, he didn't rush it. He'd rather suffer before hurting Isobel. Even now those tiny muscles rippled and fluttered over his flesh, adjusting to his penetration. Tremors quaked through her petite frame, and whimpers slipped past her lips.

"Shh," he soothed, pausing. Keeping one hand braced on her hip, he cupped her cheek with the other, tipping her head down. "Your pace, sweetheart. Tell me what you need, and it's yours," he said against her lips.

"Kiss me."

She tilted her head, opening for him, and he twisted his tongue with hers, sucking on it. She joined in the duel, thrusting and parrying. Pursuing and eluding. It turned wild, raw.

Before the kiss ended, she sat fully and firmly on his cock.

With a snarl, he tore away from her, tipping his head back against the couch. She was…perfect.

"Isobel," he growled, raising his head again, unable to *not* see what she did to him. How she took him.

Cradling her hips, he lifted her, stared in rapt fascination as she unsheathed him, leaving his length glistening with the evidence of her desire. Then when just the head remained inside her, he eased her back down, still watching as she parted for him, claiming him.

Branding him.

"After that night in the hallway," he gritted out, pulling free again. "I regretted not taking you. Not knowing how it felt to bury myself inside you. But now," he rasped, lowering her. "Now I'm glad I didn't. Because then I would've missing seeing how you so sweetly spread for me. And that, sweetheart…that would've been a crime."

"Darius," she whispered, and the sound of his name on her lips tattered the remnants of his control.

He drove inside her, snatching her down to him. Not that he needed to. She rode him, fierce and powerful, and in that moment, she was the one doing the claiming. And he surrendered, letting her incinerate him. And he held on, thrusting, giving, willingly being rendered to ash.

"Please," she begged, her body quaking. She clung to him even as she surged and writhed against him. "Please, Darius."

He didn't need her to complete the thought; he already knew what she wanted. Reaching between them, he stroked a path down her belly and between her legs. Murmuring, he rubbed the pad of his thumb over her swollen clit. Once. Twice...

Before he could reach three, her sex clamped down on him, a strangling, muscular vise that dragged a grunt out of him. She exploded, seizing his cock, spasming and pulsing around him as she flew apart in his arms.

He rode her through it, thrusting hard and quick, ensuring she received every measure of the release that gripped her. Only when the quakes eased into shivering did he let go.

Pleasure—powerful, intense and brutal—plowed into him. His brain shorted, his vision grayed as he threw himself into an orgasm like a willing sacrifice, wanting to be consumed, obliterated, reshaped.

But into what? The unknown terrified him.

Then, as the darkness submerged and swamped him, he didn't think.

Couldn't think.

Could only feel.

And then, not even that.

Nine

Isobel released a weary sigh as she pulled into an empty spot in the four-car garage.

Darius had moved one of his luxury vehicles so she could have a parking space, and had invited her to drive one of them. But she had yet to take him up on the offer. She'd already invaded his house, and she and Aiden were living off his money. Taking one of the cars as if she owned it edged her one step closer to being the gold-digging creature she'd been called. So no, she'd continued driving her beat-up but trusty Honda Civic. Even if parking it next to his Bugatti Chiron seemed like blasphemy.

Climbing out of her car, she inhaled the early evening air. Though she'd left work at the grocery store without wearing her jacket, she now drew it around her, the black collared shirt and khakis of her uniform not fighting off the nippy breeze.

Glancing down at her watch, she picked up her pace and strode toward the front door of Darius's home. It was just nearing five o'clock, and like the previous days, she was hoping she'd beat him home from work. Since she no longer had to work a second shift with her mother to make ends meet, she'd switched her hours at the store. Four days a week, she left the house at eight to arrive for her nine-to-four shift. Isobel liked the nanny, Ms. Jacobs, just fine. She was grateful for her, because her presence allowed Isobel to continue working even when she couldn't ask her mom to watch Aiden. Still, she missed her son fiercely when she left.

And yet over the last few days, she'd been thankful for her job. Concentrating on customers, price checks and sales prevented her from obsessively dwelling on...other things.

Other things being the cataclysmic event of sex with Darius.

A flush rushed up from her chest and throat, pouring into her face. She loosened her collar as the memories surged forth, as if they'd been hovering on the edges of her subconscious, waiting for the opportunity to flood her.

Her step faltered, and she stumbled. "Damn," she muttered.

No matter how many times those mental images flashed across her brain, they never failed to trip her up—literally and figuratively. She vacillated between cringing and combusting. Cringing at the thought of her completely abandoned and wild reaction to him.

Combusting as she easily—too easily—recalled how his mouth and hands had pleasured her, marked her. How he'd triggered a need in her that eclipsed any previous sexual experience, rendering all other men inconsequential and mediocre.

He'd spoiled her for anyone else.

And she'd committed a fatal error in letting him know just how much she craved him.

So yes, she'd been avoiding him, trying to reinforce her emotional battlements. And surprisingly he'd allowed her to evade him. The few times they'd been in the same room since That Night, he'd treated her with a distant politeness that both relieved and irritated her. Pretending as if they'd never shook in each other's arms, him buried inside her to the hilt.

Pinching the bridge of her nose as she entered the house, she deliberately slammed the door on those memories, and not just locked it but threw three dead bolts just for good measure.

"Where have you been?"

She skidded to a halt in the foyer at the furious demand, her head jerking up. Shock doused her in a frigid wave, and she stared at Darius. Anger glittered in his amber gaze, tightened the skin over his sharp cheekbones and firmed the full curve of his mouth into a flat line.

"Hello to you, too, Darius," she drawled with acid sweetness.

"Where. Have. You. Been?" he ground out, his big body vibrating with emotion. It flared so bright in his eyes, they appeared like molten gold.

"At work, although I don't see how that's any of your business," she snapped. "Which is becoming a common refrain between us. I might be in your home, but no clause in that contract mandated me having to run my every movement by you."

A snarl curled the corner of his lips, and he shifted a step forward but stopped himself. "I beg to disagree with you on that, Isobel. When it has to do with Aiden's care and no one knows where the hell you've been for hours, and you don't answer your cell phone, then it most definitely. Is. My. Business." He pivoted away from her, the action sharp, full of anger. His fingers plowed through his hair, fisting it, before he turned back to her. "Aiden started coughing and became irritable, and when Ms. Jacobs took his temperature, he had a low-grade fever. She tried to call you to see if you wanted her to make a doctor's appointment for him. When she couldn't reach you, she called me. Damn it, Isobel," he growled. "I didn't know if something had happened to you or if you were in trouble or hurt…" Again, he glanced away from her, a muscle ticking along his clenched jaw. "No one could find you," he finally growled.

Worry for her son washed away her annoyance and propelled her forward. "Is he okay? I can take him to an after-hours clinic…"

"He's fine. I had a doctor come out and examine him. He has a virus, probably a twenty-four-hour bug, but nothing serious. I've just looked in on him, and he's sleeping."

Relief threaded through her concern, but didn't get rid of it. As a cashier, she wasn't allowed to have a cell phone on the floor. When her mother had been watching Aiden, this hadn't been a problem, as she'd trusted her mother to handle anything that came up. Not to mention that the store had been minutes from her mom's place. Maybe she should've given Darius her work schedule, or told him she was continuing to work at the store, period. And she'd just told Ms. Jacobs she was going to be out.

Damn. She turned toward the staircase, her thoughts already on her baby. But Darius's voice stopped her.

"I'll be in the library, Isobel. After you look in on him, come find me. This conversation isn't finished." The "don't make me come find you" was implicit in the order, but she ignored it, instead rushing up the stairs to her son.

Fifteen minutes later, after she'd satisfied herself that he was resting and breathing easily, she headed toward the library. Her heart thudded against her chest, her blood humming in her veins. Returning to the scene of the crime. She'd barely glanced at the entrance to the room since she'd last left it, and now she had to reenter it. Maybe sit on the same couch where she'd lost her control, her pride and possibly her mind.

She hated having to enter this room again and be reminded of how she'd come apart. Of how she'd cemented his belief that she was an immoral whore who would screw anyone. After all, she'd claimed not to want him, but at his first touch, she'd surrendered.

Break it... Break me.

Hadn't those been the words she'd uttered as she begged him? *Break the no-sex rule she'd instituted. Break her with his passion.*

Briefly, she closed her eyes, attempting to smother the humiliation crawling into her throat, squatting there and strangling her.

Deliberately keeping her gaze off the couch, she strode into the room and located Darius, who was in front of his desk, with his arms crossed and his eagle-eyed scrutiny fixed on her.

"Isobel."

"Can we get this over with so I can return to Aiden?"

He didn't move, but she could practically *see* him bristle. "How is he?" he asked, surprising her once more with his concern for her son.

"Sleeping, as you said," she murmured. "He's still warm, but he seems to be resting okay." Drawing in a breath, she mimicked his pose, crossing her arms over her chest. "I'm sorry you couldn't reach me. That was my fault. I was at work, and management doesn't allow us to have our cells on us. And I didn't even notice I had missed calls when I left. So I apologize for worrying...everyone."

"Work?" he asked, his voice dropping to a low rumble. "What 'work'?"

"I'm sure the private investigator you hired included my job in his or her report," she said, sarcasm dripping from her tone. "If not, you might want to request a refund for his shoddy performance."

He shook his head, dropping his arms to slash a hand through the air. "Don't tell me you're still going to that supermarket?"

"Of course I am," she replied. "That contract didn't require me to give up my job."

"Why?" he demanded. "You don't need the job, especially when it pays basically pennies. And yes, I do know how much you make, since my investigator's report included not only where you work but how much you're paid," he added.

"There's nothing wrong with ringing up groceries. It's good, honest work." She thrust her chin up. "Maybe you're so far removed from that time in the mail room, you don't remember what that's like."

"No, there's nothing wrong with your job." He frowned, cocking his head to the side. "But what do you need it for, Isobel? If there's something you want, why don't you just come to me and ask?"

His obvious confusion and—hurt?—smoothed out the ragged edges of her anger. How could she make him understand?

After his parents had died, he might've lived with the Wellses, but he'd never been totally dependent on them. Not with a multibillion-dollar empire waiting on him. Not with homes scattered around the country and money in bank accounts. He didn't know the powerlessness, the helplessness of being totally reliant on someone else's generosity... or lack of it.

She'd learned that particular lesson the hard way with Gage. Yes, she might've held down the job when she'd been married, but Gage had considered his role to be manager of their finances. And he'd been horribly irresponsible with them. And later, when his parents had parceled out sympathy money to him, he'd stingily doled that out to her, holding money for things like groceries and diapers over her head.

Never again would she be at the mercy of a man.

And if that meant keeping a low-paying job with good hours so she could maintain a measure of independence, then she would do what was necessary. If it meant losing some time with Aiden while she squirreled away her wages, well, then sacrifices needed to be made. She needed to be able to provide for them when Darius's charity finally reached its limits.

She was a mother first. And any good mother did what needed to be done.

"Then enlighten me, Isobel. Because I don't understand. You have a home. You don't have to pay any bills. You even have cars at your disposal if you'd stop being so damn prideful and use them—"

"No, you're wrong," she interrupted, her voice quiet but heavy with the emotion pressing against her sternum. Frustration, irritation and sadness. "*You* have a home. *You* have cars at your disposal. *Your* money pays the bills. None of this is mine. Even after we sign that marriage certificate and exchange vows, it still won't be. If you put me out, I couldn't leave with any of it. Couldn't lay claim to it. And you could put me out at any time, on any whim, because of any conceived sin on my part. And I would be on the street, homeless, with no money or resources for me and my son. No." She shook her head. "I won't allow that to happen."

He stared at her, shock darkening his eyes. His lips parted, head jerking as if her words had delivered a verbal punch.

"I would never abandon you or Aiden like that," he said, the words uttered like a vow.

She knew only too well how vows could be broken.

"I know you believe you wouldn't. But minds change,

feelings change," she murmured. Then, suddenly feeling so tired that her limbs seemed to weigh a hundred pounds, she sighed, pinching the bridge of her nose. "Are we done here? I need to get back to Aiden."

"No," he said, the denial firm, adamant. As if it'd pushed through a throat coated in broken glass. "You don't believe me."

"I wanted to return to college. Did you know that?" she asked softly. Without waiting for him to reply, she continued, "One of my regrets is that I quit school. I would've been the first one in my family to earn a degree if I'd stayed. So graduating from college was a dream of mine, but when I broached it with Gage, he convinced me to wait until after the baby was born. At the time, I thought him wanting that time for the two of us was sweet. So I agreed. But after Aiden came, I couldn't go back. Working a full-time job, being a mom..." She shrugged. "College would've been too much, so I had to place it on the back burner. But I've always wanted to go back. To obtain that degree. To have a career that I love. And when Aiden is older, I'll show him that no matter how you struggle, you can do anything you desire."

Scrubbing her hands up and down her arms, she paced to the wide floor-to-ceiling window and stared sightlessly at the view of his Olympic-size pool, deck and firepit. Her admission made her feel vulnerable, exposed.

"Did Gage support your dream?" Darius asked quietly.

She didn't turn around and face him. Didn't let him see the pain and anger she couldn't hide. Darius didn't want to hear the truth. Wasn't ready to hear it. And he wouldn't believe her anyway. College, money for tuition—those had been givens in his and Gage's worlds. He wouldn't understand or see how his friend would begrudge his wife that same experience.

"Gage had specific ideas about the wife he wanted," she

whispered instead. "A wife like his mother." One to cater to him. Be at his beck and call. Place him as the center of her universe, at the exclusion of everyone else.

Images from that time flashed across her mind, and she deliberately shut them down, refusing to tumble back into that dark time when she'd been so helpless and powerless.

Silence descended on the room, and she swore she could feel Darius's confusion and disbelief pushing against her.

"If what you say is true, how—"

She'd expected him not to believe her. But she *hadn't* expected the dagger-sharp pain to slice into her heart. Uttering a sound that was somewhere between a scoff and a whimper, she turned, unable to stand there while he doubted every word that came out of her mouth. This is what she got for opening up and letting him in even a little.

Lesson learned.

"Wait. *Damn it, Isobel*," he growled, his arms wrapping around her, his chest pressing to her spine. His hold, while firm, wasn't constrictive, and it was this fact that halted her midescape. "That came out wrong. Just give me a minute. Don't I have the right to ask questions? To try to understand?"

A pause—where the only sound in the room was the echo of their harsh breaths. He loosened his arms, releasing her and taking his warmth with him. Turbulent emotions surged up from the place deep inside her that remained wounded and bruised. The place that cried out like a heart-sore child for satisfaction, for someone to hear her, for acceptance. That place urged her to lash out, to hurt as she'd been hurt.

But flashes of Darius being so affectionate with Aiden, of him upset on her behalf after the dinner with the Wellses, of him kissing and touching her—those flashes filled her head. And it was those flashes that tempered her reply.

"Love blinds us all."

Unable to say any more, unable to hear him defend his friend and family, she left the study and climbed the stairs to return to Aiden.

How they could ever forge a peaceful, if not loving, marriage when the past continued to intrude?

And to that question, she didn't have an answer.

Ten

"No, Mommy!"

Darius heard Aiden's strident, high-pitched objection before he stepped into the doorway of the boy's room. Isobel sat on one of the large beanbag chairs, Aiden curled on her lap, reading a book. Well, Isobel was reading anyway, Darius mused, humor bubbling inside him.

"No," Aiden yelled again, stabbing a chubby finger at one of the pages. "Nose." He twisted around and declared, "Eye," nearly taking out hers with his enthusiastic poke. "Nose," he repeated, squishing his with the same finger.

Isobel laughed, dropping a kiss on his abused nose. "You're right, baby. Nose. Good job!"

"Good job," he mimicked, clapping.

Warmth slid through Darius's veins like liquid sun. The previous evening had left him confused, and the maddening cacophony of questions lingered.

Gage had specific ideas about the wife he wanted.

She'd made it sound like she hadn't met Gage's standard.

If so, had there been consequences? What had those consequences been? Had he and Gage's family been so fixated on Gage's side that they'd missed clues about the truth of Gage's marriage?

Darius closed his eyes, but when the image of Isobel's face, filled with sadness, hurt and resignation, just before she left the study, flashed across the back of his lids, he opened them again.

Nothing could excuse breaking one's marriage vows. But if her dreams had been crushed, if her marriage had been less than what she'd expected, if her husband had changed, was that why she'd turned to other men? Had she been seeking the affection and kindness she believed her husband hadn't given her?

Darius longed to ask her, because these questions tortured him.

"Darry!" Aiden shrieked, jerking Darius from his dark jumble of thoughts. Catching sight of him, Aiden scrambled out of Isobel's lap and dashed on his little legs toward him.

Joy unlike anything he'd ever experienced burst in his chest as he scooped the boy up and held him close. His heart constricted so hard, so tight, his sternum ached. But it was a good hurt. And not just because Aiden had thrown himself at Darius with the kind of confidence that showed he knew he would be caught. But also because, for a moment, Aiden's garbled version of his name sounded entirely too close to *Daddy.* And as selfish as it might be, he yearned to be Aiden's father. Already he fiercely loved this boy as if they shared the same blood and DNA.

He kissed Aiden's still-warm forehead. "How's he feeling this morning?" he asked Isobel.

For the first time since he'd entered the room, she met his gaze. He noted the wariness reflected in her eyes. Noted and shared it. He might have been knocked on his ass by her confession the previous night, but he still didn't—couldn't—trust her. No matter how much his body craved hers. Actually, that grinding need only cemented why he had to be cautious with her. He'd shown in the past he could be led around by his dick, and he would never be that foolish again. Especially with a woman who had already betrayed her vows of fidelity.

And that was the crux of the war waging inside him.

Though it was difficult to reconcile the materialistic gold digger with the woman he was living with—the doting, sacrificing mother, the proud fighter—loyalty came down to family.

They'd earned it.

Isobel hadn't.

"He's still running a small fever, but it's lower than yesterday, and he has more energy. As you can tell," she added dryly.

He nodded, poking Aiden in his rounded stomach and chuckling at the child's giggling and squirming. Setting the boy on his feet, Darius straightened, finding Isobel's stare again.

"Can I see you downstairs for a moment?"

"Fine," she said after a brief hesitation, rising from the floor and setting Aiden's book on his bed.

"I'll wait for you in the living room." Not waiting for her response, he retraced his earlier path down the hallway and staircase. He'd purposefully chosen the living room. Right now the study contained too many memories.

Minutes later, Isobel entered the room, and though he resented his reaction to her, his blood sang and his pulse drummed, the throb echoing in his cock. This was what she did to him by simply breathing. How did he armor himself against her?

God forbid she discovered his weakness.

"You wanted to see me," she said.

"Yes." He picked up a manila envelope from the mantel over the fireplace and offered it to her.

Frowning, she strode forward and gingerly accepted it. "What is this?"

"Open it, Isobel."

Flicking him a glance, she reluctantly acquiesced. He studied her as she withdrew the thin sheaf of papers and scanned the contract and bank documents. Bewilderment, shock and finally anger flitted across her face in rapid-fire succession. Her head snapped up, and her eyes narrowed. She pinned him with a glare.

"What. Is. This?" she repeated, her tone as hard as stone.

"Exactly what it looks like," he replied evenly, unsurprised by her response. "An addendum to our original contract. For entering our agreement, you receive one million dollars that will be deposited in an account under your name alone, as the bank documents reflect. It's yours free and clear. Even if you seek a divorce, it will still be yours."

"Like a signing bonus?" she drawled, the words acerbic.

He dipped his head. "If that's what you want to call it."

"No." She dropped the papers and the envelope on the glass table next to them as if they burned her fingers. "Hell no."

"Isobel—"

But she slashed a hand through the air, cutting off his explanation. "Is this about last night?" She shook her head so hard, her hair swung over her shoulders. "I didn't tell you that to make you feel guilty. If you hadn't pushed me, I wouldn't have said anything. At. All. But I damn sure won't take pity money from you now. If you wanted me to have that money—" she jabbed a finger in the direction of the papers "—then you would've included it during our original *negotiations*."

"You're right," he growled, and from her silence, he surmised his admission shocked her. "But at the time, I didn't want to hear anything except a yes. But now I want you to have it. And I can't unhear your fears or your dreams." Or the other things hinted at but left unsaid. "Maybe I need to give you what you missed. Your education. A father for your son. Help raising him. Time with him. Let me try to give it back to you, Isobel."

The only time in his life that he'd ever begged anyone for anything was when he'd pleaded with God to return his parents to him. But here, he came damn close.

She stared at him, and he battled the urge to turn away and evade that fey gaze that cut too deep and saw too much.

"Okay," she murmured.

He paused, her capitulation rendering him momentarily speechless. "Okay," he repeated. "And I'm not asking you to quit the supermarket or not replace it with something else. You can return to college, or I can arrange an entry-level position in a company or field of your choice that will allow you to get your foot in the door of your career. Or both college and the job. I don't want to steal your independence, Isobel. I don't want to be your jailor."

"Well, I really didn't want to ask my current manager for a reference anyway." A small smile flirted with her mouth. "Thank you, Darius."

"You're welcome," he said, his fingers suddenly tingling with the need to brush a caress over those sensual lips and feel that smile instead of just seeing it.

Silently, they stood there, snared in each other's gazes. She was the first to break the connection, and he bit back a demand for her to return to him, to give him her thoughts.

"I was going to bundle Aiden up and take him to see my mom. She's been calling nonstop since yesterday. I think she just needs to lay eyes on him." She halted, her eyes again meeting his. "Did you… I don't know if you'd like to…" Her voice tapered off, red staining the slashes of her cheekbones.

She was inviting him to come with her to visit her mother. Considering they didn't have a traditional relationship, introducing him to her family hadn't occurred. But she was offering that to him. It…humbled him.

"Why don't you invite her here instead since his fever isn't completely gone? I can send a car for her. Or go get her myself. Whichever she prefers. If you'd like, she can spend the day here with you and Aiden."

She blinked. "A-are you sure?" she stammered. "This is your home. You don't have to…"

"No, Isobel," he contradicted, injecting a thread of steel in the words. "This is our home. And it is always open to your mother, to your family."

She didn't agree with him—but she didn't refute him either.

And for today at least, it was a start.

Eleven

Isobel removed her earrings and dropped them into the old wooden jewelry box that had been a gift from her mom for her thirteenth birthday. Closing the lid, she picked up her brush and dragged it through her hair, meeting her own gaze in the mirror of the vanity. A smile curved her lips, and she didn't try to suppress it. Even if she looked like a dope wearing a silly grin for no reason.

Well, that wasn't true. She had a reason.

A wonderful day with her mom, Aiden...and Darius.

She carefully set the brush down as if it were crafted out of fragile glass instead of durable plastic. When truthfully, she was the one who felt delicate...breakable.

Inhaling a deep breath, she splayed her fingers low on her belly in a vain attempt to stifle the chaotic flutter there.

Once the car bringing her mother had arrived, she'd expected Darius to retreat to his study or even head to his office. He'd done neither. Instead Darius had stayed with them, warmly welcoming her mother and melting her reserve toward him with his graciousness and obvious adoration of Aiden. They'd watched movies, played with Aiden, cooked, ate and laughed. She'd glimpsed another side of Darius that day. Charming. Relaxed.

Like his gift of the contract addendum and the bank account with more money than she'd ever see in five lifetimes. She shook her head. She still couldn't believe that. Not only had he handed it over to like it'd been change in a car ashtray, but he'd given it to *her*, the woman he considered a money-grubbing user. When she thought on it, the shock returned, and she had to stop herself from pinching her skin like some kid.

She could take care of Aiden.

She didn't have to work at the supermarket.

She could return to college.

She had no-strings-attached options.

A whirl of electric excitement crackled inside her. In the space of minutes, her world had expanded from the size of a cramped box to a space without walls, without ceilings.

He'd done that for her. For her son.

Isobel spun on her heel, charged out of the bedroom and marched down the hall before she could change her mind. Seconds later, she knocked on the door of Darius's room. Already cracked, it swung further open under her hand.

"I'm sorry," she apologized, wincing as she shifted into the opening. "I didn't…know…it…"

The words dried up on her tongue, along with all the moisture in her mouth.

Good. Lord.

Darius stood in the middle of the room, naked to the waist. Miles and miles of golden, taut skin stretched over muscle like barely leashed power. Wide, brawny shoulders, strong arms roped with tendon and veins that seemed to pulse with vitality and strength. A solid chest smattered with dark brown hair that her fingers knew was springy to the touch. It thinned into a silky, sexy line that bisected his rock-hard stomach. Her gaze trailed that line, following it with complete fascination as it disappeared beneath the loosened belt and unbuttoned jeans.

Face heating, she jerked her head up, her stare crashing into his whiskey-colored one. Whiskey. Yes. She'd always compared it to an eagle's gaze, but whiskey was more accurate. Especially considering the punch it delivered and the heat it left behind.

"I'm sorry," she apologized again, inwardly cringing at her hoarse tone. Like sandpaper smoothed with jagged rock. "I didn't mean to interrupt…" She waved a hand up and down, encompassing his towering frame. "I'll just go," she said, already whirling around.

"Isobel." Her name halted her escape. No, it was the swell of arousal low in her belly that froze her. "Come here."

No "I'll meet you downstairs." Not "it's fine. Let me get changed and we'll talk later." Not even "come back." But, *come here.*

It was a warning. An invitation.

A threat. A seduction.

"Come here," he repeated, and she surrendered, her feet shifting forward, carrying the rest of her with them until she stood in front of him.

His heat, his cedar-and-musk scent, his almost tangible sensuality called out to her, enticed her to eliminate those scant few inches and bury her face against his chest. Inhale him *and* feel him. Somehow she resisted. But just. And even now that resistance was pockmarked, and so thin one touch would shred it.

"What do you want?" he asked, the sharp blades of his cheekbones and the hewn line of his jaw only emphasizing the blaze in his eyes. "Why did you come in here?"

"To thank you for today," she murmured. "For…everything."

"You're welcome," he rumbled, and as if in slow motion, he lifted a hand and rubbed the back of his fingers down her cheek. "Now tell me why you really came to find me."

She parted her lips to deliver a stinging reply, but it didn't come. Before she could contain it, the truth that she hadn't even acknowledged burst free.

"For you. I want you."

Another blast of flames in his eyes, and then her world tipped upside down. In one breath, she stood trembling before him, and in the next her back met his mattress, and Darius loomed over her. Her world narrowed to his big body and starkly beautiful face.

He tunneled his fingers through her hair, the blunt tips pressing against her skull. His gaze burned into hers, capturing her. Not that she wanted to be anywhere but here—his breath tangling with hers, his chest and legs covering hers, his cock branding her stomach through their clothes.

"Take it back," he ordered. When she stared up at him, confused, he lowered more of his weight onto her. She felt claimed. His flesh ground into her, teasing her with the promise of the pleasure only he was capable of delivering. "Take back your condition. Tell me you don't want me to fuck anyone else," he growled. "Tell me the thought of me touching another woman would drive you insane. Tell me I'm allowed to have you and only you."

She dug her nails into his shoulders, the words he demanded to hear crowding the back of her throat.

"Isobel," he growled.

The sexy, primal rumble unlocked her voice. "You can't touch another woman except me. You're not allowed, because it would drive me crazy," she finished on a gasp, with the word *crazy* barely out of her mouth before he swallowed it, his tongue thrusting forward past her parted lips and taking her in a kiss so blatantly carnal, so wild and possessive, it propelled the breath from her lungs.

But that was okay, because he gave her his.

He devoured her. It was wild, a clash, an erotic battle where both seized and neither lost. An ache opened wide in her, like a deep chasm that could never be filled. And yet she would never stop trying.

Did it register somewhere underneath the turbulent, consuming need that he hadn't asked her to make the same request? Yes. Did it also occur to her that he didn't ask because he didn't believe she would honor his demand of faithfulness? Yes. Did it hurt like a nagging, old wound? God, yes.

But right now, with his mouth working hers like he owned it, she didn't dwell on the pain. She submerged it beneath the waves of passion crashing over her. Later, when his hands didn't tilt her head back to receive more of him, that's when she'd think on it. But not now.

Darius abruptly straightened, tugging her up with him. With hurried hands, he balled the hem of her sleep shirt and yanked it over her head, leaving her clad only in a plain pair of black boy-short panties. Definitely not the expensive, seductive lingerie he was probably used to, but as he stared down at her, unchecked desire lighting his amber gaze, it didn't matter. Not when, without uttering a word, he told her he wanted her with a hunger that rivaled the need grinding her to dust.

Slipping a hand behind his neck, she drew his head down to her as she arched up to meet him. This time their kiss was slower, wetter. Somehow hotter.

He eased her back to the bed, his chest pressed to hers, and she undulated under him, rubbing her breasts over him, dragging her nipples across the solid wall of muscle. Correctly interpreting her message, he tore his mouth away from hers and blazed a path down her neck to the flesh that tightened in anticipation of his wicked attention.

As he cupped one breast, he nuzzled the other. She cradled his head, silently demanding he stop toying with her. And with a rumble that vibrated against her abdomen, he obeyed, parting his lips over her and drawing her in. She cried out, bowing so hard, her back lifted off the mattress. The strong pull of his mouth set off sparks behind her closed eyelids and matching spasms deep inside her. *God*, the ache. She wrapped her legs around his hips and ground against his cock, shuddering at the swell of pain-tinged pleasure. Whimpering, she repeated the action. Coupled with the mind-twisting things his mouth was doing to her breasts, she teetered close to the edge of release. So close…

"Not yet, sweetheart," he rasped against her skin.

Treating her nipple to one last kiss, he trailed his lips down her stomach, pausing to lap at her navel before continuing to the drenched center of her body. With an abrupt tug, he had her panties down her legs and tossed behind him.

Mortification didn't have time to sink its sharp nails in her as he lodged himself between her thighs, which were perched on his shoulders. She didn't have the opportunity to inform him that she'd never cared for oral sex, had never understood the allure of it. Didn't have a chance to tell him she'd just rather have him inside her because she didn't want to disappoint him.

No, she didn't say any of that because the second his mouth opened over her sex, shock and searing pleasure robbed her of the ability to think, to form coherent sentences.

"Oh, God," was all she could squeeze out of her constricted throat. He stroked a path through her folds, lapping at her, his growl humming against her. Grasping his head, she fisted his hair, to hold on and to keep him right there. He circled her clit, blowing on the pulsing knot of nerves, then he tortured her with short stabs and long sweeps. She writhed against his worshipping lips. Bucked into each stroke. Begged him to suck harder, faster, slower and gentler. She went wild.

And when release rushed forward in a flood so strong, so sharp, so potent, she didn't fight it. She surrendered to the undertow with a loud, piercing cry, chanting his name like an invocation.

Dimly, she registered the mattress dipping. Heard the soft shush of clothing over skin. Caught the crinkle of foil. Didn't have enough energy to turn her head and investigate. But when Darius reappeared over her, his big, beautiful body crouched over her like the gorgeous animal he was, desire rekindled in her veins, burning away the postorgasm lassitude. It was unbelievable. She'd just come hard enough to see stars, and now, when it should've been impossible, her sex trembled and clenched, an emptiness deep inside her begging to be filled.

She lifted her arms to him, and without hesitation, he came down over her, one hand curving behind her head and the other cupping the back of her thigh, holding her open. With her eyes locked on to his, she waited, her breath trapped in her throat. Even when he pushed forward, penetrating her, stretching her, she didn't look away. The inexplicable but no less desperate need to see his face, his eyes, gripped her. She longed to see if they reflected the same awe, rapture and relief that surged within her. To determine if she was alone on this tumultuous ride.

His full, sensual lips firmed into a line. His nostrils flared, the skin across his cheekbones tightened and in the golden brown depths of his eyes…there, she saw it. The flare of surprise, then the blazing hungry heat and something shadowed, something…more.

No, she wasn't alone. Not in the least.

Wrapping her arms tighter around his neck, she burrowed her face in the strong column, throwing herself into the ecstasy, the burn, the passion—into him. Opening her mouth over his skin, she tasted his tangy, musky flavor, mewling as he burrowed so deep inside her, she wondered how far he would go, how much he would take.

Not enough. The answer quivered in her mind. *It won't ever be enough.*

A trill of alarm sliced through her, but it was almost immediately drowned out by the carnal havoc he created within her body. After sliding his hands down her back, he palmed her behind and held her for his long strokes. He forged a path that only he could travel, dragging his thick length in and out of her and igniting tremors with each thrust. She savored each one, rolling up to meet each plunge.

"With me, sweetheart," he murmured in her ear. Tunneling his fingers into her hair, he gripped the strands and tugged her head back. His eyes so dark with lust that only flickers of gold remained, he grated through clenched teeth, "I'm not going alone. Get there and come with me."

The words, so arrogant and commanding, but strained with lust and drenched in need, were like a caress over her flesh. Clawing at his back, she slammed her hips against his, and his cock rubbed against a place high inside her, forming a catalyst, a detonator to her pleasure.

She shattered.

Screaming, she threw her head back against the pillows, propelling herself into the orgasm that claimed her like a ravenous beast, devouring her, leaving nothing. Above her, Darius rode her through it, until he stiffened and quaked. The throbbing of his flesh triggered another orgasm, rolling into the previous one like an unending explosion of ecstasy.

Darkness swept over her, pulling her under, but not before a seed of worry sprouted deep in her head. In the heat of passion, they'd become something new tonight.

But what? *Who?*

And would they survive it?

Twelve

Darius stared at his computer monitor, but he didn't see the report on the possible acquisition. Too many other thoughts crowded his mind. No, he had to be honest with himself.

Isobel.

Isobel crowded his mind, not leaving room for anything else.

Who was this woman? The selfish, devious conniver he'd believed her to be these past years? Or the woman he'd come to know since the night of the blackout? Just a week ago, he would've said both. That maybe single motherhood and being on her own had matured her from the person she'd been. But now...

Now doubts niggled at the back of his mind; perhaps he'd been wrong all along.

The things Isobel had hinted at—the controlling nature of her marriage, the lack of independence, the chameleon nature of the man Darius had called friend and she'd called husband—as well as the things she'd left unsaid. Working at a neighborhood grocery store even though she resided in one of the wealthiest zip codes in the state.

But if he believed Isobel—and God help him, he was starting to—then that meant Gage had concealed a side of himself from his family. What else had he hidden? Was it possible that Darius's best friend could've lied to them, to him? And if so, how could he have been so blind? He couldn't have been…right?

The urge to unearth the truth swelled within him, and he reached for the phone. He could have the company PI investigate for him. Contact Gage and Isobel's old neighbors or employees that had worked with Isobel at the time. It'd been years, but maybe they could give him some insight…

Just as his fingers curled around the receiver, the desk speaker crackled, and his executive assistant's voice addressed him.

"Mr. King, Mrs. Wells is here to see you."

Darius pressed the intercom button. "Thank you, Charlene," he replied. "Please let the marketing team know we're going to move our one o'clock meeting to one thirty."

"Yes, sir."

Darius rose from his chair and was already halfway across his spacious office when Helena opened his door and strode in. In spite of his unsettled thoughts, pleasure bloomed inside him at the unexpected but welcome visit. Several weeks had passed since the disastrous dinner at her home. Since then, he'd visited them several times, but without Isobel and Aiden. Though they'd asked about the boy and when they could spend time with him, Darius hesitated. First, he'd promised from the beginning that he wouldn't make arbitrary decisions about Aiden without consulting Isobel. And that included taking him to see his grandparents without her permission, even if he longed for them all to build a loving relationship.

Helena, regal in a black dress that wrapped around her still-slender figure, met him with outstretched arms.

"What brings you here today?" He led her to his office sitting area, lightly clasping her elbow.

She arched a dark, elegant eyebrow. "Do I need a reason to come see family? Especially when he's been a bit of a stranger lately?"

Darius laughed as he helped her settle on the black leather couch and then took a seat beside her. "That was subtle," he drawled. "Like a claw hammer to the head."

She smiled, but her point was well-taken. True, he hadn't been by the Wellses' home as often as he'd visited in the past. In the past weeks, he, Isobel and Aiden had settled into a cautious but peaceful routine. A truce that included Isobel in his bed, where they fucked until neither could move. God, she stripped him of his control, and that both terrified and thrilled him. Intimidated him and freed him.

It was the terror and intimidation that kept his mouth sealed shut when she slipped out of his bed in the dark, early mornings, returning to her room and leaving him alone. She never slept the night through with him. That bothered and relieved him.

Relieved him because the intimacy of sharing a bed smacked of a relationship, a vulnerability he wasn't ready to reveal to her. He'd given that trust to one woman, and she'd screwed him, literally and figuratively.

Bothered him because her sneaking out like he was her dirty secret didn't sit well with him.

"So you're here because you miss me?" he teased, deliberately dismissing his disquieting thoughts.

Helena's smile dimmed just a fraction, taking on a faintly rueful tinge. "Of course I do, darling. We all do. But I have another reason for coming to you. Next week is Thanksgiving. What are your plans?"

He stifled a sigh. Him joining them for the holidays was a tradition. But this year, it wasn't only him.

"I haven't discussed it with Isobel yet. She might want to spend the holiday with her family. And if that's her choice, I can come by the house afterward."

Anger flashed in her eyes, and she thinned her lips. "I see," she finally said. "You have a new family, whose wishes come first."

"Helena—"

"No." She sliced a hand through the air. "I'm glad you said that, it makes my next reason for being here easier to say." Her chin hiked up. "I want a DNA test for Aiden."

Shock whipped through him, and he stiffened under the blow of it. "What?"

"We want a DNA test," she repeated. "Yes, Aiden does resemble Gage, but that's not enough. In order for us to erase any doubt, we need to know he's Gage's son. And that can only be answered with a paternity test." Her features softened, and she settled a hand over his knee, squeezing lightly. "I need this, Darius."

His first reaction had been to flat-out refuse, but then reason crept in. Would having a DNA test done be so wrong? It would cement that Aiden was indeed Gage's son, and once the Wellses had the truth, they could finally lay this issue to rest and move on. He could give them that; he owed them that.

Isobel. He briefly closed his eyes.

Isobel wouldn't agree, just as she hadn't years ago. She would view it as an insult, but if it could facilitate healing… Yes, she would be angry about him going behind her back, but the results…how could she argue with the results when it meant the Wellses laying down their swords and Aiden having all of his family in his life, without doubts?

Meeting Helena's gaze, Darius nodded. "I'll arrange it."

Satisfaction flared in the blue depths. "Thank you, Darius. Another thing? Let's keep this between us for now. Baron doesn't know I'm here, and I don't want this impacting his health. So when you have the results, please contact me."

Unease over the further request for secrecy ate at him, but again he nodded.

"I should go," she murmured, standing. But then she hesitated, staring at him. "You're like a son to me, Darius," she said, steel entering her tone, belying the sentimental words. "And I love you, which is why I believe I have the right to say this to you. Gage fell for Isobel's sweet, innocent act, and look how he ended up. Betrayed, broken, angry...and dead. I would want to die myself if she did the same to you. So please, Darius, be careful, and don't succumb to the same game. Just...be aware, because Isobel is not who she pretends to be."

Darius didn't stop Helena as she left his office. After the door shut with a soft click, he slowly rose, her words of caution whirling inside his head.

Please be careful, and don't succumb to the same game... Isobel is not who she pretends to be.

He shook his head as if he could dislodge them, but they clung to him like burrs. Anger continued to dog him the rest of the day, nipping at him. He'd refused to play the fool again. But with Helena's warning ringing in his head, he couldn't shake the thought that her words had come a little too late.

Darius shoved open the front door to his house, the usual peace it brought him as he stepped into the foyer absent. His day had gone from hell to shit. By the time he left, hours earlier than his usual time, his employees had probably tossed confetti in the air as the elevator doors closed behind him. And if he were honest, he wouldn't blame them. His mood had been dark ever since Helena's impromptu visit, and even now, shutting the door behind him, he couldn't shake it loose.

He needed a drink. And time alone. Then, he mused, heading toward his study, he'd go find Aiden and Isobel. It wouldn't be fair to inflict his attitude on them.

What the fuck?

He slammed to a halt in the doorway of the study, shock winding through him like frigid sleet.

Gage fell for her sweet, innocent act, and look how he ended up. Betrayed, broken, angry... Please be careful, and don't succumb to the same game... Isobel is not who she pretends to be.

As they had all day, Helena's words tripped through his brain, growing louder and louder with each pass.

Isobel sat on the couch in his study, with her head bent close to the man perched next to her.

On the same couch where she'd straddled him, and he'd pushed into her body for the first time.

Jealousy, ripe and blistering, ripped through him. The power of it rocked him, and it was only the unprecedented intensity that unlocked its grip on him. Dragging in a breath, he forced the destructive emotion under a sheet of ice.

As if she'd heard his deep inhale, her head lifted, and their eyes met.

Surprise rounded her eyes, and an instant later, a smile started to curve her mouth, but that stopped as she scanned Darius's face. It shifted into a frown, before smoothing into a carefully blank expression.

"Darius, I didn't hear you arrive," she finally said, voice neutral as she rose to her feet.

What did that expression hide?

Isobel is not who she pretends to be.

"Obviously," he drawled, then shifted his attention to

the tall man who now stood beside her. Handsome, wearing an expensive gray suit and about Darius's age. Green-tinged acid ate at his gut.

Faith used to wait until he'd left for the office, then sneak men into their house. Their bed had been a favorite location for her trysts. She'd gleefully thrown that information at him. Part of her pleasure had been in knowing that, at night, Darius would lie in the same bed where she'd fucked other men.

And here Isobel stood with some stranger. Playing the same game? After all, she hadn't expected him home from work this early. He studied her. Seeking signs of deceit, of guilt, but not expecting to find any. She was more of an expert than that.

"Where's Aiden?" he asked.

Translation: *Where is Aiden while you're down here... entertaining?*

From the narrowing of her eyes, she didn't require a translator. "He's upstairs, taking a nap. Ms. Jacobs is with him," she replied, tone flat. Turning to the man beside her, she waved a hand in Darius's direction. "Ken, let me introduce you to Darius King. Darius, Ken Warren."

"Nice to meet you, Mr. King," the other man greeted, striding forward with his hand outstretched. "Ms. Hughes speaks highly of you."

"Does she now?" he murmured, and after a pause in which he stared down at the extended palm, he clasped it. "A shame I can't say the same."

"Thank you, Ken," Isobel said, walking forward and shooting Darius a look that possessed a wealth of *fuck you*. "I appreciate you coming all the way out here. I bet house calls are rare in your profession."

"Not as much as you'd think." He chuckled. "Call me if you have any questions." Nodding at Darius, he said, "Again, nice to meet you."

She ushered him out of the room, and Darius moved into the study, stalking toward the bar. He poured Scotch into a glass and then downed it, welcoming the burn.

With his back to the door, he didn't see her reenter the room, but he felt it. The air seemed to shift, to shimmer like steam undulating off a hot sidewalk after a summer shower. That's how aware he was of her. He could sense the moment she entered a damn room.

Pivoting, he leaned a hip against the edge of the bar, taking another sip of the alcohol as he watched her approach.

"You are an asshole," she hissed, the anger she'd concealed in front of Ken Warren now on vivid display. It flushed her cheeks and glittered in her eyes like stars as she stalked to within inches of him. "I don't know what happened at the office, but you had no right to be so rude to him and to me. What the hell is wrong with you?"

"What's wrong is that I came home to find a strange man in my house, with my soon-to-be-wife, sitting on the same couch where I've fucked her," he drawled. "So forgive me if my mood is a little…off."

"I knew it," she murmured. For a long moment, she studied him as if trying to decipher a code that baffled her. "I *knew it*," she repeated, a soft scoff accompanying it. "I took one look at your face and could've written a transcript of your thoughts. *I caught her with her latest screw. In* my *house. I knew she wouldn't be able to keep her legs closed for long.* Am I close?" The sound that escaped her lips was a perversion of laughter. "You're so predictable, Darius."

She whipped around and stalked to the couch. Leaning over the arm, she picked up a small, dark brown box and marched back to him.

"Here." She thrust the case at him. "Ken is the husband of one of the moms I met at the Mommy Center Aiden and I go to on Tuesdays and Thursdays. When I found out he was a jeweler, I thought of you. Take it," she ordered, shoving the item at him again.

A slick, oily stain spread across his chest and crept up his throat as he accepted the box. As soon as he did, she moved backward, inserting space between them that yawned as wide as a chasm.

He clenched his jaw, locking down the need to reach for her and pull her back across that space. Instead he shifted his attention to the case. It sat in the middle of his palm. A jeweler. She'd said Ken Warren was a jeweler.

With his heart thudding dully against his sternum, he pried the top off. And it ceased beating at all as he stared down at the gold pocket watch nestled on a bed of black silk. A detailed rendering of a lion was etched on the face of it, the amber jewels of its eyes gleaming, its mouth stretched wide as if in midroar. Awed, he stroked a fingertip over the excellent craftsmanship and artistry.

It was...beautiful.

"When I saw it, I knew it was yours. A lion for both your first and last names. *Darius*, which means royalty, and then *King*," she murmured. "I thought it would be a perfect addition to your and your father's collection."

He tore his gaze away from the magnificent piece and met her eyes. Awe, gratefulness, regret and sadness—they all coalesced into a jumbled, thick mass that lodged in his throat, choking him.

She'd bought a gift for him, had chosen it with care and thoughtfulness.

And he'd returned that kindness with suspicion and scorn.

He'd fucked up.

"Thank you," he rasped. "Isobel..."

"Save it." She took another step back. "You're sorry now. Until the next time when I fail some test or, worse, pass it. Is this what I have to look forward to for however long this *agreement* lasts? I spent two years walking on eggshells. At least give me a handbook, Darius. Tell me now so I can avoid the condescending comments, the scathing glares and condemning silences."

"I'm sorry," he said, trying again to apologize. "You didn't deserve that."

"I know I didn't," she snapped. "But the truth is, you can say those two words, but you obviously believed I did. You convicted me without even offering me the benefit of the doubt. Of course, me sitting with a man couldn't be innocent. Not Isobel 'The Gold Digger' Hughes."

Suddenly the anger leaked from her face, from her body. Her shoulders sagged, and a heavy sadness shadowed her eyes. The sight of it squeezed his heart so hard, an ache bloomed across his chest.

"I just wanted to do something nice for you. To show you how much I appreciate all you've done for Aiden, show you all that you…" She trailed off, ducking her head briefly before lifting it. *Finish it*, he silently yelled. *Finish that sentence*. "I'm fighting a losing battle here, and Darius, I'm tired. Tired of trying to change your mind, of proving myself, of paying the price for a sin I never committed. I'm…" She shrugged, lifting her hands with the palms up in surrender. "Tired."

Slowly, she turned and headed toward the study entrance.

"Isobel," he called after her, her name scoring his throat. But she didn't pause, and desperation scratched him bloody, demanding he *stop her*. Give her the truth he'd kept from her. Pride and honesty waged a battle inside him. Self-preservation and vulnerability. "Stop. Please."

She'd jerked to a halt at his "please." Probably because she'd never heard him utter the word before. Still, her back remained to him, as if he had mere seconds before she bolted again.

Shoving a hand through his hair, he thrust the other in his pants pocket and paced to one of the walls of windows. "I don't remember you at the wedding, but you might recall that I married. Her name was Faith." He emitted a soft scoff. "When we first met, her name had seemed like a sign. Like fate or God sending me a message that she was the one. I'd wanted what my parents had, and I thought I'd found that with Faith.

"She'd reminded me of my mother. Not just beautiful and elegant, but full of life and laughter. Faith had a way of dragging a smile out of you even when everything had gone to hell. Dad used to call it the ability to 'charm the birds right out of the trees.'" In spite of the ugly tale he was about to divulge, a faint smile quirked a corner of his mouth. He couldn't count how many times his father had lovingly said that about his mom, usually after she'd used said charm to finagle something out of him. "Faith and I only dated several months, but the Wellses loved and approved of her, and I believed we would have a long, happy marriage... I was wrong."

Isobel's scent, delicate and feminine, drifted to him seconds before she appeared at his side. She didn't touch him but stood close enough that he could feel her.

"Within six months, I realized I'd made a mistake. The affectionate, witty woman I'd known turned catty, cold and spiteful. Especially if I said no to something she wanted. I discovered a little too late that she didn't love me as much as she loved what I could afford to give her. As much as the lifestyle I offered her." He clenched his jaw. The despair, disillusion and anger that had been his faithful companions back then returned, reminding him how foolish he'd been. "But even then, I'd still been determined to salvage our relationship. Hoping she'd change back into the woman I'd married. Then..." He paused, fisting his fingers inside his pants pockets. "Then I came home a day early from a business trip. Since it'd been late, I hadn't called to let her know I was arriving. I walked into our bedroom and found her. And one of my vice presidents. I froze. Stunned. And in so much goddamn pain, I couldn't breathe. By this time, our marriage was hanging on by a thread, but I was still hopeful. Of all the things she could do—had done—I hadn't expected this betrayal. Didn't think she was capable of it."

Again, he paused, his chest constricting as the memories of that night bombarded him, the utter helplessness and grief that had grounded his feet in that bedroom doorway, rendering him an unwilling voyeur to his wife's infidelity.

A delicate hand slipped into his pants pocket and closed over his fist. He tore his sightless gaze away from the window and glanced at Isobel. She didn't face him, keeping her own stare focused ahead, but the late afternoon light reflected off the shiny track of tears sliding down her cheek.

She was crying.

For him.

Clearing his throat, he looked away, that tightness in his chest now a noose around his neck. He forced himself to continue. To lance the wound.

"I filed for divorce the next morning. We'd only been married a year and a half. A year and a half," he repeated. "I felt like a failure. Still do. I was so ashamed, I hid the truth from Baron, Helena and Gabriella. They still don't know why Faith and I divorced."

His admission echoed inside him like a clanging church bell. He'd never voiced those words aloud. Didn't want to admit that his disastrous marriage continued to affect his life years after it had ended. Thank God he hadn't been so lovestruck that he'd forgone a prenup. He wouldn't have put it past Faith to try to clean him out just from spitefulness.

"Why?" Isobel asked, her voice gentle but strong. "You made a mistake. It doesn't make you a failure. Just human.

Like all of us mortals. Wanting to believe in a person, wanting to believe in love, doesn't reflect on your intelligence or lack of it. It speaks volumes about your integrity, your honor, your heart. Just because that other person didn't have the character or dignity to respect their vows, to cherish and protect your heart, doesn't mean you're a fool or a disappointment. She didn't respect your relationship, you or herself. That's her sin, not yours. But, Darius," she turned to him, and he shifted his gaze back to her. "It's your decision, but you should forgive her, let it go."

He frowned. "I have forgiven her, and obviously I've moved on. I'm not pining for her." Hell no. That bridge had not only been burned, but the ashes spread.

"No, you haven't," she objected. "Forgiveness isn't just about cutting someone off or entering new relationships. It's deciding not to allow that person or that experience to shape your decisions, your life. It's not giving that person power over you even though they're long gone. And when your choices, your views, are influenced by past hurt, then those betrayals do have power over you." Her mouth twisted into a rueful smile. "I should know. I've fought this battle for two years. But understand—this is what I've had to come to grips with—forgiveness isn't saying what that person did was okay. It's just choosing to no longer let that poison kill you."

"Who have you forgiven, Isobel?" he murmured, but his mind already whispered the answer to him.

She didn't immediately answer, but seconds later she sighed and dipped her head in a small nod.

"Every day when I get up, I make the choice to forgive Gage. It's a daily process of letting go of the pain and anger. Especially since he's Aiden's father. I refuse to taint that for him with my own bitterness. And I refuse to be held hostage by it. Gage isn't here any longer. I'm never going to hear 'I'm sorry' from him. And even though Faith is very much alive, you most likely won't receive an apology from her either. So, what do we do? Forgive ourselves for the guilt and blame that isn't ours. But as long as we hold on to the past, we can never grab ahold of the future and all it has for us."

He stood still, her words sowing into his mind, his heart. By her definition, had he really released Faith, the past? He bowed his head, pinching the bridge of his nose.

"What about wisdom, Isobel? Only a fool or a masochist doesn't learn from his mistakes."

She slowly removed her hand from his and stepped back. He checked the urge to reach for her, to claim her touch again.

"Wisdom is applying those lessons, Darius. It isn't judging someone based on your own experiences. It isn't allowing the past to blind you to the reality even when it's staring you in the face." She lifted her hands, palms up. "Today you walked in here and jumped to the conclusion that I was sneaking behind your back with another man. That I had brought him into your home like your ex-wife. It's easier for you to be suspicious than to believe that maybe I'm not like her."

She inhaled and tilted her chin up, with defiance in the gesture, in the drawing back of her shoulders.

"I did not cheat on Gage, Darius. I never betrayed him—he betrayed me. He was the cheater, not me."

Before he could object, question her accusation or deny it—maybe all three—she pivoted on her heel and exited the room. Minutes passed, and when she returned, he remained standing where she'd left him, too stunned by her revelation. *Gage cheated? No. Impossible.* He'd loved Isobel. Hell, sometimes it'd seemed he'd loved her to the point of obsession. He couldn't, *wouldn't have*, taken another woman to his bed. Not the man Darius had known.

Did you really know him?

The insidious question crept into his brain, leaving behind an oily trail of dread and doubt.

"Here." She extended a cell phone to him. He reached for it before his brain sent the message to ask why. "It's my old phone, the one I had when I was married to Gage. I saved it for the pictures I'd taken of him for Aiden when he was older. But I want you to read this."

She pressed the screen and a stream of text messages filled the screen.

From Gage.

He tore his attention away from her solemn face to the phone.

I should divorce you. Where would you be then? Back in that dirty hole I found you. It's where you belong.

You'll never find someone better than me. No one would want you, anyway. I don't even know why I bother with you either. You're not good enough for me.

Don't bother waiting up for me. I'm fucking her tonight.

And below that message, a picture of Gage maliciously smiling into the camera, his arm wrapped around a woman.

Bile raced up from the pit of Darius's stomach, scorching a path to his throat. He choked on it, and on the rage surging through him like a tidal wave. Swamping him. Dragging him under.

She hadn't deserved the kind of malevolent vitriol contained in those texts. No woman did. And that his friend, one of the most honorable, kindest men he'd ever known, had sent them to his *wife*... The woman he'd proclaimed to love beyond reason...

Had Gage been that great of an actor? And to what end?

The questions plagued him, drumming against his skull, not letting up. Because he needed answers. He needed to understand. His heart yearned to reject the idea that Gage could've been that spiteful...an abuser.

"Tell me," he rasped. "All of it."

After a long moment, her soft voice reached him.

"I was twenty when we met. And he was handsome, charming, funny and, yes, wealthy. I didn't—still don't—understand why he chose me. And I didn't care—I loved him. Becoming pregnant so soon after we married was a little scary, but seemed right. He'd started becoming a little moody and irritable a few months after we married, but soon after the baby arrived, and I refused the paternity test, he completely changed. I didn't understand then, but now I see he hated being poor, regretted being cut off from his family and blamed me for it. Resented me. That's when the isolation started. He needed to know where I went, who I was with. He decided my every move, from who I could spend time with to what I wore. Since I just wanted to please him, I gave in. But then I couldn't see my family because they were a 'bad influence.' And if I spoke to a man for too long, or smiled at one, I was cheating. The little money I earned, and the money his parents started giving him, he controlled that, as well. If I needed anything—from personal hygiene items to new clothes for Aiden—he bought them, because he couldn't trust me to spend wisely. I was trapped. A prisoner. And my husband was my warden."

"Why did you stay?" Darius asked, desperate to understand. To punch something. "Why didn't you leave?"

"Love," she murmured. "At first, love kept me there. I foolishly believed it could conquer all. But then that fairy tale ended, and fear and insecurity stepped in. I'd left school, had no degree. A minimum wage job. At that point, the unknown seemed far more terrifying than the known. And I never stopped believing that if I learned the proper way to act and speak, if I could get Gage to love me again like he used to, everything would be okay. His family would love and accept me, too." She shook her head, letting loose a hollow chuckle that bottomed out Darius's stomach. "And I wanted our child to have a two-parent home like I didn't. So I stayed longer than I should've. The night I told Gage I wanted a divorce is the night he…"

Grief tore through Darius. And, still clutching the phone with its offensive messages, he turned and stalked away from Isobel. His thigh clipped the edge of his desk, and he slammed his palms on the top of it, leaning all of his weight on his arms.

It was a death.

A death of his belief in a man he'd called brother. The demise of his view of him. Whom had Darius been defending all these years? How could he still love Gage…?

Her arms slid around him. Her cheek pressed to his back.

The comfort—the selfless comfort—nearly buckled his knees.

"It's okay to love him," she murmured, damn near reading his mind. Her voice vibrated through him, and he shivered in her embrace. "A part of me still does. For the memory of the man I initially fell in love with, for the father of my son. With time and distance, and loving Aiden, who is a part of Gage, I can't hate him. He was a man with faults, with issues and weaknesses. But he was also everything you remember him to be. A great, loyal friend. A loving son. A brother who would literally lay down his life for you. You can love those parts of him and dislike the parts that made him a horrible husband. There's no guilt or betrayal in that, Darius."

He pushed off the desk, spun around and grabbed her close, closing his arms around her. Crushing her to him. As if she were his lifeline. His absolution.

She clung to him just as tightly.

"I have a confession," she whispered against his chest.

"Yes?" he asked, the word scratching his raw throat.

"I never betrayed Gage, but…" She hesitated, tilted her head back. He lifted his gaze, meeting hers. She studied him for several long moments before dipping her head in a slight nod. "I noticed you, admired you. Somehow I instinctively knew you would never mistreat a woman. You were too honorable. And you've always been beautiful to me."

The soft admission reverberated in the room like a shout. He stared into her eyes—eyes that had captured his imagination and attention from the first glance.

"Sweetheart," he growled. It was all he got out before he cupped her face and crashed his mouth to hers. He couldn't stop, couldn't rein himself in if he'd wanted to.

And he didn't want to.

The avalanche of emotion that had eddied inside him burst free in a storm of passion and need so sharp, so hungry that fighting it would've been futile.

Her fingers curled around his wrists, holding on to him. Maybe designating him as her anchor as she, too, dove into the tempest. She leaned her head back, angled it and opened wider for him. Granting him permission to conquer, to claim more. More. Always more with her.

He dragged his mouth from hers, and turning with Isobel clasped to him, swiped an arm across the surface of his desk, sending books, folders, the cell and his home phone tumbling to the floor. After grabbing her by the waist, he hiked her onto the desk, following her down. Covering her. Impatient, with a desperation he didn't want to acknowledge racing through him, he jerked her pants and underwear down her legs, baring her. Her trembling fingers already attacked his pants, undoing them while he removed his wallet and jerked a condom free. Within seconds, he sheathed himself and thrust inside her. His groan and her cry mingled, entwined together as tightly as their bodies.

And as they lost themselves in each other, as he buried himself in her over and over, he forgot about everything but the pleasure of this woman.

Of Isobel.

And for those moments, it was enough.

Thirteen

Isobel leaned closer to the vanity mirror, applying mascara to her lashes. When the doorbell rang, echoing through the house, she almost stabbed herself in the eye.

"Damn," she whispered, replacing the makeup wand.

It was Thanksgiving Day. Who could that possibly be?

She glanced at the clock on her dresser. One o'clock. A loud holiday meal with her mother, brothers and plethora of aunts, uncles and cousins was set for three o'clock at her mom's house. They were supposed to leave as soon as Darius returned from the store after a last-minute errand. For someone to show up uninvited on their doorstep on a holiday, it must be important.

Quickly rushing down the hall to Aiden's room, she leaned inside the doorway. "Ms. Jacobs, I'm going to get the door. But we should be ready to go in just a few."

The older woman smiled from where she played blocks with Aiden. "We're fine until then, Ms. Hughes."

"Isobel," she corrected, but the nanny just smiled and returned her attention to Aiden. Shaking her head and chuckling, she descended the steps. She'd been waging the war of getting Ms. Jacobs to call her Isobel, but to no avail. In the short time she'd known the woman, they had grown fond of each other. So much so, Ms. Jacobs was spending Thanksgiving with them since she didn't have children of her own.

It'd been Darius who had thought of that kindness.

Darius.

A spiral of warmth swirled through Isobel's chest, landing in her belly.

Ever since that evening a week ago, when he'd come home to find her with Ken and heard her full admission about Gage, a…connection had forged between them. One that, while tenuous, had her heart trembling with a cautious hope that what had started out as a marriage bargain between them might evolve into a real relationship. A relationship based on respect, admiration…trust.

Love.

The nervous snarls in her stomach loosened, bursting into flutters.

There'd been a time—not too long ago—when she wouldn't have believed herself capable of falling for another person. She hadn't thought she could ever take the risk of trusting someone with not just her heart, but with Aiden's.

But here, only weeks later, she stood on the crumbling precipice of a plunge into something powerful and dangerous—love.

And it was a beautiful, strong, loyal and fierce man who had her heart whispering with the need to take the fall.

She was afraid. Even as a fragile hope beat its wings inside her, she was *afraid*.

She reached the foyer and glanced out the window next to the door. Shock rocked through her.

Helena and Gabriella.

What…?

As if on autopilot, Isobel unlocked the door and opened it.

"Hello," she greeted, surprised at the calmness in her voice. "Please come in." As they passed by her and entered the house, she shut the door behind them. "Darius isn't here at the moment…"

"That's fine. We can wait," Helena said, turning to face Isobel with a coldly polite smile. "We apologize for showing up unannounced, but he told us you were having Thanksgiving dinner with your family. We wanted to catch him before you left."

Unease sidled through her veins, but she pasted a smile on her lips and waved a hand toward the living room. "He should be back shortly, if you'd like to wait for him in here."

Part of her wanted to run up the stairs and let Darius deal with his visitors when he returned, but at some point she had to become accustomed to being around them without Darius as a buffer. She could handle a few minutes.

"You and Darius seem to be getting along well," Helena commented as she moved into the room and settled on the couch.

Isobel nodded, stalling as she considered how to answer. As if a physical trap waited to be sprung at the end of her reply. "Darius is a kind man."

Gabriella strode over to the mantel and studied the array of pictures there. "Yes, he is. It's both a blessing and a curse," she said. "Have you two set a wedding date yet?"

Unease knotted Isobel's stomach, at both the cryptic comment and the switch in topic. "Not a definite date," she replied. But remembering the stipulations Darius had set in their contract, she added, "Sometime in January, I believe."

"You believe," Helena echoed, and Isobel couldn't miss the sneer in her words as her gaze flicked to Isobel's left hand. "No ring yet, I see. Doesn't that tell you something, Isobel?"

"No," Isobel murmured, sensing the shift in the other

woman's demeanor and steeling herself. "But I suppose you have an idea about that."

"He hasn't set a wedding date and hasn't even bothered buying you a ring." Helena cocked her head, her steady contemplation condescending, pitying. "What you said earlier is very true. Darius is a good man. The kind who would sacrifice his own happiness for those he loves. Yet he's obviously reluctant to shackle himself to you. A man who is looking forward to marriage publicly claims his fiancée."

"I'm afraid she's correct, Isobel," Gabriella agreed, strolling the few feet to stand next to the couch her mother perched on.

A smirk curved the younger woman's lips, and a sinking, dread-filled pit yawned wide in Isobel's chest. Was insulting her the purpose behind their visit? Or just a bonus since Darius wasn't home yet? She glanced toward the bottom of the staircase. *Please, God, let Ms. Jacobs keep Aiden upstairs.*

Briefly, she considered exiting the room. But that smacked too much of running, and she'd quit doing that when she returned to Chicago.

"You don't know anything about my relationship with Darius," she said, tone cool. "But why don't you go ahead and have your say so we can get all this out in the open? That way we no longer have to indulge in this pretense. You don't want me with Darius."

Helena's lips firmed into a flat, ugly line, anger glittering in her eyes. "I thought we were rid of you for good. But you found a way to sneak back in, didn't you? It wasn't enough that you used my son and took him away from us, but now you've latched onto my other son. And if we don't want to lose him or our grandson, we have to deal with *you*," she spat out.

"I would never come between you and Darius," Isobel objected.

"As if you could," Gabriella snapped. "We have a real relationship. We love each other. You don't know anything about that."

Dragging in a breath and struggling to contain her temper in the face of their venom, Isobel straightened her shoulders and tipped up her chin.

"As I was saying," Isobel gritted out. "I would never come between you and Darius. His relationship with you is yours. And if it's as strong as you say, then there's nothing I could do to harm it," she pointed out. Ignoring Helena's outraged gasp, Isobel continued, "But while you might revise history with Darius, don't look me in the eye and speak it to me. We both know I've never tried to keep you from your grandson. You were the ones who didn't believe he was a prestigious *Wells*." She uttered that name as if it were sour. "You decided he wasn't worthy of your time and attention. Your love. As for me, I don't need your approval or acceptance. I don't even want it. But now, for some reason, you've changed your mind, and I won't deprive Aiden of knowing his father's family. But if you believe for one second that I'll let you twist and poison him, then you're absolutely correct. You won't see him."

I won't allow you to turn him into his father.

"Twist him? Poison him?" Gabriella bit, her lips curling in a snarl. "That is rich coming from you of all people. You, a gold-digging wh—"

"What's going on here?"

All of them turned toward the living room entrance at the sound of Darius's voice. A steadily darkening frown creased his brow as he scanned Isobel's features before moving to Helena and Gabriella.

Relief coursed through her, but she locked her knees, refusing to betray any sign of weakness in front of the two women.

"Helena? Gabriella?" he pressed. "What are you doing here?"

Isobel desperately needed to retreat and regroup. Shore up her battered shields.

"They came by to see you. I'm just going to check on Aiden. I'll be right back." Forcing a smile that felt fake and brittle on her lips, she left without a backward glance at Helena and Gabriella.

"Isobel," Darius murmured, catching her arm in a gentle grasp as she passed him. "Sweetheart…"

"No, Darius," she said, slipping free of his hold. "Just give me a minute."

She left the room and prayed that when she returned, the two women he considered a surrogate mother and sister were gone. If not, she might not be responsible for her actions.

Fourteen

"What happened?" Darius demanded as soon as Isobel disappeared from sight. "And can one of you explain to me why I received a phone call from my nanny to return home as soon as possible because two women were attacking Isobel?"

Fury simmered beneath his skin. They both stared at him, their faces set in identical mutinous lines. Helena rose from the couch, turning fully to face him.

"Helena? Gabriella?" He strode farther into the room, halting across from them. "What. Happened? And don't tell me 'nothing' or 'everything is fine,' because both would be lies."

He'd glimpsed Isobel's face when he'd first entered the room. That cold, shuttered mask had relayed all he needed to know. She only wore that blank expression when hurt or angry. And from the shadows that had swirled in her eyes before she'd pulled away from him, both emotions had applied.

"I love you, Darius," Helena said, approaching him with her hands outstretched toward him. "You know I do. But how much longer is this supposed to go on? How much longer are we supposed to pretend that that...*woman* is welcome in our family?"

"Helena," he warned, his muscles tensing when she clutched his forearms.

He'd never pulled away from her touch before, but with those vicious words ringing in the room—no matter the pain they originated from—he couldn't take it. He stepped back, her arms dropping away. Hurt flashed across her face, her lips parting in surprise.

"Darius," Gabriella murmured, glancing at her mother, then back at him. A plea filled her gaze. "That's why we came here today. To tell you that we know you went through this farce of a relationship so we could have Aiden in our lives. You've sacrificed for us, but you don't have to anymore. Mother told me about the DNA test. And now that we have the results back—"

He slashed his hand through the air, dread spiking in his chest. "Did you tell Isobel about the DNA test?" he growled. Driving his fingers through his hair, he glanced away from the women. His motives—bringing closure to the family—had been pure, but Isobel would see it as a betrayal. He needed to talk to her first, to explain. "Gabriella, did you say anything to Isobel about the test?"

"No, I didn't say anything to your precious Isobel," she snapped, whipping around and pacing away from him. "But you should know that we've been talking and have come to some decisions."

The unease that had coiled inside him slowly unfurled. "What are you talking about?"

For a heartbeat, Helena and Gabriella didn't respond, just stared at him. The tension thickened until it seemed to suck all the air out of the room.

"Answer me," he grated out.

"Now that we know for certain that Aiden is Gage's son, we intend to go forward with the suit for sole custody," Helena announced. "We've already contacted our attorney."

"You. Did. Not," he snarled. Betrayal, rage and despair churned in his chest, and he fought not to hurl curses and accusations that would irrevocably damage his relationships with these people. "That wasn't my plan or my agreement with Isobel. The terms of which I expressly discussed with you."

Helena scoffed, waving a hand. "That was before we knew that Aiden was our grandson. *Ours*," she stressed, pressing a fist to her heart. "Gage would've wanted him raised with us. By *us* and not that…that deceiver, that liar. And no judge on this earth wouldn't see that we're much more fit parents than her."

"Darius, don't you see?" Gabriella implored, moving closer to him. She clutched his upper arm, and he curbed his automatic reaction to shake her off. And that reaction sent a blast of pain through him. "This is for you, too. Now you can break off this joke of an engagement. You did all this for us, and we love you for it. But now, with us suing for custody, you don't have to chain yourself to a woman you hate. We know you might not agree with this, but we believe it is for the best."

"For the best," he repeated. "Do you know all Isobel has been through with her marriage to Gage? He wasn't a loving, faithful husband. He emotionally beat her down, cheated on her. He mentally abused her. Now, after she survived that, you want to rip her child away from her."

"How dare you?" Helena hissed, anger mottling her skin. She advanced on him, eyes narrowed and glittering. "I love you like a son, Darius, but I won't allow you to speak ill of my son in this house. Who told you these lies that you're so willing to swallow? Isobel?" She spit the name, her mouth twisting into an ugly sneer. "So, you believe her over a man who you loved as a brother? Did she warp your mind? Is that it, Darius? Do you think you're in love with her?"

He parted his lips, but no words emerged. His pulse pounded in his ears, and his tongue suddenly seemed too thick for his mouth. Helena's question ricocheted off the walls of his skull.

Do you think you're in love with her? Do you think you're in love with her?

Over and over. *No*, his mind objected. *Not possible.*

He pivoted sharply on his heel and strode to the bank of windows. After Faith, he hadn't believed himself capable of having deep feelings for another woman. Just the idea of opening himself and risking that kind of pain once more... He'd vowed never to make himself vulnerable—*weak*—again. And Isobel...

She had the power to hurt him like Faith never did.

If he gave her the chance, and she betrayed him, she could wreck him.

The knowledge had fear and anger cascading through him. Could he take a chance? Could he crack himself open and lose not just his family—because the Wellses would view him as choosing her as the biggest betrayal—but also risk losing himself?

No.

Coward that he was, no, he couldn't risk it.

"Darius."

He jerked his head up, spinning around.

Isobel stood in the doorway. *How long had she been standing there? How much had she overheard?* He moved towards her, but she shifted backward.

And that one movement supplied the answers.

"Isobel, please let me explain."

She stared at him, numb. The blessed nothingness had

assailed her from the moment she'd returned to the living room and overheard his conversation with Helena and Gabriella.

Did you tell Isobel about the DNA test?

We intend to go forth with the suit for sole custody.

No judge on this earth wouldn't see that we're much more fit parents than her.

Do you think you're in love with her?

That awful, damning silence.

The two women had left soon after she'd appeared in the room, but she hadn't moved. Hadn't been able to. And now, as pain invaded her body, she prayed for the return of the numbness.

"Yes," she agreed, voice hoarse. "You're right. Which should we talk about first? The violation of running a DNA test on my son behind my back? Or how *your family* intends to take my son away from me?"

He closed his eyes, and a spasm of emotion passed over his face. But it disappeared in the next instant.

"I'm sorry for not telling you about the DNA test, Isobel," he murmured.

"You're sorry for not telling me, but not for doing it," she clarified. A sarcastic chuckle escaped her. "You promised me we would make decisions regarding Aiden *together*. Without interference from the Wellses. You betrayed my trust."

"I didn't..." He broke off his sentence, briefly glancing away. "Yes, I did break that promise. And I'm sorry," he said, returning his gaze to her. "I am, Isobel. But my motives weren't to hurt or betray you. I thought if Baron, Helena and Gabriella knew for certain that Aiden was their grandson and nephew, he could bring healing to them. To this family. I wanted to give them that. But also, knowing you told the truth about him being Gage's would start to change their view of you, as well. Not only do they need to know their grandson and nephew—they need to begin to know you."

"No, Darius. Now they just think it was luck that Gage fathered him, out of all the other men I supposedly screwed." She shook her head. "But this isn't about them. It's about how you lied to me. It's about how you put them—their feelings, their welfare—above Aiden." *Above me.* "And you handed them cause to take him away from me."

"I won't allow that to happen," he growled, moving toward her, his arms outstretched. As if to touch her.

No. No way could she allow that. Not when she was so close to crumbling. She shifted backward, steeling herself against the glint of pain in his eyes.

"Agreeing to marry you, to move in here, to put my son under your protection was supposed to stop it from occurring. But it didn't. I still find myself at their mercy. A place I vowed two years ago I would never be again. And all because I trusted you."

"Do you really believe I would throw you to the wolves? That I would abandon you to face this alone? Do you think I'm capable of that?" he demanded, stalking forward, but he drew up several feet shy of her.

"Would you want to? No," she whispered. "But would you do it all the same? Yes. If Baron, Helena and Gabriella made you choose between them and me, I have no illusions about whose side you would come down on. And I'm so tired of waging a losing battle between the past, your mistrust and Gage's family. *Your family.* Because I'll never be considered a member of that perfect unit."

"That's bullshit," he snapped, his features darkening in anger. "We've been building something here. Something good. Our own place, our own family. You can't deny that."

She shook her head once more. Desperately needing space, she backpedaled, then caught herself midstep. She was through running. Through letting others dictate her life, her truth.

"What we've 'been building' was founded on blackmail, lies and mistrust. It'll never be 'something good.'"

Raising her head, she committed every one of his features to memory. Though she might wish she could evict him from her heart, she never would.

That didn't mean she wouldn't try. She had to. For her peace. For her sanity. For her future.

"I love you, Darius," she admitted quietly.

His body stiffened, and lightning flashed in his eyes, brightening them so the gold almost eclipsed the dark brown. "Isobel," he rumbled.

"No." She slammed a hand up, though he hadn't moved toward her. "Let me finish. I didn't think I would ever be able to open my heart to another man. But you did the impossible. You made me trust again. Love again. Made me believe in second chances. And I thank you for that. And I might hate you for that," she whispered. "Because you showed me what happily-ever-after could be, then snatched it from me."

"Isobel," Darius rasped again, erasing the distance between them and cradling her cheek.

And for a moment, she cupped her hand over his, pressing his palm to her face and savoring his touch. But then she dragged his hand away from her.

"Do you love me?" she asked, staring into his eyes. Glimpsing the surprise flicker and then the shadows gather in them.

Darius stepped backward, a dark frown creasing his brow. But he said nothing. And it was all the answer she needed.

"You awakened something in me," she said softly. "Something I wish would fall back asleep, because now that it's alive, I hurt. I...hope. The Isobel from two years ago would believe she could change you, make you accept her. Fight for her, if she just loved you hard enough. That Isobel would be happy with the parts of yourself you were willing to give her. But I'm not that woman anymore. I deserve to be a man's number one and to be loved and cherished and valued and protected. I deserve a man who will love me beyond reason, and though I'm not perfect, he will love me perfectly."

"What you want, I..." he trailed off.

The raw scrape of his voice and the sorrow in his gaze should've been a balm to her battered soul, but it did nothing.

"I'm not telling you this to emotionally blackmail you, Darius. I'm admitting this for *me*, not you. So when I walk out of here, I won't have regrets."

"Walk out of here?" he repeated on a low growl. His arms lifted again, but once more he dropped them, his fingers curling into fists. "We had an agreement. A contract. You can't just break it."

"We've been breaking the contract from the beginning. Becoming lovers. The DNA test. Falling in love with you." The contract was supposed to have been a defense against that. A reminder of who she was marrying and why. But it hadn't shielded her heart, just as Darius hadn't protected her and Aiden. "Do what you feel you need to do regarding the consequences. But I won't remain in this home, in this... arrangement knowing I can't trust you. That I will continue to pay the price for Gage's lies and the Wellses' grudges. I refuse to be someone's emotional and mental punching bag again. And every time you side with Gage's memory and his family, you deliver another blow. No, Aiden and I will be leaving today. But I won't keep him from you. He loves you, and I know you feel the same. We'll set up a schedule after we're settled..."

Her arms tingled with the need to throw themselves

around him. Her throat ached with the longing to ask him to say something, to beg her not to go. To declare his love and loyalty.

But nothing came from him.

She straightened her shoulders and inhaled past the pain. Then she turned, exited the room and climbed the stairs. Once she entered her bedroom and shut the door, her back hit the wall and she slowly slid to the floor. The tears she'd been reining in fell unchecked down her cheeks. How long she sat there, quietly sobbing and hugging herself, she didn't know. But during that time, her resolve to do right by Aiden, and by herself, firmed until it resembled a thick, impenetrable wall.

She might be losing Darius, losing the future she'd so foolishly allowed herself to imagine for her and Aiden, but she was gaining more.

Her self-respect.

Her dignity.

Her.

And it was more than enough.

Fifteen

Darius stared down into the squat glass tumbler and the amber-colored bourbon filling it.

At what point would the alcohol send him tumbling into oblivion, where the memories from Thanksgiving couldn't follow? He'd been seeking the answer to this for four days now. But while he'd been fucked up, that sweet abyss of forgetfulness had eluded him. No matter how many bottles he'd gone through, he could still see Isobel's beautiful face etched with pain and fierce determination as she confessed she loved him—and then left him. Could still hear the catch in her voice as she accused him of betraying her trust. Could still hear the sound of the front door closing behind her and Aiden that afternoon.

Closing his eyes, he raised the glass to his lips and gulped a mouthful of the expensive but completely useless liquid. But he was desperate to not just escape the mental torture of his last, devastating conversation with Isobel, but the terrible, deafening silence of his house. It'd chased him into his study, where he'd shut himself away. But there was no refuge from the emptiness, from the *nothing* that pervaded his home.

I deserve a man who will love me beyond reason, and though I'm not perfect, he will love me perfectly.

If Baron, Helena and Gabriella made you choose between them and me, I have no illusions about whose side you would come down on.

You betrayed my trust.

Do you love me?

Her words haunted him, lacerated him...indicted him.

But goddamn, he'd been crystal clear that he hadn't gone into this arrangement for love. He'd been more than upfront that he'd wanted to save the Wellses and her from an ugly custody battle. To protect Baron from any future health risks that a custody suit could inflict. To provide for Aiden. To unite the boy with his father's family. And everything he'd done—the engagement, the dinner with the Wellses, the DNA test—had been to work toward those ends.

He'd never lied. Never had a secret agenda.

He'd never asked for her love. Her trust.

When you let people in, they leave. He'd learned this lesson over and over again.

Isobel had left him.

Like his parents.

Like Faith.

Like Gage.

Anguish rose, and he bent under it like a tree conceding to the winds of a storm.

She'd begun to hope. Well, so had he.

In this dark, closed-off room, he could admit that to himself. Yes, he'd begun to hope that Isobel and Aiden could be his second chance at a family. But just when he'd had it within his grasp, he'd lost it. Again. Only this time... This time didn't compare to the pain of his marriage ending.

As he'd suspected, Isobel had left a gaping, bleeding hole in his world. One that blotted out the past and only left his lonely, aching present.

A knock reverberated on his study door, and Darius jerked his head up. Before he could call out, the door opened, and Baron appeared. Surprise winged through Darius, and he frowned as the older man scanned the room, his gaze finally alighting on Darius behind his desk.

With a small nod, Baron entered, shutting the door behind him. Darius didn't rise from his seat as Baron crossed the room and lowered himself into the armchair in front of the desk.

"Darius," Baron quietly said, studying him. "We've been trying to contact you for the past few days, but you haven't answered or returned any of our calls. We've been worried, son."

The apologies and excuses tap-danced on his tongue, but after taking another sip of bourbon, "Isobel left. Her and Aiden. They left me," came out instead.

Baron grimaced, sympathy flickering in his eyes. "I'm sorry, son. I truly am."

"Really?" Darius demanded, emitting a razor-edged chuckle. "Isn't this what the plan was from the moment I announced my intentions to marry her? Trick her into complying with my proposal long enough to order a DNA test. And once the results were in, take her son and free me from her conniving clutches?" he drawled. "Well, you can tell Helena and Gabriella it worked. Congratulations."

He tipped his glass toward Baron in a mock salute before downing the remainder of the alcohol.

"I'm sorry we've hurt you, Darius. I truly am," Baron murmured. "Their actions might have been...heavy-handed, but their motives were good."

"Why are you here, Baron?" Darius asked, suddenly so weary he could barely keep his body from slumping in the chair. He didn't have the energy to defend Helena and Gabriella or listen to Baron do it.

Baron heaved a sigh that carried so much weight, Darius's attention sharpened. For the first time since the other man had entered the room, Darius took in the heavier lines that etched his handsome features, noted the tired slope of his shoulders.

Straightening in his chair, Darius battled back a surge of panic. "What's wrong? Are you feeling okay? Is it Helena? Gabrie—"

"No, no, we're fine." Baron waved off his concern with an abrupt shake of his head. "It's nothing like that. But I..." He faltered, rubbing his forehead. "Darius, I..."

"Baron," Darius pressed, leaning forward, bourbon forgotten. Though his initial alarm had receded, concern still clogged his chest. "Tell me why you're here."

"This isn't easy for me to say because I'm afraid to lose you. But..." He briefly closed his eyes, and when he opened them, a plea darkened the brown depths. "I can't keep this secret any longer. Not when the reasons for keeping it are outweighed by the hurt it's inflicting."

The patience required not to grab Baron and shake the story from him taxed his control. Darius curled his fingers around the arm of his chair and waited.

"On Thanksgiving, you told Helena and Gabriella about Gage and Isobel's marriage. That he'd been cruel, abusive and faithless. Everything you said..." He dragged in an audible breath. "It was true. All of it. Their marriage was horrible, and Gage's jealousy, insecurity and weakness were to blame."

Shock slammed into Darius with an icy fist, rendering him frozen. He stared at Baron, speechless. But his mind whirred with questions.

How do you know? Why didn't you say anything to your wife and daughter?

How could you not say anything to me?

"How?" he rasped. "How do you know?"

Another of those heavy sighs, and Baron turned away, staring out the side window. As if unable to meet Darius's gaze.

"Gage told me," Baron whispered. "The night he died, he told me the truth."

"What?" Darius clenched the arms of his chair tighter. If they snapped off under the pressure, he wouldn't have been surprised.

Baron nodded, still not looking at him. "Yes, he found me in the library that evening and broke down, confessing everything to me. Isobel had demanded a divorce, and he'd been distraught. I'd barely understood him at first. But as he faced losing Isobel and Aiden, he'd come to me, horrified and ashamed."

Baron finally returned his attention to Darius, but the agony on the older man's face was almost too much to bear.

"My son... He was spoiled. Yes, he had a big heart, but Gage was entitled, and the blame for that rests on Helena's and my shoulders. He'd defied us by marrying Isobel but hadn't been prepared for the separation and disapproval from his family. Hadn't been ready to live on his own without our financial resources. But instead of faulting himself, he blamed Isobel. Yet he loved her and didn't want to let her go. So he'd alienated her from us physically and with his lies of mistreatment and infidelity. He admitted he lied about the cheating, but at some point he'd started to believe his own lies. Became bitter, resentful, jealous and controlling. It transformed him into someone he didn't know, someone he knew I wouldn't be proud of. Who he'd become wasn't the man I'd raised him to be. And I think that's why he confessed to me. His shame and guilt tore at him, and in the end it drove him out into the night, where he crashed his car and died." Baron swallowed, his voice hoarse, and moisture dampening his eyes. "Do I think Gage killed himself that night? No. I don't think it was intentional. But I also believe he was reckless and didn't care. He just wanted the pain to stop."

Air whistled in and out of Darius's rapidly rising and falling chest. A scream scored his throat, but he didn't have enough breath to release it. He squeezed his eyes shut, battling the sting that heralded tears. Tears for Isobel's senseless suffering at her husband's and family's hands. Tears for the man he'd loved and obviously hadn't known as well as he'd thought. Tears for the agony of conscience Gage succumbed to at the end.

"I'm sorry, Darius," Baron continued. "Sorry I lied to you, to Helena and Gabriella. Gage didn't ask me to keep the truth a secret, but I did because I couldn't bear causing them more pain on top of losing him. Even if keeping the secret meant standing by while Isobel was villainized. I made a choice between protecting his memory and protecting her, and now I realize my lie by omission is hurting not just my wife, daughter and Isobel, but *you*, a man I love as a second son. I can't continue to be silent. I can't allow her to be crucified when she's been guilty of nothing but falling in love with my son. Both of my sons."

Trembling, Darius shoved to his feet, his desk chair rolling back across the hardwood floor. He pressed his fists to the desktop, wrestling against the need to lash out, to rail over the injustice and torment they'd all inflicted on Isobel.

Stalking across the room, he tunneled his fingers through his hair, gripping the strands and pulling until tiny pinpricks of pain stung his scalp.

"You're going to tell Helena and Gabriella the truth," he demanded of Baron, who'd also stood, silently watching him.

"Yes," he murmured. "I planned on doing it today, but I felt you deserved to hear it first. Darius." Baron lifted his hands and spread them out in a plea of mercy, of surrender. "I'm so sorry."

"Sorry?" Darius laughed, the sound crackling and brittle with cold fury. "Sorry doesn't give her back the years where she was abandoned, left to raise a child on her own. If you knew Aiden was Gage's, why didn't you help her?"

"Gage said he believed Aiden was his, but I didn't know for sure. And she'd refused the paternity test, which deepened my doubts. And honestly, I hated her after Gage's death. I wanted her to suffer because I no longer had my son. I didn't want any reminders of him around—and that included her and a baby that might or might not have been Gage's. It was selfish, spiteful. Yes, I know that now, and I don't know if I can forgive myself for it. Gage told me I'd raised him to be a better man. But I don't know if I did."

Darius clenched his jaw, choking on his vitriolic response.

Helena and Gabriella might not have known the truth, but their behavior toward Isobel since she'd reentered their lives had been spiteful, hurtful. So unlike the gracious, kind, affectionate women he'd known for over a decade.

And he'd excused it.

Which meant he'd condoned it, just as Baron had.

Grief and searing pain shredded him.

He'd told Isobel he would never leave her out to dry. Throw her to the wolves. But he'd done it. He'd broken more than a contract. He'd shattered her trust, his word.

His concern had been about betraying the Wellses, when he'd ended up betraying and tearing apart the family he'd created, the family he'd longed for—with Isobel and Aiden. The roar he'd been trying to dam up rolled out of him on a rough, raw growl. Every moment they'd shared since the night of the blackout bombarded him.

Laughing together in the hallway.

Sharing the stories of his parents' death and Gage in the dark.

Touching her.

Her fiery defiance in her apartment.

Her surrendering to the incredible passion between them.

Her quiet dignity as she confessed about her marriage.

Her resolute pride as she admitted she loved him, but could, and would, live without him.

Jesus.

He slammed a fist against the wall, the impact singing up his arm and reverberating in his chest. He'd marched into her apartment, self-righteous and commanding, accusing her of being deceptive and manipulative, when he'd been guilty of both to maneuver her into doing what he wanted. He'd entered their agreement acting the martyr. When in truth she'd been unjustly persecuted. It'd been he who'd entered their relationship without clean hands or a pure heart.

She was the only one—out of all of them—who could claim both.

And he loved that purity of heart. Loved that spirit and bravery that had looked at all the odds stacked against her and plowed through them one by one. Loved the passion that had stealthily, without his knowledge, thawed and then healed the heart he'd believed frozen beyond redemption.

He loved her.

The admission should've knocked him on his ass. But it didn't. Instead it slid through him, warm and strong, like a spring nourishing a barren field.

He loved her.

Maybe he'd started falling from the moment she'd coaxed him out of his panic attack with talk of movies and Ryan Reynolds. No doubt he'd fought his feelings for her, but if he were brutally honest with himself, the inevitable had occurred when she'd embraced him and assured him his love for his friend—her abusive husband—wasn't wrong.

A weight that had been pressing down on his shoulders lifted, and he could breathe. He could suck in his first lungful of air unencumbered by the past. Turning, he faced Baron. Darius loved him. But if it came down to a choice between him, Helena and Gabrielle, and Isobel and her son—*their son*—then Isobel and Aiden would win every time.

"I'm going to go find my family," Darius said.

His family. Isobel and Aiden.

From the slight flinch of Baron's broad shoulders, the emphasis hadn't been lost on him.

"I don't know what this means with you, Helena and Gabriella in the future. Maybe after you tell them the truth, they can find it in their hearts to forgive Gage and let the past go, including their hate of Isobel. But right now, that's not my issue—it's theirs and yours. If they can't, then we won't be a part of your lives. And that includes Aiden. I won't allow them to poison him, and you can inform them that if you continue in the pursuit of custody, I'll stand beside Isobel and fight you."

Darius pivoted and strode out of the study without a backward glance, steady and determined for the first time since Isobel and Aiden had left.

He had his family to win back.

If they'd have him.

Sixteen

Isobel pushed open the front entrance to her mother's apartment building, shivering as she stepped out into the cold December air. Her arms tightened around Aiden for a second before she set him on the ground.

"You're okay?" she asked, kneeling next to him and making sure his jacket was zipped to the top. "Warm?"

Aiden nodded as she tugged his hat lower. "See Darry?" he asked, his eyes wide, hopeful.

A dagger of pain slipped between her ribs at his expectant question. Just as it did every time he asked about Darius. Which was at least five times a day since they'd moved out of the house. At least. Aiden missed Darius, and to be honest, so did she. It'd been a long week. One where she forced herself not to dwell on him every minute of the day. She only succeeded a quarter of the time.

She smothered a sigh, shaking her head. "No, baby," she said, crying inside as his little face fell, the sparkle of excitement in his eyes dimming.

He didn't understand that they were no longer living with Darius, that he would no longer be a permanent part of their lives. And it crushed her to hurt and disappoint her son. Darius had called a few times, but as soon as she saw his number, she'd passed the phone to Aiden.

Hearing his voice, talking to him—she wasn't ready for it yet. Didn't believe she would still have the courage and determination to say no if he asked her to return home.

Home.

She'd constantly told Darius his house wasn't hers, but somewhere along the way, she'd started thinking of it as home. And she missed it. Missed Ms. Jacobs.

Missed him.

"See Darry," Aiden whined, tears pooling in his eyes. His bottom lip trembled.

She hugged her son tight, as if she could somehow squeeze his hurt and confusion away. "I know, baby. But right now we're going to see the lights and animals at the zoo, okay?"

She'd kept Aiden—and herself—busy with outings. They'd visited the Children's Museum at Navy Pier, the Christmas tree at Millennium Park and the model trains at Lincoln Park Conservatory. And now they were headed to Zoolights at Lincoln Park Zoo. Yet, during all the trips, she couldn't help but imagine how different they would be if Darius had been by her side. As a family.

Standing, she forced the thoughts away. Yes, she loved Darius. Maybe she always would. But he didn't return the feeling, and there was no getting past that.

They weren't a family.

"Good," she said, injecting cheer into her voice for Aiden's benefit. "Let's go—"

"Darry!" Aiden's scream burst in the air seconds before he yanked his hand out of hers and took off across the tiny courtyard.

"Aiden!" she yelled, but her footsteps faltered, then jerked to a complete stop as she took in the man stooping low to catch her son and toss him in the air before pulling him close for a hug.

And the love on that face as he cuddled Aiden... It stole what little breath her baby's mad dash away from her hadn't.

Darius.

Oh, God. Darius. *Here.*

Stunned, she watched as he kissed Aiden's cheek, grinning at whatever Aiden chattered about. Joy, sadness and anger filled her, and heat pulsed in her body at the sight of him. The wind flirted with his hair, and her fingers itched to take its place. Hair that just passed the five-o'clock shadow covered his jaw and emphasized the sensual fullness of his mouth. A long black, wool coat covered his powerful body. But she remembered in vivid and devastating detail what was beneath it. She craved the strength of it at night.

Darius shifted his attention away from Aiden and pinned her with that golden gaze. The intensity of it snapped her out of her paralysis. Still, her feet wouldn't move, and she stood, immobile, as he approached her, carrying her son in his arms.

"Isobel," he said, and she worked not to reveal the shudder that coursed through her at the velvet sound of her name.

"What are you doing here?" she whispered. Damn it. Clearing her throat, she tried again. "What are you doing here, Darius?"

Sighing, he lowered Aiden to the ground, and turning, pointed in the direction of the curb where his town car idled. "Aiden, look who came to see you."

The window lowered, and Ms. Jacobs popped her head out, waving to him. Shrieking, he ran to the car, and the older woman opened the door, scooping him up. In spite of the emotional maelstrom whirling inside her, Isobel smiled. Aiden had asked about her only slightly less than he had asked about Darius.

Rising, Darius slid his hands into his coat pockets. "I hope you don't mind. I didn't want him to overhear our conversation."

"No. He's missed her," she admitted softly. Shifting her gaze from the ecstatic pair back to him, she murmured. "You, too."

Darius nodded, studying her face as if he, too, were cataloging any changes that had taken place in the last week. "You look tired," he observed in a gentle tone.

She hardened her heart against his concern, shielding herself against the tenderness that immediately sprang to life. "What are you doing here, Darius?" she repeated her question.

"To see Aiden. And you," he said, his eyes gleaming. "I've missed you both. I just needed to lay eyes on you." Then he loosed a short bark of laughter that fell somewhere between self-deprecating and rueful. "That's not quite the truth. I came to find you and beg you to come back home. To give me—give us—a second chance."

Beg you to come back home.

The words echoed in her head and her chest, and swirled in her belly. A yearning swelled so high, so strong, that it nearly drowned out the steely resolve to not give in. She wanted to—God, she wanted to just walk into his arms and have him hold her.

But she couldn't live a life without love, acceptance, trust and loyalty.

She refused to settle anymore.

"Darius, we can't," she murmured, but he clasped her hand, and the *goodness* of his touch cut her off. But just as quickly as he'd reached for her, he released her.

"Please, sweetheart. I know I don't have the right—don't deserve the right—to ask you to hear me out. But I am." He paused, as if gathering his thoughts, then continued. "Everything you said to me was true. I betrayed your trust. I betrayed you. Our family. And I do mean *our family*, Isobel. Because that's who you and Aiden are to me. You two are who I look forward to coming home to when I leave the office. And that's who you are for me, Isobel—home. All these years I believed the memories of my time there with my parents made it that. But I forgot the reason I love the house so much is because it means family. It means love. And I didn't realize what was missing until you and Aiden came to live with me. The moment you left, it was empty, a shell. And I need you to come back, to return it to my haven, my sanctuary."

Her heart thudded against her chest, her pulse deafening in her ears. Hope—that stubborn, foolish hope—tried to grow. But she shut it down. Only more pain led down any road hope traveled.

"I can't…" She shook her head. "Darius, I know you love Aiden. And we…we…" God, she couldn't get it out.

"We burned together, Isobel," he supplied, and her breath snagged in her throat. "But that's not all that was between us. Is still between us. Before I knew who you were, I trusted you with things I hadn't spoken to another living soul in years. I didn't need to see your face to tell you were special, loving, kind and compassionate. You didn't change, Isobel. I did. I turned on you. I allowed the past with Faith and Gage to warp what my heart acknowledged all along."

He shifted closer, but still didn't reach for her. But his gaze… It roamed her face, and she shivered as if his fingertips had brushed her skin.

And inside…oh, inside she couldn't battle hope anymore. It broke through her shields and flowed into her chest, filling her.

"I love you, Isobel." He raised his arms, and after a moment's hesitation, he cupped her face between his palms. "I love you," he whispered. "Remember when I told you about my fear of the dark and falling asleep in our burning building?" She nodded, his tender clasp, his soft words rendering her speechless. "I didn't tell you everything. I believe I heard my mother and father shout my name, and that's what woke me up. I know how insane it sounds, but even from where they were, they saved me. And now I think it's not just because they loved me, but because they knew what waited for me. You and Aiden.

"I've waited for you. And I hate that I almost threw away our future, *us*. Sweetheart," he murmured, sweeping his thumb over her cheekbone. "I promise I'll never place anyone else above you and our son and any more children we have together. But if I've hurt you too badly and you can't give me your heart and trust right now, I understand. Know this—I'll still provide for you and Aiden until I can convince you to forgive me. Because, sweetheart, my heart *is* yours. And I refuse to give up on us ever again. I'll love you perfectly."

He'd gifted her with her own words. She blinked, trying to hold back the tears, but they slipped free. And he pressed his lips to her cheek, kissing them away.

"Talk to me, sweetheart. I need to hear your beautiful voice. You're the only thing keeping me sane," he whispered, his voice carrying her back to that dark hallway where they'd first connected. Where she'd started to fall for him.

Where they'd begun.

"I love you." She circled his wrists and held on to him. "I love you so much."

He crushed his mouth to hers, taking and giving. Savoring and feasting. Loving and worshipping. And she surrendered it all to him, while claiming him.

"Sweetheart," he said against her lips, scattering kisses to her mouth, her jaw, her chin. "Tell me again. Please."

"I love you." Throwing her arms around his neck, she jumped, and he caught her, his hands cradling her thighs. Laughing, she tipped her head back, happiness a bird catching the wind and soaring free. "Now take us home."

Epilogue

Six months later

Isobel groaned through a smile. "This is your fault. And you're going to deal with the fallout."

Beside her, Darius snorted, laughter gathering in his chest and rolling up his throat. "Do you want to go over there and tell him to leave the bouncy castle?"

She scoffed. "And face World War Three *and* Four? God, no." She elbowed him in the side. "I thought we had a conversation about this party, though. Low-key. Nothing too big or grand."

Darius scanned their backyard, where they were holding Aiden's third birthday party. The aforementioned bouncy castle claimed a place of honor right in the middle of the lawn, surrounded by a petting farm, a huge slide, games, face painting, clowns… Their place could double for a carnival.

He shrugged. What could he say? Having missed Aiden's previous two birthdays, he'd really wanted to handle this one. So, he might have gone a little...overboard. Still, as Aiden's high-pitched laughter reached Darius, he had zero regrets.

"Well, he is having a blast," Darius noted, watching their son slide down the "drawbridge" of the castle. "And look on the bright side. At least the party is out here, so in case of a blackout, no one can get trapped inside. With all these animals."

She laughed. "True." Smiling, she slid an arm around his waist and leaned her head against his shoulder. "He'll never forget this. All of his family here to celebrate him." Including Isobel's mother and brothers. They mingled with the children and parents with ease, laughing and talking.

Well, not with Darius's family. Since Baron had confessed the truth to Helena and Gabriella, they'd dropped the custody suit. Discovering Gage's faults hadn't been easy on them, and even now, months later, they still struggled with the magnitude of his lies. And his death. Though he knew Isobel held sympathy for them, relations between her and the Wellses had been put on hold. It would take a while to heal years' worth of pain, and Darius refused to push that reconciliation. Isobel had to move forward when she was ready, and until then Darius had her back. At least she'd allowed Aiden to see them, but only if Darius was there to supervise. And he would never betray her trust again.

It'd been six months since he'd gone to Isobel to plead for her forgiveness and love. Six months since she'd given him both, plus her trust, her heart and her body. She'd given him his family back. That had been the happiest day of his life. And the days that followed were just as wonderful, filled with laughter and joy.

She'd been accepted into the University of Illinois and was majoring in psychology to become a domestic-violence counselor. He wholeheartedly supported her. Isobel was living proof that a person could emerge from a destructive situation stronger, whole, and with the ability to find happiness and peace.

"And just think," Darius said, sliding behind her and settling his hands over the small bump under her tank top. "In another five months, we'll have another one to spoil. A girl. Just imagine the princesses and unicorns that will be prancing around here in another two years."

Isobel groaned, but it ended on a full-out laugh. The joy in it flowed over him.

"Thank you," he murmured, pressing a kiss under her ear. And when she tipped her head back, he placed another kiss on her generous, lovely mouth. "Thank you for filling my life with love and family. I love you."

Her grin softened, and she lifted an arm, cupping the back of his neck. "I love you, too. Always and forever."

"Always and forever."

* * * * *

SAVANNAH'S
SECRETS

REESE RYAN

To my parents, who instilled a love of reading in me at an early age. To the teachers who fostered that love. To my childhood friends who felt reading was as cool as I did—both then and now. To my husband and family, who sacrifice precious time with Babe/Mom/Nonni so that I can share the stories in my head with the world. And to the amazing readers who are kind enough to come along for the ride. Thank you, all.

One

Blake Abbott rubbed his forehead and groaned. He'd rather be walking the floor of the distillery, preparing for their new product launch, instead of reviewing market research data. Out there on the floor was where the magic of making their world-renowned bourbon happened.

His assistant, Daisy, knocked on his open office door. "Blake, don't forget the interview for the new event manager position... It's in fifteen minutes."

Blake cursed under his breath. His brother Max had asked him to handle the interview. The new position fell under Max's charge as marketing VP. But he was at a trade show in Vegas. Probably partying and getting laid while Blake worked his ass off back at the office.

Their mother—who usually handled their special events—was in Florida helping her sister recover from surgery.

Tag, I'm it.

But Blake had more pressing matters to deal with. Production was two weeks behind on the limited-edition moonshines they were rolling out to commemorate the upcoming fiftieth anniversary of King's Finest Distillery. Once an illegal moonshine operation started by his great-grandfather in the hills of Tennessee, his grandfather had established the company as a legal distiller of premium spirits.

What better way to celebrate their golden anniversary as a legitimate enterprise than to reproduce the hooch that gave them their start?

Getting the project back on track took precedence over hiring an overpriced party planner.

Blake grunted, his eyes on the screen. "Too late to reschedule?"

"Technically? No," a slightly husky voice with an unfamiliar Southern drawl responded. "But then, I am already here."

Blake's attention snapped to the source of the voice. His temperature climbed instantly when he encountered the woman's sly smile and hazel eyes sparkling in the sunlight.

Her dark wavy hair was pulled into a low bun. If she'd worn the sensible gray suit to downplay her gorgeous features, it was a spectacular fail.

"Blake, I'm sorry." Daisy's cheeks flushed. Her gaze shifted from him to the woman. "I should've—"

"It's okay, Daisy." Blake held back a grin. He crossed the room, holding the woman's gaze. "I'll take it from here, thanks."

Daisy shoved a folder into his hands. "Her résumé. In case you can't find the copy I gave you earlier."

Blake thanked his assistant. She knew him well and was unbothered by his occasional testiness. It was one of the reasons he went to great lengths to keep her happy.

"Well, Miss—"

"Carlisle." The woman extended her hand. "But please, call me Savannah."

Blake shook her hand and was struck by the contrast of the softness of her skin against his rough palm. Electricity sparked on his fingertips. He withdrew his hand and shoved it in his pocket.

"Miss… Savannah, please, have a seat." He indicated the chair opposite his desk.

She complied. One side of her mouth pulled into a slight grin, drawing his attention to her pink lips.

Were they as soft and luscious as they looked? He swallowed hard, fighting back his curiosity about the flavor of her gloss.

Blake sank into the chair behind his desk, thankful for the solid expanse between them.

He was the one with the authority. So why did it seem that she was assessing him?

Relax. Stay focused.

He was behaving as if he hadn't seen a stunningly beautiful woman before.

"Tell me about yourself, Savannah."

It was a standard opening. But he genuinely wanted to learn everything there was to know about this woman.

Savannah crossed one long, lean leg over the other. Her skirt shifted higher, grazing the top of her knee and exposing more of her golden-brown skin.

"I'm from West Virginia. I've lived there my entire life. I spent the past ten years working my way up the ranks, first at a small family-owned banquet hall. Then at a midsize chain hotel. In both positions, I doubled the special events revenue. My recommendation letters will confirm that."

She was confident and matter-of-fact about her accomplishments.

"Impressive." Regardless of how attractive Savannah Carlisle was, he would only hire her if she was right for the job. "You're a long way from West Virginia. What brings you to our little town of Magnolia Lake?"

"Honestly? I moved here because of this opportunity."

When Blake narrowed his gaze in response, she laughed. It was a sweet sound he wouldn't mind hearing again. Preferably while they were in closer proximity than his desk would allow.

"That wasn't an attempt to sweet-talk you into hiring me. Unless, of course, it works," she added with a smile. "This position is the perfect intersection of my talents and interests."

"How so?" Blake was intrigued.

"I've been fascinated by distilleries and small breweries since I worked at a local craft brewery my senior year of college. I led group tours."

Blake leaned forward, hands pressed to the desk. "And if you don't get the position?"

"Then I'll work my way up to it."

Blake tried not to betray how pleased he was with her unwavering conviction. "There are lots of other distilleries. Why not apply for a similar position elsewhere?"

"I believe in your products. Not that I'm a huge drinker," she added with a nervous laugh. "But as an event professional, King's Finest is my go-to. I also happen to think you have one of the smoothest finishes out there."

He didn't respond. Instead, he allowed a bit of awkward silence to settle over them, which was a device he often employed. Give a candidate just enough rope to hog-tie themselves, and see what they'd do with it.

"That's only part of the reason I want to work for King's Finest. I like that you're family-owned. And I was drawn to the story of how your grandfather converted your great-grandfather's moonshine operation into a legitimate business to create a legacy for his family."

She wasn't the first job candidate to gush about the company history in an attempt to ingratiate herself with him. But something in her eyes indicated deep admiration. Perhaps even reverence.

"You've done your homework, and you know our history." Blake sat back in his leather chair. "But my primary concern is what's on the horizon. How will you impact the future of King's Finest?"

"Excellent question." Savannah produced a leather portfolio from her large tote. "One I'm prepared to answer. Let's talk about the upcoming jubilee celebration. It's the perfect convergence of the company's past and present."

"The event is a few months away. Most of the plans are set. We don't expect anyone to come in, at this late hour, and pull off a miracle. We just want the event to be special for our employees and the folks of Magnolia Lake. Something that'll make them proud of their role in our history. Get them excited about the future."

A wide grin spanned her lovely face. "Give me two months and I'll turn the jubilee into a marketing bonanza that'll get distributors and consumers excited about your brand."

An ambitious claim, but an intriguing one.

King's Finest award-winning bourbon sold well in the States and was making inroads overseas. However, they faced increased competition from small batch distilleries popping up across the country in recent years.

"You have my attention, Savannah Carlisle." Blake crossed one ankle over his knee. "Wow me."

Savannah laid out a compelling plan to revamp their jubilee celebration into an event that was as reflective of the company's simple roots as it was elegant and forward thinking.

"I love your plan, but do you honestly think you can pull this off in two months?"

"I can, and I will." She closed the portfolio and returned it to her bag. "If given the chance."

Blake studied the beautiful woman sitting before him. No wonder their HR manager had recommended the woman so highly. Impressed with her after a joint telephone interview, Max and their mother had authorized him to make her an offer if she was as impressive in person.

Savannah Carlisle was clever and resourceful, everything they needed for their newly minted event manager position. There was only one problem with hiring the woman.

He was attracted to her. More than he'd been to any woman in the two years since his last relationship imploded.

Blake was genuinely excited by the possibility of seeing Savannah every day. Of knowing she occupied an office down the hall from his. But there was the little matter of their family's unwritten rule.

No dating employees.

Problematic, since he'd spent the past half hour preoccupied with the desire to touch her skin again. But he had something far less innocent than a handshake in mind.

Blake wouldn't hire her simply because she was attractive. And it wouldn't be right not to hire her because of her beauty, either.

His feelings were his problem, and he'd deal with them. "All right, Savannah Carlisle. Let's see what you can do."

They negotiated her salary, and then Blake sent her off to complete the requisite paperwork. His gaze followed her curvy bottom and long legs as she sashayed out of the office.

Blake shook his head and groaned. This time, he may have gotten himself in over his head.

Two

Savannah had never relied on sex appeal for a single, solitary thing in her life.

But today was different.

If her plan succeeded, it would correct the course of her family's lives. Money wouldn't be an issue. Not now, nor for generations to come.

Her grandfather would get justice and the recognition he deserved. Her sister wouldn't have to struggle under the crushing weight of student loans.

So failure wasn't an option. Even if it meant playing to the caveman instincts of a cretin like Blake Abbott.

He hadn't been obvious about it. She'd give him credit for that. But the smoldering intensity of his gaze and the sexy growl of his voice had made the interview feel a lot like a blind date.

His warm brown gaze penetrated her skin. Made her feel something she hadn't expected. Something she couldn't explain. Because despite the charm of the man she'd just met, she knew the truth about Blake Abbott and his family.

They were thieves, plain and simple.

The kind of folks who would cheat a man out of what was rightfully owed to him. Who didn't have the decency or compassion to feel an ounce of regret for leaving such a man and his family twisting in the wind, floundering in poverty.

So despite Blake's warm smile and surprisingly pleasing demeanor, she wouldn't forget the truth. The Abbotts were heartless and cruel.

She would expose them for the snakes they were and reclaim her grandfather's rightful share of the company.

Once she'd exited the parking lot in her crappy little car, she dialed her sister, Delaney, back in West Virginia.

"I'm in," Savannah blurted as soon as her sister answered the phone. "I got the job."

Laney hesitated before offering a one-word response. "Wow."

"I know you don't agree with what I'm doing, Laney, but I'm doing this for all of us. You and Harper especially."

"Vanna come home!" her two-year-old niece said in the background.

"Listen to your niece. If you're doing it for us, pack up and come home now. Because this isn't what we want."

"It's what Granddad deserves. What we all deserve." Savannah turned onto the road that led back to town. "This will alter our family's future. Make things better for you and Harper."

"This isn't about Harper or my student loans. You're playing to Grandpa's pride and yours."

Savannah silently counted to ten. Blowing up at Laney wouldn't get her sister on board. And deep down she wanted Laney's reassurance she was doing the right thing.

Their grandfather—Martin McDowell—had raised them after the deaths of their parents. He'd made sacrifices for them their entire lives. And now he was gravely ill, his kidneys failing.

"Grandpa's nearly ninety. Thanks to the Abbotts, his pride is all he has, besides us. So I say it's worth fighting for."

Laney didn't answer. Not surprising.

When they were kids, Savannah was mesmerized by her grandfather's stories about his days running moonshine in the Tennessee hills as a young man. But even as a child, Laney took a just-the-facts-please approach to life. She'd viewed their grandfather's stories as tall tales.

Their positions hadn't changed as adults. But Laney would come around when Savannah proved the truth.

Joseph Abbott, founder of the King's Finest Distillery, claimed to use recipes from his father's illegal moonshine business. But, in reality, he'd stolen their grandfather's hooch recipe and used it to parlay himself into a bourbon empire. And the tremendous fortune the Abbotts enjoyed.

"If the Abbotts are as heartless as you believe, does it seem wise to take them on alone? To get a job with them under false pretenses and snoop around in search of…what? Do you think there's a vault with a big card in it that says, 'I stole my famous bourbon recipe from Martin McDowell'?"

"I didn't get this job under false pretenses. I'm extremely qualified. I'm going to do everything I can to help grow the company. We're going to be part owners of it, after all." Savannah navigated the one-lane bridge that crossed the river dividing the small town.

"You're risking jail or maybe worse. If something were to happen to Granddad…" Her sister's voice trailed. "You're all Harper and I would have left. We can't risk losing you. So, please, let it go and come home."

She didn't want to worry Laney. School, work, taking care of a two-year-old and seeing after their grandfather was strain enough. But this was something she had to do.

If she succeeded, it would be well worth the risk.

"I love you and Harper, Laney. But you need to trust that I'm acting in all of our best interest. And please don't rat me out to Grandpa."

"Great. I have to lie to him about it, too." Laney huffed. "Fine, but be careful. Remember, there's no shame in throwing in the towel and coming to your senses. Love you."

"Love you, too."

After hanging up, Savannah sighed heavily and focused on the road as the colorful shops of the quaint little town of Magnolia Lake came into view.

She parked behind the small building where she was staying. It housed a consignment and handmade jewelry shop downstairs and two apartments upstairs. The shop and building were owned by Kayleigh Jemison, who was also her neighbor.

Inside her furnished, one-bedroom apartment, Savannah kicked off her heels and stripped off her jacket. Her thoughts drifted back to Blake Abbott. He was nothing like the cutthroat, ambitious jerk her grandfather had described. Blake was tall and handsome. His warm brown skin was smooth and practically glowed from within. He was charming with a welcoming smile and liquid brown eyes that made her stomach flip when they met hers.

Her grandfather had only known Joseph Abbott personally. The rest of the Abbotts he knew only by reputation. Maybe he was wrong about Blake.

"You are *not* attracted to him. Not even a little bit," Savannah mumbled under her breath. "He's the enemy. A means to an end."

But Blake was obviously attracted to her. A weakness she could exploit, if it came to it.

An uncomfortable feeling settled over her as she imagined Laney's thoughts on that.

The solution was simple. Avoid Blake Abbott, at all costs.

Three

Savannah signed her name on the final new hire form and slid it across the table.

Daisy was filling in for the HR manager, who was out sick. She studied the document and gave it a stamp of approval. Her thin lips spread in a big smile, her blue eyes sparkling. "You're officially a King's Finest employee. Welcome to the team."

"Fantastic." Savannah returned the smile. "So, what's next?"

The conference room door burst open.

Blake Abbott.

He was even more handsome than she remembered. The five o'clock shadow crawling along his square jaw made him look rugged and infinitely sexier. Uneasiness stirred low in her belly.

"Daisy, Savannah… I didn't realize you were using the conference room." His hair, grown out a bit since their initial meeting, had a slight curl to it.

"We're just leaving anyway." Daisy collected her things. "Did I forget there was a meeting scheduled in here?"

"No, we decided to have an impromptu meeting about the changes Savannah proposed for the jubilee celebration. We can all fit in here more comfortably. Come to think of it—" he shifted his attention to Savannah "—this would be a great opportunity for you to meet my family…that is… our executive team."

She wasn't in a position to refuse his request. Still, there was something endearing about how he'd asked.

It took her by surprise.

"I've been looking forward to meeting the company's founder." Savannah forced a smile, unnerved about meeting the entire Abbott clan. Especially Joseph Abbott—the man who'd betrayed her grandfather.

"I'm afraid you'll have to wait a bit longer." He sounded apologetic. "We want the changes to be a surprise. Speaking of which… I know it's last-minute, and I hate to throw you into the fire on your first day, but do you think you could present your ideas to the rest of our team?"

Savannah's eyes went wide. "Now?"

"They're all really sweet." Daisy patted her arm and smiled. "You're going to love them. I'm just sorry I can't stay to hear your presentation. Got another new hire to process. Good luck!" Daisy called over her shoulder as she hurried from the room.

"I've been telling everyone about your proposal. Got a feeling my father and brother will be more easily persuaded if you wow them the way you did me."

Savannah had anticipated meeting every member of the Abbott family, eventually. But meeting them all at once on her first day was intimidating. Particularly since she had to refrain from saying what she wanted.

That they were liars and thieves who'd built their fortune by depriving her family of theirs. But she couldn't say that. Not yet, anyway. Not until she had proof.

"I've got my notes right here." Savannah opened her portfolio. "But with a little more time, I can create a formal presentation."

"What you presented to me is fine. They'll love it." Blake slid into the seat across from her.

Her belly did a flip.

"Hey, Blake, did you eat all of the…? Oh, I'm sorry. I didn't realize you were meeting with someone," came a voice from the doorway.

"It's all right." Blake waved in the woman Savannah recognized as his sister. "Zora, this is our new event manager, Savannah Carlisle. Savannah, this is our sales VP, Zora Abbott—the baby of the family."

"And they never let me forget it." Zora sat beside her older brother and elbowed him. The woman leaned across the table and shook her hand. "Welcome aboard, Savannah. We need you desperately. You've certainly impressed my big brother here. Not an easy feat."

A deep blush of pink bloomed across Blake's cheeks. He seemed relieved when another member of the Abbott clan stepped into the room.

"Max, this is your new event manager, Savannah Carlisle," Zora informed the handsome newcomer, then turned to Savannah. "Max is our marketing VP. You'll be working for him and with our mother—who isn't here."

There was no mistaking that Max and Blake were brothers. They had the same square jaw capped by a cleft chin. The same narrow, brooding dark eyes. And the same nose—with a narrow bridge and slightly flared nostrils.

Max wore his curly hair longer than Blake's. And where Blake's skin was the color of terra-cotta tiles, his brother's skin was a deeper russet brown. Max was a little taller than his brother, with a leaner frame.

"I look forward to working with you, Savannah." Max sat beside her and shook her hand, his grip firm and warm. His smile seemed genuine. "I'm excited to hear more of your ideas for the anniversary celebration."

"That's why I invited her to join us. She can relay them much better than I can."

Two more men walked into the room. "Didn't realize we were having guests," the younger of the two said, his voice gruff.

"My brother Parker." Zora rolled her eyes. "Chief financial officer and resident cheapskate."

Parker was not amused, but the older man—whom Zora introduced as their father, Duke—chuckled and gave Savannah a warm greeting.

Parker offered a cursory greeting, then shifted his narrowed gaze to Blake.

"I thought we were going to discuss the proposal honestly." Parker sat at one end of the table. Duke sat at the other.

"We will." The intensity of Blake's tone matched his brother's. He nodded toward Savannah. "No one is asking you to pull any punches. She might as well get accustomed to how we do business around here. Besides, she can best respond to your questions about the kind of return on investment we should expect."

"Welcome, then." Parker tapped something on his phone. "I've been described as...no-nonsense. Don't take it personally."

"I won't, if you promise not to take my tendency to shoot straight personally, either." Savannah met his gaze.

Parker nodded his agreement and the other siblings exchanged amused glances.

"You found someone Parker can't intimidate." Zora grinned. "Good job, Blake."

The Abbotts continued to tease each other while Zora or Blake filled her in on the inside jokes. Savannah smiled politely, laughing when they did. But an uneasiness crawled up her spine.

The Abbotts weren't what she'd expected.

Her grandfather had portrayed them as wild grizzly bears. Vicious and capable of devouring their own young.

Don't be fooled by their charm.

"Ready to make your presentation?" Blake asked.

Parker drummed his fingers on the table and glanced at his watch.

Don't show fear.

"Absolutely." Savannah stood, clutching her portfolio.

Blake's warm smile immediately eased the tightness in her chest. Her lungs expanded and she took a deep breath.

Savannah opened her portfolio and glanced around the room.

"All right, here's what I'm proposing..."

* * *

Blake typed notes into his phone as Savannah recapped her presentation. She'd won over everyone in the room. They were all on board with her plan—even penny-pinching Parker.

The event had graduated from the "little shindig" his mother had envisioned to a full gala. One that would retain a rustic charm that paid homage to the company's history. Savannah had also suggested holding anniversary events in other key cities.

The upgrades Savannah proposed to the old barn on his parents' property to prepare for the gala would significantly increase its rental income. They could charge more per event and would draw business from corporations and folks in nearby towns. All of which made Parker exceedingly happy.

"There's one thing I'm still not sold on," he interjected. "The majority of our market share is here in the South. Why invest in events elsewhere?"

"It's the perfect opportunity to deepen our reach outside of our comfort zone," Savannah said.

Parker folded his arms, unconvinced.

"She's right." Blake set his phone on the table and leveled his gaze on his brother. "I've floated the idea with a few distributors in the UK, California and New York. They love our products and they're eager to introduce them to more of their customers. I'm telling you, Parker, this could be a big win for us."

Savannah gave him a quick, grateful smile. A knot formed low in his gut.

"Savannah and Blake have done their homework," his father said. "I'm ready to move forward with Savannah's proposal. Any objections?"

Parker shook his head, but scowled.

"Excellent. Savannah, would you mind typing up your notes and sending them to the executive email list so my wife can get a look at them?"

"I'll do my best to get them out by the end of the day, Mr. Abbott."

"Duke will do just fine. Now, I'm late for a date with a five iron."

"The gala is going to be sensational." Zora grinned. "Right, Max?"

"It will be," Max agreed. "I wasn't sure that turning Mom's low-key, local event into something more elaborate and—"

"Expensive," Parker interrupted.

"Relax, El Cheapo." Zora's stony expression was a silent reminder that she wasn't just their baby sister. She was sales VP and an equal member of the executive team. "The additional sales will far exceed the additional expenses."

"Don't worry, lil' sis. I'm in." Parker tapped his pen on the table. "I'm obviously outnumbered. I'm as thrilled as you are to expand our market and rake in more cash. I just hope Savannah's projections are on target."

"I look forward to surprising you with the results." Savannah seemed unfazed by Parker's subtle intimidation.

"C'mon, Savannah." Max stood. "I'll show you to your office. It isn't far from mine."

Blake swallowed back his disappointment as she left with Max, Zora and their father. So much for his plan to give Savannah a tour of the place.

"Watch yourself," Parker warned.

"What do you mean?" Blake stuffed his phone in his pocket and headed for the door.

"You know *exactly* what I mean. You've been stealing glances at Savannah when you think no one is looking. Like just now." Parker followed him.

"You're exaggerating."

"No, I'm your brother." Parker fell in step beside him. "I know the signs."

"Of what?" Blake turned to face his brother. "A man very impressed with his new hire?"

"It's worse than I thought." Parker shook his head. "Look all you want, just don't touch. She's our employee. A subordinate. Don't cross the line with her. And for God's sake, don't get caught up in your feelings for this woman."

"Good advice." Blake resumed the walk to his office. "Too bad you haven't been good at following it."

"That's why I know what a horrible idea it is."

"Don't worry, Parker. I won't do anything you wouldn't." Blake went into his office and shut the door.

He didn't need Parker to remind him that Savannah Carlisle was off-limits.

Four

Savannah surveyed the gleaming copper stills and the pipes running between them that filled the distillation room. "They're beautiful."

She was home. Exactly where she was meant to be, had it not been for Joseph Abbott's treachery.

"I guess they are." Daisy checked her watch again.

Blake's assistant was a nice enough woman, but her limited knowledge wasn't helpful to Savannah's cause. If she was going to take on the powerful Abbott family and prove they'd stolen her grandfather's bourbon recipe and his process for making it, she needed to learn everything there was to know about the making of their signature bourbon.

Daisy gave the stills a cursory glance. "I never really thought of them as beautiful."

"I do. I just didn't think anyone else did," a familiar, velvety voice chimed in.

Blake again.

The man seemed to pop up everywhere. Hopefully, it wouldn't be a daily occurrence.

"Didn't mean to scare you, Dais." Blake held up a hand. "Just met with Klaus—our master distiller," he added for Savannah's benefit. "I'm surprised you're still here. Doesn't Daphne's softball game start in an hour?"

"It does." Daisy turned to Savannah. "Daphne's my ten-year-old daughter. She's pitching as a starter for the first time."

"I'm sorry." No wonder Daisy had tried to rush her through the tour. "I didn't realize you had somewhere to be."

"Get out of here before you're late." Blake nodded toward the exit. "Tell Daph I'm rooting for her."

"What about the tour? We're nowhere near finished. Savannah has so many questions. I haven't done a very good job of answering them."

"You were great, Daisy," Savannah lied, not wanting to make her feel bad. "Your daughter's pitching debut is more important. We can finish the tour another day."

"Go." Blake pointed toward the exit. "I'll finish up here. In fact, I'll give Savannah the deluxe tour."

Daisy thanked them and hurried off.

"So you want to know all about the whiskey-making process." Blake turned to Savannah. He hadn't advanced a step, yet the space between them contracted.

"I mentioned that in my interview." She met his gaze, acutely aware of their height difference and the broadness of his shoulders.

His fresh, woodsy scent made her want to plant her palms on his well-defined chest and press her nose to the vein visible on his neck.

"Thought that was just a clever bit to impress me." The edge of his generous mouth pulled into a lopsided grin that made her heart beat faster.

"Now, you know that isn't true." Savannah held his gaze despite the violent fluttering in her belly.

She was reacting like a hormonal high-school girl with a crush on the captain of the football team.

Blake was pleasant enough on the surface, and certainly nice to look at. Okay, that was the understatement of the year. His chiseled features and well-maintained body were the stuff dreams were made of.

But he wasn't just any pretty face and hard physique. He was an Abbott.

E-N-E-M-Y.

Her interest in this man—regardless of how good-looking he was or the sinful visions his mouth conjured—needed to stay purely professional. The only thing she wanted from Blake Abbott was insight into the history between their grandfathers.

"So you promised me the deluxe tour."

"I did." His appraising stare caused a contraction of muscles she hadn't employed in far longer than she cared to admit. "Let's go back to the beginning."

"Are you sure?" Savannah scrambled to keep up with his long, smooth strides. "I've nearly caused one family crisis already. I don't intend to start another today. So if you have a wife or kids who are expecting you—"

"That your not-so-subtle way of asking if I'm married?" He quickly pressed his lips into a harsh line. "I mean... I'm not. None of my siblings are. Our mother is sure she's failed us somehow because we haven't produced any grandchildren."

"Why aren't you married? Not you specifically," Savannah added quickly, her cheeks hot.

"We're all married to this place. Committed to building the empire my granddad envisioned nearly half a century ago."

Blake held the door open and they stepped into the late-afternoon sunlight. Gravel crunched beneath their feet, forcing her to tread carefully in her tall spike heels.

They walked past the grain silos and onto a trail that led away from the warehouse. The property extended as far as she could see, a picturesque natural landscape that belonged on a postcard.

"Someone in town mentioned that you have another brother who isn't in the business."

"Cole runs the largest construction company in the area. With the explosion of high-end real estate around here, he's got the least time on his hands."

"Doesn't bode well for those grandchildren your mother wants."

"No, it doesn't," Blake agreed. "But she's convinced that if one of us finally takes the plunge, the rest will fall like dominoes."

"So then love is kind of like the plague?"

Blake's deep belly laugh made her grin so hard her cheeks ached.

"I can't disagree with that." He was smiling, but there was sadness in his eyes. There was a story there he wasn't willing to tell, but she suddenly wanted to hear.

The gravel gave way to a dirt path that was soft and squishy due to the recent rain. Her heels sank into the mud. "I thought we were going to start at the beginning of the tour."

"We are."

"But we already passed the grain silos." She pointed in the opposite direction.

He stopped, turning to face her. "Do you know why most of the storied whiskey distilleries are based in Kentucky or here in Tennessee?"

Savannah shook her head. She'd noticed that the industry was concentrated in those two states, but hadn't given much thought to why.

"A whiskey with a smooth finish begins with the right water source." He pointed toward a creek and the hills that rose along the edge of the property. "See that limestone shelf? Springs deep in these limestone layers feed King's Lake—our sole source of water. The limestone adds calcium to the water and filters out impurities like iron that would make the whiskey bitter."

She studied the veins in the limestone shelf. "So it wouldn't be possible to produce bourbon from another water source with the same composition and flavor?"

"Not even if you used our exact recipe." He stood beside her, gazing reverently at the stony mountain and the waters that trickled from it. "Then there's the matter of the yeast we use for fermentation. It's a proprietary strain that dates back to when my great-grandfather was running his moonshine business seventy-five years ago."

"Most distilleries openly share their grain recipe. King's Finest doesn't. Why?"

"My grandfather tweaked the grain mixture his father used. He's pretty territorial about it." Blake smiled. "So we keep our mash bill and yeast strain under tight control."

The fact that Blake's grandfather had stolen the recipe from her grandfather was the more likely reason.

"I'm boring you, aren't I?"

"No. This is all extremely fascinating."

"It's a subject I can get carried away with. Believe me, no other woman has ever used the word *fascinating* to describe it."

"You still think I'm feigning interest." Something in his stare made her cheeks warm and her chest heavy.

His lips parted and his hands clenched at his sides, but he didn't acknowledge her statement. "We'd better head back."

They visited the vats of corn, rye and malted barley. Next, they visited the large metal vat where the grain was cooked, creating the mash. In the fermentation room there were large, open tubs fashioned of cypress planks, filled with fermenting whiskey. The air was heavy with a scent similar to sourdough bread baking.

In the distillation room, he gave her a taste of the bourbon after it passed through the towering copper still and then again after it had made another pass through the doubler.

"It's clear." Savannah handed Blake back the metal cup with a long metal handle he'd used to draw a sample of the "high wine."

Her fingers brushed his and he nearly dropped the cup, but recovered quickly.

"The rich amber color happens during the aging process." He returned the cup to its hook, then led her through the area where the high wine was transferred to new, charred white oak barrels.

They walked through the rackhouse. Five levels of whiskey casks towered above them. Savannah fanned herself, her brow damp with perspiration, as Blake lowered his voice, speaking in a hushed, reverent tone.

"How long is the bourbon aged?"

"The signature label? Five years. Then we have the top-shelf labels aged for ten or more years." Blake surveyed the upper racks before returning his gaze to hers. "My grandfather made so many sacrifices to create this legacy for us. I'm reminded of that whenever I come out here."

Blake spoke of Joseph Abbott as if he were a self-sacrificing saint. But the man was a liar and a cheat. He'd sacrificed his friendship with her grandfather and deprived him of his legacy, leaving their family with nothing but hardship and pain.

Tears stung her eyes and it suddenly hurt to breathe in the overheated rackhouse. It felt as if a cask of whiskey was sitting on her chest. She gasped, the air burning her lungs.

"Are you all right?" Blake narrowed his brown eyes, stepping closer. He placed a gentle hand on her shoulder.

"I'm fine." Her breath came in short bursts and her back was damp with sweat.

"It's hot in here. Let's get you back in the air-conditioning. Our last stop is the bottling area." His hand low on her back, he guided her toward the exit.

"No." The word came out sharper than she'd intended. "I mean, I promised your father I'd get that presentation out today."

"You told him you'd try. Do it first thing tomorrow. It'll be fine."

"That's not the first impression I want to make with the company's CEO. Or with his wife, who's eagerly awaiting the information." Savannah wiped the dampness from her forehead with the back of her hand. "I gave my word, and to me, that means something."

Five

It was clear Blake had offended Savannah.

But how?

He replayed the conversation in his head. Before she'd looked at him as if he'd kicked a kitten.

They'd been talking about how his grandfather had built the company. The sacrifices he'd made for their family. How could she possibly be offended by that? Especially when she'd already expressed her admiration for his grandfather's entrepreneurial spirit.

"If sending the presentation out tonight is that important to you, I won't stop you. All I'm saying is…no one will hold it against you if we receive it tomorrow."

Savannah turned on her heels, caked in dry mud from their earlier walk. She headed back toward the main building.

Even with his longer strides, he had to hurry to catch up with her. "You'd tell me if I upset you?"

"You didn't. I'm just—" Her spiked heel got caught in the gravel, and she stumbled into his arms.

He held her for a moment, his gaze studying hers, enjoying the feel of her soft curves pressed against his hard body.

Her eyes widened and she stepped out of his grasp, muttering a quick thank-you.

"I'm angry with myself for not remembering the presentation earlier."

"You've been busy all day. That's my fault."

"It's no one's fault." She seemed to force a smile. "I appreciate the deluxe tour. What I've learned will be useful as I prepare my presentation. It's given me a few other ideas."

"That's good, then." Blake kneaded the back of his neck. "I'll walk you back to your office."

"I'd like to find it on my own. Test my sense of direction." Savannah's tepid smile barely turned up one corner of her mouth. She headed back to the building, calling over her shoulder. "See you tomorrow."

When she was too far away to hear it, Blake released a noisy sigh. He returned to his office by a different route.

Despite what Savannah said, he'd clearly upset her. He couldn't shake the gnawing need to learn why. Or the deep-seated desire to fix it so he could see the genuine smile that lit her lovely eyes, illuminating the flecks of gold.

Blake gritted his teeth.

You do not feel anything for her.

He said the words over and over in his head as he trekked back inside, past her office and straight to his.

You're full of shit, and you know it.

Why couldn't his stupid subconscious just cooperate and buy into the load of crock he was trying to sell himself?

There were a million reasons why he shouldn't be thinking of Savannah Carlisle right now. Long-legged, smooth-skinned, caramel-complexioned goddess that she was.

He shouldn't be thinking of her throaty voice. Her husky laugh. Her penetrating stare. Or the way she sank her teeth into her lower lip while in deep thought.

Blake shut his office door and loosened his tie. He dropped into the chair behind his desk, trying not to focus on the tension in his gut and the tightening of his shaft at the thought of Savannah Carlisle...naked. Sprawled across his desk.

He opened his laptop and studied spreadsheets and graphs, ignoring the most disconcerting aspect of his growing attraction for Savannah. What scared him...what was terrifying...was how Savannah Carlisle made him feel. That she'd made him feel anything at all.

Especially the kind of feelings he'd carefully avoided in the two years since Gavrilla had walked out of his life.

Since then he'd satisfied his urges with the occasional

one-night stand while traveling for business. Far away from this too-small town, where every single person knew the private affairs of every other damned person.

In painful detail.

He hadn't been looking for anything serious. Just a couple of nights in the sack. No feelings. No obligations beyond having safe, responsible sex and being gentlemanly enough never to speak of it.

But from their first meeting, he'd been drawn to Savannah. She was bold and confident. And she hadn't begged for a shot with the company. She'd simply laid out a solid case.

He would've been a fool to not hire her.

Her indomitable spirit and latent sex appeal called to something deep inside him. In a way that felt significant. The feelings were completely foreign and yet deeply familiar.

He didn't believe in love at first sight or soul mates. But if he had, he'd have sworn that Cupid had shot him the second Savannah Carlisle sashayed her curvy ass into his office.

Blake loosened the top two buttons of his shirt. Parker's admonition played on a loop in his head. It could be summed up in five words: *Don't think with your dick.*

If Parker recognized how perilous Blake's attraction to Savannah was, he was in big trouble. He needed to slam the lid on those feelings. Seal them in an indestructible steel box fastened with iron rivets and guarded by flaming swords and a den of rattlesnakes.

Because he could never go back there again. To the pain he'd felt two years ago when Gavrilla had walked out. She'd left him for someone else. Without warning or the slightest indication she'd been unhappy.

Without giving him a chance to fix things.

In retrospect, she'd done him a favor. Their stark differences—so exciting in the beginning—had been flashing red lights warning of their incompatibility.

Blake sighed. It'd been a while since he'd taken a business-meets-pleasure excursion. Experienced the adrenaline of tumbling into bed with a stranger.

He'd have Daisy schedule a meeting with a vendor in Nashville or maybe Atlanta. Somewhere he could blend in with the nameless, faceless masses.

Anywhere but Magnolia Lake.

Blake hit Send on his final email of the night—a response to a vendor in the UK. He checked his watch. It was well after seven and Savannah's proposal hadn't pinged his inbox.

She'd been determined to send it before she left for the night. That meant she was still in her office working on it.

Blake rubbed his unshaved chin. Perhaps she'd encountered a problem. After all, it was her first day. He should see if she needed help.

Blake packed up his laptop, locked his office door and headed down the hall. He almost kept walking. Almost pretended he didn't hear the tapping of computer keys.

He groaned, knowing he was acting against his better judgment.

"Hey." He gently knocked on Savannah's open office door. "Still at it?"

"Finished just now." Her earlier uneasiness appeared to be gone. "You didn't wait for me, did you?" She seemed perturbed by the possibility.

"No. Just finished up myself. But since I'm here, I'll walk you to your car."

"I thought small towns like Magnolia Lake were idyllic bastions of safety and neighborliness." Savannah barely contained a sarcastic grin as she grabbed her bags.

"Doesn't mean we shouldn't practice courtesy and good old-fashioned common sense." He opened the door wider to let her out, then locked it behind them.

They made the trip to her small car in near silence. She stopped abruptly, just shy of her door.

"About earlier." She turned to him, but her eyes didn't meet his. "Sorry if I seemed rude. I wasn't trying to be. I just…" She shook her head. "It wasn't anything you did."

"But it was something I said." He hiked his computer bag higher on his shoulder when her eyes widened.

"It won't happen again."

"Good night, Savannah." Blake opened her car door. He wouldn't press, if she didn't want to talk about it.

They weren't lovers, and they needn't be friends. As long as Savannah did her job well and played nice with others, everything would be just fine.

He stepped away from the car and she drove away.

Blake made his way back to his truck, thankful Savannah Carlisle had saved him from himself.

Savannah let herself into her apartment, glad the day was finally over.

When she got to the bedroom, she pulled a black leather journal from her nightstand. It held her notes about the Abbotts.

Savannah did a quick review of what she'd learned on the job today and jotted down everything she could remember.

Their processes. The grains used in their bourbon composition with a question mark and percentage sign by each one. The industry jargon she'd learned. Next, she outlined her impressions of each member of the Abbott family—starting with Blake.

Finished with the brain dump, she was starving and mentally exhausted. She scarfed down a frozen dinner while watching TV.

Her cell phone rang. *Laney.*

"Hey, sis." Savannah smiled. "How's my niece? And how is Granddad doing?"

"They're both fine. How was your first day?"

"Long. I just got home." Savannah shoved the last bite of processed macaroni and cheese into her mouth, then dumped the plastic tray into the recycle bin. "I made my proposal to the entire family—"

"You met all the Abbotts?"

"Everyone except their mother, Iris, and Joseph Abbott." Savannah was both angry and relieved she hadn't had the chance to look into the eyes of the coldhearted bastard who'd ruined her grandfather's life.

"What were they like?"

Savannah sank onto the sofa. Blake's dreamy eyes and kind smile danced in her head. The vision had come to her in her sleep more than once since they'd met.

In her dreams, they weren't from opposing families. They'd been increasingly intimate, holding hands, embracing. And last night she'd awakened in a cold sweat after they'd shared a passionate kiss.

She'd struggled to drive those images from her head while spending a good portion of her day in his company.

"The Abbotts aren't the ogres you expected, are they?" There was a hint of vindication in Laney's question.

"No, but I met most of them for the first time today. They were trying to make a good first impression. After all, even a serial killer can have a charming facade."

Laney didn't acknowledge her logic. "Tell me about them, based on what you observed today. Not on what you thought you knew about them."

Savannah removed her ponytail holder and shook her head. Her curly hair tumbled to her shoulders in loose waves from being pulled tight.

"It was hard to get a read on their dad—Duke. He's personable, but all business."

"What about the rest of them?"

"I met Blake, Parker, Max and Zora—the four siblings who run the distillery. There's a fifth—Cole. He has his own construction company."

"Why didn't he go into the family business?"

"Don't know." Savannah had wondered, too.

"Quit stalling and tell me more."

"Zora is sweet. Max is funny. Parker is kind of an asshole."

"And what about Blake Abbott? This was your second encounter. Did your impression of him improve?"

"Yes." She hated to admit that it was true. But Blake's genuinely warm interactions with his employees during the tour made him appear to be an ideal boss.

"So now that you see you were wrong about the Abbotts, will you please let this thing go?"

So much for Laney being on board with the plan.

"The congeniality of Joseph Abbott's grandchildren isn't the issue here."

"Savannah—"

"If they're genuinely innocent in all of this…well, I'm sorry their grandfather was such a bastard. It isn't like I plan to steal the company from under them the way he did from Granddad."

"Then what exactly do you want, honey? What's your grand plan here?"

"Our family deserves half the company. That's what I want. And if they don't want to share, they can buy us out. Plain and simple."

Laney made a strangled sound of frustration. A sound she made whenever they discussed their grandfather's claims regarding King's Finest.

"I couldn't do what you're doing." Laney's voice was quiet. "Getting to know people. Having them come to like and trust you. Then turning on them."

Savannah winced at the implication of her sister's words. "I'm not 'turning' on them. I'm just standing up for my family. As any of them would for theirs. Besides, I'm not harming their business in any way."

"You're spying on them."

"But I'm not taking that information to a competitor. I'm just gathering evidence to support Granddad's ownership claim." Savannah tamped down the defensiveness in her tone.

"And what about Blake?"

"What about him?"

"You like him. I can tell. What happens when he learns the truth?"

A knot twisted in Savannah's belly. "If he's as good a man as everyone seems to think, he should want to make this right. In fact, I'm counting on it."

Six

Savannah smiled in response to the email she'd just received from Max, who was away at another trade show. They'd secured the endorsement of a local boy who'd become a world-famous actor. With his rugged good looks and down-home, boyish charm, he was perfect.

Her plans for the jubilee were in full swing. The rustic gala, to be held in the Abbotts' old country barn, would celebrate the company, its employees and distributors and attract plenty of media coverage. The renovated barn would provide King's Finest with an additional revenue stream and create jobs in the small town.

Savannah had been working at the distillery for nearly a month. The residents of the small town had done their best to make her feel welcome—despite her desire to hang in the shadows and lie low.

Every Friday she turned down no less than two invitations to the local watering hole for drinks after work. One of those invitations always came from Blake.

An involuntary shudder rippled down Savannah's spine when she thought of Blake with his generous smile and warm brown eyes. Savannah shook her head.

She would *not* think of how good Blake Abbott looked in the checkered dress shirts and athletic-fit slacks he typically wore. Each piece highlighted the finer points of his physique. A broad chest. Well-defined pecs. Strong arms. An ass that made it evident he was no stranger to lunges and squats.

His clothing was designed to torture her and every other woman with a working libido and functioning set of eyes. It tormented her with visions of what his strong body must look like beneath that fabric.

A crack of thunder drew her attention to the window. She checked the time on her phone. It was barely after seven, but dark clouds and a steady downpour darkened the sky, making it feel later.

Savannah worked late most nights. The gala was quickly approaching and there was so much to do.

Plus, being the last member of the administrative team to leave each night gave her a chance to do some reconnaissance. She could access files she didn't feel comfortable perusing when Max, Blake or Zora might pop into her office at any minute.

Then there was the surprising fact that she thoroughly enjoyed the work she was doing. She was often so engrossed in a task that time got away from her.

Like tonight.

Outside the window, increasingly dark clouds loomed overhead. The steady, gentle rain that had fallen throughout the day was now a raging downpour.

Another flash of light illuminated the sky. It was quickly followed by a peal of thunder that made Savannah's heart race.

It was lightning that posed the real danger. Savannah knew that better than most. The thunder was just sound and fury.

She loathed driving in inclement weather. Tack on the steep hills, narrow roads, one-lane bridge and her vague familiarity with the area, and it was a recipe for disaster.

One wrong turn, and she could end up in a ditch, lost in the woods, undiscovered for months.

Stop being a drama queen. Everything will be fine. Just take a deep breath.

Savannah took a long, deep breath.

She'd hoped to wait out the storm. Her plan had backfired. Engrossed in her work, she hadn't noticed that the rain had gotten much heavier. And it didn't appear to be letting up anytime soon.

After composing and sending one final email, Savannah signed off her computer. She gathered her things and headed for the parking lot, as fast as her high-heeled feet could carry her.

Shit.

She was without an umbrella, and it was raining so hard the parking lot had flooded. No wonder the lot was empty except for her car.

If it stalled out, she'd be screwed.

A flash of lightning lit the sky like a neon sign over a Vegas hotel.

Jaw clenched, Savannah sucked in a generous breath, as if she were about to dive into the deep end of the pool. She made a mad dash for her car before the next bolt struck.

Despite the warm temperatures, the rain pelted her in cold sheets as she waded through the standing water. Her clothing was wet and heavy. Her feet slid as she ran in her soaking-wet shoes.

Savannah dropped into the driver's seat and caught her breath. Her eyes stung as she wiped water from her face with the back of her hand, which was just as wet.

She turned her key and gave the car some gas, grateful the engine turned over.

There was another flash of lightning, then a rumble of thunder, followed by a heavy knock on the window.

She screamed, her heart nearly beating out of her chest.

A large man in a hooded green rain slicker hovered outside her window.

She was cold, wet, alone and about to be murdered.

But not without a fight.

Savannah popped open her glove compartment and searched for something…anything…she could use as a weapon. She dug out the heavy tactical flashlight her grandfather had given her one Christmas. She beamed the bright light in the intruder's face.

"Blake?" Savannah pressed a hand to her chest, her heart

still thudding against her breastbone. She partially lowered the window.

Even with his eyes hidden by the hood, she recognized the mouth and stubbled chin she'd spent too much time studying.

"You were expecting someone else?"

Smart-ass.

If she didn't work for the Abbotts, and she wasn't so damned glad not to be alone in the middle of a monsoon, she would have told Blake exactly what she thought of his smart-assery.

"What are you doing here? And where'd you come from?"

"I'm parked under the carport over there." He pointed in the opposite direction. "Came to check on the building. Didn't expect to see anyone here at this time of night in the storm."

"I didn't realize how late it was, or that the rain had gotten so bad. I'm headed home now."

"In this?" He sized up her small car.

She lifted a brow. "My flying saucer is in the shop."

Savannah knew she shouldn't have said it, but the words slipped out of her mouth before she could reel them back in.

Blake wasn't angry. He smirked instead.

"Too bad. Because that's the only way you're gonna make it over the bridge."

"What are you talking about?"

"You're renting from Kayleigh Jemison in town, right?"

"How did you know—"

"It's Magnolia Lake. Everyone knows everyone in this town," he said matter-of-factly. "And there are flash-flood warnings everywhere. No way will this small car make it through the low-lying areas between here and town."

"Flash floods?" Panic spread through her chest. "Isn't there another route I can take?"

"There's only one way back to town." He pointed toward

the carport. "The ground is higher there. Park behind my truck, and I'll give you a ride home. I'll bring you back to get your car when the roads clear."

"Just leave my car here?" She stared at him dumbly.

"If I could fit it into the bed of my truck, I would." One side of his mouth curved in an impatient smile. "And if there was any other option, I'd tell you."

Savannah groaned as she returned her flashlight to the glove compartment. Then she pulled into the carport as Blake instructed.

"Got everything you need from your car?" Blake removed his hood and opened her car door.

"You act as if I won't see my car again anytime soon."

"Depends on how long it takes the river to go down."

"Seriously?" Savannah grabbed a few items from the middle console and shoved them in her bag before securing her vehicle. She followed Blake to the passenger side of his huge black truck.

She gasped, taken by surprise when Blake helped her up into the truck.

"I have a couple more things to check before we go. Sit tight. I'll be back before you can miss me."

Doubt it.

Blake shut her door and disappeared around the building.

Savannah waited for her heartbeat to slow down. She secured her seat belt and surveyed the interior of Blake's pickup truck. The satellite radio was set to an old-school hip-hop channel. The truck was tricked out with all the toys. High-end luxury meets Bo and Luke Duke with a refined hip-hop sensibility.

Perfectly Blake.

A clean citrus scent wafted from the air vents. The black leather seats she was dripping all over were inlaid with a tan design.

A fierce gust of wind blew the rain sideways and swayed

the large truck. Her much smaller car rocked violently, as if it might blow over.

Another blinding flash of lightning was quickly followed by a rumble of thunder. Savannah gritted her teeth.

She'd give anything to be home in bed with the covers pulled over her head.

Everything will be fine. Don't freak out.

Savannah squeezed her eyes shut. Counted backward from ten, then forward again. When she opened them, Blake was spreading a yellow tarp over her small car.

Damn you, Blake Abbott.

She'd arrived in Magnolia Lake regarding every last one of the Abbotts as a villain. Blake's insistence on behaving like a knight in shining armor while looking like black Thor made it difficult to maintain that position.

He was being kind and considerate, doing what nearly any man would under the circumstances. Particularly one who regarded himself a Southern gentleman.

That didn't make him Gandhi.

And it sure as hell didn't prove the Abbotts weren't capable of cruelty. Especially when it came to their business.

But as he approached the truck, looking tall, handsome and delicious despite the rain, it was impossible not to like him.

Relax. It's just a ride home.

The storm had Savannah on edge. Nothing a little shoofly punch wouldn't soothe. She just needed to endure the next twenty minutes with Blake Abbott.

Blake stood outside the truck with the wind whipping against his back and his soaking-wet clothing sticking to his skin. He forced a stream of air through his nostrils.

Parker's warning replayed in his head.

Don't think of her that way. It'll only get you into trouble.

He'd come back to the plant after dinner with his father to make sure everything was okay. But he'd also come back looking for her, worried she'd spent another night working late, not recognizing the dangers of a hard, long rain like this. Something any local would know.

He would have done this for any of his employees—male or female. But he wasn't a convincing enough liar to persuade himself that what he was doing tonight…for her… wasn't different. More personal.

Something about Savannah Carlisle roused a fiercely protective instinct.

Keep your shit together and your hands to yourself.

Blake took one more cleansing breath and released it, hoping his inappropriate thoughts about Savannah went right along with it.

When he yanked the door open, Savannah's widened eyes met his. Shivering, she wrapped her arms around herself.

"You're freezing." Blake climbed inside the truck and turned on the heat to warm her, wishing he could take her in his arms. Transferring his body heat to hers would be a better use of the steam building under his collar. "Is that better?"

Savannah rubbed her hands together and blew on them. "Yes, thank you."

Blake grabbed a jacket off the back seat and handed it to her. "Put this on."

There was the briefest hesitance in her eyes before Savannah accepted the jacket with a grateful nod. It was heavy, and she struggled to put it on.

Blake helped her into it. Somehow, even that basic gesture felt too intimate.

"Let's get you home." Blake put the truck into gear and turned onto the road that led across the river and into town.

They traveled in comfortable silence. It was just as well. The low visibility created by the blowing rain required his complete focus.

They were almost there. Savannah's apartment was just beyond the bridge and around the bend.

Shit.

They were greeted by a roadblock and yellow warning signs. The water had risen to the level of the bridge.

"There's another way into town, right?" Savannah asked nervously.

Blake didn't acknowledge the alarm in her brown eyes. If he didn't panic, maybe she wouldn't, either, when he broke the bad news. "That bridge is the only route between here and your place."

"I can't get home?" Her voice was shaky and its pitch rose.

"Not tonight. Maybe not tomorrow. The bridge is in danger of washing out. I could possibly make it across in my truck, but the weight of this thing could compromise the bridge and send us downriver."

"So what do I do for the next couple of days? Camp out in my office until the bridge is safe again?"

"That won't be necessary." Blake groaned internally. Savannah wasn't going to like the alternative. "My house is up the hill a little ways back."

"You think I'm staying at your house? Overnight?" She narrowed her gaze at him. As if he'd orchestrated the rain, her staying late and the bridge threatening to wash out.

"You don't really have another choice, Savannah." He studied her as she weighed the options.

She pulled the jacket around her tightly as she assessed the road in front of them, then the road behind them. "Seems I don't have much of a choice."

A knot tightened in the pit of Blake's stomach. He'd hoped that she would be stubborn enough to insist on returning to the office. That he wouldn't be tortured by Savannah Carlisle being off-limits *and* sleeping under his roof.

"Okay then." He shifted the truck into Reverse, turned

around and headed back to the narrow road that led to the exclusive community where he and Zora owned homes.

As they ascended the hill, the handful of houses around the lake came into view. A bolt of lightning arced in the sky.

Savannah flinched once, then again at the deafening thunder. She was trying to play it cool, but her hands were clenched into fists. She probably had nail prints on her palms.

Why was she so frightened by the storm?

He wanted to know, but the question felt too personal. And everything about Savannah Carlisle indicated she didn't do personal. She kept people at a safe distance.

She'd politely refused every social invitation extended to her since she'd joined the company. Some of his employees hadn't taken her repeated rejections so well.

He'd tried not to do the same. After all, distance from her was exactly what he needed.

When they arrived at his house, he pulled inside the garage.

"You're sure this won't cause trouble? I mean, if anyone found out…" A fresh wave of panic bloomed across her beautiful face. "It wouldn't look good for either of us."

"No one else knows. Besides, any decent human being would do the same," he assured her. "Would you prefer I'd left you in the parking lot on your own?"

"I'm grateful you didn't." Her warm gaze met his. "I just don't want to cause trouble…for either of us."

"It's no trouble," Blake lied. He hopped down from the cab of the truck, then opened her door.

She regarded his extended hand reluctantly. Finally, she placed her palm in his and allowed him to help her down.

Blake stilled for a moment, his brain refusing to function properly. Savannah was sopping wet. Her makeup was washed away by the rain, with the exception of the black mascara running down her face. Yet she looked no worse for the wear.

Her tawny skin was punctuated by a series of freckles splashed across her nose and cheeks.

Something about the discovery of that small detail she'd hidden from the world thrilled him.

His gaze dropped to her lips, and a single, inappropriate thought filled his brain.

Kiss her. Now.

She slipped her icy hand from his, slid the jacket from her shoulders and returned it to him.

"Thank you." He tossed it into the back seat and shut the door.

When he turned to Savannah she was shivering again.

He rubbed his hands up and down her arms to warm her before his brain could remind him that was an inappropriate gesture, too.

Her searing gaze made the point clear.

"Sorry… I…" Blake stepped away, his face heated. He ran a hand through his wet hair.

"I appreciate the gesture. But what I'd really love is a hot shower and a place to sleep."

"Of course." Blake shrugged off his wet rain slicker. He hung it on a hook, then closed the garage door. "Hope you're not afraid of dogs."

"Not particularly."

"Good." Blake dropped his waterlogged shoes by the door to the house. When he opened it, his two dogs surrounded him, yapping until he petted each of their heads. They quickly turned their attention to Savannah.

"Savannah Carlisle, meet Sam—" He indicated the lean Italian greyhound who, while peering intently at Savannah, hadn't left his side. "He's a retired racing greyhound I rescued about five years ago."

"Hello, Sam."

"And that nosy fella there is Benny the labradoodle." Blake indicated the rust-and-beige dog yapping at her feet, demanding her attention.

"Hi, Benny." Savannah leaned down and let the dog sniff her hand, then petted his head. "Pleasure to meet you."

Benny seemed satisfied with her greeting. He ran back inside with Sam on his heels.

"Did you rescue Benny, too?"

"No." Blake swallowed past the knot that formed in his throat when he remembered the day he'd brought Benny home as a pup.

He'd bought Benny as a surprise for his ex. Only she'd had a surprise of her own. She was leaving him for someone else.

"Oh." Savannah didn't inquire any further, for which he was grateful.

Blake turned on the lights and gestured inside. "After you."

Seven

Stop behaving like the poor girl who grew up on the wrong side of the tracks. Even if you are.

Savannah's wide eyes and slack mouth were a dead give-away as Blake gave her an informal tour of his beautiful home.

She realized the Abbotts were wealthy. Still, she'd expected a log cabin with simple country decor. Maybe even a luxurious bachelor pad filled with gaming tables and the latest sound equipment.

She certainly hadn't expected this gorgeous, timber-built home overlooking a picturesque lake and offering breath-taking mountain vistas. The wall of windows made the pastoral setting as much a feature of the home as the wide plank floors and shiplap walls.

Rustic charm with a modern twist.

It was the kind of place she could imagine herself living in. The kind of home she would be living in, if not for the greed and betrayal of Joseph Abbott.

Her shoulders tensed and her hands balled into fists at her sides.

"You must be tired." Blake seemed to sense the shift in her demeanor. "I'll show you to your room. We can finish the tour another time."

Blake always seemed attuned to how she was feeling. A trait that would be endearing if they were a couple. Or even friends.

But they weren't. It was a reality she couldn't lose sight of, no matter how kind and generous Blake Abbott appeared on the surface.

She was here for one reason. But she'd learned little about Joseph Abbott and nothing of his history with her grandfather. If she opened up a little with Blake, perhaps he'd do the same, and reveal something useful about his family.

Maybe Blake didn't know exactly what his grandfather had done. But he might still provide some small clue that could direct her to someone who did know and was willing to talk.

But none of that would happen if she couldn't keep her temper in check. She had to swallow the bitterness and pain that bubbled to the surface whenever she thought of Joseph Abbott's cruel betrayal.

At least for now.

"I'm tired. And wet. And cold. So I'm sorry if I'm cranky." Her explanation seemed to put him at ease.

"Of course." He led the way through the house and up an open staircase to the second floor. Sam and Benny were on his heels.

"I hate to ask this, but do you think I could borrow a T-shirt and some shorts?"

"Don't think I have anything that'll fit you." Blake stopped in front of a closed door. His gaze raked over her body-conscious, black rayon dress. Soaked through, the material shrank, making it fit like a second skin. Blake made a valiant effort to hold back a smirk.

He failed miserably.

"I'll see what I can find."

He opened the door to a spacious guest room with a terrace. The crisp, white bedding made the queen-size bed look inviting, and the room's neutral colors were warm and soothing. The angle of the windows provided a better view of a docked boat and an amphibious plane.

Maybe being a guest chez Blake won't be so bad after all.

"Thanks, Blake. I'll be out of your hair as soon as I can, I promise."

Her words drew his attention to her hair, which was soaking wet. A few loose strands clung to her face.

He reached out, as if to tuck a strand behind her ear. Then he shoved his hand into his pocket.

"It's no trouble. I'm just glad I came back to check on you... I mean, the plant." His voice was rough as he nodded toward a sliding barn door. "The bathroom is there. It's stocked with everything you need, including an unopened toothbrush."

"Thank you, again." Savannah set her purse and bag on the floor beside the bed.

Neither of them said anything for a moment. Blake dragged his stare from hers. "I'll find something you can sleep in and leave it on the bed. Then I'll rustle up something for us to eat."

With the violent storm crackling around them, she hadn't thought about food. But now that he mentioned it, she was starving. She hadn't eaten since lunch.

"All right, cowboy." She couldn't help teasing him. She hadn't ever heard the word *rustle* used outside of a cowboy movie.

Blake grinned, then slapped his thigh. "C'mon, boys. Let's give Savannah some space."

The dogs rushed out into the hall and Blake left, too, closing the door behind him.

Savannah exhaled, thankful for a moment of solitude. Yet, thinking of him, she couldn't help smiling.

She shook her head, as if the move would jostle loose the rogue thoughts of Blake Abbott that had lodged themselves there.

Don't you dare think about it. Blake Abbott is definitely off-limits.

"Hey." Blake was sure Savannah could hear the thump of his heart, even from where she stood across the room.

She padded toward him wearing his oversize University of Tennessee T-shirt as gracefully as if it was a Versace ball gown. Her black hair was chestnut brown on the ends.

Ombre, his sister had called it when she'd gotten a similar dye job the year before.

Savannah's hair hung down to her shoulders in loose ringlets that made him want to run the silky strands between his fingers. To wrap them around his fist as he tugged her mouth to his.

Absent cosmetics, Savannah's freshly-scrubbed, freckled skin took center stage. She was the kind of beautiful that couldn't be achieved with a rack of designer dresses or an expensive makeup palette.

Her natural glow was refreshing.

Seeing Savannah barefaced and fresh out of the shower felt intimate. She'd let down her guard and bared a little of her soul to him.

Blake's heart raced and his skin tingled with a growing desire for this woman. His hands clenched at his sides, aching to touch her.

He fought back the need to taste the skin just below her ear. To nip at her full lower lip. To nibble on the spot where her neck and shoulder met.

Blake snapped his mouth shut when he realized he must look like a guppy in search of water.

"Hey." Savannah's eyes twinkled as she tried to hold back a grin. "Where are Sam and Benny?"

"I put them downstairs in the den. Didn't want to torture them with the food or annoy you with Benny's begging. One look at that sad face and I'm a goner." He nodded toward the orange-and-white University of Tennessee shirt she was wearing. "I see the shirt fit. Kind of."

Savannah held her arms out wide and turned in a circle, modeling his alma mater gear. "It's a little big, but I think I made it work."

That's for damn sure.

The hem of the shirt skimmed the tops of her thighs and hugged her curvy breasts and hips like a warm caress.

Blake was incredibly jealous of that T-shirt. He'd give

just about anything to be the one caressing those undulating curves. For his body to be the only thing covering hers.

The too-long sleeves hung past her fingertips. Savannah shoved them up her forearms. She lifted one foot, then the other, as she pulled the socks higher up her calves. Each time, she unwittingly offered a generous peek of her inner thigh.

Blake swallowed hard. The words he formed in his head wouldn't leave his mouth.

"Smells good. What's for dinner?" She didn't remark on his odd behavior, for which he was grateful.

"I had some leftover ham and rice." He turned back to the stove and stirred the food that was beginning to stick to the pan. "So I fried an egg and sautéed a few vegetables to make some ham-fried rice."

"You made ham-fried rice?"

There was the look he'd often seen on her face. Like a war was being waged inside her head and she wasn't sure which side to root for.

"Yep." Blake plated servings for each of them and set them on the dining room table, where he'd already set out a beer for himself and a glass of wine for her. He pulled out her chair.

She thanked him and took her seat. "I didn't realize you cooked. Did your mom teach you?"

Blake chuckled. "There were too many of us to be underfoot in the kitchen."

"Not even your sister?"

Blake remembered the day his mother decided to teach Zora to cook.

"My sister was a feminist at the age of ten. When she discovered Mom hadn't taught any of us to cook, she staged a protest, complete with hand-painted signs. Something about equal treatment for sisters and brothers, if I remember correctly."

"Your mother didn't get upset?"

"She wanted to be, but she and my dad were too busy trying not to laugh. Besides, she was proud my sister stuck up for herself."

"A lesson your sister obviously took to heart." Savannah smiled. "So if your mother didn't teach you to cook, who did?"

"I became a cookbook addict a few years back." A dark cloud gathered over Blake's head, transporting him back to a place he didn't want to go.

"Why the sudden interest?" She studied him. The question felt like more than just small talk.

Blake shrugged and shoveled a forkful of fried rice into his mouth. "Got tired of fast food."

"I would think there's always a place for you all at Duke and Iris's dinner table." Savannah took a bite, then sighed with appreciation.

What he wouldn't give to hear her utter that sound in a very different setting: her body beneath his as he gripped her generous curves and joined their bodies.

"There is an open invitation to dinner at my parents' home," he confirmed. "But at the time I was seeing someone who didn't get along with my mother and sister." He grunted as he chewed another bite of food. "One of the many red flags I barreled past."

"You're all so close. I'm surprised this woman made the cut if she didn't get along with Zora or Iris."

This was not the dinner conversation Blake hoped to have. He'd planned to use the opportunity to learn more about Savannah. Instead, she was giving him the third degree.

"We met in college. By the time she met any of my family... I was already in too deep. A mistake I've been careful not to repeat," he added under his breath, though she clearly heard him.

"Is that why things didn't work out? Because your family didn't like her?"

He responded with a hollow, humorless laugh. "She left me. For someone else."

The wound in his chest reopened. Not because he missed his ex or wanted her back. Because he hadn't forgiven himself for choosing her over his family.

Though, at the time, he hadn't seen it that way.

After college, he'd moved back home and worked at the distillery, and he and Gavrilla had a long-distance relationship. But when he'd been promoted to VP of operations, he'd asked her to move to Magnolia Lake with him.

The beginning of the end.

Up till then, his ex, his mother and sister had politely endured one another during Gavrilla's visits to town. Once she lived there full-time, the thin veneer of niceties had quickly chipped away.

Blake had risked his relationship with his family because he loved her. She'd repaid his loyalty with callous betrayal.

She'd taught him a hard lesson he'd learned well. It was the reason he was so reluctant to give his heart to anyone again.

"I'm sorry. I wouldn't have brought it up if I'd known it would stir up bad memories." Savannah frowned.

"You couldn't have known. It's not something I talk about." Blake gulped his icy beer, unsure why he'd told Savannah.

"Then I'm glad you felt comfortable enough to talk about it."

"That surprises me." He narrowed his gaze.

"Why?"

"You go out of your way not to form attachments at work."

Savannah's cheeks and forehead turned crimson. She lowered her gaze and slowly chewed her food. "I don't mean to be—"

"Standoffish?" He did his best to hold back a grin. "Their words, not mine."

"Whose words?"

"You don't actually think I'm going to throw a member of my team under the bus like that, do you?" Blake chuckled. "But that fence you work so hard to put around yourself... It's working."

"I don't come to work for social hour. I'm there to do the job you hired me to do." Savannah's tone was defensive. She took a sip of her wine and set it on the table with a thud.

"That's too bad." Blake studied her. Tension rolled off her lean shoulders. "At King's Finest, we treat our employees like family. After all, we spend most of our waking hours at the distillery. Seems less like work when you enjoy what you do and like the people you do it with."

"Am I not doing my job well?" Savannah pursed her adorable lips.

"You're doing a magnificent job." He hadn't intended to upset her. "I doubt anyone could do it better."

She tipped up her chin slightly, as if vindicated by his statement. "Has anyone accused me of being rude or unprofessional?"

"No, nor did I mean to imply that." He leaned forward. "All I'm saying is...you're new to town. So you probably don't have many friends here. But maybe if you'd—"

"I didn't come to Magnolia Lake to make friends, Blake. And I already have a family."

Savannah had given him a clear signal that she didn't want to discuss the topic any further, but she hadn't shut the conversation down completely. There was something deep inside him that needed to know more about her.

"So tell me about your family."

Eight

They'd talked so much about his family. Savannah shouldn't be surprised he'd want to know about hers.

Not in a getting-to-know-you, we're-on-a-date kind of way. In the way that was customary in Magnolia Lake. One part Southern hospitality. One part nosy-as-hell.

Had she not been determined to keep her personal life under wraps, she might've appreciated their interest.

She didn't want to discuss her family with Blake or any Abbott. But she hadn't gotten anywhere in her investigation. If she didn't want to spend the rest of her natural life in this one-horse town, she needed to change her approach.

If the quickest route to getting answers was charming the handsome Blake Abbott, she'd have to swallow her pride, put on her biggest smile and do it. At the very least, that meant opening up about her life.

"I have a sister that's a few years younger than me."

"That your only sibling?"

"Yes."

"What's she like?"

"Laney's brilliant. She's been accepted as a PhD candidate at two different Ivy League schools. All of that despite being the mother of a rambunctious two-year-old." A smile tightened Savannah's cheeks whenever she talked about Laney or Harper. "Someday my sister is going to change the world. I just know it."

"Sounds like Parker." Blake grinned. "While the rest of us were outside running amok, he had his nose in a book. For him, being forced to go outside was his punishment."

"Seems like his book obsession paid off."

"A fact he doesn't let any of us forget. Especially my mother." Blake chuckled. "You and your sister…"

"Delaney." No point in lying about her sister's name. He could find that out easily enough.

"Are you close?"

"Very. Though with our age difference and the fact that we lost our parents when we were young, I sometimes act more like her mother than her sister. Something she doesn't appreciate much these days."

"Sorry to hear about your parents. How'd you lose them, if you don't mind me asking?"

She did mind. But this wasn't about what she wanted. She needed Blake to trust her.

"The crappy little tenement we lived in burned down to the ground. Lightning hit the building and the whole thing went up in no time." She could feel the heat and smell the smoke. That night forever etched in her brain. "A lot of the families we knew growing up lost their lives that night."

"How'd you and your sister get out?" There was a pained expression on Blake's face. It was more empathy than pity.

A distinction she appreciated.

"My dad worked second shift. When he arrived home the building was in flames. He saved me and my sister and a bunch of our neighbors, but he went back to save my mother and…" A tightness gripped her chest and tears stung her eyes. She inhaled deeply and refused to let them fall. "He didn't make it back out."

"Savannah." Blake's large hand covered her smaller one. "I'm sorry."

The small gesture consoled her. Yet if not for what Blake's grandfather had done, her life would be very different.

She couldn't know for sure if her parents would still be with her. But they wouldn't have been living in a run-down housing project that had been cited for countless violations. And they wouldn't have lost their lives that stormy night.

"Thank you." Savannah slipped her hand from beneath

his. "But it was such a long time ago. I was only nine. My sister was barely four. She hardly remembers our parents."

"Who raised you two?"

"My grandfather." She couldn't help smiling. "I didn't want to go live with him. When my parents were alive he'd always seemed so grumpy. He didn't approve of my dad. He'd hoped my mother would marry someone who had more to offer financially. But after my dad gave his life trying to save my mom... He realized too late what a good guy my father was." She shoved the last of her food around her plate. "He's been trying to make it up to them ever since."

They ate in silence, the mood notably somber.

"Sorry you asked, huh?" She took her plate to the kitchen.

"No." Blake followed her. "I understand now why you don't like to talk about yourself or your family."

"I'd rather be seen as polite but aloof than as Debbie Downer or the poor little orphan people feel sorry for."

A peal of thunder rocked the house, startling Savannah. The storm had abated for the past hour only to reassert itself with a vengeance.

"It's raining again." Blake peered out the large kitchen window. When he looked back at her, a spark of realization lit his eyes. "Your parents... That night... That's why you're so freaked out by thunderstorms."

Savannah considered asking if he wanted a cookie for his brilliant deduction. The flash of light across the night sky turned her attention to a more pressing issue.

"Where do you keep the bourbon around here?"

Blake chuckled. "I was saving it for after dinner."

"It's after dinner." Savannah folded her arms. "After that trip down memory lane, I could use something that packs a punch."

"You've got it."

She followed him down to the den. Sam and Benny greeted them, their tails wagging.

This was the game room she'd anticipated. But instead

of having a frat-house quality, it was simple and elegant. There was a billiards table, three huge televisions mounted on the walls, a game table in one corner and groupings of chairs and sofas throughout the large room.

One bank of windows faced the mountains. The other faced the lake with more mountains in the distance.

Savannah sat on a stool at the bar. "This place is stunning. It isn't what I expected." She studied him as he stepped behind the bar. "Neither are you."

A slow grin curled one corner of his generous mouth. Her tongue darted out involuntarily to lick her lips in response. There was something incredibly sexy about Blake's smile.

He was confident, bordering on cocky. Yet there was something sweet and almost vulnerable about him. When he grinned at her like that, she felt an unexpected heaviness low in her belly. Her nipples tightened, and she mused about the taste of his lips. How they would feel against hers.

Blake produced a bottle of King's Finest top-shelf bourbon. Something she'd only splurged on for high-end, no-expenses-spared affairs when she'd planned events at the hotel.

"If you're trying to impress me, it won't work." She lowered her voice to a whisper. "I happen to know you get it for free."

"Not the premium stuff. I buy that just like everyone else." He chuckled. "Except for the bottle we give employees every year at Christmas. But I did use my employee discount at the gift shop."

Savannah couldn't help laughing. She honestly didn't want to like Blake or any of the Abbotts. She'd only intended to give the appearance of liking and admiring them. But then, she hadn't expected that Blake would be funny and charming in a self-deprecating way. Or that he'd be sweet and thoughtful.

Blake was all of that wrapped in a handsome package that felt like Christmas and her birthday rolled into one.

And that smile.

It should be registered as a panty-obliterating weapon.

"How do you take your bourbon?" Blake set two wide-mouth glasses on the counter.

"Neat." She usually preferred it in an Old Fashioned cocktail. But with the sky lighting up and rumbling around her, drinking bourbon straight, with no fuss or muss, was the quickest way to get a shot of courage into her system.

Before the next lightning strike.

Blake poured them both a fourth of a glass and capped the bottle.

Savannah parted her lips as she tipped the glass, inhaling the scent of buttery vanilla, cherries and a hint of apple. She took a sip, rolling the liquor on her tongue. Savoring its smooth taste.

Light and crisp. Bursting with fruit. A finish that had a slow, spicy burn with a hint of cinnamon, dark cherries and barrel char absorbed during the aging of the bourbon.

Savannah inhaled through both her nose and mouth, allowing the scent and flavors of the twelve-year-old bourbon to permeate her senses. She relished the burn of the liquor sliding down her throat.

"You approve, I take it." Blake sat beside her and sipped his bourbon.

"Worth every cent." She raised her glass.

"My grandfather would be pleased."

Savannah winced at the mention of Joseph Abbott. It was like being doused with a bucket of ice water.

She took another sip of the bourbon that had catapulted King's Finest to success. Their King's Reserve label had quickly become a must-have for the rich and famous.

Her grandfather's recipe.

"I look forward to telling him in person." Savannah smiled slyly as Blake sipped his bourbon. Her grandfather always said liquor loosened lips. She couldn't think of a more suitable way to induce Blake to reveal his family's secrets.

"Up to watching a movie or playing a game of cards? We could play—"

"If you say 'strip poker,' I swear I'll—"

"I was thinking gin rummy." The amusement that danced in his dark eyes made her wonder if the thought hadn't crossed his mind.

"Since you, and the entire town, are hell-bent on getting to know me, I have another idea." She traced the rim of her glass as she studied him. "'Truth or dare?'"

Blake laughed. "I haven't played that since college."

"Neither have I, so this should be fun." She moved to the sofa. Benny sprawled across her feet and rolled over for a belly rub. Savannah happily complied.

Blake studied her as he sipped his bourbon. He still hadn't responded.

"If 'truth or dare?' is too risqué for you, I completely understand." Having satisfied Benny's demands, Savannah crossed one leg over the other, her foot bouncing. Blake's gaze followed the motion, giving her an unexpected sense of satisfaction.

He sat beside her on the couch, and Sam settled at his feet.

"My life is an open book. Makes me fairly invincible at this game." He rubbed Sam's ears.

"A challenge. I like it." The bourbon spread warmth through Savannah's limbs and loosened the tension in her muscles. She was less anxious, despite the intense flashes of light that charged the night sky.

Thunder boomed and both dogs whined. Benny shielded his face with his paw.

Savannah stroked the dog's head. "By all means, you go first, Mr. Invincible. I'll take truth."

A grin lit Blake's dark eyes. "Tell me about your first kiss."

Nine

Blake had always considered himself a sensible person. Sure, he took risks, but they were usually calculated ones. Risks that would either result in a crash and burn that would teach him one hell of a lesson or pay off in spades.

Sitting on his favorite leather sofa, drinking his granddaddy's finest bourbon and playing "truth or dare?" with the sexiest woman who'd ever donned one of his shirts was the equivalent of playing with fire while wearing a kerosene-soaked flak jacket.

Or in this case, a bourbon-soaked one. They'd both had their share of the nearly empty bottle of bourbon.

Their questions started off innocently enough. His were aimed at getting to know everything there was to know about Savannah Carlisle. Hers mostly dealt with character—his and his family's. But as the game went on—and the bourbon bottle inched closer to empty—their questions grew more intimate.

Too intimate.

Savannah was an employee and he was part owner of King's Finest. He shouldn't be sitting so close to her, well after midnight, when they'd both been drinking. While she was wearing his shirt, her skin smelling of his soap.

Savannah folded her legs underneath her, drawing his eyes to her smooth skin.

They were playing Russian roulette. Only the six-shooter was loaded with five bullets instead of one.

Neither of them was drunk, but they were sure as hell dancing along its blurry edge.

"What's your favorite thing to eat?" he asked.

"Strawberry rhubarb pie. My sister makes it for my birthday every year in lieu of a cake." She grinned. "Your turn. Truth or dare?"

"Truth."

Savannah leaned closer, her gaze holding his, as if she were daring him instead. "Tell me something you really wanted, but you're glad you didn't get."

The question felt like a sword puncturing his chest. His expression must have indicated his discomfort. "Married."

Savannah's cheeks turned crimson and she grimaced. "If it's something you'd rather not talk about—"

"I wanted to surprise my ex with a labradoodle for her birthday." He got the words out quickly before he lost his nerve. "Instead, she surprised me. Told me she'd fallen for someone else, and that it was the best thing for both of us."

"That's awful. I'm sorry."

"I'm not." He rubbed Sam's ears, then took another sip of bourbon, welcoming the warmth. "She was right. It was the best thing for both of us. Marrying her would've been a mistake."

They were both quiet, the storm crackling around them.

He divided the remainder of the bottle between their two glasses and took another pull of his bourbon. "Truth or dare?"

"Truth." Her gaze was soft, apologetic.

"Why'd you *really* come to Magnolia Lake?" It was a question he'd wanted to ask since he'd learned she moved to town prior to being offered the position.

He couldn't shake the feeling there was more to the story than she'd told him that day. Savannah Carlisle was an organized planner. And too sensible a person to move to an area with very few employment options on the hope she'd be hired by them.

"Because I belong at King's Finest." Something resembling anger flashed in her eyes. "It's like I told you—I was compelled by the company's origin story. I want to be part of its future." She shifted on the sofa. "Now you. Truth or dare?"

"Truth." He studied her expression and tried to ignore

the shadow of anger or perhaps pain she was trying desperately to hide.

"If you could be doing anything in the world right now, what would it be?"

"This." Blake leaned in and pressed his mouth to hers. Swallowed her little gasp of surprise. Tasted the bourbon on her warm, soft lips.

A soft sigh escaped her mouth and she parted her lips, inviting his tongue inside. It glided along hers as Savannah wrapped her arms around him. She clutched his shirt, pulling him closer.

Blake cradled her face in his hands as he claimed her mouth. He kissed her harder and deeper, his fingers slipping into her soft curls. He'd wanted to do this since he'd first seen the silky strands loose, grazing her shoulders.

He reveled in the sensation of her soft curves pressed against his hard chest and was eager to taste the beaded tips straining against the cotton.

Blake tore his mouth from hers, trailing kisses along her jaw and down her long, graceful neck.

"Blake." She breathed his name.

His shaft, already straining against his zipper, tightened in response. He'd wanted her in his arms, in his bed, nearly since the moment he'd laid eyes on her.

He wanted to rip the orange shirt off. Strip her down to nothing but her bare, freckled skin and a smile. Take her right there on the sofa as the storm raged around them.

But even in the fog of lust that had overtaken him, his bourbon-addled brain knew this was wrong. He shouldn't be kissing Savannah within an inch of her life. Shouldn't be preparing to take her to his bed. Not like this. Not when they were both two glasses of bourbon away from being in a complete haze.

He wouldn't take advantage of her or any woman. His parents had raised him better than that.

Blake pulled away, his chest heaving. "Savannah, I'm sorry. I can't… I mean…we shouldn't—"

"No, of course not." She swiped a hand across her kiss-swollen lips, her eyes not meeting his. She stood abruptly, taking Benny by surprise. "I…uh… Well, thank you for dinner and drinks. I should turn in for the night."

Blake grasped her hand before he could stop himself. "You don't need to go. We were having a good time. I just got carried away."

"Me, too. But that's all the more reason I should go to bed. Besides, it's late." She rushed from the room, tossing a good-night over her shoulder.

"Benny, stay," Blake called to the dog, who whimpered as Savannah closed the door softly behind her. "Come." The dog trotted over and Blake petted his head. "Give her some space, okay, boy?"

The dog clearly didn't agree with his approach to the situation. Neither did certain parts of Blake's anatomy.

"Way to go," he whispered beneath his breath as he moved about the room, gathering the glasses and the empty bottle.

I shouldn't have kissed her. Or brought her here. Or given her that damn shirt to wear.

He could list countless mistakes he'd made that evening. Missteps that had inevitably led them to the moment when his mouth had crashed against hers. When he'd stopped fighting temptation.

Blake shouldn't have kissed her, but he wished like hell that he hadn't stopped kissing her. That Savannah Carlisle was lying in bed next to him right now.

Sam's howl and Benny's incessant barking woke Blake from his fitful sleep at nearly three in the morning.

"What the hell, guys? Some of us are trying to sleep." Blake rolled over and pulled the pillow over his head.

A clap of thunder rattled the windows and the dogs intensified their howls of distress.

Benny hated thunderstorms, but Sam usually remained pretty calm. Blake sat up in bed and rubbed his eyes, allowing them to adjust to the darkness.

"Guys, calm down!" he shouted.

Benny stopped barking, but he whimpered, bumping his nose against the closed door.

Blake strained to listen for what might be bothering the dogs. Maybe Savannah had gone to the kitchen.

He got out of bed, his boxers sitting low on his hips, and cracked open his bedroom door.

No lights. No footsteps. No running water. Aside from the storm and the rain beating against the house, everything was quiet.

"No! No! Please! You have to save them."

"Savannah?" Blake ran toward her room at the other end of the hall. He banged on the guest bedroom door. "It's me—Blake. Are you okay?"

There was no response. Only mumbling and whimpering.

"Savannah, honey, I'm coming in."

He tried the knob, but the door was locked. He searched over the door frame for the emergency key left by his brother's building crew.

Blake snatched down the hex key, glad he hadn't gotten around to removing it. He fiddled with the lock before it finally clicked and the knob turned.

He turned on the light and scanned the room.

Savannah was thrashing in the bed, her eyes screwed shut, tears leaking from them.

"Savannah, honey, you're okay." He touched her arm gently, afraid of frightening her. "You're right here with me. And you're perfectly fine."

"Blake?" Her eyes shot open and she sat up quickly, nearly head-butting him. She flattened her back against the headboard. "What are you doing here?" She looked around, as if piecing everything together. "In my room."

"You were having a bad dream. The dogs went nuts. So did I." He sat on the edge of the bed, his heart still racing from the jog to her room. "I thought you were hurt."

Her voice broke and her breathing was ragged. "Sorry I woke you, but I'm fine."

"No, you're not. Your hands are shaking, and you're pale."

"Thank you for checking on me." She wiped at the corners of her eyes. "I didn't intend to be so much trouble tonight."

"I'm glad you're here." Blake lifted her chin so their eyes met. "I'd hate to think of what might've happened if you'd been out there alone on that road tonight. Or home alone in this storm." He dropped his hand from her face. "Do you always have these nightmares during a storm?"

"Not in a really long time." She tucked her hair behind her ear. "Talking about what happened that night probably triggered it." Savannah pressed a hand to her forehead.

"I shouldn't have pushed you to talk about your family. I just wanted to…" Blake sighed, rubbing Benny's ears.

"What were you going to say?" For the first time since he'd entered the room, her hands weren't trembling. Instead of being preoccupied with the storm, she was focused on him.

"There's this deep sadness behind those brown eyes."

Savannah dropped her gaze from his.

"You try to mask it by throwing yourself into your work. And you ward off anyone who gets too close with that biting wit. But it's there. Even when you laugh."

"Let's say you're right." She met his gaze. "Why do you care? I'm just another employee."

"I would think that kiss earlier proved otherwise."

"So what…are you my self-appointed guardian angel?" Savannah frowned.

"If that's what you need." He shrugged.

Silence stretched between them. Conflicting emotions played out on her face. There was something she was hesitant to say.

Blake recognized her turmoil. He'd been struggling with it all night. Wanting her, but knowing he shouldn't. He struggled with it even now.

"Thank you, for everything, Blake. For coming to check on me." She scanned his bare chest.

Blake was suddenly conscious that he was sitting on her bed. In nothing but his underwear.

Good thing he wore boxers.

"Sorry. You sounded like you were in distress, so I bolted down here after Benny woke me up."

Savannah turned her attention to Benny's wide brown eyes and smiled for the first time since Blake had entered the room. She kissed the top of the dog's furry head.

"Were you worried about me, boy?" She laughed when Benny wagged his tail in response.

Blake chuckled softly. Benny was a sociable dog, but he'd never been as taken with anyone as he seemed to be with Savannah.

"You've earned at least one fan here." Blake's face grew hot when Savannah's gaze met his.

"Thank you both." She gave Benny one last kiss on his snout. "I won't keep you two up any longer. Good night."

"Good night." Blake turned out the light.

Savannah flinched in response to the lightning that flashed outside the window.

"Look, why don't Benny and I sleep in here tonight?"

"With me?" The pitch of her voice rose and her eyes widened.

"I'll sleep in the chair by the window."

She scanned the chair, then his large frame. "I don't think you'd be very comfortable contorting yourself into that little chair all night. Don't worry about me. Seriously, I'll be fine."

A bolt of lightning flashed through the sky, followed by a loud cracking sound.

Savannah screamed and Benny whimpered and howled, hiding underneath the bed.

"It's all right." Blake put a hand on Savannah's trembling shoulder. He went to the window and surveyed the property.

Lightning had hit a tree just outside the bedroom window. A huge section had split off. The bark was charred, but the tree wasn't on fire.

Blake turned back to Savannah. Her eyes were filled with tears, and she was shaking.

"It's okay." He sat beside her on the bed. "There was no real damage, and no one was hurt."

Blake wrapped an arm around her shoulders. He pulled her to his chest, tucked her head beneath his chin and rocked her in his arms when she wouldn't stop crying.

"You're fine, honey. Nothing's going to happen to you, I promise."

"What if I want something to happen?" She lifted her head. Her eyes met his, and suddenly he was very conscious of the position of her hand on his bare chest.

The backs of her fingertips brushed lightly over his right nipple. "What if I want to finish what we started earlier?"

Electricity skittered along his skin and the muscles low in his abdomen tensed as his shaft tightened.

He let out a low groan, wishing he could just comply with her request and give in to their desire. He cradled her face in his hand.

"Honey, you're just scared. Fear makes us do crazy things."

"Wanting to sleep with you is crazy?" She frowned.

"No, but getting into a relationship with a member of the management team is ill-advised."

"I'm not talking about a relationship." She seemed perturbed by the suggestion. "I'm just talking about sex. We're adults, and it's what we both obviously want. I'm not looking for anything more with you."

He grimaced at the indication that it was him specifically she didn't want more with. For once in his life, he longed for a good *It's not you, it's me.*

"That won't work for me." He sighed heavily. "Not with you."

They were way past the possibility of meaningless sex. He felt something for her. Something he hadn't allowed himself to feel in so long.

"Why not with me? I'm here, and I'm willing." She indicated his noticeable erection. "And unless you're hiding a gun in your boxers, it's what you want, too."

"Savannah…" Blake gripped her wrists, holding her hands away from his body. "You aren't making this easy for me."

"I thought I was." She grabbed the hem of the shirt and tugged it over her head, baring her perfect breasts. The brown peaks were stiff. Begging for his mouth. Her eyes twinkled. "Can't get much easier than this."

Blake's heart raced as the storm raged around them. He wanted to take the high road. But right now, it wasn't his moral compass that was pointing north.

Blake tightened his grip on Savannah's neck and something about it sent a thrill down her spine. Her core pulsed like her heartbeat.

The cool air tightened the beaded tips of her breasts. His gaze drifted from the hardened peaks back to her.

"You're scared. You've been drinking. You're not thinking clearly right now. Neither am I."

"We slept off the bourbon hours ago," she reminded him, pressing a kiss to his jaw. His body stiffened in response. "Besides, you kissed me last night." She kissed his neck, then whispered in his ear, "And don't pretend you haven't thought about us being together before tonight."

Savannah relished Blake's sharp intake of breath when she nipped at his neck. She wanted his strong, rough hands to caress her skin. And she longed to trail her hands over the hard muscles that rippled beneath his brown skin.

Adrenaline rushed through her veins, her body hummed with energy and her brain buzzed with all of the reasons she shouldn't be here doing this.

Just for tonight, she wanted to let go of her fear and allow herself the thing she wanted so badly.

Blake Abbott.

Sleeping with him would complicate her plans, but weren't things between them complicated anyway? Whether they slept together tonight or not, things would never be the same between them.

Maybe she didn't want them to be.

If it turned out her grandfather was confused about what had transpired all those years ago, she need never tell Blake why she'd really come to Magnolia Lake. And if her grandfather was right…and Blake's family had used him cruelly… why should she feel the slightest ounce of guilt? The Abbotts certainly hadn't.

Either way, she wanted him. And she had no intention of taking no for an answer when it was clear he wanted her, too.

Savannah wriggled her wrists free from Blake's loose grip. She looped her arms around his neck, her eyes drifting shut, and kissed him.

Blake hesitated at first, but then he kissed her back. He held her in his arms, his fingertips pressed to her back.

The hair on his chest scraped against her sensitive nipples. She parted her lips and Blake slipped his tongue between them, gliding it along hers.

Savannah relished the strangled moan that escaped his mouth. The way it vibrated in her throat. That small sound made her feel in control in a moment when she'd normally have felt so powerless.

As helpless as she'd felt when she'd watched the building burn. Unable to save her parents.

Her parents. Her grandfather. Laney.

What would they think of what she was doing right now? Giving herself to the grandson of the man who had taken everything from them?

Savannah's heart pounded in her chest as she tried to push the disquieting thoughts from her head.

They wouldn't understand, but she did. She wasn't giving herself to Blake Abbott. She was taking what she wanted… what she needed…from him.

She'd gotten lost in her thoughts. Blake was the one driving the kiss now. Both of them murmured with pleasure as his tongue danced with hers. Then he laid her back and deepened the kiss.

Savannah glided her hands down Blake's back and gripped his firm, muscular bottom.

His length hardened against her belly and he groaned, his mouth moving against hers.

Savannah kept her eyes shut, blocking out the lightning that periodically illuminated the room, and the thunder that made poor Benny whimper. Instead, she focused on the beating of her own heart. The insistent throb and dampness between her thighs.

Savannah couldn't control what was happening outside. But she could control this. How he felt. How he made her feel.

Powerful. Alive. In control.

She slipped a hand beneath his waistband and wrapped her fingers around the width of his thick shaft. Blake moaned against her open mouth, intensifying the heat spreading through her limbs. She circled the head with her thumb, spreading the wetness she found there, relishing the way his breathing became harder and faster in response.

He grabbed her wrist, halting her movement as she glided her fist up and down his erection.

"Neither of us is ready for what happens next if you keep doing that, sweetheart." His voice was low and gruff.

"Then we should stop wasting time and get down to business."

Blake shooed the dogs from the room and locked the door behind them before returning to bed. He cradled her cheek.

"Savannah, you know I want you. But I don't want you to do this for the wrong reasons."

"Does it matter why?"

"Yeah, baby. In this case, it does." He swept her hair from her face. "Because this isn't a typical one-night stand for me."

"Why not? I'm sure you've done this lots of times before." She tried to rein in her frustration. In her limited experience, it had never been this difficult to get a guy to have sex with her.

"Not with someone who works for me."

Suddenly an Abbott is worried about being ethical?

"It'll be our little secret. And it'll be just this once." She hated that an Abbott had reduced her to groveling.

"I can't promise that, because I'm already addicted to your kiss." He kissed her mouth. "Your taste." He ran his tongue along the seam of her lips. "And if I get more...and make no mistake about this—I do want more...there is the definite risk of becoming addicted to having you in my bed."

It was the sweetest, sexiest thing any man had ever said to her.

She wanted to hear more of it while Blake Abbott moved inside her, making her forget her worries and fears and replacing the tragic memory associated with thunderstorms with a pleasurable one.

"I can't promise what's going to happen tomorrow." She kissed him again, trying to convince him to let go of his worries, too. "I can only tell you that this is what I want.

It isn't the liquor or my fear talking. It's me. I want you. Period."

His body tensed, and his eyes studied hers there in the dark. Then he claimed her mouth in a kiss that shot fireworks down her spine, exploding in her belly. Her core throbbed with a desire so intense she ached with the emptiness between her thighs.

An emptiness only he could fill.

Blake trailed kisses down her neck and ran his rough tongue over one sensitive nipple. He gripped the flesh there and sucked the hardened nub. Softly at first, then harder. She moaned as he licked and sucked, the sensation tugging at her core.

"Oh, Blake. Yes." She arched her back, giving him better access. His eyes met hers and he smiled briefly before moving on to the other hardened peak, making it as swollen and distended as its counterpart.

He trailed kisses down her belly and along the edge of the waistband of her panties. Suddenly, he pulled aside the fabric soaked with her desire for him and tasted her there.

Gripping a handful of his short, dark curls, Savannah gasped and called out his name. She spread her thighs, allowing her knees to fall open and providing Blake with better access to her swollen folds and the hardened bundle of nerves he was assaulting with that heavenly tongue.

He reached up, pinching one of her nipples as she rode his tongue. Every muscle in her body tightened as a wave of pleasure rolled through her hard and fast.

She was shivering and trembling again. This time, it wasn't because of the storm. It was because Blake Abbott had given her an orgasm that had struck her like a lightning bolt.

And left her wanting more.

Ten

Blake groaned as the sunlight filtered through the window of the guest bedroom. He peeked one eye open and lifted his arm, which had been draped across Savannah as she slept. He looked at his watch.

It was well after seven. Normally he would've worked out and walked the dogs by now. He was surprised Sam and Benny weren't already...

His thoughts were interrupted by Benny's moaning and scratching at the door.

Savannah sighed softly, her naked bottom nestled against the morning wood he was sporting.

Hell, his erection had probably never gone away after his night with Savannah. A night in which he'd brought her to pleasure with his mouth and fingers so many times that her throat was probably raw from calling his name.

He hadn't made love to her, and he hadn't allowed her to give him so much as a good hand job. A decision his body—strung tight as a piano wire—bemoaned. But he had to be sure her head was in the right place. That she wasn't just acting out of fear.

Blake sucked in a deep breath, inhaling the scent of her hair. He wanted to run his fingers through the silky curls again, brush her hair back so he could see her lovely face.

But he didn't want to wake her. He wasn't ready to burst the bubble they'd been floating in.

He couldn't bear for her to wake and regret their night together. A night he didn't regret in the least.

Blake slipped out of the room, got dressed, fed the dogs and took them for their usual walk, avoiding all the water-logged areas. He surveyed the damage to his property and the neighborhood. There were a few downed branches and lots of upended lawn furniture. A tree had fallen through one neighbor's roof. Shingles littered their front lawn, and a yellow tarp, draped over the roof, billowed in the wind.

But for Blake, the storm hadn't been a bad thing. It'd brought Savannah to his home and into his bed.

Blake hoped she hadn't been serious about making this a one-off. He liked her. A lot.

Dating Savannah would ruffle his family's feathers. He wouldn't tell them right away. Not until he knew whether this was serious. If it was, he'd just have to deal with the consequences of breaking their unwritten rule.

Blake opened the side garage door and let the dogs in, wiping their muddy paws on a rag. As they went back into the house, he paused to listen.

The house was silent. Savannah was evidently still sleeping. He washed his hands and checked the kitchen for breakfast food. He cursed under his breath for putting off grocery shopping.

Every Southerner knew you stocked up on basic goods when there was an impending storm of any kind.

Luckily, there were his mother's and sister's refrigerators to raid. Both of them kept their pantries and deep freezers well stocked. His mother's deep freezer likely contained a side of beef and enough chicken to feed the entire company. Zora's would be filled with frozen meals and store-bought goodies.

Right now, he'd settle for either. But since Zora lived closest, he'd start with her.

"You two be good." He patted Sam's and Benny's heads. "I'll be back before you know it. And don't bother Savannah. She's sleeping." He headed back toward the garage. "That means you, Benny."

Benny whimpered, dropping on the floor in the corner and resting his head on his paws.

Blake hopped in his truck and drove the five minutes to

his sister's home on the other side of the lake. She was out-side gathering broken tree limbs.

"If you came to help, you're too late. I'm just about done here." Zora stepped on a long branch, snapping it in two. Then she snapped each piece in half again.

Blake hugged his sister. It didn't surprise him that she hadn't asked for assistance. Since she was a kid, Zora had been determined to prove her independence.

"Well, since you've already got everything under control, maybe you can help me out. I don't have anything for break-fast back at the house. I was gonna go grocery shopping this weekend but the bridge is out." He shoved his hands in his pockets, hoping to avoid his sister's usual forty questions.

Zora stopped breaking branches and eyed him. "Why don't you fix breakfast here for both of us?"

"Because."

"I'm not twelve, Blake. That doesn't work anymore." Zora propped a hand on her hip.

Blake sighed. "Okay, fine. I have company."

Zora stepped closer. "Female company?"

Blake tried to keep his expression neutral.

"You don't have women over to the house. Ever. Not since you broke up with Godzilla."

"Gavrilla." But he didn't correct the part about him ini-tiating the breakup. They both knew it wasn't true, but say-ing it seemed to make his family feel better.

"Whatever." She waved her hand. "This must be seri-ous if you brought one of your out-of-town hookups home."

"How did you—"

"I didn't, but I always suspected that's why you never take Daisy when you travel." Zora looked more proud of herself than she had when her team had posted record sales numbers the previous quarter.

"Don't you have anything better to do than to worry about who I'm sleeping with?"

"People around here talk. If they're not talking, nothing's

happening. I haven't heard about you hooking up with anyone around here and...well...you are a guy."

"Zora, *enough*."

He was *not* going to have a conversation with his sister about his sex life. Though Zora was an adult, she'd always be his baby sister.

"I can't help it if I'm smarter than you." She shoved him playfully.

"You're the Jessica Fletcher of who is doing who in this town. Congratulations, Brat." He dug up her childhood nickname. "Now, can we get back to my request?"

"Right. You need to shop my pantry."

Zora removed her work gloves and headed toward the garage of her colonial. The place was newer than his, though a bit smaller and far more traditional-looking.

"Let's find something you and your girlfriend can eat for breakfast."

"Didn't say she was my girlfriend." Blake gritted his teeth.

Zora turned to him. "She woke up at your house, presumably in your bed. Just let that sink in for a minute."

"I'm seriously starting to wish I'd gone to Mom and Dad's house. Besides, they have real food. Not just crap that comes out of a box."

"That hurts." Zora punched his arm. "Besides, that's no way to talk to someone you want a favor from, big brother."

Zora opened her well-stocked fridge. She cut an egg carton in half and gave him half a dozen eggs. Then she took out a mostly full package of thick-cut maple bacon and an unopened jug of orange juice. She arranged everything in a reusable shopping bag.

"Please tell me you at least have the basics...cheese, milk, maybe an onion and some mushrooms."

"I'm the one who actually cooks for myself," Blake reminded her. "But I think I used my last onion making fried rice last night."

"You cooked dinner for her, too?" Zora's eyes lit up like a Christmas tree that had just been plugged in. "After you left Mom and Dad's last night?"

Ignoring her question, Blake accepted two sweet onions from his sister and dropped them in the bag, careful not to crack the eggs. "Thanks, Brat."

"You're not even going to give me a hint who I'm feeding?" She leaned one hip against the fridge.

"I don't kiss and tell." He hoisted the bag. "And I didn't sleep with her."

"Then why won't you tell me who it is?"

"Because it's none of your business."

"Speaking of business...your mystery guest wouldn't happen to be a certain not-so-Chatty-Cathy employee who you can't seem to keep your eyes off, would it?"

Blake froze momentarily, but recovered quickly. Zora was fishing, hoping to get a reaction out of him. If he played it cool, she'd move on to another theory.

"Thanks for the food," he called over his shoulder. "Holler if you need help with the yard."

"Only if you'll bring your girlfriend over."

Blake shook his head and climbed back in his truck.

Brat.

He waved and backed out of his sister's drive. As he headed toward home, his neck tensed in anticipation of seeing Savannah.

Savannah's eyes fluttered open. She was floating on a warm cloud of indescribable bliss, and her entire body tingled with satisfaction. Her mouth stretched in an involuntary smile.

Last night, Blake had given her mind-blowing pleasure, and he'd done it without removing his boxers.

He'd focused on making their encounter special for her. Even if it meant denying himself.

No one had ever given her such intense pleasure or focused solely on her needs. Savannah groaned. She'd finally met a man who made her want *things*. Things she hadn't allowed herself the luxury of wanting.

God, why does he have to be an Abbott?

Because apparently the universe hated her.

As she'd given in to her desire for him, she'd convinced herself she could remain detached and keep their encounter impersonal. Transactional.

But when he looked into her eyes, all she'd seen was Blake. Not his family versus hers. Not the history of their grandfathers. Nothing but him.

For a few hours, she'd allowed herself to buy into the delusion that she could have him and still get justice for her family.

But she couldn't have both. At some point, she'd have to choose. And her allegiance was to her own family.

Savannah sighed and rolled over. Blake wasn't in bed. She got dressed and went down to the kitchen.

No Blake.

She walked through the house, calling him without response. His truck wasn't in the garage. When she returned to the kitchen, she saw his note.

Gone to rustle us up some breakfast.

She couldn't help smiling. *Smart-ass.*

Why couldn't he stop being funny and thoughtful and all-around adorable? He was making it difficult to focus on her mission. Which was the only thing that mattered.

She was alone in Blake Abbott's house. She'd never get a better opportunity to see if there was anything there that could shed light on what had happened between their grandfathers.

She went to Blake's office. The door was unlocked, but the moment she opened it, the dogs ran down the hall and greeted her.

Savannah shut the door and stooped in front of the dogs, petting them and giving Benny a peck on his nose.

"Stay here. I just need to take a quick peek." Savannah slipped inside, shutting the door behind her. The dogs yipped in protest.

A loud thump nearly made her jump out of her skin. One of the dogs had jumped against the door.

Benny. The thud was too heavy to be Sam.

She glanced around. The neat, organized room was flooded with sunlight.

She had no idea how long it would be before his return. There was no time to waste.

Savannah searched the bookshelves. She looked through drawers and scanned files for anything related to the company's origin. She sifted through his desk drawers, hoping to find something...anything.

There was nothing out of the ordinary.

She spotted his laptop. The same one he used at work.

Frustrated, Savannah sat down at the large oak desk and groaned. She bumped the mouse and the screen woke.

It was unlocked.

He'd obviously used it that morning and hadn't been gone long. Savannah rummaged through the computer directories. All she found were the same files she accessed at work.

Savannah pulled open the desk drawer again and lifted the organizer tray. A photo of Blake, Sam and a woman was wedged in back.

The ex.

She was pretty, but something about her didn't feel real. *Hypocrite.*

She was under Blake's roof, sleeping in his bed and trying to stage a coup at his family's company.

At least his ex had been up-front with her treachery.

Guilt gnawed at Savannah's gut. She replaced the photo and then put the drawer back in order.

There were few personal photos elsewhere in the house,

but the office walls and shelves were filled with family pictures and photos of King's Finest employees—many of whom had worked for the Abbotts for decades.

Savannah was struck with deep, painful longing for her own family. The parents she'd never see again. The ailing grandfather who'd raised her. Her sister and young niece. They were the reasons she was doing this.

She had no desire to hurt Blake, but this was war. And in war, there were always casualties.

Her family hadn't started it. But she sure as hell would finish it.

Even if it meant hurting Blake.

She was a spy working on the side of right. Sometimes trickery and deceit were required. And sometimes people got hurt. Good people. People you liked. But wasn't getting justice for her family more important than hurting Blake Abbott's pride?

He was a big boy. He'd get over it. Just as he'd gotten over his ex.

Or had he?

Savannah glanced at the drawer where the woman's photo was hidden.

She sighed softly. He'd never forgive her once he learned that she was the granddaughter of his grandfather's enemy.

But maybe he'd eventually understand.

Joseph Abbott hadn't given her a choice. This was what she had to do, even if what she really wanted now was Blake Abbott.

The garage door creaked. Savannah peeked through the window. Blake's big black pickup truck was approaching.

Savannah made a quick sweep of the room, ensuring everything was as she'd found it. She hurried into the hall past the dogs.

"Stay." She held up a hand when they tried to follow her. Benny's paw prints were all over the door, but there was no time to clean them.

Savannah hurried upstairs and got into the shower. She pressed her back against the cool tiles and reminded herself she'd done what she had to do.

So why was her chest heavy with guilt? And why did her eyes sting with tears?

Because she couldn't stop wishing last night had been real and that she could have Blake Abbott for herself.

Eleven

Their tails wagging, Sam and Benny ambushed Blake when he stepped through the garage door.

"Calm down, you two." Blake set the grocery bag on the counter and unloaded it.

The house was quiet, but the note he'd left for Savannah had been moved, so she'd been downstairs.

Blake put the bacon in the oven and set up an impromptu omelet bar. When the bacon was done, he grabbed another shirt for Savannah and headed toward the guest room. The room where he'd awakened with her in his arms.

He knocked on the door. "Savannah, you up?"

She opened the door wearing a bath towel wrapped around her curvy frame. Her hair was wrapped in another. "Sorry. I just hopped out of the shower."

"Then you'll be needing this." He handed her another shirt, this one a gray short-sleeve T-shirt.

"Thanks." She clutched the garment to her chest. "That was thoughtful of you."

"Breakfast is set." He shoved his hands into his pockets, feeling awkward, as if they were strangers who hadn't been intimate the night before. "Hope you like omelets and bacon."

"I love them." Her smile was polite. Distant. "Be down in a sec."

"Okay then." Blake rubbed the back of his neck. He wasn't sure where things stood between them, but their awkward morning-after conversation didn't bode well.

He jogged down the steps and paused, head tilted, noticing paw marks on the office door. He obviously hadn't done a thorough job of cleaning Benny after their walk.

Blake grabbed a rag and some wood cleaner and wiped

the door down. Then he cleaned Benny's paws again and tossed the rags into the laundry room.

Why was Benny trying to get into the office?

He wouldn't unless someone was in there. The muddy prints weren't on the door when Blake left. That meant Savannah had been inside.

But why?

Blake returned to his office. Everything was exactly as it had been that morning. Still, she'd been there. He was sure of it.

He returned to the kitchen and cut up some fruit, his mind turning.

"Smells delicious." Savannah stood at the entrance of the kitchen with Sam and Benny at her feet.

Traitors.

They dropped him like a bad habit whenever Savannah was around, Benny more so than Sam.

"Thanks. I made bacon, set up an omelet bar and made a fruit salad." Blake poured himself a glass of orange juice. He lifted the container. "Juice?"

"Please." She sat at the breakfast bar. "But let me make the omelets. I insist."

"The stove is all yours." He handed her a glass.

Savannah sipped her juice, then melted butter in a pan and sautéed vegetables.

"I hope you were able to get some sleep," Blake said finally. He wanted to ask why she'd been in his office.

"Didn't get much sleep." She flashed a shy smile. "But I certainly have no complaints."

"Glad to hear it." The tension in Blake's shoulders eased. He parked himself on a stool.

"One other thing…" Savannah pulled an ink pen from the breast pocket of her T-shirt and handed it to him. "I borrowed a pen from your office. Hope you don't mind."

"Of course not." Blake breathed a sigh of relief. Savannah did have an innocent reason for being in his office. It was good he hadn't accused her of snooping. "Glad you found what you were looking for."

He tapped a finger on the counter after an awkward silence fell over them. "About what happened last night," he began.

Her posture stiffened. She didn't turn around. "What about last night?"

"It was amazing."

"For me, too. Believe me." Savannah's cheeks were flushed but she seemed relieved. She moved to the counter and cracked eggs into a bowl.

"I like you, Savannah. I have since the day you walked into my office and called bullshit on me for trying to reschedule your interview."

She looked at him briefly and smiled before washing her hands at the sink with her back to him. "But?"

"But I shouldn't have kissed you or let things get as far as they did."

She turned off the pan with the vegetables, then heated butter in another pan.

"I get it. I work for your family. Last night was my fault. You tried to show restraint. I should apologize to you." She glanced over her shoulder at him. "It won't happen again."

"That's the thing." Blake stood, shoving his hands into his jean pockets. "I don't want it to be over. I don't think you do, either."

Savannah turned to him slowly. She worried her lower lip with her teeth.

"It doesn't matter what we want. You're an Abbott, and I'm…" She sighed. There was something she wouldn't allow herself to say. "I'm your subordinate. If anyone knew about what happened last night…it wouldn't look very good for either of us."

She wasn't wrong.

Blake groaned, leaning against the counter. "I've never been in this position before."

"You've never been attracted to one of your employees before?" she asked incredulously.

"Not enough to risk it."

Her teasing expression turned more serious. She returned to her task. "You're worried I'll kiss and tell, like everyone else in this gossipy little town."

"That isn't it at all."

"Then there's no problem. Once the bridge opens, you'll take me back to my car and we'll pretend this never happened."

Blake wanted to object. But Savannah was right. It would be best if they pretended last night never happened.

But that was the last thing he wanted to do.

"Thanks for breakfast," Savannah said as she ate the final bite of her omelet. "Everything was delicious."

They'd endured the awkward meal, both acting as if walking away from each other was no big deal. The heaviness in the air between them indicated otherwise.

"Your omelet especially." Blake gathered their plates and took them to the sink. "Good thing I raided my sister's refrigerator."

"You told Zora I was here?"

"Of course not." He turned to scrape the plates. "She hinted that she thought it was you, but she was just fishing. Trust me."

Savannah joined him at the sink. "What did she say *exactly*?"

"I don't recall her exact words."

Savannah was supposed to be a fly on the wall. Working in the background, hardly noticed. Now she had the full attention of Blake and she'd be on Zora's radar, too.

And if Zora suspected, did that mean she'd already told the rest of his family?

"But your sister asked specifically if it was me you were entertaining for breakfast?"

"She didn't mention your name. And if she had any real reason to believe it was you, she would've told me. There's nothing to worry about."

"Maybe for you. Your family won't fire you over this."

"No one is getting fired. I promise." He dried his hands on a towel and gripped Savannah's shoulders. "Look at me."

She did, reluctantly.

"I'd never let you get fired because of me. Trust me. All right?"

Savannah nodded, her breath coming in quick, short bursts. She'd come so far, and she was so close. She wouldn't let anything derail her plans—not even Blake Abbott.

"When do you think I'll be able to leave?"

"Got a weather alert on my phone." Blake pulled it out of his pocket. "The bridge is still closed. According to the alert, it'll be a couple of days. My dad already emailed us to say that if the bridge isn't open by tomorrow, the plant will be closed on Monday."

"I can't stay here all weekend."

"You don't really have a choice." He held her hand. His voice was quiet and calm.

"I don't want to complicate things for either of us."

"And I don't want you to leave." Blake lifted her chin. He dragged a thumb across her lower lip, his gaze locked with hers.

"I don't want to, either." The truth of her admission shocked her. They weren't just words, and she wasn't simply playing a role. "But we've discussed all the reasons I should."

"I know." He stepped closer. His clean, masculine scent surrounded her. "But I don't care."

"I do." She stepped beyond his reach. "And one of us needs to be the adult here."

"You walking away right now won't resolve our feelings for each other."

"What do you expect me to say, Blake?"

"Say you'll stay. That you'll spend another night in my bed." He slipped his arms around her waist and hauled her against him. "This time, I know you're making the decision with a clear head. So I won't hold back."

Her belly fluttered and her knees were so weak she could barely stand. She held on to him. Got lost in those dark eyes.

"Say it." Blake pressed a gentle kiss to one edge of her mouth, then the other. Then he kissed the space where her neck and shoulder met. "Say you'll stay."

Savannah wanted Blake so badly she ached with it. Despite who his family was. Despite what she'd come there to do.

Blake Abbott was the last man in the world she should want. Yet she'd never wanted anyone more.

"Yes." Her response was a whisper.

"Yes, what?" His gaze followed his hand as it trailed down her arm.

Her skin tingled wherever he touched it. "Yes, I'll stay with you."

"Where?"

It wasn't a question. It was a demand issued in a low growl that caused a trembling in her core. Her knees wavered slightly.

"In your bed." Her eyes met his.

Blake's pull was as strong as the earth's gravity. She was too close to escape its effects. And she wouldn't want to, even if she could.

He grinned. "Good girl."

Even as she gave in to him, she needed to prove she wasn't a pushover. "But I'll only stay until—"

He covered her mouth with his, swallowing her objection as if it were a morsel that had been offered to him. Blake tugged her hard against him as he laid claim to her mouth.

Savannah gasped at the sensation of his erection pressed to her belly. She had zero willpower where this man was concerned. The dampness between her thighs and hardening of her nipples were evidence of that.

Blake tugged the T-shirt up over her hips, planted his large hands on her waist and set her on the cold quartz countertop. She shivered in response. He stepped between her legs, spreading them. Blake stripped off her shirt and dispensed with her bra. He assessed her with his heated gaze.

"Beautiful," he murmured.

He'd seen her naked the night before. So why did she feel so exposed? As if she was standing on a stage naked?

He surveyed her full breasts and tight, sensitive nipples that were hungry for his mouth, his touch. Her belly knotted and electricity skipped along her spine, ending in a steady pulse between her thighs.

Blake stepped as close as the countertop would allow him. He kissed her neck and gently nipped the skin, as if marking his territory.

He palmed the heavy mounds. Sucked a beaded tip into his warm mouth.

A soft gasp escaped her lips. She slipped her fingers into his short, dark curls as he sucked, then laved the hypersensitive nub with his rough tongue.

Her mind flashed back to how delicious it had felt to have that tongue attending to more sensitive areas of her body. How it had felt inside her.

"Blake, please." She hardly recognized her own voice as she made the urgent plea for him to relieve the deep ache between her thighs. "I want you."

He trailed kisses down her belly as he laid her back on the cool surface. "Don't worry, babe. I know exactly what you want."

Blake slid her back on the counter and pulled her legs up so that her heels pressed against the countertop. Starting inside her knee, he kissed his way down her inner thigh to her panties.

He tugged the damp fabric to one side and kissed the

slick, swollen flesh. Each kiss sent her soaring higher, making her want him more. In any way he wanted to take her.

She arched her back, lifting her hips off the cool quartz. Blake cupped her bottom and sucked on her distended clit, bringing her close to the edge. Then he backed off, lavishing the surrounding flesh with slow, deliberate licks before sucking on it again.

Savannah was falling. Hurtling toward her release. She covered her mouth and tried to hold back the scream building in her throat.

"No." He lifted his head, leaving her aching for his mouth. His hooded gaze locked with hers. "Don't hold back. Whatever you're feeling… I want to hear it. Every murmur. Every scream."

He slowly licked the swollen flesh again, his tongue moving in a circular motion, hitting everywhere but where she needed him most.

Teasing her.

"Understand?" His eyes met hers again.

She nodded. "Yes."

He went back to sucking on her slick bud. She trembled, bucking her hips and clutching his hair.

She let go of embarrassment and fear. Of her worries about what would happen next. Instead, she floated on the sea of bliss surrounding her.

She let go of every moan. Every curse.

Until she couldn't hold back the river of pleasure that flooded her senses, shattering any remaining control.

She called his name. Her back arched as she rode his tongue until she'd shattered into a million tiny, glittering pieces.

Savannah lay there afterward, her breathing rapid and shallow. Her chest heaving. Feeling both satisfied and desperate for more.

Blake placed delicate kisses on her sensitive flesh. Each kiss caused another explosion of sensation.

He kissed his way up her belly and through the valley between her rising and falling breasts, as he pulled her into a seated position. His eyes met hers momentarily, as if seeking permission. Then he pressed a kiss to her open mouth. The taste of her was on his tongue.

Blake lifted her from the counter and led her up the stairs and to the opposite end of the hall.

His bedroom.

The decor was rustic, but elegant, in keeping with the style of the house. A king-size bed dominated the space. Large windows flooded the room with light and provided a nearly unobstructed view of the lake and the mountains in the distance.

Before Savannah could admire the space, he'd taken her in his arms and kissed her again. His tongue delved into her mouth. His hands drifted over her body. Her hands explored his body, too, and traced the thick ridge beneath his jeans.

Savannah loosened his belt, eager to touch the silky head of his velvety shaft again. She slipped her hand inside his pants, gripping the warm, veiny flesh. He grunted and shuddered at her touch before breaking their kiss.

Blake turned her around abruptly and nestled her bottom tight against him. His groan of pleasure elicited a sigh from her.

Pinning her in place with one strong forearm slung low across her stomach, Blake kissed her neck and shoulder. He glided the backs of his fingers up and down her side. The featherlight touch made her knees shake. Her sex pulsed with need.

Had the few men she'd been with before been doing it all wrong?

Blake hadn't entered her. Yet he'd found countless ways to bring her such intense pleasure she wanted to give him everything.

All of her.

He slid his fingers into the hair at the nape of her neck,

turning her head. His mouth crashed into hers. She gasped when Blake grazed one painfully hard nipple with his palm.

The contact was so slight. A whisper against her skin. But it made her want to drop to her knees and beg for more.

She considered doing just that, but Blake pinched her nipple, sending a bolt of pleasure to her core. She cried out, though she wasn't sure if it was from the pain or the pleasure.

He toyed with her nipple—so sensitive she could barely stand it. Then he glided his hand down her belly, dipping it beneath her waistband.

She gasped against his hungry mouth when he slipped two fingers through her wetness. He massaged the sensitive, swollen flesh, avoiding her needy clit.

Savannah moaned, moving against his hand. He swallowed her cries, intensified them with his movements.

His long fingers drifted from the back of her neck and lightly gripped her throat. Not enough to cause constriction or bruising. Just enough to let her know he was in control.

There was something about his grip there that was primal and erotic. A surprising turn-on that brought her closer to the edge.

"You like that, don't you?" His warm lips brushed her ear as he whispered into it, his voice tinged with deep satisfaction. "I knew you would."

"Blake, please, I'm so close." Her words were clipped, her tone breathy.

He used four fingers, massaging her clit and the sensitive flesh around it. His hand moved faster, until she shattered, her knees buckling as she cried out his name.

Savannah Carlisle coming apart in his arms was probably one of the most erotic things Blake had ever seen.

Her caramel skin glistened with sweat. Her small, brown nipples had grown puffy and rock-hard after his ministra-

tions. So sensitive that the slightest touch had her ready to
fall apart.

Savannah's body was perfect. Womanly curves in all
the right places. Smooth, creamy skin. Long, shapely legs.

Her responsiveness to him was a thing of beauty. The
way her skin flushed, from head to toe. The slow grinding of her hips against him. The little murmurs that grew
louder as she became more aroused. How wet she'd gotten
for him—even before he'd laid a hand on her.

Then there was the air of mystery about her. Something
Blake appreciated after living most of his life in this tiny
town.

He liked that he knew very little about this woman. That
he had to earn every bit of knowledge he'd gathered about
her. Savannah Carlisle was an enigma he'd enjoy unraveling.

Bit by bit.

They moved to his bed, where Blake lay on his side, his
head propped on his fist as he stroked her skin.

Savannah had given him her trust. Something he didn't
take lightly.

Until now, he'd focused on her satisfaction. It was no
selfless act. He'd relished the control. But he ached with
his desire for her. His body was taut with need.

Savannah released a long, slow breath and opened her
hazel eyes. Her lopsided smile was adorably sexy.

One look at her kiss-swollen lips and the vivid image
of Savannah on her knees flashed through his brain. He
groaned, his shaft stretching painfully.

"That was amazing. I can't wait to find out what comes
next."

He dragged a thumb across her lower lip. "And I can't
wait to give you what comes next."

Savannah's eyes danced. She accepted the digit, sucking
it between her soft lips, her gaze locked with his.

Blake pulled his thumb from her mouth with a pop. He

kissed her as Savannah removed his shirt, and he shed his remaining clothing.

The widening of her eyes, followed by an impish grin as she glided her tongue across her upper lip, made his erection swell. He swallowed hard, needing to be inside her.

Blake rummaged through his nightstand, praying he'd find at least a handful of condoms. He didn't stock them at home.

Hookups were something that happened elsewhere. Outside of this tiny town.

Blake wasn't sure how to categorize what was happening between them. But it definitely wasn't a one-off, meaningless hookup.

Finally, he found a strip of three condoms. He took one and tossed the others on the nightstand.

He fumbled with the foil packet, finally ripping it open and sheathing himself as quickly as his fingers would allow.

Blake knelt on the bed. Savannah's mouth curved in a smile, but her eyes held a hint of sadness.

Whatever it was…a painful memory, a bad experience… he wanted to wipe it away. He'd make her forget whoever had come before him. Men who probably hadn't shown her the sincerity and respect he would.

He dragged the lacy panties down her legs and pitched them on the floor. He admired her glistening pink center as she spread her thighs for him.

Blake groaned. A delicious sensation rippled through him as he slipped the head of his erection through her wetness. He pushed his hips forward, then drew his shaft back over her firm clit.

Savannah's belly tensed and she made a low keening moan. The sound became more pronounced with each movement of his hips.

He needed to be inside her. Now.

Blake pressed his shaft to her entrance. Inched his way inside her warm, tight walls.

They both murmured at the incredible sensation. He cursed as he moved inside her, his motions measured, controlled.

So. Fucking. Good.

He went deep. Hit bottom. Then slowly withdrew. Beads of sweat formed on his brow and trickled down his back as he tried to maintain control.

He refused to give in until he'd brought her to pleasure once more with him deep inside her.

Blake took her by surprise when he flipped their positions so he was lying on his back. She dug her knees into the mattress on either side of him and leaned backward, bracing her hands on his thighs. Her gaze locked with his as she moved her hips furiously, her breasts bouncing.

The sight of this beautiful woman grinding her hips against him was almost too much for him to take.

Suddenly, she leaned forward and planted her hands on his chest. Blake reached up and slipped the tie from her ponytail. Her loose curls cascaded forward, shielding her face like a dark curtain.

He gripped a handful of her hair, flipping it out of the way so he could watch as she got closer. He gritted his teeth, tried to slow his ascent as her mouth formed an O, euphoria building on her face.

She was close, and he was ready.

He rolled her onto her back again. Kneeling on the mattress, he leaned forward, increasing the friction against her hardened nub as he moved between her thighs.

Savannah cried out. Digging her heels into the mattress, she arched her back and clutched the bedding. With her eyes screwed shut, her head lolled back as she gave in to sweet ecstasy.

Pleasure rolled up his spine as her inner walls spasmed. He continued to move his hips. A few more strokes and Blake cursed and moaned as he came hard inside her. He shuddered, then kissed her softly, still catching his breath.

Savannah looped her arms around him. He settled the weight of his lower body on her and supported himself on his elbows as he kissed her. Slowly. Passionately.

It was something he'd never do with a hookup. Something he hadn't realized he missed...until now.

Blake pulled away, but Savannah tightened her grip on him.

"Can't we stay like this just a little while longer?"

Blake lay on his side and pulled Savannah against him, cradling her in his arms. He tucked her head beneath his chin and pulled the cover over them.

They lay in silence, enjoying the warmth and comfort of each other's bodies. Savoring everything they'd just shared.

As he drifted to sleep, his only thought was the need to keep Savannah in his bed.

Twelve

Savannah had awakened in Blake's arms for the second morning in a row. At least last night they hadn't made the mistake of falling asleep without discarding the condom, as they had the night before. To make matters worse, her birth control pills were at her apartment. She hadn't taken them for the past three days.

What if you're...?

Her heart beat furiously whenever she considered the possibility. So she couldn't allow herself to consider it. Not even for a moment.

When Blake received notice that the bridge had reopened, she was relieved. Blake had taken her to pick up her car, and she'd followed him in his truck back across the river.

Her time with Blake had been amazing, but it was a weekend fling. Two people confined together in a storm.

Shit happened.

That didn't make them a couple.

Yet Blake believed they could be more than a fling.

Savannah pulled into the parking lot behind her apartment building and got out of her car, wishing the circumstances were different.

She tugged down the hem of the too-tight, wrinkled rayon dress, ruined the night of the storm. She approached Blake, who leaned against the truck, waiting for her.

"I appreciate your insistence on seeing me home." She scanned the parking lot and a nearby street, which was a main thoroughfare in town. "But I think I'm good now."

"Don't worry. I'm maintaining my distance." His tone was laced with irritation. "But I know the history of this building." He nodded toward it. "It flooded during storms like this a few times before. Kayleigh needs a new roof, but she can't afford one and she's too damned stubborn to let my brother Cole fix it for her."

"Fine." She glanced around again. "But remember—"

"You're just an employee. Got it." He narrowed his gaze, his jaw tight. Blake headed toward the back entrance that led to her apartment, without letting her finish.

If he wanted to be that way…fine. It would absolve her of the guilt she might have felt when she finally exposed the Abbotts for who they really were.

She unlocked the main door, and Blake trailed her up the stairs to her apartment.

"Kayleigh's done a good job with the place." He glanced around the small space. The entire apartment was probably smaller than his great room.

"It's not a house on the lake with mountain views, but it's home." Savannah closed the door behind him and dropped her bags on the sofa.

"You think I'd look down on you because you have a smaller place?" Blake's brows furrowed. "Is that why you keep trying to push me away?"

Savannah didn't respond.

"You can't convince me this weekend didn't mean anything to you."

Savannah's throat tightened and her lungs constricted. "I thought I'd been clear. I'm not looking for a relationship. That would cause problems for both of us."

"I'm not saying we should run out and tell the world."

"You don't want your family and friends to know you're slumming it."

"I never said that." The vein in his neck pulsed. He raked his fingers through his hair. "You're purposely being combative."

"But it's the truth." She sank onto the sofa. "Besides, I doubt that Iris Abbott would want any of her precious boys to fall under the spell of some poor girl from the wrong side of the river."

Blake shoved aside the magazines on the coffee table and sat in front of her. He lifted her chin, forcing her gaze to meet his. "You don't really believe that."

"Because you know me so well." She pulled free of his grip.

"I know you better than you think. I know your fears, what turns you on..." He leaned in closer, his voice low. "I know how to satisfy you in ways no one else has."

Blake was too close. He was taking up all of the air in the room, making it difficult for her to breathe.

"So what?" She shrugged. "You haven't known me long. Maybe you wouldn't like me if you really knew me."

He leaned in closer, his gaze softer. "That's something I'd like to find out for myself."

She swallowed the lump in her throat. "Why is getting to know me so important to you? Most men would be content with a no-strings weekend." She forced a laugh. "You don't even have to pretend you're going to call."

"I'm not most men. Not when it comes to you." Blake kissed her.

She held back, at first. But when he took her face in his hands, Savannah parted her lips to him and pulled him closer, needing more of the connection they'd shared.

When he pulled away, one edge of his mouth curled in a smirk. "Is that your way of admitting that this weekend meant something to you, too?"

"If I say yes, will you take me to bed?"

"No." He stood, the ridge apparent beneath his zipper. "But it does mean I'm asking you on a date."

"Around here? Are you crazy?" She stood, too. "Everyone will know before dessert."

He sighed heavily. "True."

"Then where do you propose we have this date?"

"My place for starters." He tucked her hair behind her

ear. "But pack for the weekend. I've got something special in mind."

He kissed her, made a quick inspection of the apartment, as promised, and left.

Savannah closed the door behind him and exhaled.

What have I gotten myself into?

She needed to vindicate her grandfather and get the hell out of Magnolia Lake before she fell any deeper under Blake's spell.

She'd barely sat down when there was a knock at her door.

Had Blake changed his mind?

"Savannah, it's me—Kayleigh." A wall separated their apartments, though there were separate staircases leading to each.

Savannah opened the door. "Hi, Kayleigh. Is everything okay?"

"I bought too much food and I thought you might be hungry."

"Starving." She let the woman in. "Thanks for thinking of me."

"Haven't seen you around since the storm. I was worried." Kayleigh set containers of barbecue chicken, wedge fries and coleslaw on the table.

"Got caught on the other side of the river." Savannah gathered plates, napkins and silverware.

"I hope someone put you up during the storm." Kayleigh was trying to figure out where she'd spent the past few days.

"Thankfully, yes." Savannah put the dishes on the table and sat across from her landlord and neighbor.

"Well, that's a relief."

Savannah was eager to change the subject and avoid the question she knew would come next. "Everything smells delicious. Thanks for sharing."

"My pleasure." Kayleigh spooned coleslaw onto her plate.

Savannah fixed a plate for herself, hoping the other shoe didn't drop.

"I noticed that Blake Abbott followed you home today."

The other shoe dropped.

Savannah couldn't deny what Kayleigh had seen with her own eyes. But she could spin it.

"I'm about the only person in town who doesn't have a truck or SUV. Blake was nice enough to make sure I made it back across the river safely."

"And it was kind of him to see you inside."

Didn't the people in this town have anything else to do with their time?

"He mentioned that the building's roof has leaked in previous storms."

"Damn Abbotts think they're better than everyone else."

"He mentioned that you won't let his brother fix the roof."

"I'm not one of their charity cases." Kayleigh opened a jar of preserves and spread it onto her biscuit. "I can afford to get my own roof repaired…eventually."

They ate in companionable silence. But even the delicious food wasn't enough to keep Kayleigh quiet for long.

"It's none of my business what you do and who you do it with." The woman took a sip of her sweet tea. "But getting involved with an Abbott isn't too smart, if you ask me."

Savannah chewed her food. She had no intention of confirming her involvement with Blake Abbott, but she didn't bother denying it, either.

"You've made it clear you don't like them," Savannah said. "But you've never said why."

Kayleigh's scowl briefly shifted to a pained expression. Then her mask of anger slipped back in place.

"They're always throwing their money around like they can buy anyone they want."

"Did they do something to you specifically?"

Maybe the Abbotts had a pattern of cheating business partners. If she could prove that, it would go a long way toward supporting her grandfather's claim that Joseph Abbott had done the same to him.

"I went to school with Parker." She groaned. "That one is a piece of work."

Savannah couldn't disagree with that. Parker was smart, but his people skills were nonexistent. Everyone at the distillery seemed to understand that was simply who Parker was. No one took his overly direct approach personally. She'd learned to do the same.

"Is Parker the reason you don't like the entire family?"

"Parker is only part of the reason." Kayleigh's mouth twisted. She dropped her fork, as if she'd lost her appetite. "The other reason has to do with my father."

"What happened?"

The fire that always seemed to blaze in Kayleigh's eyes faded. "When I was growing up, my dad was the town drunk. In and out of the local jail all the time. Generally horrible to my mother, my sister and me."

"That must've been difficult for you. Especially in a small town like this one."

"There wasn't a week that went by when I wasn't humiliated by some kid talking shit about my dad's latest antics."

"Kids like Parker?"

"Not at first. At first, he and his brothers were about the only kids who didn't tease me. But then Parker started hanging with a different crowd... He wanted so badly to fit in back then."

"Doesn't sound like the Parker Abbott I know." Savannah tried to imagine the abrasive man as an impressionable kid who just wanted to fit in. She couldn't. "The guy I know doesn't care much what anyone thinks of him."

"It's true. Parker was different from the other kids. Smarter. More direct. Way too honest." Kayleigh shook her head and sighed. "So he tried to be part of the crowd. That meant embarrassing me, like all the other 'cool' kids." She used air quotes to emphasize the word.

"I see why you dislike Parker, but why don't you like the rest of the Abbotts?"

"Because Duke Abbott is a liar and a thief." The fire was back in Kayleigh's eyes. The icy tone returned to her voice.

Now we're getting somewhere.

Savannah leaned forward. "What did Duke Abbott steal from you?"

"We didn't have much, but my grandfather had left my mom a ton of property adjacent to the distillery. The old house and barn were dilapidated, but when my dad was sober we'd take a ride out there and walk around. He wanted to fix the place up. Make it a working farm again." She swiped angrily at the corner of her eye.

"In those moments when my dad was completely hammered, those walks on my grandfather's property were the one good memory I held on to. The only hope I had that one day he'd finally come through and be a real father to us."

"What happened to the farm?" Savannah knew the answer before she asked the question. Why else would Kayleigh hate the Abbotts when everyone else in town fawned over them?

"While my sister and I were away at college, Dad got really sick. Sicker than he or my mother were telling us. His liver couldn't take any more. My mother didn't want to burden us with their financial problems. So she sold the property to Duke Abbott for a fraction of what it was worth to pay hospital bills and help with our tuition."

"Must've been a tough decision for your mother."

"Selling her dad's property for a song broke her heart. She died not a year later. That's when I learned that greedy bastard Duke Abbott had bought it." Kayleigh paced the floor. "He'd already torn down the old house and put new buildings up."

Like father, like son.

The sound of her own heartbeat filled Savannah's ears. She was getting closer to establishing a pattern of the Abbotts cheating neighbors and friends. It evidently hadn't been much consolation to Kayleigh, but at least her family had received *something* for their property. That was more than her family could say.

"Sorry—I don't want to dump my issues on you. And I don't mean to be the kind of petty person who doesn't want her friends to have any other friends." Kayleigh returned to her chair and nibbled on a wedge fry. "But I had to warn you. The Abbotts seem like sunshine and roses. But when it comes to something they want, they'd as soon stab you in the back as smile in your face."

Savannah was surprised Kayleigh had referred to her as a friend. She hadn't thought of the woman that way. Kayleigh always seemed closed off, and Savannah hadn't been eager to make new friends, either. But maybe together they could form an alliance against the Abbotts.

She opened her mouth to tell Kayleigh who her grandfather was, and the reason she loathed Joseph Abbott. But the truth was, she didn't really know Kayleigh.

What she did know was that Kayleigh was part of the town's gossip circle. If she told her the truth it would be all over town by morning. She'd lose her one advantage over the Abbotts: the element of surprise.

Blowing her cover wasn't worth the risk.

Instead, she thanked the woman for her advice and turned the conversation elsewhere, while her grandfather's advice played on repeat in her head.

Never trust an Abbott farther than you can throw one.

Not even Blake.

But that didn't mean she couldn't enjoy whatever it was that they had. For now.

Thirteen

"Hello, darlin'. Miss me?"

Blake glanced up from his laptop to find the whirlwind that was Iris Abbott in his office.

"Mama." He met her in the middle of the room so she could give him one of her trademark bear hugs. "Dad didn't tell me you were back."

"I wanted to surprise you."

"How's Aunt Constance?" Blake straightened his collar and sat behind his desk.

"Much better." She sat in one of the chairs across from him. "She'll only need me for a few more weeks. Then I'll be home for good."

"How long are you staying?" Blake studied his mother's face. Iris Abbott considered flying a necessary evil. If she took a voluntary plane trip, she had a damn good reason for it.

"A few days." Her eyes roamed the space, as if it were her first visit. "Just long enough to have a couple of meetings with this Savannah girl."

The hair on the back of Blake's neck stood up. "Thought you two were holding video conferences about the gala."

"We have been, and we've gotten lots done. She's sharp, and she's not just talk. She makes things happen."

Blake crossed one leg over the other. "Sounds like the arrangement is working. So why the surprise trip?"

"What, you didn't miss your mama?"

"I did." Blake leaned on the armrest. "But you haven't answered my question. Why make a special trip just to meet with Savannah?"

His mother shifted in her chair, brushing imaginary crumbs from her summery floral skirt. "Technology is great, but it doesn't replace sitting across the table from someone and getting a good read on them."

"And why do you suddenly need a better read on Savannah?"

She folded her arms. "A little birdie told me her car was here all weekend."

"We had one heck of a storm. The bridge was closed, and she lives on the other side of the river. She obviously got stuck on this side."

"And *where* do you suppose she spent all that time?"

"Why are you asking me?" Blake composed an email to Savannah, warning her of his mother's suspicions.

"Tread carefully, son." Iris flashed her you-ain't-fooling-me smirk. "I saw the video of you bringing her back to her car on Monday afternoon."

Damn blabbermouth security guards.

"What if I did?" He shrugged. "She's new to the area. Didn't know it's prone to flooding. I wanted to make sure she was all right. What's wrong with that?"

His mother hiked one brow. "You still haven't answered my question. Where did she spend that long weekend? In your bed?"

"Just so we're clear, that question will *never* be okay." His cheeks flooded with heat. "Who I sleep with—or don't—is my business."

"Except when it threatens *our* business."

"You're being melodramatic, Mother."

"Am I?" She folded her arms. "You remember how ugly things got when Parker made a mess of things with his secretary?"

Blake groaned, recalling how angry the woman had been when Parker broke it off.

"This situation isn't the same."

"So you *are* sleeping with her."

He wasn't a good liar, which was why he preferred to

take the it's-none-of-your-business approach. But his mother never had trouble getting to the truth.

Still, what happened between him and Savannah wasn't up for family discussion.

"Blake, you were the one son I could count on to not break the rules. What happened? Did she seduce you?"

"I'm a grown man. Nothing happened I didn't want to happen. Let's leave it at that."

She folded her arms, pouting.

"I need you to promise me something, Mama." He moved to sit beside her.

"And what is that?"

"Don't mention this to Savannah."

"Now you want to dictate what I can say to her? This is why I made the rule in the first place, son. Can't you see the problems this is causing already?"

"Do this for me. Please."

"Fine." She stood, flipping her wrist to check the time. "I won't say anything—"

"To anyone," he added.

"For now." She leaned down and kissed him. "Come by for dinner tonight. I promise you and your little girlfriend won't be the topic of discussion."

"I'll be there around six."

Blake groaned in relief as his mother left.

His weekend with Savannah made him realize that his feelings for her were deeper than he'd imagined. Savannah evidently had feelings for him, too. Yet she was hesitant to explore them.

If she found out what his mother knew, it would only spook her. She'd pull away again.

Blake returned to his desk and discarded the email to Savannah. He could handle his mother, and what Savannah didn't know wouldn't hurt her.

Fourteen

Savannah pulled her car into Blake's garage and parked, as he'd requested. She'd spent the previous weekend at his place out of necessity. But this was a deliberate decision.

She'd crossed the line and the guilt bored a hole in her gut. Savannah could only imagine what Laney would say, if she knew.

Her sister would be gravely disappointed in her.

But she hadn't slept with Blake as part of some grand scheme to elicit information from him. What had happened was precipitated by the very real feelings that had been developing between them.

But didn't that make what she was doing worse?

She was giving him hope. Making him believe something could come of the game they were playing. Only Blake had no idea he was playing a game.

Savannah got out of her car, her hands shaking.

This was a mistake. I should go.

Blake stepped into the garage, a dish towel thrown over one shoulder. He seemed to know she was grappling with the decision to come inside.

His welcoming smile assured her everything would be okay.

"Hey." He took her bag and kissed her cheek.

"Hey." She slipped her hand into his and let him lead her inside. The house smelled like roasted vegetables and baked goods. "Are you sure this is a good idea? Your sister or one of your brothers could pop by at any—"

Blake set the bag on the floor and pulled her into a kiss that ended her objections. Her heart raced and warmth filled her body.

She forgot all the reasons she shouldn't be there as she

tumbled into a morass of feelings she might never be able to escape.

A buzzer sounded in the kitchen. Blake reluctantly suspended their kiss.

"We'll finish this later." He gave her a lingering kiss before removing a pie from the oven.

"Smells delicious. What kind of pie is it?"

"Strawberry rhubarb." He removed his oven mitts. "Hope you like it."

He remembered.

"You made it?"

"It's my first one." He grinned. "So I want you to be brutally honest. If it tastes like crap, don't pull any punches. It's the only way I'll learn to make it the way you like it."

"You did this for me?"

"Why else?" Blake tugged her against him and kissed her again.

It was just a silly little pie. So why was she so moved by the gesture?

Because Blake cared about what she wanted. About what was important to her.

And all she cared about was getting revenge for her grandfather and hurting his family in the process.

She pulled away, tears burning her eyes.

Blake cupped her cheek. "Did I do something wrong?"

"No." Savannah's neck and face tingled with heat. She swiped away warm tears and forced a smile. "Anyone ever tell you you're a little too perfect?"

"No." He chuckled, then kissed her again. "Certainly not any of my siblings."

"Brothers and sisters are there to rein us in when we get a little too big for our britches."

"At that, they excel." Blake grinned. "But they're also there when I need someone to help me get my head back on straight. Or to remind me that things aren't as bad as they seem." He moved to the counter and uncovered the steaks. "I imagine you and your sister do that for each other, too."

"Laney does her best to keep me on the straight and narrow. Doesn't always work, but she tries."

"And what about you?"

"I'm the pit bull." Savannah sat at the counter, watching him prep the steaks. "Even when our parents were still alive, it was my job to protect my sister." She swallowed past the thickness in her throat. "It still is. Even when it requires me to make difficult choices."

"Like what?" He held her gaze.

Savannah's heart felt heavy. It was a lead weight pulling her beneath the sea of guilt washing over her. Blake's reaction to learning the truth flashed in her head. Would he be hurt or angry? Probably both.

He'd regret the day he laid eyes on her.

She'd always anticipated that the day she finally vindicated her grandfather would be the happiest day of her life. Now she could only envision heartbreak and pain.

She'd have to explain to Blake why she'd misled him about her reasons for coming to King's Finest. Her only comfort was knowing she hadn't lied to him. Which meant she couldn't answer his question now.

Blake put the steaks in a skillet and washed his hands. When he turned around, she handed him a towel.

"It's been a long week." She looped her arms around his waist, tugging his lower body against hers as she gazed up at him. "I'm not in the mood for talking or eating right now."

She guided Blake's lips to hers and kissed him.

Blake gripped her bottom, hauling her closer. She accommodated his silent request by grinding her body against his until he grew hard against her belly.

Savannah broke their kiss and whispered in his ear. "I want you, Blake. Now."

"What about dinner?" His voice was as rough as his

beard, which scraped against her skin as he trailed hot kisses up her neck.

"It'll be just as good if we have it later…in bed." She unfastened his belt and slid her hand beneath his waistband. Savannah took his steely length in her palm and stroked his warm flesh.

Blake groaned against her throat, his body tensing. He pulled away just long enough to turn off the broiler and put the steaks in the fridge. Then he grabbed her bag and followed her to his bedroom as quickly as their legs would carry them.

They stripped each other naked. Blake tried to lead her to his bed, but Savannah urged him into a brown leather chair.

Her gaze fused with his as she slowly sank to her knees. She swirled her tongue around the head of his thick erection before taking just the tip in her mouth.

Blake cursed and his thighs tensed. He gripped the arms of the chair, as if it took every ounce of self-control he could muster to refrain from palming the back of her head and urging her to take him deeper.

She gripped the base of his shaft and ran her tongue lazily along the underside before taking him in her mouth again. Until she could feel him at the back of her throat.

Blake swore under his breath. He loosely gathered a handful of her hair in his fist so it wouldn't obstruct his view of her taking him deep.

"Do you have any idea what you're doing to me, Savannah?"

She ran her tongue along a bulging vein. "I'd like to think so."

"That's not what I mean." His expression became serious. "It's been a really long time since I've cared for anyone the way I care for you."

Savannah froze, her heart racing. She'd done this to remind them both that this was only sex. They were mutually satisfying each other's needs.

She hadn't expected Blake to say she meant something to him. What did it matter if she felt the same? She couldn't say it back. It would only make it hurt more once he knew the truth.

"Blake…" Her mouth went dry and her chest ached. "I can't—"

"It's okay." He pressed a kiss to her mouth. "My mother always says I'm the kid that goes from zero to a hundred in sixty seconds flat." He sighed, then stood, pulling her to her feet. "Forget I said anything."

But she couldn't forget.

It was all she could think of as he took her into his arms and kissed her.

When he made love to her.

Fire and passion spread through her limbs. Her body spasmed with intense pleasure. Her heart was overwhelmed with the emotions that sparked between them.

Blake Abbott had turned her inside out. Made her feel there was nothing in the world he wanted more than her.

He'd left her wishing desperately that this was more than an illusion, born from deception and half-truths.

Unable to sleep, Savannah lay in Blake's arms after their late-night dinner, listening to him breathe as he slept. Blake Abbott had ruined her. Her life would never be the same without him.

If only she could reclaim her grandfather's legacy and have Blake Abbott, too.

Fifteen

Blake straightened his tie and adjusted the cuffs of the suit jacket Savannah had helped him pick out for the jubilee gala. His jaw dropped as he surveyed the barn.

He'd witnessed the slow transformation of the structure as his brother Cole's construction crew renovated and painted it over the past month. He and the rest of the team had assisted with the execution of Savannah's party plans and decor over the past three days.

Still, he was floored by the remarkable beauty of what had once been a run-down building at the edge of his parents' property. His brother's company did excellent work. But this had all been Savannah's vision.

It was everything she'd promised when she'd pitched her idea. An upscale event with down-home roots. An event that honored their past while celebrating the future.

"The place is beautiful. I had no idea this old barn had so much potential." His mother suddenly appeared beside him, dabbing the corners of her eyes with a handkerchief. "Your Savannah is a genius."

"She isn't *my* Savannah, Mother. She's very much her own woman." Blake wasn't being evasive or ambiguous. He'd spent the past month trying to convince Savannah to formalize their affair. He cared deeply for her, but he was tired of being her dirty little secret.

He and Savannah had spent lazy weekends getting to know each other better. They cooked together, ate together and spent their nights making love.

Bit by bit, he was falling for her, diving headfirst into emotions he'd spent the past two years actively avoiding.

"Women who maintain a sense of self make the best

mates." Iris squeezed his hand reassuringly. "Ask your father."

They both chuckled and the tension in his shoulders eased. He squeezed his mother's hand back, appreciative of her underlying message. She wouldn't stand in the way of him being with Savannah.

Now if only he could convince Savannah it was time to take the next step.

"Can you believe this place?" Zora's eyes danced with glee as she approached. "It's incredible, and I've been dying for a good reason to dress up."

Not many occasions in Magnolia Lake called for elegant attire. The typical town event required a well-worn pair of jeans and a sturdy pair of boots.

"Will Dallas be here tonight?" Iris elbowed Zora.

"Said he wouldn't miss it for the world."

Zora's eyes sparkled when she talked about Dallas Hamilton—her best friend since kindergarten. Though Dallas still had a home in Magnolia Lake, he and Zora didn't see each other much.

Dallas's hobby of building stunning handmade furniture pieces in his family's run-down work shed had exploded into a multimillion-dollar business. He was frequently overseas attending trade shows, visiting with vendors and presiding over the setup of new retail stores in some of the world's most glamorous cities.

Sometimes Blake envied the guy. He was a self-made millionaire who'd built an empire out of nothing with a vision and hard work.

"Make sure Dallas comes to see me as soon as he gets here." Iris beamed. "There's a spot in the entry hall just begging for one of his custom pieces."

"Dal is here as our guest, Mother. Not to work. Let him enjoy himself, please," Zora pleaded.

"That means she plans to keep Dallas to herself all

night," Iris whispered to Blake loudly, fully aware Zora could hear her.

His attention shifted to Savannah as she flitted about the space. Tonight she was simply stunning.

She wore a black one-shoulder blouse and a high-waisted, long, flowing gray skirt with a bow tie at the back of her waist.

He loved her enticing curves. Had memorized them. But tonight, the cut of the blouse emphasized her bustline. Not that he was complaining. The generous flow of the skirt made her curvy bottom seem fuller, too.

Her hair, swept to one side, fell on her creamy, bare shoulder in loose curls. Blake's hand clenched at his side, his body tensing with the memory of combing his fingers through those soft curls as she lay naked in his bed.

"Seems your brother is more impressed with Ms. Carlisle than with what she's done here tonight."

Blake's cheeks warmed. He shifted his gaze back to his mother and sister. Zora giggled, likely glad their mother was temporarily distracted from her attempts to pair her and Dallas.

"I'm monitoring how she handles herself under pressure." Blake congratulated himself on his quick recovery. "Maybe you two haven't noticed who Savannah is talking to."

His mother and sister carefully assessed the tall, dark-haired man who hovered over Savannah.

"Wait a minute. Is that—"

"It's Dade Willis," Zora squealed. "I knew a couple B-and C-list Tennessee celebs had RSVP'd. I had no idea Dade Frickin' Willis would be here."

A tinge of jealousy gnawed at Blake as the man flirted with Savannah. The Tennessee native was country music's latest phenom. His single had topped the country charts for the past ten weeks. That didn't mean Blake wouldn't rearrange his pretty, surgically-enhanced face if he didn't back off Savannah.

"I'd better go greet our guest." His mother hurried toward Dade.

"Not without me you aren't." Zora caught up to their mother.

Blake went to the bar to check on their stock for the event. As Savannah rushed past him holding a clipboard, Blake stopped her with a discreet hand on her hip.

"Everything looks great, Savannah. You've done well. Take a breath and relax."

"I forgot to bring Dade's badge. He was a last-minute addition, so I made it in my office this morning."

"Not a big deal. Send one of the guys to get it."

"I need everyone here. There's still so much to do. The first band is already late and guests will arrive shortly." The words rushed from her mouth.

"Then I'll get it." Blake fought the urge to kiss her. He held out an open palm. "Give me the key to your office."

Savannah dropped her keys in his hand, her eyes filled with gratitude. "There's a small crate on the edge of my desk. My cell phone is in there, too. Thanks, Blake."

"Anything for you, babe." He lowered his voice so only she could hear him. "Now stop being such a perfectionist, or you won't get a chance to enjoy your own damn party."

Savannah seemed surprised he'd called it *her* party. She smiled gratefully, then made a beeline for the caterer.

Blake's gaze followed the sway of Savannah's hips as she crossed the room. He turned in the opposite direction when someone squeezed his shoulder.

"Gramps." Blake gave his grandfather a bear hug. "I wondered when you'd get here." He gestured around the room. "So what do you think?"

"It's remarkable." The old man removed his thick glasses and wiped them on a hankie he produced from his inside pocket. The corners of his eyes were wet with tears. "I didn't expect all this."

"But you deserve it, Gramps." Blake draped an arm

around his shoulders. "We wanted to show you what you and King's Finest mean to us and to the community. And this is only the beginning."

His grandfather's eyes widened. "What do you mean?"

"This gala kicks off a yearlong international celebration of our brand. The entire thing was envisioned by the new events manager we hired a couple of months ago—Miss Savannah Carlisle." Blake nodded in her direction.

"Oh, I see." His grandfather chuckled. "The pretty little thing you were cozied up with here at the bar. The one you couldn't take your eyes off when she walked away."

Blake didn't bother denying it, but refused to throw any more logs on the fire.

"We were discussing a small problem, which I promised to handle." Blake's gaze met Savannah's. Her mouth pinched and her eyes narrowed. "But first, let me introduce you to the woman behind all of this."

Blake walked his grandfather toward Savannah and she met them halfway, forcing a smile as she got closer.

"Don't worry—I'm headed out to take care of that errand in just a minute," Blake said quickly. "But my grandfather arrived, and I know you've been dying to meet him."

"For longer than you know." Savannah's smile was tight and her shoulders stiff. Her hand trembled slightly when she placed it in his grandfather's palm.

His grandfather clasped her hand in both of his and smiled broadly. "My grandson tells me I have you to thank for all of this. Can't begin to explain how much it means to me."

"The look on your face when everything's said and done... That's all the thanks I'll ever need." Savannah's attention turned to members of the band finally arriving. "I look forward to chatting with you at length later, but right now I need to show the musicians where to set up. Excuse me."

They both watched as she approached the band and guided them to the stage.

"I see why you're so taken with her, son." The old man chuckled. "You go on and take care of whatever it is you need to." His grandfather smiled at Zora, who was walking toward them. "My granddaughter will keep me company until you return."

Blake drove the short distance to the distillery. He retrieved the small crate from Savannah's desk and checked to make sure the badge and her phone were there.

Her phone buzzed, indicating a text message. The message scrolled across the screen, capturing his attention.

It's been two months. Give up and come home. I feel icky lying to Gramps. Giving you one week. Won't do it anymore.

Blake scanned the screen quickly before the message disappeared. It was from Savannah's sister, Laney.

A rock formed in Blake's gut.

What did Laney want Savannah to give up? Her job at the distillery? Her relationship with Blake? And why was Savannah asking her sister to lie to their grandfather?

Uneasiness skittered along his spine.

Blake couldn't ignore the text. His feelings aside, if there was a risk of Savannah leaving them in the lurch, he needed to know. They'd scheduled a year's worth of events to celebrate the King's Finest jubilee. Savannah was the point person on every one of them.

What if there was a simple, harmless explanation?

Savannah would be furious he'd read her private text message. Even if he'd done so inadvertently.

Blake had been burned before by getting involved with someone who wasn't as committed to the relationship as he was. Perhaps Savannah's reluctance to take their relationship public went beyond worries over her career.

And then there was the day she'd been in his home office, ostensibly to find a pen. Could there have been another reason?

Blake groaned.

He was being paranoid. Admittedly, her sister's text message didn't look good. But it wasn't as if Savannah had initiated a relationship with him. Or even wanted to come back to his house that night. Both had been his idea.

Blake grabbed the crate and returned to his truck. Whatever the truth was, he'd find a way to get to the bottom of it.

Sixteen

Savannah sat down at the bar for a moment and ordered an energy drink.

Most of the night's pomp and circumstance had already played out. The Abbott family had taken the stage and thanked everyone—including the town of Magnolia Lake—for its support for the past half century. A handful of celebs, business executives and longtime employees had shared anecdotes about King's Finest bourbon.

A few other big names circulated throughout the crowd. They mixed it up with employees, townsfolk, distributors and the numerous reporters she'd invited.

Savannah had been moving at warp speed for the past seventy-two hours. It wasn't surprising she was tired. But tonight, she was unusually exhausted. And she'd felt slightly nauseous all day.

She finished her energy drink. Then she ordered a ginger ale to allay the queasiness.

"Everything okay?" Blake sat beside her.

There was something going on with him. He'd been slightly aloof since he brought the crate to her.

She'd tried to create distance between them in their public dealings. But there was something about Blake's sudden indifference that made her feel she was standing naked in a blizzard, desperate to come in from the cold.

Blake wore the expensive sand-colored suit and navy-and-white gingham-check shirt she'd selected for him during a recent visit to Nashville. It suited the man and the occasion. Serious and elegant with a bit of playfulness beneath the refined surface.

"Everything is fine. It's just been a really long couple of days. I'm a little run-down."

"Anything else wrong?" He turned slowly on the bar stool to face her. For the first time, he was sizing her up.

Judging her.

A chill ran down Savannah's spine. She wasn't imagining it. Something was wrong. Had she left an incriminating note on her desk?

Impossible.

She didn't handwrite notes about the Abbotts or the distillery. She captured digital notes in her phone.

My phone.

It'd been in the box Blake delivered to her. Had he gone through it and found her notes?

Savannah forced a smile. No point in panicking without good reason. That would only make her seem guilty.

"Everything is good. Nearly everyone who RSVP'd made it. All of the staff and musical acts showed up. Things are running smoothly." As she spoke, Savannah inwardly ticked off possible reasons for Blake's change in attitude. "People seem to be enjoying themselves, especially your grandfather."

"Haven't seen him that emotional since my grandmother died ten years ago." Blake's stony expression softened. His eyes met hers. "I can't thank you enough for giving him all this."

Savannah's spine was as stiff as her smile. When she'd proposed this event, she'd hoped it would be the night she humiliated the Abbotts. The night when she pulled back the curtain and revealed the ugly truth that they were cruel, heartless liars and thieves who'd taken credit for her grandfather's work.

"My pleasure." Savannah finished her ginger ale and stood. "I have to go powder my nose." Her bladder was clearly unable to keep up with the amount of liquids she'd consumed throughout the day. "See you later."

Blake caught her hand in his and pulled her closer. He

searched her eyes, as if seeking an answer to some burning question.

"What is it, Blake?" Savannah glanced around, her cheeks hot. She ignored the bartender's sly grin. "There's obviously something you want to say."

He averted his gaze. "Wrong place. Wrong time." He nodded toward the restrooms. "We can talk later."

Savannah made a beeline for the bathroom. But she couldn't help thinking that whatever it was Blake wanted to ask her would be the beginning of the end.

As Savannah exited the restroom, a hand reached out from the doorway of the back office and pulled her inside. She immediately recognized the scent and the hard body pressed against her.

"What on earth is going on?" Savannah whispered angrily. Blake had nearly given her a heart attack.

"We need to talk, and I'd rather do it without my mother and sister staring at us."

"Why would they be staring at us? Wait… Does your mother suspect, too?"

Blake didn't respond.

"That's why she's been looking at me like that all night. Why didn't you tell me?"

"That's not the pressing issue right now." Blake was agitated.

Her heart beat faster. "What is?"

"What's happening between us… It isn't a game for me. And regardless of what you say, this isn't just about sex for you, either." He took a deep breath. "So I want you to tell me the truth. Is there something you're keeping from me?"

Savannah's blood ran cold, and her throat was dry.

"What are you asking me, Blake?"

"Are you unhappy at King's Finest?" He frowned.

"Of course not. I told you, I belong here. I've never had a job I enjoyed more."

"Are you entertaining another job offer?"

Savannah felt a sense of relief. "How could you ask me that? Hasn't tonight's gala proven how important this company is to me?"

"It would appear so. Still—"

"Still…what?" Savannah wouldn't blink first. If Blake thought he knew something, he'd have to ask her directly. She wouldn't volunteer information unnecessarily and compromise the mission. Not when she finally had a chance to question Joseph Abbott.

Blake gripped her shoulder, his fingers warm against her skin. His eyes demanded the truth. Something she couldn't give him.

Not yet.

"Savannah, it's been a long time since I cared this much for anyone. So if this doesn't mean the same to you, tell me now. Before I get in deeper."

Her hands trembled. Blake's expression was so sincere. It reminded her of all the things she adored about him.

Why did she have to hurt him?

"I… I…" She swallowed what felt like a lump of coal. "I can't answer that right now. Please, give me some time. This relationship is still new. What's the rush?"

"Is that what this is, Savannah? A relationship?"

"Yes." She nodded, pushing her hair behind her ear. "And it's all I can offer right now. Please, just be patient."

Blake palmed her bottom and pulled her closer. His mouth crashed against hers in a searing kiss that took her breath away.

Her body filled with heat. The hardened tips of her breasts were hypersensitive as they grazed his rock-solid chest.

"Blake…" Her objection died on his lips.

He turned her around, jerking her against him. His erection was pinned between them. Blake squeezed her full breasts. They felt tender, almost sore. Yet she craved more of his touch.

"I've never wanted anyone the way I want you, Savannah." His voice was thick as he trailed kisses along her shoulder. His beard sensitized her skin.

He kissed the back of her neck, his hand lightly gripping her throat. Blake hiked her skirt and glided his hand up her inner thigh. He palmed the drenched space between her thighs.

She moaned with pleasure as he ran firm fingers back and forth over the silky material that shielded her sex.

When Blake kissed her ear, Savannah nearly lost all control. Her knees quivered as Blake slipped his hand inside the fabric. Her flesh was so sensitive she could barely stand it.

"Blake, yes. Please."

She needed him inside her. Her mind was so clouded with lust, she didn't care about the risk they were both taking.

She only cared about Blake Abbott making love to her. Making her feel as only he could. As if there was no one in the world but the two of them.

Blake unfastened his pants and freed himself. She lifted her skirt higher to accommodate him as he shifted her panties aside and pressed his thick head to her slick entrance.

Savannah nearly lost it when he massaged her clit.

She pressed back against him, needing him inside her.

"You sure about this, baby?" Blake breathed the words in her ear.

She nodded, wanting desperately to bear down on his thick length. She hadn't missed a single day of her birth control since the storm.

With one hand still moving over her sensitive flesh, he grabbed the base of his shaft with the other. He pressed himself inside her.

They both groaned with pleasure.

Whatever happened between them later, they would always have moments like this.

Moments in which she couldn't deny how much she cared for him. That she was falling in love with him. And maybe he was falling in love with her, too.

Savannah braced herself against a cabinet as Blake brought her closer to the edge. His hand moved over her slick flesh as he thrust inside her. Taking them both higher.

Her legs trembled and her whimpers grew louder. Blake clamped a hand over her mouth, muffling her cries as he whispered in her ear, telling her all of the deliciously dirty things he wanted to do to her once he got her back to his place.

The sounds of people laughing and talking outside the door didn't deter either of them from their singular goal: to bring each other pleasure.

Savannah was floating higher. Dizzy with her desire for him. Finally, pleasure exploded in her core. She shuddered, weak and trembling, muttering his name against his rough palm still pressed to her lips.

Soon afterward, Blake stiffened, cursing and moaning. He held her in his arms, their chests heaving and their breath ragged. Both of them seemed reluctant to be separated from the other's warmth.

He'd made her feel incredible. Yet she was quickly overcome by a wave of sadness. Tears burned the backs of her eyelids.

Would this be the last time he'd hold her, make love to her?

"I'll leave first," he said after they'd made themselves presentable. "Wait a few minutes before you come out."

Blake reached for the doorknob. He paused and turned back to her. "Are you sure you don't need to tell me anything?"

She shook her head, her heart breaking. "Nothing at all."

It was a lie from which they would never recover.

Eyebrows drawn together and lips pursed, he turned

and slipped out of the door, leaving her alone with the bitter tears that spilled down her cheeks.

When she got back to the party, Savannah hid in the shadows near the back of the room, trying to regain her composure and make sense of the change in Blake's mood. Her skin prickled and her breasts still throbbed from her encounter with Blake.

"This is quite the affair you've orchestrated, young lady."

Savannah nearly dropped her clipboard and cell phone. "Mr. Abbott."

Joseph Abbott stood beside Savannah as she surveyed the crowd, the smell of bourbon heavy on his breath. "My granddaughter tells me that even the decision to renovate this old barn was your idea."

Savannah's fists clenched so tightly she wouldn't have been surprised if blood dripped from her palms. Her throat seized, rendering her mute. She swallowed hard, forced herself to smile in the face of the devil who'd been the catalyst for every devastating thing that had happened in their lives.

"Yes, sir. It was. I'm thrilled you're pleased." Once the muscles of her larynx relaxed enough for her to speak, she oozed warmth. Like honey. Sticky and sweet. Because she was more apt to catch a fly with honey than vinegar. "I must admit, I'm obsessed with the story of how you started King's Finest all those years ago with nothing more than your father's bourbon recipe and his moonshine stills."

There was a flash of something across the old man's face. Sorrow? Regret? Whatever it was, for an instant, he looked every bit of his seventy-plus years.

"It's not that simple, I'm afraid. Nothing worthwhile ever is. I had the support of my family. Of people who helped me make this happen."

Savannah turned to the man. Her heart racing. "Like who?"

His gaze didn't meet hers. There was a far-off look in his eyes. One that would've made her feel sorry for the old man, if he hadn't destroyed her family's lives.

He didn't answer her, and for a moment they both stood in silence.

"My father died in a car accident when I was young. I wanted to revive his moonshine business, but I didn't know much about it. I partnered with someone who could teach me the ropes."

Savannah's stomach churned. Her fingers and toes tingled. Time seemed to slow.

She was finally going to get her proof from the mouth of Joseph Abbott himself. Savannah turned on the recording app on her phone.

"There's no mention of a partner in the company story on the website." Or anywhere else she'd looked.

"We dissolved the partnership before I incorporated King's Finest."

That explained why Savannah hadn't been able to find proof that her grandfather was a partner in the distillery.

But if Joseph Abbott had used her grandfather's recipe, wouldn't that still give him claim to part of the company's profits?

"Who was your partner, Mr. Abbott?"

The seconds of silence between them seemed to stretch for an eternity.

Joseph Abbott rubbed his forehead, finally raising his gaze to hers.

"Forgive me, Miss Carlisle. I'm afraid this lovely affair has been a bit too much excitement for an old man like me after my travels yesterday."

"But, Mr. Abbott—"

"Please, excuse me." The old man nodded his goodbye, then made his way across the room to where Duke and Iris stood.

Savannah's belly clenched and her hands shook. She'd

been so close to learning the truth. To getting the information she needed to change her family's fortune.

She'd pushed too hard and spooked the old man. Now he'd never tell her the truth. Worse, there was a wary look in his eye before he'd fled. As if he'd seen her intentions.

Joseph Abbott wouldn't tell her anything more.

Savannah wiped away the hot tears that leaked from her eyes. Giving up wasn't an option. Not when she was this close. She'd find another way.

Her phone buzzed. It was a text message from Laney.

Did you get my previous text?

Laney knew how important the gala was to her. She'd obviously forgotten this was the night of the event. Otherwise, she wouldn't have expected a timely reply.

Savannah scrolled up the message chain.

It's been two months. Give up and come home. I feel icky lying to Gramps. Giving you one week. Won't do it anymore.

If her grandfather learned what she'd been doing, he'd insist that she stop putting herself at risk by working in what he referred to as "a den of hyenas."

Just when she was so close to finding answers.

Savannah quickly typed a reply.

Please think about what you'll be doing, Laney. I'm so close. Nearly got Joseph Abbott to admit everything just moments ago.

Savannah stared at her phone, as if that would make Laney's response come any faster.

Another alert came.

Two weeks. No more.

Savannah huffed. That didn't give her much time, but two weeks was better than one.

It was time to beat the Abbotts at their own game. She'd have the same level of callous disregard for them as Joseph Abbott had for her grandfather. She'd be as ruthless as Duke Abbott had been when he'd acquired Kayleigh Jemison's family property for a song.

She'd do whatever it took to resolve the issue once and for all.

Even if the truth would hurt Blake.

Seventeen

Blake stood at the window in his office, watching as a gentle breeze stirred the water on the lake. He shut his eyes for a moment, but it made no difference.

Eyes wide open or tightly shut, Savannah Carlisle had taken up residence in his head.

Blake groaned and returned to his chair. He finished his third cup of coffee and scrolled through his emails.

He'd made a couple of phone calls and answered a few emails. Otherwise, he'd gotten very little done. Instead, he'd been rehashing Laney's text message to Savannah. He imagined a dozen different scenarios her message could have alluded to. None of them good.

Blake picked up his desk phone to call Savannah. She'd been avoiding him since the night of the gala, more than a week before. And she'd made every excuse imaginable for why she couldn't come to his place.

Regardless of the consequences, they had to have this conversation. He'd confess to reading the text message and demand an explanation.

The door to his office burst open.

Blake hung up the phone. "Parker, don't you ever knock?"

His brother slipped into a chair on the other side of his desk, not acknowledging his complaint. "We need to talk."

"About what?"

"About whom," Parker corrected him. "Savannah."

Blake's spine stiffened and the muscles in his back tensed. He took another gulp of his coffee and shrugged. "What about her?"

"I'm concerned."

"About?"

Parker leaned forward, his voice lowered. "She's been asking a lot of questions."

"She's inquisitive. That's her nature." Blake had expected Parker to let him have it with both barrels over his affair with Savannah. "I'd say it's served us well."

Parker stood and paced. "It has when she's used it for us, not against us."

Blake sat on the edge of his desk. "What are you talking about?"

"She's been asking a lot of questions about our company. About how it got started and whether Gramps ever had a partner. Why is she suddenly so interested?"

"She works here." An uneasy feeling crawled up Blake's spine. Still, he folded his arms and shrugged. "That information could be useful as she prepares for the remaining jubilee events and news coverage."

"But why is she so fixated on some nonexistent business partner of Granddad's?" Parker shoved a finger in his direction.

That was odd. If she wanted to know, why hadn't she just asked him? It was one more thing they needed to discuss.

"I'll get to the bottom of it, Parker. Don't worry. Besides, it's not as if we have anything to hide." Blake studied his brother's face. "Do we?"

"No, but I still don't like it. Feels like she's got her own agenda. One that isn't aligned with ours." Parker sank into his chair again.

"Then why come to me? Dad's CEO of the company, and she reports directly to Max." Blake's eyes didn't meet his brother's.

"You hired Savannah, and I know…" Parker ratcheted down the judgment in his voice. "I know how fond you are of her."

Blake's jaw tensed. "I'd never jeopardize this company. Nor will I allow anyone else to. So if you think we have reason to be wary of Savannah…"

"That's not what I'm saying." Parker crossed an ankle over his knee.

"Then what are you saying?" Blake pressed his brother. If he was going to make an accusation against Savannah, he'd damn sure better be clear about it.

Parker tapped on the arm of the chair. "One of us needs to find out exactly what she's trying to uncover and why."

"Are you willing to possibly burn this bridge?" It was the same question he'd been forced to decide where he and Savannah were concerned.

"Dammit, Blake, none of us wants to lose her." Parker sighed heavily. "She's been good for us. Made a major impact in a short period of time. But our first job is to protect this distillery, and to protect the family. Even if that means losing Savannah."

Blake nodded. "Let's talk to Max about this when he returns from Philly tomorrow. Then we'll decide how to approach it."

The situation between him and Savannah had just become exponentially more complicated. If he gave her an ultimatum on their relationship, and she turned him down, the company's inquiry into her behavior would seem like retaliation.

That would be devastating to their reputation. Something he'd never allow.

Eighteen

"I'm going on my dinner break now. Do you think I'll be able to clean your office when I return?" Maureen stood in the doorway in her housekeeping uniform, doing her best not to look annoyed.

"I'll try to finish up for the night before you come back." Savannah smiled at the woman, and she turned and left.

When the elevator doors closed, Savannah rushed to Maureen's cleaning cart.

Savannah had worked late every night since the gala, looking for her opportunity to search the archived files that predated the company's use of computers.

It was her last hope of finding something useful before her sister's looming two-week deadline.

Savannah retrieved the large key ring from Maureen's cart and made her way down to the file room. She tried nearly every key before she found the right one.

She slipped inside the large, windowless space and switched on her flashlight. The room smelled stale and dust floated in the air. Steel file cabinets lined the brick walls in the first portion of the room. Antique wooden furniture was pushed up against the back wall.

Savannah checked her watch. She had little more than half an hour. She moved to the file cabinet marked with the earliest dates and pulled out a drawer stuffed with yellowed files. Most of the papers were typed. Some were handwritten.

By his own admission, Joseph Abbott had dumped her grandfather as his partner before starting the company. Maybe the files contained information about the origin of the company's recipes and procedures.

Savannah checked her watch again and cursed under her breath. Fifteen minutes left.

She was dirty, sweaty, and had gotten several paper cuts during her frantic search through the files. She finally found a pad with notes written in familiar longhand.

Her grandfather's.

She removed the notebook and continued sifting through the files. Savannah opened an envelope marked "Old Photos." She recognized her grandfather in one of them. "Joe and Marty" was scribbled on the back.

Savannah froze at the sound of voices in the hall.

Someone's coming.

She quietly closed the drawer and hid in the shadows, crouching between a tall bookcase and a large antique bureau desk. She clutched her grandfather's notebook and the photo of her grandfather and Joseph Abbott.

Keys jangled in the door, and then the hinges creaked.

"Switch on the light. I just walked into a spiderweb."

Savannah's blood ran cold.

What's Parker doing here?

He'd never been her biggest fan, but lately he'd been grumpier and questioned everything she did.

Had he followed her down here?

The light switched on.

"So where's this stuff Mom just had to have tonight?"

Max. He'd left hours ago. Why had he returned? And what were they searching for?

Had her conversation with Joseph Abbott prompted them to destroy evidence of their theft?

"Mom had a few of the guys set the pieces she wants aside in the back."

Blake.

"Wait—do you guys smell that?" Blake sniffed, then glanced around the room. "Someone's been in here, and I know that scent."

Savannah pressed a hand to her mouth to muffle her

gasp. She was wearing the perfume Blake had bought her. Her heart beat furiously as footsteps crept closer.

Blake made his way through the maze of furniture until he was standing in front of her.

"Savannah, what are you doing in here? And why are you hiding?"

Her knees shook so badly she could barely stand. Blake didn't offer to help her up, so she braced herself on the wall and climbed to her feet.

"Blake, I'm so sorry." She could hardly get enough air into her lungs to say the words.

All three brothers stood in front of her.

"I knew something was going on with her." Parker's nostrils flared. His entire face had turned crimson. She got a chill from his arctic stare. "You aren't authorized to be down here. You're trespassing. You'd better have a damn good explanation for being here or I'm calling the sheriff."

Max almost looked amused. "Don't tell me this is how you've been spending all those late nights."

"I've never been down here before tonight. I swear."

"Why should we believe anything you say?" Parker demanded. "And where'd you get these keys?"

"From Maureen's cart. I recognize her key ring." The heartbreak in Blake's voice and the pained look in his eyes were unbearable.

Blake didn't deserve this. And nothing she could say would fix it.

"What's that you're holding?" Max asked.

"They're mine." She clutched the photo and notebook, her hands shaking.

"Hand them over." Blake held out his hand, his voice jagged.

Savannah released a long, agonizing breath. She had no choice. There were three of them and one of her. They weren't going to let her leave with the notebook and photo. She handed both items to Blake, who handed them to Max.

"That's it. I'm calling the sheriff. We'll have them search her. Who knows why she was down here or what else she might be hiding." Parker gestured wildly.

"Calm down, Park. Why don't we ask her what she's doing down here?" Max kept his voice calm. "Maybe Savannah has a logical explanation."

The three brothers turned to her.

Savannah stared at each of them, her gaze lingering on Blake's face. Tears stung her eyes and rolled down her cheeks.

"I was… I was looking for…" Savannah stammered.

She couldn't tell the Abbotts the truth. Not until she was sure she had solid documentation to support her grandfather's claim. Once they learned her reason for being there, they'd surely destroy any potential evidence.

The truth wasn't an option.

She'd tell them she was looking for info to use in the yearlong celebration of the company's inception.

"I came down here because…" Savannah snapped her mouth shut, stopped cold by the pain and disappointment in Blake's eyes.

She couldn't tell Blake the truth, but she wouldn't lie to him, either. Which left her out of options.

Savannah turned her attention to Parker. She held out the keys. "If you're going to call the sheriff, call him. I don't have anything else to say."

"Gladly." Parker pulled out his phone.

"Don't." Blake took the phone from him.

"Why not? We caught her stealing irreplaceable archival documents. Who knows what else she's taken since she's been here? She's obviously a thief." A vein twitched in Parker's forehead. "Likely a corporate spy. She was probably sent here by one of the Kentucky distilleries."

"Blake's right, Park. We don't need the bad publicity. It'll counter all the positive press we're getting now." Max clapped a hand on Parker's shoulder. "Most of it thanks to her."

"All right." Parker snatched the key ring from her open palm. "But I'm filing a complaint with the sheriff. So don't think of skipping town until everything has been accounted for."

"Of course." Savannah extricated herself from the small space, unable to bring herself to meet Blake's wounded gaze.

"Where do you think you're going?" Parker held up a hand, his large body blocking her exit. "A member of the security team will escort you to clean out your desk. It should go without saying that you're fired."

"Is that really necessary?" Blake turned to his brother.

"Very. Who knows what else she'll try to take on the way out," Parker insisted.

"No." Blake made it clear the topic wasn't up for debate. "We're not causing a scene. I'll walk her to her office, then to her car."

"Good idea." Max stuck his hand out. "Give me the key to your truck. Parker and I will load those tables and lamps Mama wanted for the barn."

Blake handed Max the truck key and took Maureen's keys from Parker. He gripped Savannah's arm and led her out the door to the elevator.

"Blake, I can't tell you how sorry I am."

"Then don't." He wouldn't look at her. The tone of his voice was icier than Parker's eyes had been moments earlier. Shivers ran down her spine.

When they got on the elevator, she plastered her back against the wall.

"I never meant to hurt you, Blake, I swear. This isn't what it seems."

"Then what is it, Savannah? Do you have a reasonable explanation for stealing the housekeeper's key, breaking into our archives and cowering in the corner? If so, I'd love to hear it."

Her eyes met his, tears spilling down her cheeks. Her answer caught in her throat.

She'd imagined the misery of the day when Blake would learn she was a fraud. But the pain in his eyes and the pain exploding in her chest were so much worse.

For an instant, she wished she'd never come to Magnolia Lake. But if she hadn't, she wouldn't have uncovered the hand-scribbled notes and photo that proved her grandfather had worked closely with Joseph Abbott.

"I wish I could tell you everything…but I can't. Not yet."

"You lied to me. Made a fool of me."

She'd misled Blake. Taken him off guard. But he wasn't the fool. She was. Because she'd fallen for him. Hard.

"I had no choice. Believe me."

"I wish I could." He stepped off the elevator and led the way to her office.

"Blake, what are you doing here?" Maureen looked up from searching her cart.

"I had to retrieve something from the archives. I forgot my key." He held out her key ring. "Hope you don't mind— I borrowed yours."

Savannah's breath hitched.

Blake was protecting her, even now. Allowing her to save face with Maureen.

"Of course not." Maureen grinned as she accepted the keys from Blake and dropped them into the pocket of her smock. "I was afraid I'd lost them some—" Maureen paused, her head tilted. She'd noticed Savannah had been crying.

"Savannah isn't feeling very well." Blake spoke up before Maureen could inquire. "We'll be ten or fifteen minutes. Then we'll be out of your way."

"Hope you feel better, Savannah." Maureen nodded and rolled her cart away.

Blake closed the door and shoved his hands in his pockets. He leaned against the wall, maintaining maximum distance between them.

"I'll help you carry your things down." His voice was stripped of the warmth and affection she'd come to adore. He was looking through her. Past her. Probably wondering what it was he'd ever seen in her.

The wave of nausea she'd been feeling for the past week rose. Savannah grabbed a half-full bottle of ginger ale from her desk and chugged it.

She dropped her planner, phone and a few other items from her desk into her bag and grabbed her purse. She held it up. "This is everything. Do you need to check it?"

Blake sighed, as if repulsed by, then resigned to, the idea of needing to search her.

He did a cursory search through the two bags she held open. Then he patted her pockets while she held her arms out wide and turned her back to him.

"One more thing." Savannah pulled a small package from her desk drawer and handed it to Blake. "I've been meaning to give this to you. It's one of those calming shirts for Benny, so he doesn't freak out during the next thunderstorm. Unfortunately, they didn't have one in my size."

Her crushed heart inflated the slightest bit when a small smile curled the edge of Blake's sensuous mouth.

The same mouth that had kissed hers. That was acquainted with her most intimate parts.

"Why didn't I see this coming?" Blake laughed bitterly as he scanned her office. "Your office is as nondescript as your apartment. No family photos. Nothing personal. You never intended to put down roots here. You used me, and I was such a fool that I begged you to do it."

Tears stung her eyes again and her nose burned. But Savannah bit her lower lip, refusing to let the tears fall. She had no right to cry. In this, she'd been the one who was heartless and cruel. Blake had been innocent.

And she'd hurt him. Just as his ex had. Only Savannah

was worse. She'd always known this was inevitable. That they would both be hurt.

It was a sacrifice she'd been willing to make for her family.

As Blake's eyes searched hers, demanding an answer, her conviction that the sacrifice was worthwhile wavered.

"I know you don't believe me, but I honestly didn't intend to hurt you. I swear." She swiped angrily at her eyes and sniffed.

"Say I'm crazy enough to believe that's true." His voice vibrated with pain and anger. "Then tell me why you did this. What did you hope to gain?"

Savannah lowered her head, unable to answer him. She'd betrayed Blake and lost the best man she'd ever known. And without the notepad and photo, she didn't have a single thing to show for it.

Nineteen

Savannah pulled the covers over her head, blocking out the sunshine spilling through the curtains. It was nearly noon and she'd spent the entire morning in bed for the second day in a row.

She was stressed, scared, miserable and missing Blake. Her body wasn't handling the wave of emotions well. It rebelled.

She'd made countless trips to the bathroom and felt so tired and weak she could barely get out of bed. All of which was out of character for her. She prided herself on being able to endure just about anything. After watching their rattrap apartment burn to the ground with her parents inside, there was little else that could faze her.

Until now.

The attachment she felt to Blake Abbott was powerful. Unlike anything she'd experienced before.

She'd been in a handful of relationships. She'd even imagined herself to be in love once or twice before. But the end of those relationships hadn't shaken her to her core, the way losing Blake had.

She missed his intense, dark eyes, mischievous grin and sense of humor. She missed the comfort she felt in his presence—even if all they were doing was watching a movie together in silence.

Savannah clutched at the hollowed-out emptiness in her belly. She'd lost Blake and a job she actually loved. And she'd gained nothing. Except possibly an arrest record if Parker Abbott had his way.

She made another trip to the bathroom. After more retching, she rinsed her mouth and splashed cool water on her face, sure there was nothing left for her body to reject.

Savannah crawled back into bed and dialed her sister.

"Thought you weren't talking to me anymore." There was a smile in Laney's voice when she answered the phone.

Savannah was about to make a smart remark in reply, but the instant she heard her sister's voice, tears welled in her eyes. She whimpered softly.

"Savannah? What is it? What's wrong?"

Savannah told her sister about everything, including her relationship with Blake and how she'd hurt him.

"You're in love with him, aren't you?"

Savannah cried harder, unable to answer the question.

"Vanna, why would you do something so risky?"

"I only had two weeks to make something happen, so I switched to a more aggressive approach."

"Will the Abbotts press charges?"

"I don't know. Blake and Max won out against Parker that night. But in a full family meeting, I don't know if the two of them will be enough. If they don't take legal action, it'll only be because they don't want the bad publicity."

Her chest ached with the pain of letting down her family and losing Blake.

Why does it hurt so badly when he was never really mine?

Savannah hated herself for descending into a weepy, hot mess. She was the one who'd always taken care of Laney. Like she'd promised her father when she was a girl.

"What did Blake say when you told him about Granddad's claim?"

"I didn't tell him." Savannah dabbed her face with a tissue. "It would blow any chance of us getting proof down the road."

"What did you tell him?"

"Nothing. I couldn't look in his face and lie."

"You pleaded the fifth?" Laney groaned. "No wonder you nearly ended up in jail."

"And I still might."

"I'm sorry, Savannah. I know you'd hoped for a different outcome, but at least this is over and you can come back home. Harper and I miss you."

"Yeah." Savannah's response was flat. She hadn't expected to fall in love with Magnolia Lake and its town full of quirky people. But she'd begun to enjoy her life there. "Miss you, too."

"Wait… You haven't just fallen for Blake. You actually like living there, don't you? And I know you loved your job. No wonder you're miserable."

"And sick as a dog. Plus, I promised not to leave town until I get the okay from Parker and the sheriff."

Laney was silent for a few beats. "You're sick how?"

"A virus maybe. I've been run-down and exhausted. Nauseous. Haven't been able to keep my breakfast down the last couple of days." Savannah burrowed under the covers again. She felt nauseous just talking about it.

"Sweetie, you aren't late, are you?"

"For work? You do realize they fired me?"

"Not that kind of late."

"Oh!" Savannah bolted upright in bed when Laney's meaning sank in. "I can't be. We used protection and I'm on the pill."

"Protection isn't foolproof. Nor are the people who use it. Besides, if you slept with him that weekend you got trapped there by the storm…well, did you suddenly start carrying your birth control around with you?"

Savannah's forehead broke into a cold sweat. They both knew the answer to that question. She hadn't had her pills with her that weekend. And then there was that night they'd fallen asleep with the condom on.

"Shit."

"What is it?"

"I need to make a trip to the pharmacy."

"So there is a chance you might be pregnant."

"Can you at least *pretend* not to be excited about the

prospect?" Savannah paced the floor. "This entire situation is already a disaster. How on earth would I explain this to Blake?"

"Tell him the truth."

"Everything?" The thought made Savannah nauseous again. "Once he learns the truth, he'll never believe I didn't plan this."

"It's your only play here."

Savannah's chin trembled and tears flowed down her face. "Blake will never forgive me for what I've done. For how I hurt him."

"Calm down, honey. It isn't good for the baby if you're stressed out."

"Pump your brakes, sister." Savannah stopped pacing. "We don't know there is a baby."

The grin returned to Delaney's voice. "Well, it's time you find out."

"Did the lessons on knocking before entering begin and end with me?" Blake looked up from his computer as his brother Max slid into the seat on the other side of his desk.

"I need to tell you something, and it couldn't wait." Max's brows drew together with concern.

It had to be about Savannah.

"Did Mom and Dad decide whether to press charges?"

"Not yet, but I discovered something and I wanted to tell you before I tell the rest of the family."

"What is it?" Blake's heart thumped against his rib cage.

"Since Savannah wouldn't tell us why she was in the archives or why she wanted that photo and notepad, I did some digging."

"And?"

"The photo was of Gramps and a man named Martin McDowell. The notepad was his, too. Did she ever mention the name to you?"

"No." Blake shrugged. "Who is he, and why would she want his old stuff?"

"This is only a copy." Max handed him a file. "But I'm sure Gramps has the original locked away somewhere safe."

Blake quickly scanned the document, reading it three times. It felt like a cannonball had been launched into his chest. Blake fell back against his chair, speechless.

"Marty McDowell was Granddad's partner in the moonshine business. *Before* he opened the distillery," Max said.

"I had no idea he had a partner." Blake rubbed the back of his neck. "But that still doesn't explain why Savannah would want the guy's old stuff."

"I couldn't explain it, either, so I looked at her employee file. Take a close look at her birth certificate." Max indicated the file folder he'd given Blake earlier.

Blake studied the birth certificate carefully.

"Her mother's maiden name was McDowell." His heart thundered in his chest. "She's Martin McDowell's grand-daughter."

Blake dragged a hand across his forehead. He really had been a fool. Savannah Carlisle wasn't interested in him in the least. She'd used him to get information about the distillery and their processes. And to gain access to his grand-father—the company's founder. She'd talked to him the night of the gala.

"McDowell must've sent her here to spy on us." Max leaned forward, his elbows on his knees.

"But why? What did they hope to gain?" Blake racked his brain for a reason.

"Sabotage?"

Blake rubbed at his throbbing temples. Savannah was clever and resourceful. If she'd come to work for them with a plan to sabotage the distillery and its reputation, there were any number of ways she could've done it. Yet she hadn't. Why?

"If sabotage was their aim, they're playing the long game. Because everything Savannah has done since she's been working for us has boosted our sales and gotten us good press."

"Hmm…that's difficult to explain." Max leaned back in his chair and perched his chin on his fist. "Guess there's only one way to find out exactly why she came here."

"You want me to talk to Savannah?"

"If you can't handle it…no problem." Max shrugged nonchalantly. "I'm sure Parker would be happy to do it."

"No." Blake shot to his feet, then cursed silently when Max chuckled. He sighed. "You knew I wouldn't let Parker do it."

"You care for Savannah, and she obviously cares for you. Maybe you can turn up that charm you think you have and get some straight answers from her."

Blake sank into his chair again and blew out a long, slow breath. He'd spent the past two days trying to scrub every happy memory of Savannah Carlisle from his brain.

It was an abysmal failure.

Her laugh and broad smile crept into his daydreams. At night, he'd been tormented by memories of her body—naked, in all its glory. Her gentle touch. The sound she made when she was close. The way she'd called his name.

Blake had cared deeply for Savannah. He'd been willing to break the rules for her. But she'd used him and was ready to toss him aside, while he'd been prepared to give her his heart.

"Look, I don't know what's been going on with you two." Max's voice stirred Blake from his thoughts. "Frankly, I don't need to know. But if talking to Savannah would be too difficult for you, it's okay. I'll talk to her."

"No." Blake's objection was much softer this time. "I'll try to get the truth out of her."

"Sorry things didn't work out." Max clapped a hand on his shoulder. "We all liked Savannah. Even Parker, in his own way. That's why he's so angry."

"Thanks, Max. I'll let you know what I find out."

When Max left, Blake loosened his top button and heaved a sigh. He was ready to face Savannah again. Only this time, he was the one who held all the cards.

Twenty

Savannah sat on the edge of the tub, rooted to the same spot she'd been in for the past ten minutes. She'd taken three different pregnancy tests. Each had given her the same answer.

I'm pregnant.

Savannah got up and stood in front of the mirror, staring at her image. Red, puffy eyes. Hair pulled into a frizzy, low ponytail.

She looked a hot mess, had no job and had let down everyone who cared about her. Her grandfather, Laney, Harper and Blake.

Now she was growing a human being inside of her. A tiny little person for whom she'd be responsible.

Savannah braced her hands against the sink, her head throbbing and her knees unsteady.

I'm going to be a mother.

Being a parent wasn't something Savannah had ever really considered. Not the way Laney had. Yet the moment she'd seen the word *Pregnant* on that third test, she knew instantly she wanted this baby.

Suddenly, nothing was more important than her child. And there was one thing Savannah knew for sure. She'd never use this child as leverage against Blake and his family.

She'd tell Blake about the baby, because he deserved to know. But only once a doctor had confirmed the test results.

She owed Blake the truth. And she owed her child the chance to know its father—if that was what Blake wanted.

After Savannah called her sister to relay the news, she stared at the phone in her hand. She wished she could call Blake and tell him they were going to be parents. And that he'd be genuinely happy about it.

She decided to call her grandfather instead. She wouldn't

tell him where she'd really been or about the baby. Not until she was 100 percent sure. But she needed the comfort of hearing his voice.

Still, she couldn't help thinking about her grandfather's reaction when he learned the identity of his great-grandchild's father.

How do I explain this to him?

Savannah screwed her eyes shut. Her grandfather would be hurt and angry. Of all the men in the world, she'd chosen to make a child with an Abbott.

His mortal enemies.

Savannah wiped angrily at the tears that wouldn't stop falling. No matter how much the truth would hurt her grandfather, she wouldn't lie.

She was exhausted by deception. Weary from trying to walk the line between truth and an outright lie.

When she returned to West Virginia, she'd tell her grandfather everything.

Before she could dial his number, there was a knock at the door.

Kayleigh.

Savannah hadn't moved her car or left the apartment in two days. Until this morning, when she'd made her run to the pharmacy looking a disheveled mess. Kayleigh would have noticed and been worried.

Plus, it was Magnolia Lake. News of her firing was probably all over town by now.

Savannah counted to three and opened the door.

"Blake?" Her heart nearly stopped.

He was as handsome as ever in a pair of gray dress pants and a baby blue checkered shirt. Yet there was something in his face and eyes. He looked tired and as miserable as she felt.

"What are you doing here? Did your family decide to—"

"Nothing's been decided yet." His response was curt. "That's why we need to talk. Now."

Savannah let him in. "Have a seat."

"No, thank you. I won't be long."

Another wave of nausea rolled over her. She sat on the sofa, her legs folded beneath her as Blake paced the floor.

Finally, he turned and glared at her.

"I'm so angry with you, Savannah. I don't know where to begin."

She chewed on her lower lip. "Then let me start by saying I am truly sorry. I honestly never meant to hurt you. Even before I knew—"

"How easily you could manipulate me?"

That hurt.

"Before I knew what an incredible man you are. That you'd never purposely hurt anyone. I was wrong about you."

"Not as wrong as I was about you." He dropped into the chair across from her, as if his legs had buckled from the weight of the animosity he was carrying.

"I deserve that."

"You're damn right you do." His eyes blazed. "You're not the first corporate spy we've encountered. But none of them seemed willing to take things as far as you did."

"I didn't intend to get involved with you. I came here to do a job. And maybe in the beginning, I didn't care who got hurt. But then I got to know you. All of you. Suddenly, things weren't so simple."

"Not that you let that stop you."

"There was too much at stake. I couldn't let my feelings for you get in the way."

His steely gaze cut through her. "You still haven't told me why you did this. What was your endgame?"

"You wouldn't understand." Savannah went to the kitchen and poured herself a glass of ginger ale.

He stood, too, and turned to her, his arms folded. "Try me."

"Why does it matter?" She put the glass down roughly.

"What I did was wrong, but I swear to you, I did it for an honorable reason."

They stared at each other in silence. They were playing a game of chicken and waiting for the other person to blink.

Savannah walked around Blake, back toward the couch.

"How's your grandfather?"

She froze, then glanced over her shoulder at him. The hair stood on the back of her neck and her hands trembled. He wasn't making a friendly inquiry about her family.

Blake knew who she really was.

Still, she wouldn't blink first. "I was about to call him before you arrived."

"Why? To tell him his little spy got pinched?" Blake shook his head. "What kind of man would send his granddaughter to do his dirty work for him?"

"My grandfather didn't send me." She folded her arms over her chest. "He'd never have allowed me to put myself in jeopardy this way."

"You expect me to believe Martin McDowell didn't send you here? That he was oblivious to your little plan?"

"It's the truth."

Blake stepped closer. "Your word doesn't hold water around here anymore."

Savannah lowered her gaze. Her voice was softer. "Grandpa didn't know, I swear."

"Maybe we're going after the wrong person." Blake folded his arms and rocked back on his heels. "The marionette instead of the puppet master."

"No, please…my grandfather didn't have anything to do with this. It was all me. My sister can testify to that."

"And was she involved, too?"

"Laney never wanted me to come here, and she's been begging me to give up and come home."

Blake rubbed his chin. "You want to keep them out of this? Then tell me the truth. Why did you come here? What does Martin McDowell have against our family?"

Savannah fought back tears. If she showed her hand to the Abbotts, she'd lose the element of surprise and jeopardize any chance of making a claim against them. If she didn't, her sister and grandfather would be pulled into the mess she'd made.

"Tell me the truth, Savannah, or I swear I'll do whatever it takes to make your grandfather pay for this."

"It isn't my grandfather who needs to pay for his sins." She blinked back the tears that made Blake a blur. "It's yours."

Twenty-One

"What are you talking about?" Blake returned Savannah's defiant gaze. Her expression had morphed from fear and concern to righteous indignation.

"I'm talking about how he betrayed my grandfather. Cheated him. Is stealing from him even now."

Now Blake was furious. He knew his grandfather well, had worked beside him as long as he could remember, learning the business of making premium bourbon. He had so much affection for the old man. Joseph Abbott was a generous and loving man, and a pillar in his adopted community of Magnolia Lake, where he'd raised his children and grandchildren.

"How dare you accuse my grandfather of being—"

"A thief."

"That's a lie. My grandfather didn't steal anything from anyone. Why would he need to? He's a wealthy man. He can buy whatever he wants."

"He's a wealthy man *because* he's a thief." Savannah stepped closer. "Why don't you ask him where he got that recipe for his world-renowned bourbon?"

"That's what you were looking for? The recipe for our bourbon."

"Unlike most distilleries from here to Kentucky, you've taken great pains to conceal your grain bill." Her tone was accusatory.

"Even if you had our mash bill, that's only part of the recipe. There's the water source, our proprietary yeast strain and so many other factors."

"Then why is it so top secret, Blake? Ask yourself, and really, truly allow yourself to consider the answer. No matter where it leads you."

"No." Blake ran a hand through his hair. "Gramps would never do that. He'd never steal someone else's work. If you knew anything about him, about his work ethic, you'd know that's not possible."

"Let's forget about your grandfather for a minute. Tell me how your father acquired the land you expanded on."

Blake narrowed his gaze. "The Calhouns' old place?"

"How'd your father acquire the property?" She repeated the question.

"Ownership fell to Mae Jemison—Kayleigh's mother. She was the last of the Calhouns still living around here. She sold the place to my father."

"You mean your father swindled her out of it. Paid her pennies on the dollar because Kayleigh's father was dying, and her mother needed the money to help her girls finish college."

"Who told you—" The question answered itself when he remembered he was standing in the middle of an apartment owned by Kayleigh Jemison.

That explained why Kayleigh had been so cold toward his family since she'd returned to town a few years earlier. Not that she'd had any great love for them before. She and Parker had bumped heads for as long as he could remember.

Still, he had no idea Kayleigh harbored such ill will against them. Especially since they'd barely broken even at the time of the purchase, with the amount they'd had to invest in it.

"That property was an overgrown mess. It was littered with rusted, broken-down machinery and a couple of run-down shacks. Large tanks had been leaking fuel onto the property for years. It cost us a fortune to clean it up and make it usable again."

"Of course you'd say that." Savannah folded her arms.

The move framed her breasts, which looked fuller than he remembered. Or maybe it was his brain playing tricks on him. Making him want her even when he knew he shouldn't.

"It's true."

"Why would Kayleigh lie about it?"

He shrugged. "Maybe that's what her parents told her. Or maybe that's just what she chooses to believe. I don't know, but I do know my father. And he wouldn't have cheated them."

"You're just blind where your family is concerned." Savannah propped her hands on her hips. "The mighty Abbotts can do no wrong."

"Never said that. No one is perfect, and we've all made our fair share of mistakes."

He narrowed his gaze at her, chastising himself. Even now, what he regretted most was that he couldn't be with her.

"Maybe you should talk to your grandfather and father before you dismiss what I'm saying. Find out what they have to say to these accusations. You might not like what you hear."

Savannah turned around and bumped into the table, knocking her glass onto the floor, where it shattered.

She stood there, her hands shaking.

"Where do you keep the broom and dustpan?"

Savannah shook her head, as if she were coming out of a daze. She stooped to clean up the mess. "I've got it."

"You're in your bare feet." He gestured toward her. "You're going to—"

"Ouch." She lifted her bleeding foot; a shard of glass was embedded in it.

"Sit down," he instructed, glad she complied without further argument. "There must be a first-aid kit around here. Where is it?"

"In the linen closet in the hall." She drew her foot onto her lap and examined it.

Blake went to the hallway and opened the closet. He spotted the white metal box with red lettering on the top shelf. He pulled it down and looked inside. There were bandages, gauze, alcohol wipes and a few other items. He grabbed a clean washcloth and went to the bathroom to wet it. When he wrung it out, he knocked something to the floor.

Blake froze, his eyes focused on the white-and-blue stick. *A pregnancy test.*

His heart thudded against his rib cage. He retrieved it from the floor and read the word on the screen over and over. As if it would change if he read it one more time.

Savannah is pregnant.

Blake swallowed hard, his mouth dry. Was that the whole point of this game? For Savannah to bear an Abbott heir?

His head was in a dense fog and the room was spinning. He returned to the living room, his steps leaden.

He handed her the first-aid kit and washcloth. "You still haven't told me. What was your objective in coming here?"

Savannah seemed to sense the anger vibrating off him. She pulled a set of tweezers from the first-aid kit and tugged the piece of glass from her foot.

"To restore my grandfather's legacy and get what's owed to him."

"Money. That's what this is all about." He'd encountered lots of women whose only interest in him had been his family's fortune and name. Until now, he'd never imagined Savannah Carlisle was one of them. "That's all it's ever been about for you."

Her chin dropped to her chest and her eyes—already red and puffy—looked wet.

"Don't look at me as if I'm some moneygrubbing gold digger. I'm not here for a handout. I only want what's owed to my grandfather."

"You want King's Finest." His gut churned as the realization dawned on him. "That's why you've worked so hard to grow the company's sales. You hope to acquire it."

"Only the half that belongs to my grandfather." She sat taller, meeting his gaze. "We don't want anything we didn't earn."

"And how exactly is it that you *earned* half of King's Finest?"

"By providing your grandfather with the recipe he's used to build his fortune." She narrowed her gaze at him. "And I think I'm being generous in saying we're only entitled to half the company. A jury might make the argument that all of the profits should go to our family."

"Bullshit." Blake's face was hot and his heart beat like a war drum. "If you thought you had a legitimate claim, why not take it to court? Why all of the cloak-and-dagger corporate espionage?"

"My grandfather doesn't have any proof."

"If the recipe is his, it should be easy enough to prove." He gestured angrily. "Take a bottle of King's Finest to a chemist to see if his recipe and ours are the same."

"It isn't that simple." Savannah lowered her gaze, focusing on cleaning her wound and opening a bandage. "He no longer has the recipe. It got lost in the fire at our apartment."

"Why would your grandfather have entrusted something so important to someone else?"

Her cheeks reddened. "I… I don't know."

"Then how did you intend to prove that our bourbon recipe is his?" He stepped closer.

She bit her lower lip and avoided his gaze.

"Remember our deal? Tell me the truth, in its entirety. Or we'll go after your grandfather and sister, too."

Savannah repositioned herself on the sofa. "I hoped to find evidence that would corroborate Granddad's story."

"That's why you were in the archives that night. Looking for proof of your grandfather's involvement in creating the original recipe." Her expression confirmed his theory. "And did you find anything besides the photo and notepad?"

"No, but maybe if I'd had more time to search the files or to talk to more people—"

"Like my grandfather." Blake swallowed hard, remembering that his grandfather had looked perturbed and had gone home soon after his conversation with Savannah.

"What did my grandfather tell you?" Blake had an unsettling feeling in his gut.

"That he did have a partner in the moonshine business before he started King's Finest. I was *this* close to getting him to name my grandfather as the partner he left behind."

"I don't know what role your grandfather played, but my grandfather inherited that moonshine business from his father. And he kept his father's recipe."

"Your grandfather knew nothing about the business when his father died. He was too young. My grandfather taught him the business and tweaked the recipe."

"Even if that was true, you just said he helped tweak my great-grandfather's recipe. That still makes it *our* recipe."

Savannah blinked rapidly. It seemed she hadn't considered that before. "The courts will determine that."

"If you've known about this story all your life, why wait until now to try and get proof?"

"My grandfather is gravely ill." Her eyes filled with tears. "I couldn't bear the thought of him never realizing his dream. Never getting the recognition he deserved."

Blake sighed. For all he knew, they were a family of grifters who'd pulled this stunt on other wealthy families.

He could hear his mother's voice in his head. *And that's why we don't date employees, son.*

Savannah shoved her feet into a pair of shoes and got a broom and dustpan to clean up the glass.

She stooped to the floor, her short shorts providing an excellent view of her firm, round bottom.

He had zero self-control, which was exactly how he'd ended up in this mess in the first place.

She's a liar and a user. Best not forget that.

"Anything else you need to tell me?"

Savannah's shoulders stiffened. She shook her head and finished sweeping up the glass before returning to the sofa.

Blake's heart contracted in his chest. His limbs felt heavy.

He was desperate to believe some part of Savannah's story. To believe she'd been sincere in their moments of intimacy, which had evidently led to the conception of a child.

His child.

He wanted a reason to believe their relationship hadn't been part of Martin McDowell's calculated effort to swindle his family out of half their fortune.

But even now, when she'd agreed to put all her cards on the table and level with him, she wasn't capable of telling the complete truth.

Blake pulled the blue-and-white indicator from his back pocket. The one that declared the truth in a single, devastating word.

"Then how the hell do you explain this?"

Savannah gasped, her fingers pressed to her lips. "What are you doing with that?"

He ignored the question, asking one of his own. "Is it mine?"

Her head jerked, as if she'd been slapped. "Of course."

"You say that like I can just believe you, no questions asked." The pained look in his eye hurt even more than his question had. "How do I know this isn't part of the sick game you're playing?"

She felt the tears rising. "I'd never lie to you about this... about our child."

"You just did. I asked if there was anything else you needed to tell me and you said no. I'm pretty sure the fact that I might be a father qualifies as something I'd need to know."

"I wanted to be sure."

"There were two more of these in the garbage." His voice boomed, making her jump. "That wasn't confirmation enough?"

"I wanted indisputable confirmation from a doctor. I

didn't think you'd believe me otherwise. I was afraid you would think—"

"That this was your backup plan all along?"

Hot tears burned a trail down her face. She wiped at them angrily. "You don't honestly believe I'm capable of that."

Blake huffed, sinking onto the sofa beside her. "A few days ago, I wouldn't have believed you were capable of any of this. I was stupid enough to think you actually cared for me."

"Oh, Blake, I do." Savannah placed a hand on his arm, but pulled it away when he glared at her. "I never intended to get involved with you. But there you were. Handsome and funny. Sweet. Persistent." She wrapped her arms around herself, an inadvertent smile playing on her lips. "I honestly couldn't help falling in love with you."

She'd admitted she'd fallen in love with him, and he hadn't so much as blinked.

"Did you know about the baby the night we found you in the archives?"

"No." Her voice was barely a whisper. "I only found out this afternoon. I have the receipt from the drugstore across the street, if you don't believe me."

"I can't believe anything you've said, since the moment we met." Blake shot to his feet and paced.

"Everything I've told you is true. About my grandfather and parents. About my sister. Even my résumé. All of it's true. Check."

"Believe me, I will." He tossed the pregnancy test on the table in front of her and left, slamming the door behind him.

Twenty-Two

Blake left a trail of burned rubber in his wake as he exited the parking lot behind Savannah's apartment.

He was a complete idiot.

Savannah Carlisle had played him like a fiddle from the moment she'd first sashayed into his office.

She'd been smart and confident with just the right amount of Southern sass. She'd flirted with him, then feigned a lack of interest, posing a challenge he simply couldn't resist.

Then the storm had given him the opportunity to ride in like the hero on a white horse and save her.

She didn't ask to be rescued. You insisted on it.

A little voice in the back of Blake's head refused to let go of the belief that, on some level, what he and Savannah shared had been real. He was hurt by what she'd done. Furious that she and her grandfather had taken aim at their company. And still, something deep inside of him couldn't accept that she'd purposely used him as a pawn.

Martin McDowell had obviously filled his granddaughter's head with lies her entire life. Built up some crazy fantasy that they were the rightful owners of King's Finest.

Maybe Savannah really hadn't intended to get involved with Blake. But once she had…how could she allow things to escalate, knowing how he felt about her?

How could the woman he thought he knew use him that way?

Blake pulled into the drive of his grandfather's log cabin by the lake and knocked at the door.

"Well, this is a surprise." The old man chuckled. "Didn't expect to…" He shoved his glasses up the bridge of his nose. "What's wrong, son? You look like you've lost your best friend."

"We need to talk, Granddad." Blake followed his grandfather into the house and sat beside him on the plaid sofa in the den.

"About what?"

Blake was embarrassed to relate Savannah's accusations. Afraid there may actually be some truth to them.

"Blake, whatever you need to tell me...it isn't the end of the world." His grandfather gave him a faint smile. "So just say it. We'll get through it."

"You already know what happened with Savannah."

"Yes." His grandfather nodded gravely as he rubbed his whiskered chin. "Shame. I liked the young lady quite a lot. Seems you did, too."

Is there anyone who doesn't know what a fool I was?

"Max did some digging. He discovered that Savannah is the granddaughter of Martin McDowell."

The man's mouth fell open, his large eyes widening. He seemed to be staring into the past. "There was something familiar about her. Couldn't put a finger on it then, but now... now it all makes sense. She has her grandfather's nose and eyes. His boldness and spirit. But she has more business acumen than Marty ever had."

A knot clenched in Blake's belly. "I thought you inherited the business from your father when he died in his accident. When did you have a partner?"

"I was quite young when your great-grandfather died. Barely even a teen. Papa had wanted to teach me the business, but Mama wouldn't hear of it. White lightning was the reason she was so unhappy, despite the money and comforts we had. Eventually, it was the reason my father died."

"He'd been drinking." Why hadn't he realized that before?

"Wrapped his car around a tree coming home from a juke joint in the wee hours of the morning." His grandfather groaned. "Not the kind of thing I was proud to talk about."

"So you learned the business from Martin McDowell."

"He was a bit older than me, but he'd worked with my father. A couple years after my father died, we were just about broke. I found Martin, and I made a deal with him for a sixty/forty partnership split if he taught me everything he knew...everything my father had taught him. He was the muscle and he negotiated deals for us. Together we tinkered a bit with Papa's recipes."

Blake could barely hear over the sound of blood rushing in his ears. "Granddad, Martin is claiming that our bourbon recipe is his. That you stole it."

"That's a goddamned lie." His grandfather shot to his feet, his forehead and cheeks turning bright red. "That was Papa's recipe."

"But you just said..."

"I said we tinkered with the recipe while he was my partner. But I kept perfecting it, even after I bought him out."

"You bought him out as your partner?"

"Still got the paperwork in my safe-deposit box at the bank."

"That's good. You have proof." Blake heaved a sigh of relief.

"Why do I need it?" His grandfather raised a wiry, white brow.

"Because Martin's got it in his head that half of King's Finest should be his. That's why Savannah came to work for us. To find proof that her family should be part owners."

The old man averted his eyes and grimaced.

"What is it, Granddad?" Blake gripped his grandfather's wrist and the old man shifted his gaze to him. "Like you said, whatever it is, we'll get through it. We always do."

Joseph Abbott groaned and sank down on the sofa again. He dragged a hand across his forehead.

"By the time I was twenty-one, I got tired of Martin trying to boss me around. The business had belonged to my father, and I wanted it back."

"So you bought him out."

His grandfather nodded. "Even as a kid, I dreamed big. But Marty wanted to stick to what we'd always done. I wanted to start a proper distillery. Become a respectable citizen with no need to dodge the law. Martin had no interest in doing that."

"If you bought him out fair and square, he has no claim," Blake pointed out.

"True." His grandfather's voice lacked conviction. "But I wasn't very fair to him, either." He lowered his gaze. "He was a heavy gambler, and I knew he'd go for a lump-sum payout, despite it being less than half of what was probably fair at the time."

His grandfather ran a hand over the smooth skin of his head. "Always felt bad about that. Especially after he gambled most of it away. Got in debt to some pretty shady characters. He and his wife left town in the dead of the night. Haven't heard from him since."

"If you felt so bad, why'd you…?" Blake stopped short of using the word *cheat*. "Why'd you shortchange him?"

"Didn't have enough saved to buy him out at a fair price. Not if I was going to buy my building, get new equipment and hire workers. I used his vice against him. It's not one of my prouder moments, son."

"So Martin was aware you wanted to start a legal distillery?"

"Like I said, he didn't have the vision his granddaughter has. Martin thought it was a terrible idea. He expected the venture to go up in flames, as it had for a few other moonshiners who'd tried to take their business legit."

"So he made a choice." Blake needed to believe his grandfather was the upstanding man he'd always thought him to be. That he hadn't wronged Savannah's grandfather. Joseph Abbott had always been his hero. Even more than his own father.

"He did. And when he signed the contract, he relinquished everything. Including the right to take up a similar business in the state for at least fifty years."

The answer to the question he'd posed to Savannah earlier. Why now?

"So legally, he has no claim to King's Finest."

"No. Got myself a damn good lawyer to draw up that contract." His grandfather's voice was faint and there was a faraway look in his eye. "It's airtight."

"But?"

"But I do feel I owe him something. I was a young man making gobs of money. I got a little bit full of myself, and I wasn't as fair as I should've been to Marty after everything he'd done for me." His grandfather rubbed his chin. "We certainly wouldn't be what we are today without him."

"But technically, Martin sold all of the recipes, all of the processes to you."

"Legally, yes." His grandfather nodded. "Morally... I've always felt like I gave the guy a raw deal."

"There's something else you need to know." Blake sighed. "Savannah...she... I mean, we..."

"Go on, son." His grandfather prodded. "At this rate, I'll be called home before you get the first sentence out."

"She's pregnant."

"And you're the father, I assume."

"Yes." The word was a harsh whisper.

"Sounds like we both need a drink." His grandfather moved to the bar and poured two glasses of their top-shelf bourbon. The same drink Blake had shared with Savannah the night of the storm. Joseph handed him a glass and returned to the sofa.

"Congratulations are in order, I suppose." His grandfather sipped his bourbon.

"It hasn't sunk in yet." Blake sipped from his glass.

"So you didn't know who Savannah was or why she was here?"

Blake shook his head. "I only learned the truth today."

His grandfather stared into his glass for a moment before meeting his gaze. "Do you love her, son?"

"I think I do. At least, I did before I realized it was never about me. It was about the money and restoring her grandfather's legacy."

"Can't it be about both?"

"Sir?"

"Maybe she did come here with the sole purpose of getting what she felt her family was owed…a noble thing, in my mind. But that doesn't mean she didn't fall for you along the way."

"What makes you believe that, Granddad?"

"Explains the tortured look in her eyes the night we met. When she was grilling me about the history of the company. Now I understand what I saw in her eyes. She probably hated me. Wanted revenge. But then there were her feelings for you. Must've been a mighty struggle for her."

Blake didn't directly address his grandfather's conjecture. "Do you think Martin McDowell is the kind of man who would've sent her here, hoping that one of us would get her pregnant? It'd be a slam-dunk way to ensure their family got a stake in the company."

"Never. In fact, I'm shocked he would've agreed to her coming here at all. He was too proud a man to let his granddaughter fight his battle."

Blake sighed in relief. "She claims he doesn't know she's here or what she's been up to."

"Does Savannah seem to you like the kind of person who'd trick you into getting her pregnant?" His grandfather took another sip of his drink.

"No." Blake finished his bourbon and put the glass down. "Then again, I wouldn't have thought her a spy. So what do I know?"

"You know you care about the girl and that she, like it or not, is carrying the first of the next generation of Abbotts." His grandfather's mouth curled in a reserved smile.

Blake's head spun. Not from the bourbon, but from the idea that he would be a father. It certainly wasn't under the circumstances he would've wished, but still…he was going to be a father.

He poured himself another glass and topped off his grandfather's drink before settling on the sofa again. He studied the ceiling, his mind spinning.

"The question is, is it possible for you two to get past this? If you really care for this girl, maybe you can salvage it," his grandfather said. "If not, you still need to have an amicable relationship for the sake of the child."

"I don't know if I can get past what Savannah did. I know she felt she had good reason, but how can I ever trust her again?"

"Only you can answer that, son." His grandfather's voice was filled with regret. "I'm sure Marty will probably always distrust me, too."

"What are you going to do?"

"Not sure. I find it best to sleep on decisions like this." Joe tapped a finger on his glass. "But call your parents, brothers and sister. Tomorrow morning, we need to have a family meeting."

Twenty-Three

Savannah was going stir-crazy.

It'd been nearly a week since Blake had learned of her pregnancy. Two days of silence since she'd left him a message informing him a doctor had confirmed the test results. And still no word as to whether they planned to press charges.

There was a knock at her door and she answered it.

"Got a surprise for you." Kayleigh beamed, opening the signature pink box from the local bakery. "Sticky buns."

"My favorite. Thank you. C'mon in and I'll make you a cup of coffee. I can't eat these all by myself."

Savannah gave the woman whom she'd fast become friends with a grateful smile. She'd told Kayleigh the truth about why she'd come to Magnolia Lake and about the Abbotts discovering her plot. But she hadn't told Kayleigh about her and Blake. Or about the baby.

"I've gotta get downstairs and open the shop, but I brought you some company. That's the other surprise."

Kayleigh stepped aside to reveal her sister and niece in the doorway.

"Auntie Vanna!"

"Harper!" Savannah stooped to hug and kiss her niece. Then she stood and wrapped her sister in a hug. "Laney! I can't believe you guys came all this way."

Savannah's eyes filled with tears. She'd desperately missed her sister's face, so similar to her own. Laney's hair was styled in an adorable pixie cut, top-heavy with shiny, dark curls.

After turning the television to a kids' channel for Harper and setting the little girl up with her favorite snacks, Laney slid onto the couch beside Savannah.

"You ready for this?" She indicated Harper, singing along with her favorite educational show.

"I will be." Savannah's hand drifted to her belly and tears stung her eyes.

"Aww, honey, don't cry." Laney squeezed her hand. "Everything's going to be all right."

"Everything is *not* all right. I really screwed up." Savannah shot to her feet and paced the floor. "I still don't have anything to support Gramps's claim. I'm apparently the worst burglar in the history of burglars. There is still the very real possibility the Abbotts could send me to jail. Then let's not forget that I'm unemployed and pregnant... by an Abbott."

She dropped onto the sofa again, cradling her face in her hands. Her heart squeezed in her chest as she remembered Blake's face. How hurt he'd been to learn the truth. The tears started again.

"And my baby's father hates me. He doesn't want anything to do with either of us." Savannah wiped away tears.

"Did Blake tell you that?"

"No. But I got the hint from his radio silence." Savannah sighed. "I honestly don't believe things can get any worse."

A soft smile played on Laney's lips. "Then they can only get better."

Savannah loved how her sister saw the good in people and had an optimistic view of the world. But in the midst of her personal hell, with the world crumbling around her, she had no desire to pretend everything would be okay.

"Laney, maybe you missed some of what I just said." Savannah swiped a sticky bun from the box, took a bite and murmured with pleasure. "So far, the only upside to this has been that I can eat whatever I want without an ounce of guilt."

Her sister's smile grew wider. She stood and extended a hand to her. "You've been cooped up in this apartment too long. You need some fresh air. Let's go for a ride."

"I'm not supposed to leave town, and believe me, Magnolia Lake is so small that by the time we start the car, we'll already be out of it."

"I made an appeal to the sheriff. Got permission to take you on a little field trip." Laney pulled Savannah off the couch and steered her toward the bedroom. "Now take a shower and put on something nice. We'll take a little ride and get something to eat. You'll feel better. I promise."

Savannah shoved her sunglasses on top of her head and returned her seat to the upright position as Laney pulled her rental car into the parking lot of a medical center in Knoxville.

"Why are we coming here?" Savannah turned to Laney. "Are you all right? Is Harper?"

"We're both fine." A wide grin spread across her sister's face. "As for why we're here…you'll see. C'mon."

Savannah and Harper waited in a sitting area while Laney spoke to the attendant at the front desk. Then they had their pictures taken for temporary badges and rode the elevator to the fourth floor.

Laney tapped on a partially open door.

"Yes?"

Savannah's heart nearly stopped when she heard the familiar voice. She turned to her sister.

Laney nodded and smiled, taking Harper from her arms. "You two need to talk. Harper and I will be in the cafeteria."

Savannah burst through the door. "Grandpa, what on earth are you doing in Knoxville? And why were you admitted here? Is everything okay?"

"You won't believe me when I tell you." He chuckled, raising his arms to her. "Come here and give me a hug."

Savannah gave him a bear hug, hesitant to let him go. Delaying what she needed to do next.

Come clean and tell him everything.

She sat beside his bed, gripping his hand. "I have so much to tell you."

"It'll have to wait." He sighed as he rubbed his beard. "Because there are a few things I'd better tell you first."

"Like what?"

"Your sister told me why you came to Magnolia Lake, Vanna." He squeezed her hand, halting her objection. "Don't be mad at Laney. She did the right thing by telling me. If you should be upset with anyone, it's me."

"Why?"

"Because I left out an important piece of the story." His shoulders hunched and his chin dropped to his chest. "Joseph Abbott bought me out as a partner."

"You mean he already paid you?"

Her grandfather nodded. "A lump-sum payout to dissolve the partnership and secure full ownership of any recipes I helped develop."

"That changes everything, Grandpa. How could you not tell me that?" Savannah stood, her hand to her mouth. No wonder Blake thought they were crooks, trying to get one over on his family. "What happened to the money?"

His eyes didn't meet hers. "I had terrible drinking and gambling habits back then. Within a year, I'd gone through it all."

Savannah dropped into the seat again, too weak to stand. She'd risked everything based on a lie. A lie that led her to a man and a career she loved, but then had cruelly snatched them away.

"How could you let me believe all this time that you'd been cheated by the Abbotts?" Her body vibrated with anger.

"I may not have told you the entire truth, Vanna. But I did feel I'd been cheated. Joe didn't pay me my fair share. Then when he went on to make a fortune off formulas I helped create..." He sighed and shook his head.

Savannah was furious with her grandfather. And miserable over losing Blake.

"Do you have any idea what I've done to try and make things right for you? How much I've lost?"

"Laney told me." Her grandfather's eyes were shiny. He clutched her hand. "And I'm so sorry, dumplin'. To you and to the Abbotts. It was easier to blame them than to admit I'd chosen unwisely. That I'd only thought in the short term when I accepted that lump sum from Joe rather than being patient."

Savannah cradled her forehead in her palm, her lips pressed together to repress the scream building inside.

"I had no idea you'd take my words to heart, Savannah. That you'd act on them. You and your sister and little Harper... You mean everything to me. I couldn't protect your mama, but I've done everything I could to look after the two of you. I didn't want you to see me as a horrible failure. A man that never amounted to much of nothing."

"I never thought that, Grandpa. If it wasn't for you taking us in...who knows what might've become of Laney and me?"

"Still, what I done wasn't right, and I'm ashamed."

They were both silent for a moment. Savannah narrowed her gaze at her grandfather. "You still haven't explained what you're doing here in Knoxville."

"Joe Abbott."

"You talked to him?"

"He came to West Virginia to see me, a few days ago. Told me everything about you, about his grandson...and about the baby."

"You know about the baby?"

"I do. And I'm sorry about the split between you and the Abbott boy."

"Why? You always said not to trust an Abbott any farther than I can throw one." She folded her hands. "If Joe

Abbott cheated you out of a fair price for your share of the partnership, that only proves you were right."

"We both made mistakes back then, but I've compounded them by misleading you." Martin ran his free hand over his head. "And maybe Joe wasn't fair then, but he's making it up to me...to all of us, Savannah."

"What do you mean?"

A slow smiled curved the edge of his mouth. "I mean you did it, honey. Joseph Abbott and his family are giving us a stake in King's Finest. Not half, of course. But he's giving me a five percent stake in the company and he wrote me a check outright."

"For what?" Savannah couldn't believe what she was hearing. Surely it was a dream.

Her grandfather dug a piece of paper out of his wallet and handed it to her. She unfolded it and read it twice. It was a check for $1.5 million.

"Is this real?"

"Yes." He smiled, tears in his eyes as he cradled either side of her face and kissed her forehead. "I can't believe the chance you took for me. Or Joe's generosity. He brought me here on his dime to see if I'd be a good candidate for the therapy program they're conducting."

"That's incredible, Grandpa. I'm really happy for you." Savannah handed him back the check. She forced a smile, but tears brimmed, spilling down her cheeks.

She'd gotten everything she wanted for her grandfather and lost everything she never knew she wanted for herself. Her job with the Abbotts, her relationship with Blake, a chance for them to be a family.

"I'm glad Joseph Abbott is a decent man after all." Savannah wiped away the tears.

"I don't think that's why he did this at all." He folded the check and returned it to his wallet.

"Then why?"

"He did it for your beau, Blake. And for you." A smile softened her grandfather's face.

"Me? We only met once. Why would he care about doing anything for me?"

"He was impressed with you. With what you were willing to do for me. And what you've already done for his company. Not to mention the fact that you're carrying the first Abbott great-grandchild." Her grandfather's smile widened. "And my second."

Savannah forced a smile in return, determined not to shed any more tears.

"Then they won't press charges against me?"

Something Blake hadn't bothered to tell her. Just as he hadn't bothered to return the message she'd left confirming her pregnancy. A clear indication he wanted nothing to do with her or their child. It was a reality she needed to accept.

"Don't worry about that anymore. As soon as I'm out of here, we can go back home to West Virginia, if that's what you want."

"Of course it is." Pain stabbed her chest. Memories of the nights spent in Blake's bed played in her head.

He nodded sadly. "All right then, Vanna. You go on home. Get some rest now that you know everything is okay. Come back and see me tomorrow, if you have time."

She had nothing but time.

"See you tomorrow, Granddad." She kissed the old man's whiskered cheek before making her way to the cafeteria to find her sister.

I honestly, truly did it.

So why was she more miserable than she'd ever been?

Because Blake wouldn't answer her calls or return her messages. But she wouldn't leave town without thanking him and Joseph Abbott for what they'd done.

Twenty-Four

"Can I talk to you, son?" Iris Abbott stuck her head in Blake's office.

"Sure. Come in." He finished typing an email to a group of distributors before giving her his full attention. "What can I do for you, Mama?"

She fiddled with her scarf, her expression apologetic.

"Whatever it is, Mother, just spit it out." He sat on the edge of his desk.

She paced the floor. "It's about Savannah."

"What about her? Is something wrong with her or the baby?"

"No, it's nothing like that."

Blake was still furious with Savannah. She'd lied to him. Gotten involved with him under false pretenses. Hid her pregnancy. Yet he couldn't stop thinking of her. Wanting her.

"What is it, then?"

"Let's just say she did too good of a job around here." His mother sighed. "I'm plumb exhausted from trying to pick up where she left off."

"I see." Blake returned to his seat. "Ask Max to run the event manager ad again. Hopefully, we can find a replacement before you get too swamped. In the meantime, Zora and I will help however we can."

"I suppose that's one way to go."

Blake put down his pen and cocked his head. "You're not suggesting that we—"

"Who better to carry out these plans than the brilliant mind that devised them?" his mother interrupted. "Besides, the distributors liked working with her. I didn't dare tell them she wasn't here anymore. I said she was out for a few weeks on personal leave."

"How could you even suggest we bring Savannah back?"

"Because she did exactly what we hired her to do and more. Did you know she'd already booked several corporate events and weddings at the old barn?" Iris wagged a finger. "We'll need to hire permanent event staff out there just to keep up."

The storage room at the barn. That was the last time he'd been with Savannah. His body hummed with electricity at the erotic memory.

He tried to push the sights and sounds of that night from his brain.

"So we'll hire permanent staff for the space. But that doesn't justify bringing back someone we can't trust."

"But I do trust her, honey. You're right—she should've told us the truth. But she had free rein while she worked here. If she'd wanted to harm our company or sell our secrets, she could've. But she didn't, because that was never her intention."

"She's a liar with a heart of gold, is that it?"

"Something like that." His mother smiled sadly. "Did I ever tell you that when I was about ten years old a man came to town and swindled my daddy out of a good portion of his savings?"

"No." Blake had learned more about his family's financial past in the last week than he had in more than three decades.

"It nearly broke him, and to be honest, he was never quite the same after that. He felt he'd failed us. I guess in some ways he had, going for a get-rich-quick scheme like that."

"Must've been tough for Grandpa Gus."

"It was tough for all of us. Especially for my mom. She'd never trusted the man to begin with and she'd begged my daddy not to invest with him."

"Did Grandpa Gus ever get his money back?"

"No. And I used to dream about tracking down that man and making him pay for what he did to my father. And to us." She leaned back in her chair, her eyes steely. "I'd have done just about anything to bring him peace again."

"I can't believe you and Gramps admire what Savannah did, as if she's some modern-day Robin Hood. Don't forget that would make us the villains in this story."

"I do admire her. Look, honey, I know this isn't what you want to hear. She deceived us and she hurt you, even if she didn't intend to. But from what I hear, she's hurting, too. You know Grandpa Joe already gave Martin his money and his stake in the company. If that's all Savannah cared about, would she still be walking around looking miserable?"

"How do you know that?"

"It's Magnolia Lake, darlin'," his mother said matter-of-factly. "I know everything that goes on around here."

"Maybe she should've considered that before she put herself in this position. Before she put us all in a compromising position."

"Maybe so. But let me ask you a question. And I want you to be completely honest, if not with me, then at least with yourself."

"Shoot."

"If the shoe had been on the other foot, how far would you have gone to get justice for your grandpa Joe?"

Blake's attention snapped to hers. His mother knew how much he loved and admired his grandfather. He would've gone to hell and back to protect the old man, if he believed someone had wronged him.

Apparently, Savannah had the same level of love and affection for her grandfather. Unfortunately, he hadn't told her the whole truth. But then again, neither had his.

"What does Parker think about giving Savannah her job back?"

When their family had met to discuss the situation, they'd all been angry at first. But when his grandfather explained the history between him and Martin McDowell, most of them had softened their stance. Only Parker had objected to giving McDowell a stake in the company.

Surely, Parker would be Blake's one ally.

"Your brother says that if you can deal with Savannah coming back here, he can, too." A slow smile lit his mother's eyes. "Parker says that for him, it's about the bottom line. And she's certainly proven she's good for that."

"It would be awkward, us working together and having a child together, but not actually being together."

"It's important that you two get along. There's my grand-child to consider, after all. So perhaps this is a good way to force your hand." Her voice softened. "Of course, there is another option."

Blake raised an eyebrow. "Which is?"

"Things wouldn't be so awkward if you two were actu-ally together."

"Mother…"

"I know you love her, son. You're just being stubborn, because your feelings and your pride were hurt."

"You make it sound as if I'm being unreasonable. Aren't you the one who always told us that honesty is the very least we should expect in a relationship?"

"True." She nodded gravely. "But then I also told you that we sometimes do the wrong thing for all the right reasons. Can't you see that's what Savannah has done?"

"I appreciate what you're doing, Mother, but it's not that simple." Blake tapped his thumb lightly on the desk. "Parker is right, though. This is about the bottom line. Savannah's impact in her short time with the company is undeniable. I'll consider it, I promise."

Blake loved Savannah. He honestly did. But he didn't know if he'd ever be able to trust her again.

He ruminated on the question for the rest of the day. It was still spinning in his head when he approached his drive-way and found Savannah, parked there, waiting for him.

* * *

Savannah climbed out of her car as Blake pulled into the drive. She'd been parked there for an hour, determined not to leave until she'd said what she came to say.

"Hello, Blake." She was undeterred by his frown.

"Savannah." The iciness of his tone made her shudder. "Surprised you're still in town. After all, you got everything you came for."

His words sawed through her like a jagged blade.

"I needed to thank you and Mr. Abbott for everything you've done for my grandfather." Her mouth was dry and there was a fluttering in her belly. "You couldn't possibly know how much what you've done means to him and to our family."

"It means you won. Perhaps deservedly so," Blake acknowledged as he swiped the dogs' leashes from their hook on the wall. He opened the door and Sam and Benny raced toward her.

"Sam! Benny!"

The larger dog jumped on her, nearly knocking her backward. Blake was suddenly there with his arms around her, ensuring she didn't fall.

Her heart raced as her gaze met his.

Blake held her in his arms, his chest heaving. Sam poked her leg with his wet nose and Benny barked. Yet, in Blake's arms, it felt as if the world had stopped. It was only the two of them and the baby they'd made growing inside her.

"Thank you, Blake."

Blake released her without response. He grabbed the leashes he'd dropped, clamping one on Benny and the other on Sam.

"I missed you two." She showered the dogs with hugs and kisses. Their tales wagged and Benny licked her face. Savannah stood, meeting Blake's gaze. She swallowed the lump in her throat. "I've missed you, too, Blake."

Hurt and disappointment were etched between his

furrowed brows. Yet there was a hint of affection in his dark eyes.

If she could peel away the layers of pain and distrust, maybe they could salvage the warmth and affection buried beneath. Grow it alongside the love she felt for him and for their child. Nurture it until it turned into something beautiful and lasting.

He didn't acknowledge her admission. Instead, he gestured toward the path by the lake. "I have to walk Benny and Sam."

"Blake, I... I love you." The words stumbled from her lips.

"I would've given anything to hear you say that a couple of weeks ago." He sighed. "Now, how can I trust that it's not just another ploy to manipulate me?"

"I never used what happened between us to manipulate you. Everything I said to you...everything we did... For me, it was real. All of it." She bit back the tears that stung her eyes. "I never intended to fall for you. But I couldn't help wanting to be with you."

Benny and Sam started to whine.

"Walk with us?"

She fell in step beside them.

"If you feel...the way you say you do...why didn't you tell me before?"

"I felt guilty because of the secrets I was keeping. Making one confession without the other wouldn't have been fair to you."

"So what was the plan? To string me along until you found something?"

"There was no 'plan' where you were concerned." She wrapped her arms around herself as they stopped for the dogs.

"Then why did you get involved with me?" He studied her.

"It wasn't a choice." She couldn't help the involuntary

smile or the tears that leaked from her eyes. "How could I not fall for you? You're the most amazing man I've ever known."

"But you couldn't trust me with the truth?"

"I was torn between what I felt for you and doing right by my family. After I lost my parents, I promised myself I'd never stand by and do nothing again. I was determined to protect my family at all costs. Even if that meant losing what I wanted most. You."

"So you used me to get what you wanted, and I played right into your hands." Blake turned on his heels and headed back toward the house.

"I wasn't trying to use you, Blake." She scrambled to keep up with his long strides. "You were just...this vortex that pulled me in. I couldn't resist, and after a while, I didn't want to because you were incredible. And you made me feel special in a way I never had before. You made me want things I never wanted before."

He stopped and turned to her. "Like a baby?"

"Yes." Her mouth curved in a soft smile. She wiped away tears. "I didn't plan this baby, but the instant I knew, there wasn't a question in my mind about what I should do. I was given the most amazing gift. A piece of you. *Our* baby."

His gaze dropped to her hand on her belly. He swallowed hard, neither of them saying anything for a moment.

Blake walked away without a word.

Savannah wanted to dissolve into tears, but she had no right to expect forgiveness. All she could do was hope that someday he'd want to be part of their child's life.

Blake took the dogs inside. Savannah's words pierced the hardened shell that had formed around his heart. Reminded him of the incredible moments they'd shared.

During the past week, he'd been forced to question every moment. Every kiss. Wondering if any of it was real.

Something deep inside him believed it had been, and that

she truly did love him. He wanted to forgive her and to be excited about the child they were having.

But could he ever trust her again?

Blake stepped out into the garage again as Savannah opened her car door. The sight of her leaving triggered something in him. Maybe he didn't know for sure how things would end between them, but he knew he couldn't let her walk away.

"Where are you going?" He approached her.

"Back to my apartment, for now. Back to West Virginia once Grandpa is done with his treatments."

"Just like that...you're walking away?"

Savannah blinked, her brows scrunched in confusion. She shut the car door and walked toward him.

"You obviously don't want me here, and I don't want to make things worse. I just want you to know that you're welcome to be as involved in this child's life as you choose. I'd never stand in the way of that."

Blake took a few steps closer and swallowed the lump in his throat, unable to speak.

It was fear, plain and simple.

He wanted to be with Savannah. To raise their baby together. It would be difficult to get past this. To trust her implicitly. But it couldn't be worse than the torment that seized him as he watched her turn and walk toward her car again.

"Does that mean you don't want your job back?"

She turned toward him, eyes wide. "Your family would trust me to work for you again?"

Blake rubbed the back of his neck. "My mother, Max, Zora...even Parker... They all want you back. You're good for King's Finest. There's no disputing that."

"And what about you, Blake? What do you want?" She stepped closer and studied him. "As much as I love working with your family at King's Finest, I won't come back if it'll be too painful for you. I couldn't do that to you. I've already hurt you so much. I won't do it again."

Tightness gripped his chest as he stared into her lovely eyes, glistening with tears. His throat was raw with emotion.

Blake could see the love in her eyes. Hear it in her voice. He'd been right all along. Her feelings for him were real. Now that there were no more secrets between them, what remained was the love and friendship they'd been building. It ran deep, and it was as sweet and clear as the waters of King's Lake.

"What I want, Savannah, more than anything, is to be with you and our baby." He slipped his arms around her waist. "Because I love you, too."

He kissed her. Savored the taste of her sweet lips and salty tears. Then he took her inside, determined to make up for lost time. To make love to her and get reacquainted with every inch of her glowing skin.

Later, as they lay sleeping, he cradled Savannah in his arms, his hands perched protectively over her belly. His heart overflowed with the love he felt for her and for the child she carried.

Their child.

He pulled her closer, determined to never let them go.

Epilogue

Eleven months later

The old barn had become a popular wedding venue, and it had never looked more elegant than it did now.

Blake surveyed the crowd of people who'd assembled in their Sunday best to help him and Savannah celebrate their special day. Family, friends, employees and townsfolk. Most of whom he'd known his entire life.

Blake's hands were shaking. His breath was ragged and labored. A stone lodged in the pit of his stomach.

But he didn't have an ounce of doubt about marrying Savannah Carlisle. Aside from the day little Davis was born, it was the happiest day of his life.

So why was he so nervous?

Maybe he was afraid Savannah would come to her senses, turn tail and run. That she'd decide she didn't want to be part of this big, noisy, opinionated family.

Blake clenched his hands together in front of him and released a slow breath.

He was letting his nerves get the better of him.

Savannah loved him and their son. With a love he felt in every fiber of his soul.

He'd seen that love, true and deep, in Savannah's hazel eyes each morning. Felt its warmth as they played with their child.

Was rocked by its power when he made love to her. Felt it surround him as they fell asleep in each other's arms each night.

No, he didn't question the authenticity of her love for him.

And unlike the feelings he'd once had for Gavrilla, what

he shared with Savannah wasn't contained within the small unit they formed. It encompassed both of their families.

"You ready for this?" Max, his best man, stood beside him.

"Never been more ready for anything in my life." Blake smiled at Davis, who waved his arms at him as his great-grandfather bounced him on his knee.

As the ceremony began, Blake's pulse raced. He watched their family and friends march down the aisle. His mother, Daisy, arm in arm with his cousin Benji. His brother Cole and his cousin Delia. Dallas Hamilton and Zora. Kayleigh Jemison and Parker—who had managed to be civil to each other through most of the proceedings. Then Savannah's sister, Laney.

His grandfather carried little Davis—the honorary ring bearer—down the aisle.

Laney's three-year-old daughter, Harper, scattered rose petals onto the white, custom aisle runner printed with his and Savannah's names and the words *Always and Forever*.

When the music changed and everyone stood, his heart felt as if it would burst. Savannah stood at the head of the aisle on her grandfather's arm.

The love of his life was an incredible vision to behold in an off-shoulder, antique white lace wedding gown. The mermaid silhouette hugged the curves that had mesmerized him the moment he laid eyes on them.

Savannah's hair was pulled into a tousled, messy bun low over one shoulder. A spray of flowers was intertwined in her hair.

She floated down the aisle toward him. All eyes were on her, but her gaze was locked with his. As if only the two of them were there in that old barn.

Savannah turned and kissed her grandfather's cheek, and Blake shook the old man's hand. Mr. McDowell was grateful he'd lived to see his granddaughter get married, and that he had the health and strength to walk her down the aisle.

Blake extended his palm and Savannah placed her delicate hand in his.

"You ready for this, baby?" he whispered as they turned and stepped onto the stage.

Savannah grinned, her eyes glistening with tears. "Blake Abbott, I can't wait to become your wife."

They stood before the magistrate in a room filled to capacity with the people they loved most, and she did just that.

* * * * *

FROM SEDUCTION
TO SECRETS

ANDREA LAURENCE

One

As weddings go, it was a nice enough one. Sawyer Steele hadn't been to many, but knowing his parents, it was probably an extravagant and expensive affair. Perhaps the greatest wedding ever held in Charleston. He wouldn't know the difference. It wasn't exactly Sawyer's thing. But his baby sister, Morgan, was celebrating her big day, so of course he was there to smile for pictures and eat cake. Not everyone could get shipped off to work a deal in China and miss it like Finn did.

It was probably strategy on Trevor Steele's part to have his most troublesome son out of the country for the event. Sawyer's twin was the one most likely to cause the bulk of their father's headaches. He could count on Sawyer and Tom, the oldest son, to attend and behave. As such, Sawyer had had his tuxedo dry-cleaned, his dark blond curls cut short and found a suitable date to bring with him. That was all that was really required of him tonight. Behave. Don't make a scene. Make sure Morgan is happy. Easy enough.

Now the event was starting to wind down. They'd eaten, said a million toasts, had all the requisite dances and cut into the towering ivory-and-gold confection his sister had chosen for her cake. A few more dances and they should be waving sparklers and seeing his sister and her new husband off to start their lives together. He was good with that. The bow tie he was wearing felt like it was getting tighter around his throat with each passing hour.

Glancing over, he noticed his date, Serena—a woman he'd met a few weeks earlier at a conference—eyeballing the people on the dance floor. He decided it was time to take her for a spin at last. Sawyer wasn't a dancer by any stretch, but he could manage a simple waltz for formal occasions. All the Steele children had been forced through junior cotillion to pick up some basic skills like that. They lived in the South, after all, and etiquette was paramount in the social circles he was forced into as one of the Steeles.

"Would you like to dance?" he asked Serena. The buxom blonde had chosen a low-cut, pale blue sheath dress that gave off some Cinderella vibes with her golden hair pulled up into a bun. She looked very pretty. At the same time, he just couldn't muster up much enthusiasm for her. She didn't have a very memorable personality. She actually reminded him of one of his mother's beautiful, priceless antiques. Lovely to look at, but mostly decorative.

His brother Finn preferred a sports car type girlfriend. Sexy, high performance and exciting to drive, so to speak. Those women were as high maintenance as the cars and likely to get Finn in trouble before too long.

Sawyer's ex, Mira, had been a Ferrari if ever he saw one. After that, he'd decided that maybe a roomy, luxury SUV was more his speed. Beautiful, adventurous, flexible, and if you took good care of it, it would reward your efforts for years to come.

But Serena looked so much like Mira that he instinctively wanted to call her by his ex's name, and had to stop himself each time. They looked so similar that his feelings about how things had ended with Mira may have been souring how he felt about Serena. Or maybe Serena just wasn't as much fun on the road as she appeared in the dealership.

"Sure, I'd love to dance," she said with a smile.

Oh well. There was nothing he would or could do about it tonight. He took her hand and led her to the illuminated dance floor, where at least twenty other couples were gliding along to a romantic old Sinatra song. He wrapped his arm around her waist and they started to sway slowly to the music.

It was then, with her pressed close against him, that he realized taking a woman to a wedding on a third date was way too soon. He had to bring a plus one, but it made things feel more serious than they were. They'd had drinks and dinner so far, and if this wedding hadn't come up, they might've gone to a movie. Maybe not even that, so he certainly didn't need her getting overly romantic notions when he didn't plan on a fourth date.

His gaze fell on a woman entering the ballroom. Even from this distance, she instantly captured his attention with fair skin that stood out against her black cocktail dress and bright auburn hair. She looked around the room, searching for someone. And then their eyes met. In an instant, it was like Sawyer had been hit directly in the gut. He'd never felt anything like that before. It was powerful. It made him forget all about the woman in his arms. At least for a moment.

Then he noticed the angry look on the newcomer's face and wondered if it wasn't attraction he was feeling so much as a woman's fury.

She moved quickly through the crowd toward him. Sawyer was frozen in place on the dance floor—unable to pull away from the hold the redhead had on him even though his brain was telling him to escape.

Then, at last, she arrived. "You skeevy little prick!"

The angry shout cut through the sounds in the ballroom like a knife. The dancers paused, and even the orchestra was startled into an awkward silence. Everyone turned to see the stunning redhead standing at the edge of the dance floor. Now she was only a few feet away from Sawyer, with her eyes still focused directly on him.

He'd thought for a moment that maybe he was in someone else's line of fire. He looked over his shoulder, but no one was there. Was she really talking to *him*? Shouting at him? That wasn't possible.

"Who is that woman, Sawyer?" his date asked.

That was a really good question. He'd never seen her before in his life. He certainly would've remembered a woman with hair like waves of fire and skin as flawless and pale as a porcelain doll. Even as angry as she was, he wanted to know more about her. Sawyer shook his head. "I have no idea. Can I help you, miss?"

"Can you help me?" she repeated bitterly. "Yes. You can hold still." The angry woman walked up to him and slapped him hard across the face.

He was too stunned to respond for a moment. He'd never been slapped before. Somehow, being hit by a stranger made it that much worse. She hadn't hurt him, not really. It just stung, but he could feel the emotion behind the slap. She'd wanted to hurt him, and for good reason. He just didn't know what that was.

There was a collective gasp as the whole ballroom seemed equally aghast, then a murmur as everyone started discussing what was going on. Out of the corner of his eye, Sawyer could see a couple brawny security guards his father had hired for the party making their way across the room to deal with the situation. Given that the last two events at the house had ended in a kidnapping and a bombing, respectively, it was a good move to have a little extra help in that regard.

"I'm going to have to ask you to come with us, ma'am," one of the guards, wearing a black suit and an earpiece, said.

The redhead hesitated for only a moment before she

spun on her heel and marched out of the ballroom with the two guards right behind her. She'd done what she'd come here to do, apparently.

Although he knew he shouldn't abandon his date to chase down the stranger, he had to go after the woman and figure out what was going on. "I'll be right back."

Serena nodded, and he jogged out of the ballroom and into the entry hall to see if he could find where security had taken the woman. Sawyer glanced around, catching a blur of movement out of the corner of his eye as the men escorted the woman out the front door.

He chased her across the marble entry and pushed past the guards as they came back inside without her. At the top of the front stairs, he looked down and saw the woman waiting for a parking attendant to bring her car.

"I told you to keep it close!" she shouted at one of the men his parents had hired to manage all the cars at the wedding. "This wasn't going to take long. Especially with those goons seeing me out after less than a minute." She nervously glanced over her shoulder, and that was when she spied Sawyer standing at the top of the stairs.

"Do you normally wear black to weddings?" he asked. Asking why she'd slapped him seemed like jumping ahead in a conversation he wasn't ready to wrap up so quickly. "Isn't that against the rules or something?"

She sighed and crossed her hands over her chest. "It was the only nice dress I had that still fit. No offense to your sister. Anyway, don't mind me," she said.

"Security has made it clear I'm not welcome, so I'm leaving. Go on back to your hot blonde. You've obviously moved on."

Sawyer took a few steps down the stairs to get closer, but out of arm's reach of the woman. He wasn't getting hit twice in one night. "I'm sorry, there's been some kind of mistake, I think. Do I know you?" The stinging welt on his cheek suggested that he did, but he was certain he'd never laid eyes on her before. She was stunning, even in the plain strapless black dress and simple makeup she was wearing. Her red hair shimmered in the moonlight, and fat curls cascaded over her bare shoulders.

No, he would remember meeting her.

"Are you serious?" She rolled her eyes, which were a dark shade of green like antique emeralds, and shook her head. "You ignored me for weeks after we got together, then when I finally track you down, you act like you have no idea what I'm even talking about. What? Are you going to tell me your evil doppelgänger slept with me, not you?"

Sawyer opened his mouth to argue, then stopped cold. Now it all started to make sense. Why hadn't he realized this sooner? Women slapped his brother all the time. Or at least they should. It might help things. "I think you're actually looking for my twin brother, not me."

"That's an even better excuse," she said.

"It's not an excuse. Ask anyone in the party and they'll tell you I have an identical twin brother. Most people can't tell us apart."

She narrowed her gaze at him for a moment. "So you're saying you're not Sawyer Steele?"

Sawyer stopped as he opened his mouth to answer. It was one thing for her to confuse him with his brother, but this was different. "No, I *am* Sawyer Steele. But I think you're looking for my twin, Finn Steele."

The woman turned to him with her hands curled up in fists at her sides. "Are you implying that I'm some kind of slut?"

His eyes grew large with surprise. Sawyer was usually pretty good with people, very diplomatic at handling bad situations, but he couldn't say the right thing to this woman for some reason. Her hair was as fiery as her temper, it seemed. "What? No, of course not."

"You just told me I don't know the name of a man I had sex with," she said, pointing at him accusingly.

"That's not what I meant." He held out his hands in surrender and slowly came down the stairs to stand on the brick patio where she was waiting. He hoped that she would take a minute to breathe and calm down. "People get my brother and me mixed up all the time, is all. I'm telling you I've never seen you in my life, so that's the only explanation that makes sense. What is your name?"

"Katherine McIntyre." She said it with an insulted tone, as though he should know her name. "I go by Kat, if that helps jog your memory."

Sawyer frowned. To be honest, the name did sound familiar, but he was certain he'd never seen her before, much less had sex with her. He glanced down over the tightly fitting black dress, which clung to her curves and stopped just above the knee to highlight her shapely legs. He was decidedly disappointed that she'd spent the night with his brother and not him. He wasn't entirely sure that he had a type, but Kat set off all the right bells and whistles. She was a bright red Lamborghini if he'd ever seen one.

When his face didn't light up with recognition, she continued speaking. "We met at the Charleston's Best awards at the aquarium about three months ago. We had a lot of champagne, we talked, and when we got tired of looking at fish, we got a hotel room and got... better acquainted." Kat looked at him with a pointed expression.

Sawyer didn't remember going to an event at the aquarium. Actually, he was certain he hadn't, although he remembered something was being held there a while back. That was it—he hadn't been feeling great that day. He'd gotten a stomach bug, but he was supposed to attend as the Steele family representative to accept their award while his parents were wrapped up in finalizing wedding details. He hadn't gone. In fact, he'd bribed his twin brother to go to the event in his place. Finn hadn't wanted to attend, either. Sawyer had been forced to give him his new Jet Ski in exchange for going to the party.

Damn it to hell.

The realization of what really happened washed over him like a wave. Sawyer brought a hand to his face and rubbed furiously at it in frustration. It had been years since Finn had done something like this. Maybe even since college. Back then, he'd liked to meet girls at bars and give them Sawyer's name instead of his own. He was never sure if his brother just did it for a laugh, or to keep the girls from tracking him down, but Sawyer had earned quite a reputation on campus without doing a single thing to get it. But now they were in their thirties. Thirty-three, to be exact. Way too old for this kind of childish bullshit.

"I think I know what the problem is."

"The sex was so amazing you blocked it from your memory because you knew you'd never experience anything that good again?"

His jaw dropped open for a moment, then he shook his head. He'd never been so jealous of Finn in his whole life. "Uh, no. I was supposed to attend that event, but my brother went in my place. Apparently he didn't bother to tell anyone he wasn't me."

"He was wearing a name tag that said Sawyer Steele," she argued.

Sawyer wasn't surprised. "Yeah. Knowing Finn, he just went with it and pretended to be me so our father wouldn't know I bailed on the party."

Kat stopped for a moment, her mind visibly racing to process what he was telling her. "And when he kissed me? When he got a hotel room? Wouldn't that have been a good time to mention that he wasn't really you?"

"A perfect time, and I have no idea why he didn't. Listen, I'm really sorry about all this. My brother is… the trickster of the family. If he were here right now, I'd drag him outside and make him apologize for lying, but he's actually in Beijing for business. He'll be there a few weeks more, but I'll be sure to pass along your message, slap included, when he gets back."

The redhead's bravado seemed to deflate as she listened to him talk. With her anger no longer aimed at Sawyer, she seemed smaller somehow. Almost petite compared to a moment ago. "So you're saying that the man I met was actually *Finn* Steele? I can't believe, after everything that happened, that he wouldn't tell me his real name."

Sawyer could believe it. Masquerading as his brother gave Finn free license to do what he wanted without consequence. "If you don't mind me asking, was it just a one-night thing between the two of you?"

She looked at him with conflict in her eyes. "Yes. That was the plan, at least."

That was his brother's style. Love 'em and leave 'em, regardless of what name he used. "Then I doubt he would bother to correct you if you thought he was me. In the end, what would it matter? It's just a one-night stand."

Kat's expression softened for a moment as she glanced down at the ground, her eyes hidden beneath her thick auburn lashes. "It does matter, Sawyer. That's why I've crashed this party even though it's obvious he doesn't want to see me again. It matters because I'm pregnant with his child."

Katherine McIntyre had never seen a man's face blanch to a ghostly white so quickly. Even at night, with the patio light behind him, she could see the blood drain from his face and his attractive tan fade. If he hadn't seemed so steady on his feet until now, she might worry that he was about to pass out.

She wasn't sure why he was so upset about the news. He wasn't the father. He wasn't pregnant. He hadn't just found out he'd slept with a lying cheat. She was the one having a terrible night. Sure, he'd been slapped by mistake and would have a lot of explaining to do when he saw his date again, but this was hardly his problem.

The valet brought her car around at last. "I'm sorry. It took a few times for it to turn over," he said.

Kat glanced to where the valet was waiting and then back at the dumbstruck Steele heir. "I'd better go."

He reached out to her, almost appearing to surprise himself as he did it. "Wait. Come back inside and we can talk some more."

She was tempted to say yes. There was a kindness in his eyes that beckoned her to climb the steps and chat with him. It was different than what she'd seen in those familiar eyes before, so his story seemed to hold up. While identical in appearance, the Steele twins were very different men. But talking made no sense when Sawyer wasn't the one she needed to talk to. At least about the baby.

A white Rolls Royce started up the driveway and the front doors of the house opened. People started pouring out onto the stairs. It must be time for the bride and groom to make their exit. Kat wasn't going to stay around for that. Even if her old Jeep wasn't in the way.

"I can't," she said. "But Saw—I mean *Finn*—should know how to reach me when he gets back to the States. Please have him call me." She reached into her purse and pulled out a business card. She'd given Finn one before, but it had likely ended up in the trash the next morning.

Sawyer glanced over his shoulder at all the people coming toward them and his jaw flexed with what looked like irritation as he reached to take the card from her hand. He sighed and nodded as he glanced down at it. "I'll make sure he calls you *before* he gets back. I'm actually going to phone and wake him up right now. He deserves it."

Kat nodded and walked around her Jeep to get inside. She told herself not to look in the rearview mirror as she pulled away, but she did it anyway. She watched Sawyer Steele as his gaze followed her into the distance. He was still watching as she turned out of the driveway and the big house disappeared from sight.

With a groan, she wrapped her fingers tightly around the steering wheel and pressed down the gas pedal. This was not how she had envisioned this night playing out. She'd just wanted to pin Sawyer—*Finn*— down to talk, the same as that first night. Pregnancy was not what she had been going for back then. Far from it. But now that it was done, she wanted to do the right thing and tell the father. If he wasn't going to return her calls, she had to find another way to reach him.

The idea was to locate him, pull him aside to talk, and take things from there. Slapping the father of her child hadn't been a part of her plan, but when she saw him dancing with that beautiful blonde, she couldn't help it. Between morning sickness and pure exhaustion, she'd been uncomfortable for the last few weeks. He could be uncomfortable for a moment or two himself.

Then she'd found out she'd hit the wrong guy and everything just unraveled. China. Her baby's father was in China and that was the least of her troubles. Her baby's father was also a "trickster" in his own brother's words, one who had no problem seducing a woman using his brother's name. That was not the kind of man she wanted in her child's life, but it was too late now. It was done and she would have to find a way to deal with the aftermath.

Kat slowly pulled into her narrow driveway and turned off the Jeep's engine. She looked over at the historic Charleston-style house she called home. Located in the heart of the Peninsula, it had always been enough for her. The twelve-hundred-square-foot structure was the perfect space for a free-spirited artist. It had plenty of light, the traditional piazza patio allowed her to work outside sometimes and, best of all…the place was paid for.

She climbed from her Jeep and went inside. Her little abode was no Steele mansion, but what was? To be honest, she really hadn't understood what kind of family she'd gotten involved with until she pulled into that driveway and got her first view of the house. The Corinthian columns, the whitewashed stone, the lane of old live oak trees dripping Spanish moss on the long drive to the house…it was like something out of a Southern gothic novel. In this day and age it was the kind of place that was usually a museum, or rented out for weddings and events. But no, the Steeles actually lived there.

Kat wasn't a stranger to money. Both her parents had been successful, her father a famous mystery writer and her mother a celebrated painter. They'd done well for themselves, and when they were both killed in a car accident, their estates and life insurance policies had supported Kat through art school and allowed her to be an artist herself without worrying about starving or working a day job. Yes, she needed a new car. And yes, the house probably needed a new coat of paint, but she didn't want for much.

She tossed her purse onto the couch beside a box of woodworking tools and wood scraps. It would go with her Monday morning when she went down to the District to work. The old warehouse-turned-artist-community was where she spent most of her days. She rented a studio in the building even though she had room at the house to work. Woodworking was messy, but being there was more about community and exposure than anything else. If she wasn't working there or selling pieces to folks strolling by, she was hanging out with the other artists, who had become her family since her parents died.

Honestly, losing that place would be like losing her parents all over again. And that was what she was facing. That was why she'd gotten all dressed up and gone downtown to that stupid awards ceremony the night she'd met Finn. Because she was going to lose it all to the wheels of progress and commerce.

Four months ago, the owner of the District passed

away and his children sold the building to a developer. The place would be gutted and renovated. It would remain an artist community—at least that's what the letters they all received said—but it would be more about selling than creating, by necessity. The rent would be tripling to cover the costs of the renovations and bring the place more in line with the new owner's vision.

Kat had the money to pay the rent at the new building, but most artists weren't so lucky. When the District reopened as a fancy, funky downtown venue for people to shop and be seen, most of the people she knew and loved would be long gone.

Walking up the stairs to her bedroom, she unzipped her dress and let it slip to the floor on the landing. Kat stepped out of it and turned sideways to admire her slightly rounding tummy in the hallway mirror. She'd just started to show in the last week or so. Her normally flat belly had begun to curve out, making her favorite jeans uncomfortably tight at the waistband. She'd told Sawyer the truth when she said this was the only dress she had that fit. Most formals weren't made of particularly forgiving fabrics.

Life didn't always turn out the way she expected it to. This baby was evidence enough of that. Kat had gone to that award ceremony to try and talk some sense into the District's new owner, Sawyer Steele. Instead, she was having his brother's baby.

Two

"You're a real piece of work, you know that?"

"What?"

As always, Finn's voice didn't betray even the slightest bit of guilt for what he might have done. There was only an edge of sleepiness, which was to be expected given the hour in China. At least where Finn was concerned. The average Beijing citizen was likely preparing to eat lunch by now, but his brother had still been asleep after a late Saturday night of high jinks that probably involved beautiful Chinese women and too much *baiju* to drink.

"Sawyer, you know I'm half asleep and half hungover. Why don't you just tell me what you think I've done wrong instead of making me guess. Then we can move straight on to you yelling, and I can take some ibuprofen and go back to sleep."

"You're not going back to sleep, Finn. And I don't *think* I know what you did, I'm certain of it. And it's a big one this time."

"I doubt that. You're prone to overreaction, like Father."

Sawyer swallowed an insult. He wasn't going to let his brother bait him. Finn knew how much he hated being compared to their father. Yes, they shared an affinity for keeping the peace and avoiding drama, but that was about it. "You know, when I gave you that Jet Ski for going in my place to the Charleston's Best awards, it was because I wanted the night to go smoothly."

"As I recall it did go smoothly," Finn replied. "I picked up a nice plaque for the company awards case, Dad didn't figure out you skipped, and I got a new Jet Ski. Win-win."

"Yes, well, that was because everyone at the party thought you were me. I thought we were past the childish identical-twin games, Finn."

There was a moment of silence on the line, but Sawyer knew it wasn't out of guilt. Knowing Finn, he was trying to figure out how to weasel out of getting into trouble.

"Okay, who told on me? There's no way you could know that I let everyone think I was you," he said at last. "It's been months since that party and there hasn't been a peep about it since then."

"Well, that's not entirely true. Apparently the red-head you seduced that night while you were pretending to be me has been trying to get in touch with you. Me. *Us*."

Finn groaned and audibly flopped back against the pillows. "The redhead. Yeah. That was a hell of a night, but I wasn't really interested in seeing her again. She's gorgeous, don't get me wrong, but she's not my usual type. She's too artsy and academic. She's more your type, I think."

That was true enough, but Sawyer wasn't interested in walking into the hot mess his brother had left behind. "Well, to be honest, I don't think she was wanting to see you again, either, but she doesn't have a choice."

Finn chuckled. "And why is that? She can't get enough of me? She wouldn't be the first."

"No, because she's having your baby, you thoughtless idiot. How could you not take precautions for a one-night stand? You know better than that."

"Whoa, whoa, whoa," Finn said, suddenly sounding very awake on the other end of the call. "My baby? The redhead is pregnant? Well, it can't be mine."

"Her name is Kat," Sawyer corrected with an irritated tone. For some reason it grated on him that Finn was starting a family with a woman whose name he couldn't remember. "And she says it's yours. Actually, she thought it was mine until I figured out what you did and got her straightened out."

"No, it's not my baby," Finn insisted. "Listen, you may think I'm stupid, but that is one area where I don't take chances. In all these years, I've never even had a scare. Nothing was different about my night with her. She's mistaken. It's someone else's baby."

Sawyer would've liked to believe that his brother took anything seriously, especially something like this. But he'd seen the pained look in those big green eyes. She believed her story, and he wanted to believe her. But belief and trust were two different things. "Are you sure? There were no rips, no slipups?"

"No, I'm telling you, I know how to use one properly."

"Fine." There had to be another explanation for why it failed. "Did you bring the condoms or did she?"

There was a pause as Finn lay in bed, likely sorting through his romantic memory bank. "Usually I do, but I remember I didn't have any on me that night. It was supposed to be a boring party, which is why I pretended to be you, to spice things up. She had the condoms."

That made Sawyer's stomach ache with worry. If Finn wasn't in control of them at all times, anything could happen. "That means she could've sabotaged them if she wanted to. Maybe poked holes in one."

"You think she got pregnant on purpose?"

Sawyer sighed and sat back in the leather wingback chair of the family library. He didn't know. Their father had raised them to be suspicious of women's motives. Getting pregnant was an easy way to weasel into the family, and more importantly, into their fortune. "I don't know. You know her better than I do."

"Hardly," Finn scoffed. "We flirted and looked at fish in the aquarium. I don't really know anything about…"

"Kat," Sawyer repeated. "Please remember the name of the woman who's carrying your child."

"*Might* be carrying my child," Finn corrected. "I'm not as convinced as you are."

"Yeah, well, until we know otherwise, you need to handle this situation as though it were true."

"Handle it how, Sawyer? I'm in Beijing. I couldn't even come back for Morgan's wedding. I can't just fly home in the middle of constructing the new manufacturing plant and deal with... *Kat*. Dad placed a lot of trust in me when he gave me this project. I can't screw it up or I won't get a second chance."

"And if Dad finds out that you've knocked up some stranger and walked away from the situation, it will be even worse."

Finn groaned aloud. "Please don't tell him until I have some time to think on this."

"You'd better think fast. He'll find out soon. She made quite a scene at the wedding tonight. Everyone will want to know what it was about."

"A scene?"

"Yeah." Sawyer's cheek still stung from the slap Kat had given him. "When you get back to Charleston, I'll pass her message along." He intended to hit his brother harder than Kat ever could.

"Does anyone else know?" Finn asked.

"No. I thought I'd tell you first, since she's been unsuccessful in telling you personally."

"Okay, good. Can we keep it that way for a while until I can figure out what I'm going to do?"

"I'll hold out as long as I can, but I'm not going to lie for you, Finn."

"That's fair enough. I'll give my attorney a call

and see what he recommends, then take it from there. Knowing him, he'll tell me to make a big opening offer, something she can't refuse, then she'll be happy and hopefully things won't escalate. I'll keep you posted."

"Fine. But one last thing before you go, Finn."

"What's that?"

Sawyer considered his words before he said them, speaking with slow, deliberate intention. "If you ever, *ever* pretend to be me again, I'm going to mess up your face so badly no one will be able to confuse us. Am I clear?"

There was a long silence before Finn answered. "Crystal."

The line disconnected and Sawyer slipped his phone into his coat pocket. By the time he stepped out of the library and into the grand foyer, he was surprised to find that the wedding appeared to be over. Once the happy couple left, things must have wrapped up. The guests were gone, the orchestra was breaking down and the caterers were bussing the tables. He glanced around for a blonde in a pale blue gown, but Serena was nowhere to be found.

Looking at his watch, he winced when he realized how late it was. So much for telling Serena he'd be right back. She'd probably given up on him long ago. And for good. For all she knew, he'd abandoned her on the dance floor and run off with some redhead. Serena deserved someone who couldn't get thoughts of her out of his mind.

Kind of like the feisty and mysterious Kat was on Sawyer's mind right now.

He strolled into the abandoned ballroom, heading

toward the wedding cake, or what was left of it. A few pieces were still sitting on china plates, waiting to be eaten, even as the caterers worked to disassemble and pack up the remaining tiers. He picked up a slice and carried it with him into the kitchen. After brewing a cup of coffee and slowly savoring his prize, he remembered the business card he'd thoughtlessly tucked into his breast coat pocket.

When he fished it out and looked down at it at last, a piece of the fluffy white cake caught in his throat. Sawyer coughed for a moment, fighting to breathe again. Then he picked up the card and reread the words that had surprised him so much the first time.

Katherine McIntyre, Artist.
The District, Floor 2, Studio 210

Suddenly he remembered why her name had sounded familiar. He hadn't lied when he said they hadn't met. He'd never laid eyes on her before. But she had emailed him, written him and called his office so many times in the last four months that his assistant had asked for a raise.

Kat was the voice of the District's resistance group. They were not happy about his plans for the building he'd purchased, and no amount of talking was budging either side of the argument. So far.

It was then that Sawyer was absolutely certain Kat's appearance at that party three months ago, and possibly in his brother's bed, was no coincidence.

Kat frowned at the misshaped hunk of wood in front of her. This was not her best work. Far from it. Honestly, it was crap. All she'd managed to produce was crap since the day she'd taken that pregnancy test and got a positive result. The creative zone had eluded her ever since then. She understood now why her parents had each been so protective of their work time and space. It was a fragile ecosystem, susceptible to imbalance when a sticky-fingered child was introduced to the situation.

That didn't bode well for her future work, but she refused to worry about it now. She would figure it out. And not the way her parents had. Locked office doors and nannies were effective, but not particularly warm and loving for a child who wanted nothing more than her family's love.

"So…" A familiar voice sounded from the entryway of her studio. "How'd last night go?"

Setting down her chisel, Kat turned to find one of her fellow artists and friends standing there in old overalls, fireproof gloves and a welding helmet. Hilda Levy rented the studio across from Kat, and despite the constant sounds of metal banging and sparks flying, she couldn't ask for a better friend to work nearby. That said, she also kept a fire extinguisher on hand in case her wood shavings and Hilda's blazing hot sparks collided.

"It went terribly," Kat confessed.

Hilda pushed her helmet up, exposing the laugh lines and quirky black cat-eye glasses she was known for. "Well, shit. What happened?"

Kat plopped down onto an old futon she kept in the corner of her studio, and Hilda followed suit. "Well, for one thing, I had the wrong guy."

Few things seemed to faze Hilda, but this caused her brow to knit in confusion. "What's that, now?"

"I didn't have sex with Sawyer Steele."

The older woman looked over the top of her glasses at Kat. "Then who the hell was it?"

"His twin brother, Finn. He just let me think he was Sawyer, for kicks or something."

"The plot thickens," Hilda said, as she leaned in with interest. "So did you talk to Finn?"

"Uh, no. After crashing the wedding and slapping Sawyer, I hightailed it out of there, after I found out the truth. I was so embarrassed by the whole thing, I wouldn't stay a moment longer. But I did find out that Finn is half a world away at the moment. So that complicates matters."

"Does it? I know I'm old, but I have heard tell of this fancy internet thing that lets people communicate around the world."

Kat rolled her eyes at her friend's deadpan commentary. "You're not old. And I'll talk to him. Eventually. Right now I'm still trying to wrap my head around the whole thing. I mean, I slept with the wrong guy. The whole reason I went to that stupid award ceremony was to talk to Sawyer. To try and convince him that his plans for the District would be detrimental to the whole art community."

"Not sleep with him," Hilda added.

"No, not sleep with him," Kat agreed. "That was… accidental. I went down in person to put him on the spot, because he wasn't returning any of my calls and I couldn't get past his stupid secretary. And it got us nowhere in the end, because not only did we never discuss his plans for the District that night, the man I met wasn't even the one who bought it."

"You didn't bring it up that night?"

Kat thought back to the dark aquarium, the blue tank lights and the dimpled smile that had lulled her into doing something stupid. "I tried. But whenever I did, he'd change the subject. Probably so I wouldn't figure out he wasn't Sawyer and had no idea what I was talking about." She groaned and dropped her face into her hand. "I'm such an idiot."

"You're not an idiot. You were swept away by a charming billionaire after drinking too much champagne. That's no crime. Personally, I'd love to make a mistake like that. It's been a long time."

Kat couldn't help smiling at her friend. Hilda always had an outlook on life that could pull her out of the dumps when she was wallowing there. She honestly wasn't sure how she would've gotten on after her parents died without Hilda. Without everyone here at the District, actually. Hilda was like her surrogate mother now. Except she gave advice like a girlfriend, not a mom. Since Hilda had never married or had kids of her own, maternal advice wasn't her strong suit. Or so she said.

"We need to get you some," Kat said. She was a little relieved to shift the topic off herself, even for a short time.

"Oh, Lordy," Hilda exclaimed. "That shop has been closed down for so long it would take more than a good dusting to get it up and operational again."

"I'm pretty sure it all still works. There's someone out there for you. And when you meet him, you won't be able to dust off that equipment fast enough."

"I'm not so sure," Hilda replied. This time when she spoke the smile in her eyes dimmed slightly. She was lonely. Kat knew it. Her smile and attitude tried to hide the fact, but Kat knew better.

"I've seen Zeke watching you work with more than a little appreciation in his gaze."

Hilda rolled her eyes and shook her head. "Zeke? You've got to be kidding me. He just likes my work."

"Are you sure?" Kat wagged her eyebrows suggestively. The older man was a sculptor with a studio on the other side of their floor. With Kat and Hilda at the back of the building, opposite the stairs and the restrooms, there was no reason for Zeke to be over on their side. But for some reason, he always seemed to be hanging around Hilda's studio. It couldn't be just because of her metalwork.

"No," she argued. "But even if there was more to it, I'm not interested."

"Why?" Kat challenged. Hilda had spent more than a few working hours over by Zeke's studio herself.

"Because he's a widower. His wife has been gone for a year now. Men his age don't date for love. They date because they can't function without a woman to cook and clean for them. I've avoided being someone's maid for fifty-eight years and I have no interest in starting now."

"You don't know what he wants until you ask."

Hilda sputtered for a moment before turning to Kat

with a disgruntled expression on her face. "Why are we talking about my love life? You're the one in the midst of a crisis."

"Thanks for the reminder." Kat pushed herself up from the couch and walked over to the table, where she'd left a bottle of water earlier. She took a sip and shook her head. "His brother said he'd get in touch with Finn, and hopefully, I'll hear something soon."

"And when you do hear from him, what exactly are you going to say? Have you decided what you want to do about the whole situation yet?"

Kat frowned. "Yes and no. My baby is my baby, end of story there. But as far as Finn and his role in our lives… I don't know. I just… My whole life I've had this vision of my future and my family. It includes marriage. It always has."

"From what you've said so far, this Finn guy doesn't really sound like marriage material."

"He's not. Absolutely not. But the more I think about it, the more I've come to realize that it doesn't change how I want things to be. I refuse to have my child born a bastard like I was. Regardless of the circumstances."

"Your parents were together for twenty-five years," Hilda argued.

"And never married," Kat added. For whatever reason, they'd never felt it was important to do so. She got the feeling they'd actually avoided it deliberately because of the stickiness of comingling their artistic property and intellectual rights. It was such a silly reason in her eyes.

"So what? It's not the 1950s anymore. Most of those

Karwashians aren't married and they're having kids left and right."

"It's Kardashian," Kat corrected, wishing she didn't know enough about them to notice Hilda mangling their name. "And some of them are married. But it's not the point."

"Then tell me what is the point, honey."

"I want my child to have a family."

"You hardly know this guy."

"Maybe it's better I don't. Maybe we should just jump in with both feet and see what happens. It's possible we only stay married a year. Or we barely make it past the baby's birthday before we call it quits. I can't tell you how it will end up. But I can't help but think it's the right thing to do for my baby."

"I'm not sure the Steele family is going to be as receptive as you're wanting them to be. They have more money than the state of South Carolina. Even if Finn agrees to marry you, there's going to be lawyers involved at every step. Prenuptial agreements. Custody arrangements. It's not going to be the least bit romantic."

"I don't care about romance and I don't care about the money. I have enough of that. I only want my baby to have what's his or hers. I don't need anything other than a father for my child. I want better for my baby than I had."

"Okay." Hilda gave a heavy sigh. "If you're determined, then I wish you the best of luck marrying into that family. As for me," she said, pushing up from the low futon with a groan, "I've got to get some work done. The clock is ticking on our time here and it's going to be a nightmare hauling all my scrap metal away."

Kat looked around her own studio, feeling guilty that she could afford to stay when others couldn't. She'd still have to pack up and move out for a few months while they renovated, but she could come back. "You're not moving out for good, Hilda. I promise. No matter what happened between Finn and myself, I still intend to pin down that jerk Sawyer Steele, and get him to change his mind about the District. Of course, now he probably thinks I'm just some gold-digging slut and won't take me seriously."

Hilda's gaze shifted over Kat's shoulder as her eyes widened behind her thick black glasses. She bit at her lip and gently shook her head.

Kat realized she was standing with her back to the entrance of her studio. "He's right behind me, isn't he?"

Hilda nodded and Kat groaned aloud.

"I might be a jerk, but if it's any consolation," a man's voice said from over her shoulder, "I don't think you're just a gold-digging slut."

Three

Kat turned slowly to look at him and he couldn't wipe the smug grin from his face. Sawyer's timing couldn't have been better if he'd tried. He'd caught her in the middle of a tirade about him, and that was fine, because he had a few choice words for her, too.

Most of those words dissipated from his mind when she was facing him. He thought she had looked beautiful at the wedding, but it didn't hold a candle to how she looked today. Her copper hair was twisted into a messy bun, with two pencils holding it in place and sawdust, like glitter, sprinkled over the top. Her face was devoid of makeup, unless you could count the smear of white paint on her cheek and a splatter of yellow paint dots across her forehead. She was wearing a tank top and a pair of denim cutoff shorts that fell at the perfect length to highlight her firm, smooth thighs.

He expected her to say something, but she stood motionless, obviously in shock at his timely appearance. Before he could say anything else, the older woman standing nearby opted to excuse herself.

"I'll let you two talk. I've got a piece to finish and five years of crap to pack up." She looked pointedly at Sawyer as she went by.

He was used to that by now. He was the big, bad real estate developer out to destroy all they held dear. At least, that was what most of the voice mail and phone messages seemed to say. Sawyer wished he could convince them that he was trying to help, but they would never see it from his point of view. They either didn't know or didn't care that the building was crumbling around them. The electrical was old and not up to code. The plumbing was putting out rust-colored water and the pressure was almost useless. The freight elevator barely passed inspection. Before long, the District was going to be condemned and they would all lose their precious studio community.

Sawyer intended to fix things. Making those fixes required a few big concessions on the tenants' parts: one, that they move out temporarily for the work to be done, and two, that their rent increase to cover the costs. When it was all said and done, he wasn't renovating this place out of the goodness of his heart. He was a businessman. He saw the potential of the District. With some improvements, it could be not only a studio community, but a place where people wanted to come. Customers. Those people would spend money.

It was a win-win in his eyes. He wished he wasn't the only one who saw that his plan was necessary to save the institution as a whole. Yes, some people might not be able to afford the rent at the new location, even with increased sales. But he'd learned a long time ago that he couldn't make everyone happy, so he'd stopped trying.

He watched the older woman leave, then turned back to where Kat was standing, red-faced, in front of him. "You know, when we first met, your name sounded familiar, but I didn't connect the dots. It wasn't until I looked at your business card." He fished it from his pocket and held it up. "Then all the pieces came together."

"What are you doing here, Sawyer?" She wiped self-consciously at her face, but the paint stayed stubbornly in place. "Have your lawyers put together some payoff package to make me go away?"

Sawyer smiled and turned toward the collection of works in progress she had scattered around her studio space. "I'm not sure what the lawyers have in mind. Or if anyone has told them yet. I told Finn he had to deal with all that." He stuffed his hands into his pockets and strolled over to admire an intricate carving of an owl on a nearby table. It was the size of a large watermelon, with big, lifelike eyes and feathers etched so delicately it seemed he could reach out and they would feel real. She was a very talented artist.

"So you've told Finn?"

He pulled away from the owl and turned to see Kat biting anxiously at her lower lip. He wanted to run his thumb across that same lip to protect it from her abuses. Instead, he kept his hands deep in his trouser pockets where they belonged. "The minute you left. I couldn't wake him up fast enough with the good news."

"He hasn't reached out to me."

Sawyer wasn't surprised. "I wouldn't let that worry you. I'm sure he wants to get his ducks in a row before he calls. And he has very unruly ducks. They're basically squirrels on a sugar high. It may take some time."

"I'm kinda on a set time line here," Kat said, with one hand protectively covering the slight curve of her belly. "I hope he doesn't take too long, because like it or not, his baby is going to be here come winter."

"I'm sure he'll be in touch. Once the shock wears off. He really wasn't expecting to hear from you again."

"Well, considering he didn't give me the right name, I'm not surprised."

"Yes. I think that's the last time he'll play that game, though. He's far too fond of his good looks to risk them by pretending to be me again. I do have to wonder, though."

"Wonder what?"

Sawyer turned and looked at Kat, who was standing a few feet away. He could easily imagine her in some slinky dress, all dolled up to go to the party and hunt down Sawyer Steele. She intended to get her way, no matter what it took. "It made me wonder how the night would've ended if it had been me there and not Finn."

To be honest, the thought had haunted him the last few days. She had come to the party to see him. To talk to him. Perhaps to seduce him. And somehow the spoils went to Finn instead. Just like usual.

"I'm sure it would've ended very differently," Kat said.

"Would it?" he asked with an arched eyebrow.

"I think so. For one thing, you probably wouldn't have dodged my questions about the District and we could've had a real dialogue about it. And for another, you don't have Finn's...*charisma*."

"Is that what you call it?" Sawyer chuckled. "I typically describe that skill set a little differently. I'm sure that played right into your hands, though."

Kat narrowed her gaze at him, her nose wrinkling in thought and a line creasing between her auburn eyebrows. "What's that supposed to mean?"

"I mean, if you went to that party with the intention of doing whatever it took to get your way... Finn made it easier. I would've been a more difficult mark."

"Wait a minute," Kat said, her hands held out defensively. "Are you suggesting that I deliberately went to the party to seduce you? As though I could be so good in bed that you would just change your mind about the District renovations and do whatever I asked?"

Sawyer shrugged. "I don't know what you were thinking. It does seem pretty convenient, though, the more I think about it. Nothing you were doing was yielding any results. If angry calls and letters didn't work, sympathetic news articles didn't work, protests didn't work…why not try a little honey instead of vinegar?"

"I did not go to that party with the intention of giving you any…*honey*! I went to that event to talk to you, because you wouldn't return any of my calls. It was the only way I could think of to pin you on the spot and make you listen to my side of the situation."

"And yet somehow you ended up sleeping with the man who claimed to be me. Sounds like you're quite the overachiever."

The steam was practically coming out of Kat's ears, and he found he quite liked her when she was angry. The flushed cheeks, the bright eyes, pursed lips…he imagined it wouldn't be much different from how she'd look in the throes of passion. He could just envision her auburn hair across the pillowcase, her sharp nails digging into the flesh of his back…

"Of all the arrogant, insulting things you could say!" Kat sputtered for a moment, at a loss for words before she shook her head. "I was a damned fool to go down there that night. A fool to think that you could be reasoned with. All you rich people care about is your bottom line. The people here are just walking, talking rent payments to you. You don't give a damn about what this place means to the tenants here. You don't care about the community that's grown here over the years, or how you're going to destroy it to make a buck!"

Her anger suddenly wasn't so attractive anymore and she was starting to rub Sawyer the wrong way. She wanted to know why he was doing what he was doing? Well, he was going to tell her. He closed the gap between them and spoke with cold, quiet anger, mere inches from her face. "And you don't seem to care that the rent I'm currently collecting barely covers the utilities for this place. There certainly isn't enough left over to do any repairs and it's falling down around you."

Sawyer pointed to the peeling plaster overhead. "That's going to come crashing down on you sooner or later. The sewer lines are going to fail and flood the ground floor. That wood lathe of yours could overtax the electrical circuits at any moment and set the building on fire. Who is going to fix that? Who is going to pay for all that? The previous owner just ignored the place and cashed the checks. Sure, rent was cheap, but there's a cost, and the building has paid the price for all of you. It's your turn to pay up, and no amount of sweet-talking or seduction is going to change that."

Kat was at a loss for words. It didn't happen very often, but Sawyer seemed to be able to render her mute. Especially when he stood this close to her. Yes, his words were icy cold with restrained anger and frustration, but she could feel the heat radiating off his body. His words were just static noise in the background, with her pounding heart drowning out everything but its sensual rhythm. She knew she should take a step back, reclaim her personal space and counter his argument with more pointed words, but she couldn't make herself do it. Her body wanted to move nearer and close the gap between them.

It was ridiculous. Foolish. But she couldn't help but be confused whenever she was around Sawyer. She was haunted by memories of a night in a downtown hotel room...memories of a man who looked like Sawyer. A man she'd thought *was* Sawyer. Somehow it felt like the most natural thing in the world to reach out and touch him like she had before. Her libido couldn't tell the difference between the two identical men.

But her brain knew. And it knew that was all a lie. Those memories, that man... It wasn't Sawyer she remembered. And no matter how familiar those dark eyes or that dimpled smile, it wasn't the same person. This man was a stranger. A stranger who intended to take away everything she held dear to make a buck. Sure, he wanted to make necessary improvements, but the fancy, downtown art scene he had in mind was a far cry from what the tenants truly needed. The necessary repairs weren't the changes driving the rent out of the realm of possibility for most of the artists. It was the coffee shop, the concert venue, the paved parking lot and the high-end landscaping with dancing fountains.

It was a great response, exactly what she wanted to say, but the argument eluded her when Sawyer gazed at her this way. It wasn't how Finn had looked at her. And yet it was the way she'd always wanted a man to look at her. Like he wanted to consume her, body and soul.

Even in his anger, Sawyer seemed almost as though he was on the verge of kissing her. A part of her wished he would, even if just to end this fight.

Okay, not *just* to end the fight.

Kat's gaze met Sawyer's. In the quiet stillness between them, they seemed to be even closer now. She could feel his breath softly brushing over her skin. Something had changed in the silence and it seemed that he noticed it, as well. It was almost an electricity.

"Aren't you going to say anything?" he asked.

"What do you want me to—"

That's when his lips pressed into hers and a warm tingle shot down her spine. His heat spread quickly through her veins, making her aware of every feverish beat of her heart. Kat didn't pull away from Sawyer. She couldn't even if she wanted to. Her body leaned into him instead, craving more even though it was the last thing she needed right now.

His arms slipped around her waist and pulled her tight against the hard wall of his body. It was then, with every inch of her curves molded against his hard angles, that Kat knew for certain appearances were deceiving. For one thing, Sawyer might look like Finn, but he certainly didn't kiss like him. His twin might have the reputation of being a playboy, but Sawyer had obviously gone for quality over quantity where women were concerned. As he deepened the kiss, his tongue slid leisurely along her bottom lip as though he had all the time in the world to study every inch of her. It elicited a groan of pleasure deep in Kat's throat— a sound she didn't even know she could make until that moment.

This buttoned-up businessman was hiding a skilled lover beneath that boring exterior. And the longer he touched her, the more she wished that it really had been Sawyer Steele in her bed that night three months ago.

But it wasn't.

The thought that was like a lightning bolt of reality. What the hell was she doing? Kissing Sawyer Steele when she wanted to marry his brother?

It took every ounce of determination she had, but she pulled away from his embrace and stepped back out of Sawyer's sphere of influence. Once she got some distance between them again, it was easier to control her impulses and regain what little composure she had left.

This was the wrong Steele twin. They looked alike, but they acted very differently, and like it or not, Sawyer was not the one she needed in her life. Finn was her baby's father. Kissing his brother did nothing but muddy the waters and make an already complicated situation even more so.

Kat covered her lips with her hand, hoping she could somehow wipe away the tingle that lingered there from Sawyer's kiss. It didn't work.

"Did I do something wrong?" Sawyer asked, seeming almost startled by her sudden retreat.

No. Somehow he'd done everything right. Yes, Finn was charming, but Sawyer had different powers that Kat couldn't resist. "No, you didn't. I just… I think that was probably a mistake."

She watched Sawyer's jaw flex and tighten as if he was holding something in. She wished he would just say it, but he didn't seem like that kind of man. He knew when to use restraint, unlike his twin, who did or said whatever he wanted whenever he liked.

His gaze followed her hand as it dropped protectively to her belly on reflex. Then his eyes squeezed shut for a moment and he nodded. "You're right. I overstepped."

"You didn't. We both—"

"No." He held up his palm to halt any further argument from her. "It's my fault. You're having my brother's child. There's no excuse for my behavior."

"And *my* behavior is okay?" she asked. It had been only a moment since they kissed, and her memory still served her pretty well. Whether or not she should've been an active and enthusiastic participant, she was.

"It's not your fault. You were attracted to my brother, obviously. I look exactly like him. I can imagine it's confusing. It's an easy mistake for you to make in the moment, feeling like you're attracted to me when you're not." Sawyer stuffed his hands in his pockets and took a step backward.

"I'm not so blinded by desire as to not know who I was kissing. You two don't look exactly alike," Kat argued.

Sawyer hesitated a moment and shook his head. "We're identical twins."

Kat shook her head in turn. "Maybe genetically, but there are subtle differences. You're mirror images of each other. Your dimple is on the opposite cheek from Finn's. And your eyes…" Her voice drifted off. "There's something there that I didn't see in him."

She wasn't sure what it was yet. He was the more serious, responsible brother, but that wasn't it. Beneath all that there was a kindness in Sawyer's eyes. A softness when he looked at her that faded when he looked

at anyone else. Finn's eyes had reflected only desire.
At the time, that had been enough. Now that she was
hoping for a future and a family with Finn, she wished
she would see more when she looked in his eyes.

More like she saw in Sawyer.

That was a dangerous thought. There was no way
to go back in time and choose a different brother. No
way to go back and stop this whole pregnancy from
happening to begin with. She had made her bed, as
her mother used to say. Now she had to lie in it. With
Finn.

"I'd better go," Sawyer said, as though he'd heard
the thoughts in her head.

Before Kat could say another word, Sawyer Steele
turned on his heel and vanished from her shop, leaving
her more confused than she'd been when he arrived.

Well, that hadn't gone the way he'd intended. It had
started out well enough, but kissing Kat was one of the
dumbest things he'd ever done. This woman was his
nemesis at the District. She was having his brother's
baby through potentially nefarious means. She couldn't
be trusted.

And yet, he'd done it anyway.

Sawyer walked quickly out of the building, trying
to ignore the disgusted looks from the tenants as he
went by. They knew exactly who he was with his expensive suit and his dark sunglasses. He was the one
who was ruining everything.

As he stepped outside into the summer sun, he could
finally breathe again. As hot as it was in the parking

lot, the old building was stifling without air conditioning and only a few old windows for a cross breeze. He didn't know how anyone could work here in the summer. That was number one on his list of things to fix, and if he was a tenant here, he'd be happy to pay more not to sweat to death.

As he climbed into his Audi, his cell phone rang and his brother's number came up on the screen. "Finn," he said as he answered.

"Twin," Finn responded. "How are things going at home?"

"Hmm…let's see… Our parents are badgering me relentlessly about the mystery woman at the wedding. Grandma Ingrid is home from Europe for good. Oh, and it turns out the mother of your child is the one trying to shut down my District renovations."

"Really? That must've been why she kept asking me about it that night. I dodged the questions because I didn't know the answers."

It would've been nice if his brother had bothered to mention the inquisitive woman from the party three months ago. "Yes, apparently she came there looking for me to talk about changing my plans. Sleeping with you was just a…"

"Bonus?" Finn suggested.

"I was going to say *mistake*, but use whatever word you like."

"I've been talking to my lawyers. They recommend coming in with a high offer to keep things quiet, so they're working on a package now."

Sawyer was surprised his brother was moving

so quickly with his attorneys. He'd asked his future brother-in-law, Harley Dalton, to run a background check on her, but the report wasn't back yet. "This seems awfully premature. Are you sure you want to do that before you know if the baby is yours?"

"Well, actually, that's why I'm calling. I could use your help. They can do a prenatal paternity test with a blood sample from the mother and the father. But to speed things along, it would help if you could pop by the lab and do that for me."

Sawyer shook his head in the empty cab of his SUV. "Are you serious?"

"Come on, for a standard paternity test, we share all the same markers as identical twins. It's not a murder case, it's a baby, so unless you've slept with her, too, your DNA would be enough to determine if I'm the father. Doing the testing in China and trying to send the sample to the States would be a hassle and would take forever. This can't wait until I get back either."

"Finn…"

"Please. I've got an appointment all set up if you can swing by. I'll text you the lab address. Just donate some blood and I'll handle the rest. I just need to know for certain before I tell Mom and Dad."

Somehow Sawyer doubted that Finn would be handling much of anything. "When is the appointment?"

"This afternoon at three."

Sawyer glanced at the console of his car. It was almost two, so Finn expected him to drop everything for him, per usual. "You have no idea how much you owe me for this, Finn."

"If it's a boy, we'll name him after you," Finn offered brightly.

In irritation, Sawyer hit the button to hang up the
phone. "You're welcome," he snapped as he drove the
car out of the District parking lot and headed for the
lab.

Four

Kat came home to find a FedEx package on her doorstep. She hadn't ordered anything, so when she picked up the envelope, she eyed the return address with curiosity.

Carson, Turner and Leeds. Attorneys at Law.

Lovely. She'd been expecting this package since someone from the lawyer's office called and asked her to take a paternity test. She'd complied but thought perhaps she might actually *speak* to Finn before she received anything else from them. Guess not.

With a sigh, she carried it in and let the hand-carved wooden door to the piazza swing shut behind her. Dumping her things onto the nearest patio chair, she sat down on the chaise and looked at the envelope again. Taking a deep breath, she pulled the tab to open it and removed the contents.

A thick pouch of paperwork slid out, clamped together with a heavy-duty binder clip. Her eyes scanned the cover letter, but it was what she expected. Finn's first volley in the legal battle ahead. She could've saved him a lot of time if he'd just called her instead of running to his attorneys at the first word of a child.

Flipping through, she eyed the paragraph about the paternity test results—surprise, it was Finn's baby. Then she moved on to the topics of shared custody arrangements, monthly financial support, a trust fund for the baby, and even an offer to purchase and maintain a residence for them both. To say that Finn was being generous was an understatement. She was stunned by the numbers she was seeing. He wasn't a man to walk away from his responsibility, but was the kind willing to pay enough to keep everyone quiet and happy. This was more than she ever expected. And absolutely nothing she wanted.

Maybe she was stupid and naive to hope for more, but she did. Not just a weekend daddy and a big check for her child. She wanted a family. A real, legitimate family. If she had to choose her future husband from a catalog, no, Finn wouldn't be the one she would pick, but she had to play the hand Fate had dealt her.

Hearing her cell phone ringing inside her purse, Kat tossed aside the paperwork with disgust and reached for it. It wasn't a number she recognized, or even a local number, but she answered, figuring a telemarketer might be a welcome distraction.

"Hello?" she answered with a heavy sigh.

"Um, Katherine?" a man's voice asked with uncertainty. "Kat?"

"Yes?" It wasn't a telemarketer. They never called her Kat. Only her friends and family called her by that name. She pulled the phone away from her ear to look at the number again. It wasn't local. It wasn't even a US number, from the looks of it.

"This is Finn Steele," she heard, as she pressed the phone back against her ear.

"Oh."

That wasn't what she expected to say. Or what she'd planned to say once she finally got in touch with the father of her child, but that was what came out. "I got the love letter you sent."

"The *what*?"

"The offer from your attorneys."

"Oh." Finn chuckled nervously. "I was hoping it hadn't arrived yet. I wanted to talk to you first and let you know it was coming, but my lawyer is more efficient than I expected for someone paid by the hour."

"I'm sure he has a standard template he uses for all his rich clients and their pregnant mistresses." Kat couldn't help the bitter tone from leeching into her voice. She even winced at the sound of it, compared to Finn's friendly, conversational tone. No matter what, being ugly to him wouldn't help matters. Slapping Sawyer certainly hadn't. "I'm sorry," she stated, when he didn't respond. "It's the pregnancy hormones. And calling me just as I was reading the legal paperwork didn't tip things in your favor."

"What's wrong with it? Patrick said he was going to put together a very generous offer."

"It was. Very generous. Maybe too generous, under the circumstances. I can't help but feel like you're trying to sweep us under the rug. You can't write a check and make this all go away, Finn. This isn't a fender bender. It's a child. Our child. And it deserves a family."

There was a long silence on the line. Kat was tempted to keep talking, but stopped herself. It was the truth and he needed to hear it, understand it, and respond accordingly. So she waited for him to answer.

"I'm sorry. You're right. You're not a dirty secret. You're carrying a Steele grandchild. It's not an ideal situation, but it's not the end of the world, either. I just wish I wasn't in China right now. There's only so much I can do from here. But I'm going to talk to my parents. I'll tell them everything tonight and I'm sure they'll be eager to meet you as soon as they can."

"You want me to meet your parents? Without you?"

"Yeah, sure. You'll be fine. You'll get to know everyone and by the time I get back stateside, I'm sure you'll feel better about having a family that accepts our child as one of their own."

That was nice, but that wasn't exactly what she had in mind. "I was actually thinking of something a little bit more legally binding on the family front, Finn."

"I can assure you that the offer my attorneys sent you is the best for everyone, Kat."

"Not for me, Finn. I want to get—"

"You don't want to marry me," he interrupted.

Kat was stunned into momentary silence by his abrupt response. She was expecting him to give her a reason why he couldn't or wouldn't marry her, not the other way around. "I don't?"

"No. Listen, you've spoken to my brother. I'm sure he was all too eager to tell you about all my flaws. He revels in them."

"I'm not concerned with your flaws," Kat argued.

"You should be. There's a lot of them. I know that in your head getting married and raising this family together is the practical, responsible thing to do. But I am neither practical nor responsible. Ask anyone who has ever met me. Marrying me would...not be the fantasy you have in your mind."

She could hear Finn sigh on the other end of the line before he continued. "This isn't the old days where we have to marry to cover up the fact that we sinned together. I doubt many happy marriages resulted from that practice back then, and it wouldn't result in a happy marriage now. If I thought that I would be a good husband and father, I would get down on one knee the moment I saw you again. But I can't offer what I don't have. What I can offer you is support, and my last name for our child. He or she will be a Steele, and will be raised as such. You can meet my family and be as involved with them as you'd like. But believe me when I say you don't want to compound this mistake with marriage."

It was a good argument. And Finn sold it well. And if marriage hadn't been such a firm fixture in Kat's mind since she was a small child, she might even be swayed by his words. But what Finn didn't understand, what none of them understood, was what it was like to grow up with parents who weren't married. It wasn't the fifties then, and it still made her feel different. As though she wasn't good enough. Kat never wanted her child to feel like that. Especially just because the father was being selfish.

"Are you sure you're not just saying all this because you don't want to get married?" she countered.

"Of course I don't want to get married!" he shouted over the line. "That's one of the reasons I'll be so terrible at being a husband. Kat, I am not the marrying kind of guy. I've never even considered the possibility. I love the ladies too much to pick one for the rest of my life. I've always known this about myself, and that's why I've always tried to be very careful where contraception was concerned. I never wanted to put myself or a woman in this position, and until now I've been successful. I don't know why it happened this time, but I can't change it, or me. I'm saying this for your sake, for our child's sake and for my own sake. None of us will be happy if we get married."

"Let's table that discussion for now," Kat said. "What about being a father? Let's set aside talk of child support and trust funds and discuss what being a father really means to you. Do you intend to be involved?"

"Absolutely. I believe my lawyer submitted a request for visitation every other weekend, alternate holidays and a week during the summer. That seemed to be pretty standard."

Kat sighed. "And what about the rest of the time?

What about school plays and ball games? Recitals, science projects? Playing in the park? Sitting up with him or her all night when our child has a fever and can't get comfortable?"

"To be honest, I didn't expect you to want me to be that involved. I'm willing to do as much or as little as is needed. I work long hours, and travel a lot, too. I may not be able to make every after-school game and class party. But if you really need me to be there, I will do what I can."

At this point, his words felt like a win to Kat. It wasn't all that she wanted, but it was a big step for their first talk. Maybe once he returned home from China, they could spend more time together. There was still a chance he might change his mind and want to be more involved in not only their child's life, but hers, too. She wouldn't give up hope yet.

"Look over the paperwork, Kat. It doesn't cover everything, but it does cover a lot. We can talk about it more in a few days. In the meantime, I'm going to talk to my parents. Keep an eye out for a mushroom cloud over Mount Pleasant. I'll talk to you soon."

Kat hung up the phone and leaned her head against the back of the seat. After everything that had happened the last few days with Sawyer and now with Finn, she was emotionally and physically exhausted. It didn't take much lately. The tiny human inside her seemed to sap her of any energy she might have. She wasn't sure how she was going to handle it when the baby got bigger, or worse, after it was born and mobile.

The idea of having a child alone was terrifying. It

was a thought she hadn't really allowed herself to entertain. Every time the scary what-ifs crept into her mind, she would tell herself that Finn would marry her and they would be one big, happy family. But was she just lying to herself? If she accepted the fact that she was doing this on her own, would she be better prepared to face the eventuality?

Kat glanced down at the legal papers she'd set aside. Finn's attorneys had promised her a great deal of security. As much as money could buy. That was something. But Finn's money wouldn't hold her at night or get up and change the baby at 2:00 a.m. when she was too exhausted to get out of bed.

She tried to picture Finn doing just that. She could see him in a pair of boxer shorts, clutching a small baby to his chest. Both he and the infant had the same golden-blond curls as he bent to kiss the baby on the top of the head. It was a touching image. One that nearly made her tear up at the thought. But as she let the fantasy play out in her mind, she knew one thing was different in this scenario.

It wasn't Finn holding her baby in her mind.

It was Sawyer.

Sawyer stood awkwardly on Kat's doorstep, holding a large box with a bow on it. He'd gotten the address from Finn's attorneys, but it felt weird to stand here on the piazza steps of her home with a gift. Unannounced. Like he was asking her to the prom or something. He suppressed that comparison lest the image of her in a slinky beaded dress completely derail why he was here today.

This visit wasn't about his brother. Or the District. Or his undeniable urge to see her again. And kiss her again. No. It was about his family.

He rang the doorbell, stopping to admire the intricate engravings on the front door. The edges were done in a Celtic knot design that ran all the way around, with leaves, acorns, chipmunks and other woodland creatures carved into the dark wood. It was incredible, and no doubt one of her pieces.

Kat opened the door, a look of confusion wrinkling her nose as she eyed him and the box in his arms. "Sawyer? What are you doing here?"

Considering he hadn't seen her since they kissed in her workshop and now he was at her home without prior warning, that was a valid question. To be honest, he hadn't called ahead because he thought she might tell him not to come. That was the smart thing to do. Let the lawyers handle the situation and stay far from the temptation of Kat McIntyre. And yet here he was, on a mission he'd volunteered for.

"I'm here today on official Steele family business," he said. At least that might ease any concerns she could have about him being here for less than altruistic reasons. He wasn't at her home to kiss her again. Although he'd have a hard time turning her down if she wanted him to. Kat was apparently the Achilles' heel he never knew he had until their lips touched that afternoon at the District. Since then, he'd thought of little else.

"What official business is that?" She crossed her arms over her chest and leaned against the door frame.

"Well, news of you and the baby has spread to the immediate family." Sawyer hadn't been at the house the night Finn called, so had heard the tale secondhand from Lena, their housekeeper. Apparently, they'd had to call the doctor, because his father had turned bright red as his blood pressure went through the roof. Sawyer wouldn't tell Kat that, though.

"Everyone is very excited to meet you and they don't want to wait until Finn gets home, so my parents have asked me to invite you to a little thing they're putting on this weekend at the house."

"A little thing?"

Sawyer knew well enough that nothing his parents ever did could be described as little. Perhaps in their mind a garden party for a hundred of their closest friends was an intimate get-together, but normal people knew better. "My grandmother is coming home. She's spent the last three years traveling around Europe after my grandfather passed away. I guess she finally got tired of Paris and has decided to come back to Charleston. They're throwing a welcome-home party for her Saturday afternoon and they'd like you to come."

He could tell by the look on Kat's face that she wasn't excited by the invitation. Some people dreamed of being invited to a Steele party. But some people weren't carrying the illegitimate child of the family's problem son. He imagined that, for someone in her position, a party like that would be akin to being dropped in a shark tank wearing a chum bikini. This might take some convincing.

"Can I come in?"

Kat nodded and stepped back to allow him up the stairs and inside the piazza. He followed her into the house, and as she shut the door and turned to face him, he held out the large box to her. "This is for you."

"What is it?" she asked cautiously.

Sawyer shrugged. "I think it's a dress. It's from my sister Jade, so I'm not entirely certain. She just told me to give it to you."

Kat accepted the box, but the line between her brows deepened with thought as she eyed the sizable package. "Why would she give me a dress? Or anything at all for that matter? We've never even met before."

"Well, that's true, but Jade is technically new to the family, too. I don't know if you follow the news, but she and my sister Morgan were switched at birth as part of some kidnapping and ransom scheme. Jade is my biological sister, but no one knew it until recently. When she heard about your situation, she told me she wanted to help out. She knows what it's like to walk into a room of Steeles as a stranger."

Kat carried the box over to the coffee table. "That's sweet of her. But why a dress? I have clothes. Is she worried I'm going to show up to this thing in cutoffs and flip-flops?"

"No, of course not. But she knows you're expecting. And I mentioned how you'd complained about your nice clothes not fitting at Morgan's wedding. Really, I don't know why. I didn't ask. She just gave me a box. It's her way of welcoming you to the family, I guess."

"I suppose I should be happy that someone is welcoming me," Kat muttered, as she opened the lid to expose the tissue-wrapped outfit inside.

It was coral-colored lace, and when she held it up, Sawyer could see why his sister had chosen it. It would flatter Kat's new curves nicely with its high waist, plunging V-neckline, and hem that would fall just above her knee. Her shapely calves would be on display all afternoon, and he couldn't complain about that. He was undoubtedly a leg man.

"This is beautiful," she said. "And just the right size. How did she know?"

He shrugged. He wouldn't even begin to guess what size a woman wore. It was a losing game for a man anyway, so he chose not to play. "She saw you hit me at the wedding reception and took a guess. She has an eye for clothes."

"I'll have to tell her thank-you when I see her at the party." Kat folded the dress and placed it neatly back inside the box.

"So you're coming?"

Kat sighed and sat back on her sofa. "I don't suppose I can say no or I'll be starting off on the wrong foot with Finn's family. Your family," she added, with a wistful look in her eye he didn't understand. "I wish it wasn't such a big, public spectacle, though."

"That's better, really." Sawyer sat on the sofa beside her. "There will be a lot of people there and the focus won't be on you. It will be on Grandma Ingrid. You'll be able to mingle and meet people, but you won't be trapped in the dining room with the immediate family grilling you over dinner."

Sawyer had been witness to one such family dinner in recent memory. His older brother, Tom, had brought home a woman to meet the family. He'd seriously been considering proposing to her. But watching her melt to a puddle under the scrutiny had changed his brother's mind. If she couldn't handle dinner, she couldn't handle being a Steele.

"Okay, I guess. What time?"

"Three o'clock at the house."

Kat nodded and picked up her phone to put the information into her digital calendar. "Is there anything else I should know?" she asked.

"I'd recommend wearing shoes that won't sink into the lawn. And wear some good sunscreen and insect repellant. My parents have the yard sprayed, but it's still summer in Charleston."

Kat smiled and shook her head. "Thanks, but that's not exactly what I meant."

He was afraid of that. "What do you want to know?" he asked. "I'll answer you as honestly as I'm able to."

"Your parents… Finn told me he was going to tell them. Are they okay with this? I can't imagine they took the news well."

Sawyer sighed. "They didn't. At least at first. My family has always been very focused on their public image. They're getting better, though. I think my father has finally come to terms with the fact that we are all adults now, and the more he meddles in our lives, the worse it can make things."

Kat's lower lip trembled just slightly as she turned away and looked at the dress on the table. "So they hate me," she said matter-of-factly.

Sawyer wanted to reach out to her. To brush his thumb across her lip and kiss her until she forgot about his parents and what they might think. In the end, that mattered very little. Not as much as seeing her smile again. He compromised with himself and instead reached out to place a comforting hand on her denim-clad knee. "No. They don't hate you, Kat. They don't know you. But they want to get to know you and see what kind of person you are."

"They may not hate me, but they blame me for this. They think I'm just after their money and their name."

"Again, they don't know you. I'm sure they have their concerns, but they're polite enough not to confront you with them. Their future grandchild is at stake. They want to like you, I promise. Honestly, in this situation they blame Finn. I'm sure they're surprised it's taken this long for something like this to happen."

The frown line returned between her brows. It seemed to whenever he spoke about his brother. He understood her concern. She hadn't said anything to him about Finn, but he could tell that his twin's reputation bothered her. One night together wasn't enough time to decide if someone is going to be a good parent or partner.

"Just be yourself, Kat. Come and meet everyone. It

will be fine. You'll get through Saturday and I'm sure it will be easier after that. My family isn't that scary."

"You're pretty scary." Kat gave him a shady bit of side eye and a knowing smirk as she said the words. It was enough to make him pull away his hand.

"I am. As you will soon learn, Morgan is the princess, Tom's the golden boy, Finn's the fuck-up and I'm the hard-ass." Sawyer stood and shoved his hands into his pockets. "Welcome to the family, Kat."

Five

The second time Kat drove up to the Steele mansion, the circumstances were very different. It had been only a few weeks and the live oak–lined drive with its dripping Spanish moss was just the same, but this time she had been invited. And hopefully, she wouldn't cause a scene.

There were already a lot of cars parked in the field when she pulled up and handed the keys of her Jeep to the valet. Another man directed her down a path along the side of the house to the backyard. She could hear a string quartet playing and the melody of voices and laughter in the distance.

But it wasn't until she rounded the corner of the house and caught a glimpse of the party that the wave of nerves hit her. She wasn't sure how many people she was expecting, but this was hardly a *little thing* Sawyer had invited her to. The event sprawled across the manicured lawn behind the house. A huge, white tent covered a portion of the tables and she could see a large buffet laid out in the shade.

There were more than a hundred people milling around in their garden party finery and flashy hats, with almost as many staff in white tuxedos catering to their every need.

As she stood at the edge of the crowd, trying to force herself to officially enter, one of the staff approached her with a tray of crystal flutes. "Would you care for some champagne, miss?"

Kat stopped herself from reaching out on impulse and dropped her hand to her stomach instead. Her baby belly was still little more than a bump, but the gown Jade had bought her for the party highlighted what she did have. "I'm not drinking."

"Of course, miss." The man snapped his fingers and another waiter appeared with a different tray of drinks. "The elder Mrs. Steele doesn't drink, so we also have sparkling cider and sparkling fruit waters available for guests."

Kat was surprised, but pleased. Alcohol was what she probably needed to calm her nerves, but at least she could have a crystal flute to hold, and feel like she belonged. She reached out and selected a glass of faintly pink bubbling water with a plump red strawberry wedged on the rim. "Thank you."

The waiters nodded and left, leaving Kat no choice but to finally move on. She slowly followed the trail toward the crowd, ignoring the drag of her feet, which felt almost as heavy as concrete. She knew it wasn't the shoes. If she allowed herself to turn and leave, she could probably sprint. She just didn't want to go to this party.

"Katherine?"

Kat wasn't used to people using her full name. Her mother was really the only one who ever called her Katherine. She stopped and turned her head toward the voice, seeing a stunning young blonde heading her direction. She immediately tensed. She didn't know who this woman was, but could tell in an instant that this was perhaps the most beautiful woman she'd ever seen in person.

Her hair was platinum blond, and she had big doe eyes and a wide grin, her fuchsia-colored lipstick matching her dress. She was tall, thin and elegant, moving with a swift grace in Kat's direction despite the four-inch heels she was wearing.

"You *are* Kat, aren't you?"

Kat took a breath and did her best to return the smile. "I am."

"I'm Jade, Finn's sister. I recognized you in the dress I sent over with Sawyer for the party."

With a sigh of relief, Kat felt the muscles in her shoulders start to unwind. At least she had one friendly face in the sea of strangers. "Oh! Thank you so much for sending this. You didn't have to, but it's lovely."

"Yes, I did have to. It fits you perfectly, I'm so glad. Asking Sawyer about your measurements was like asking a tiger how to prepare a five-course vegetarian meal."

Kat looked down to admire the coral lace and smiled. "I appreciate you thinking of me. Honestly, I'm not sure if I would've come today if you hadn't sent the dress over with Sawyer. I'm so nervous."

"I understand. The first time I met the Steeles, I was almost thirty years old. I was their biological daughter, and yet I'd never laid eyes on any of them, or them me. Seeing them face-to-face and finally learning the truth about our family and what happened was so stressful. But I don't regret it. Now I have two amazing families, four brothers and a sister of sorts that I adore."

"It's different for me," Kat replied, feeling her smile fade ever so slightly. "You were taken from them, but you belonged here. I'm an outsider who could be using their grandchild as a means of shoehorning her way into the family fortune."

Jade narrowed her gaze at Kat for a moment. "Is that what you're doing?"

Kat shook her head. "No, but I wouldn't believe me if I were in their shoes. Sawyer is certainly suspicious enough of my motives."

"Sawyer is suspicious of everyone. That's just the way he is. Ignore him."

Kat bit her tongue, but she wanted to say that was easier said than done. The serious Steele twin had gotten under her skin. Whether he was accusing her of something terrible or looking at her with blatant desire in his eyes, Kat couldn't help but want to be nearer to him. She'd never had that happen with a man before.

Being aggravated by and attracted to a man at the same time was infuriating and confusing. Never mind having all those thoughts about the wrong person.

"Have you met Grandmother yet?"

"I haven't met anyone. I just got here."

"Well then." Jade grinned. "Let's go find ourselves some Steeles." She reached out and took Kat's hand, leading her across the lawn to the tent.

It was probably just as well that Jade was virtually dragging her through the party, because Kat wasn't certain she could do it herself. The farther into the crowd they went, the more curious gazes she could feel upon her. No one knew who she was or why she was at such an exclusive event, she guessed. She wasn't really sure why she was there, either.

"Mother Patricia? Guess who I found loitering near the car lot."

Another pale blonde turned toward them and Kat would swear she was the spitting image of what Jade would look like in twenty-five years. They actually could've been confused as sisters. The woman took a moment to study Kat, and after her gaze fell on the slight curve of her stomach her dark eyes immediately shot back up to her face. "You must be Katherine," she said, with a smile that was warmer than expected, yet a little formal and stiff at the same time.

"Please call me Kat," she said, reaching out to shake the woman's hand.

"Kat, this is Patricia Steele, our mother."

Kat could've guessed that much without being told. "It's nice to meet you, Mrs. Steele."

Patricia looked around the crowd and frowned. "I think Trevor just slipped away into the house to talk business. He hates these dull affairs. Until he shows up again, I can introduce you to his mother, Ingrid. This party is in her honor. She's just returned to Charleston after several years in Europe."

Kat nodded blankly and let herself be carried along to meet someone else. She didn't expect what she found, however. Sitting in a chair near the stage was an older woman with the carriage of the queen of England. She was wearing a light pink suit dress with a matching blazer, white gloves and sensible white flats. There was a single strand of pearls around her throat and teardrop-shaped ones hanging from her ears. Her white hair was elegantly curled and coiffed, missing only a tiara to complete the look.

When the woman turned to look her way, Kat felt a surge of nerves worse than anything she'd felt before. This was the family matriarch, the guest of honor, and likely the one whose opinion would weigh the heaviest where Kat was concerned. Making a good impression was paramount.

"Mrs. Steele," the younger Mrs. Steele said. "I'd like to introduce you to Katherine McIntyre. This is Finn's lady friend."

The woman narrowed her dark brown eyes at Kat and smirked. "Judging by that little tummy, she's more than just his lady friend, Patricia." She turned away from her daughter-in-law to focus her full attention on Kat. "Come closer, dear. Have a seat beside me."

She patted the empty chair beside her with a gloved

hand and Kat knew better than to decline. The older woman was no cookie-baking granny—she was sharp-tongued and quick-witted. Kat needed to stay on her toes with Finn and Sawyer's grandmother, she could tell.

"It's lovely to meet you, Mrs. Steele. I've been told you just returned from Europe? That sounds amazing. I've always wanted to travel more."

The older woman shrugged nonchalantly, as though she hadn't been globe-trotting for the last few years. "Sometimes you need to run away from home to get some perspective. Though most people don't wait until they're eighty to do it. Katherine, is it? Or Kate, perhaps?"

"Kat."

"Kat. I like it. I'm Ingrid. There's too many Mrs. and Miss Steeles around here. It gets confusing. So just call me Ingrid to keep things simple."

Kat nodded, noticing Patricia stiffen beside her. It made her wonder if she was allowed to call her mother-in-law by her first name.

"Why don't you run along, Patricia. I'm sure you have guests to tend to. I want to get to know this young lady better."

Patricia looked at Jade with a bit of concern, then pasted a smile on her face. "Of course. We will have plenty of time to spend with Kat. Call me if you need anything, ladies." She took Jade's arm and led her daughter to the other side of the tent, where some ladies in decorative hats were chatting.

Ingrid turned to Kat and placed a gentle hand on

her knee. "Relax, dear. I know it's stressful, but I'm not going to bite. It's never easy being the wife of one of the Steele men. It's been over sixty years and I still remember the night Edward—that's Trevor's father—introduced me to his parents. It was nerve-racking to say the least, but I held my own. And so did Patricia. And so will you. Becoming Mrs. Steele is like taking on a new identity."

Her words were kind and reassuring, but Kat wondered why Ingrid was telling her this. Yes, she wanted to do the right thing and marry Finn, but she hadn't said as much to anyone aside from Finn himself. Then again, the family probably assumed that was what Kat would want: a diamond ring and a piece of the Steele pie for herself. That wasn't exactly the way she envisioned it.

"When my husband died three years ago," Ingrid continued, "I realized I didn't know who I was any longer. Who was Mrs. Steele without Mr. Steele? I was just some grandmother shuffling around the house having tea and waiting to die myself. That's why I left. I went to Europe to mourn Edward and find out who Ingrid was now. I went to London, to Barcelona, to Florence and finally to Paris. I sat on my balcony on the Île Saint-Louis overlooking the Seine and listened to the bells of Notre Dame cathedral ring every day. I sipped cafe crème, ate whatever I liked, and took long strolls down streets without knowing where I was headed. I found Ingrid again in Paris. And the night the cathedral burned, I decided it was time to come home."

Kat couldn't imagine living a life like that, but it

sounded like the kind of thing that would feed an artist's soul. She wondered if Ingrid had some artistic talents, as well.

"It was time to come back to my family. And now I know why. I needed to come back here for you."

At that, Kat perked up in her chair. "For me?"

The older woman smiled and nodded. "Yes. As I said, it isn't an easy road to becoming Mrs. Steele, especially in your situation. People will talk, as though they have any room to judge someone else. You need someone on your side. The minute I laid eyes on you, I decided I was that person."

Kat's nose wrinkled and she took a nervous sip of her drink. "Shouldn't you be on your family's side?" she asked, when she worked up the nerve.

"I am," Ingrid said with a curt nod. "They just don't know it yet."

Sawyer wasn't sure how Kat did it. He'd seen people nearly pass out from anxiety when meeting his grandmother. She didn't mince words, always speaking her mind whether she should or not. She also had an uncanny ability to see through people's bullshit. Her words, not his. Anyone approaching her with an ounce of haughtiness would be quickly cut down to size, his own mother included.

And yet, there Kat was at his grandmother's side. She'd been there almost all afternoon. The party was to welcome his grandmother home from Europe, and he was certain there were people anxious to speak with her, but Ingrid Steele simply didn't care. She seemed to be entranced by the young Miss McIntyre.

Sawyer knew exactly how she felt.

Leaning against one of the aluminum posts that held up the gigantic tent, Sawyer had watched over the two of them—Kat in particular—for quite a while. He'd argued with himself about why he was keeping such close tabs on his brother's lover. Of course, he told himself that he was waiting for the truth to come out about her and her motives. If anyone could get to the bottom of Kat and what she was after, it would be Grandmother. And yet the two of them were chatting, laughing and nibbling on tea cakes like old friends.

In that case, Kat was either an incredibly skilled con artist or she was telling him the truth. Despite his suspicious nature, he hadn't found out anything about Kat that would raise a red flag. Jade's fiancé, Harley Dalton, owned a security and investigations firm and had personally done a background check on her. She came back squeaky clean. Probably even cleaner than Sawyer would.

She'd been orphaned in her late teens when her parents were killed in a car accident. She'd inherited a tidy sum from her parents' estates and insurance policies. From what he could tell, she'd left most of it invested and lived on the interest after buying her house. No police record. No bad debts. They couldn't even find an off-color social media post that could come back to haunt her.

Unless she'd suddenly decided to better her position by seducing and getting impregnated by the richest guy she could find, it was probably truly an accident, as she'd said. He hated to admit it, but all the evidence pointed to that outcome. Even Finn had mentioned that Kat was reluctant to accept any of the things his lawyers had offered her. If she was a scam artist, she was either terrible at it or positively diabolical.

Deep down, Sawyer knew she was innocent of the things he'd accused her of. Of course, once he stopped looking at her with suspicion, he couldn't help but look at her in a way that could only cause trouble for everyone involved.

"If I didn't know better, I'd say you were checking out that hot redhead with Grandmother."

Sawyer turned at the sound of his sister's voice. "That's just what Morgan would say if she were here, instead of on her honeymoon, gallivanting about."

Jade laughed. "Today, the role of the Steele daughter will be played by the understudy, Jade Nolan."

Sawyer wrapped his arm around her and tugged her close. "You're not an understudy. You originated the part for a short run before leaving the production for a gritty indie role."

"Cute. But don't change the subject." Jade tilted her chin in the direction of Ingrid and Kat. "Why are you over in a corner leering at Finn's baby mama?"

"I am not leering." Sawyer pulled away and crossed his arms over his chest. "I told Finn I would handle things for him and keep an eye on her until he got back from China."

"I don't think he intended for you to keep *that* good a watch on her. I suppose you can't help it, though. If you built a woman in a computer to your precise specifications it would come out Kat McIntyre."

Sawyer turned toward his sister with an irritated scowl. "You don't know what you're talking about."

Jade arched an eyebrow and nodded. "If you say so."

"Besides," he argued, "she's not available even if she was my type. She's with Finn."

"Do you really think so?" Jade looked over at Kat and narrowed her gaze in intense study. "I never pegged him for the settling-down type. Even with a baby in the mix. I don't imagine those two are going to ride off into the sunset together when he gets back from China."

Finn *wasn't* the settling-down type. But in this family people didn't always get to do what they wanted to. If they did, Morgan wouldn't have had to marry her husband, River, twice. "You never know what will happen. Something brought them together once, so it could happen again. And even if they just end up as co-parents or whatever…that doesn't mean there's a blank space in her life ready for me to occupy."

"Why don't you let her be the one to make that decision?" Jade asked. "I've seen her look at you a few times this afternoon when you were distracted."

"What does that mean? I look exactly like Finn. She was probably just glancing at me and thinking about him. Or wondering if their baby will look like her or Finn. Even if she was staring me in the face, it'd be like she was looking at him."

"But she *wasn't* looking at him. She was looking at

you. And appearances and birthdays aside, there's very little in common between the two of you."

Sawyer sighed heavily. "What's your point, baby sister?"

"*My point* is that if Kat had to choose between the two of you to be her husband and father to her child, the rebellious, irresponsible playboy probably wouldn't be her first choice. That's all." Jade gave Sawyer a pointed look and slowly strolled off in the direction of her fiancé.

Sawyer watched her head over to where Harley was standing and slip comfortably into his strong embrace. The man was huge, ex-navy, and intimidating enough to get a confession out of the toughest insurgent. And yet with Jade, he was like a big teddy bear. If she could turn a bad boy like that into marriage material, there might be hope for Finn and Kat.

That's what he should want, right? For things to work out between them? That was what Kat seemed to want. And it was best for the child to be with its father, after all.

But that wasn't what Sawyer wanted when he looked at Kat. When he saw her, all he could think about was kissing her again. That afternoon in her studio had haunted him. Her soft mouth against his, the curves of her body pressed into him, the taste of her lingering on his lips long after he'd left the District... He'd lived the moment over and over in his mind.

She'd pulled away, but he wasn't sure she'd really wanted to. Maybe Jade was right and Kat was interested in him, but she had a guilty conscience. Or the desire to do the right thing for her child outweighed everything else.

Sawyer knew about trying to do the right thing. Sometimes he thought he was the only one in his family who even attempted to do what was right. For all the good it did him. It didn't garner him any additional praise from his parents. No additional promotions or important assignments at work. It was almost like it was taken for granted that Sawyer would do the right thing, and he was ignored because of it.

Glancing back at Kat and his grandmother, he found Kat looking at him. Jade had been right about that, at least. When she realized she was caught, she smiled softly and wiggled her fingers at him in greeting.

No, kissing Kat hadn't been the right thing to do. But it had certainly felt right. Right enough that he wanted to do it again the moment he got her alone.

For once in his responsible life, Sawyer wanted to do the wrong thing.

Six

"Come on, you stupid Jeep!"

The valet had returned a few minutes ago, after attempting to bring her car around, and given her the bad news—her Jeep wouldn't start. With a groan of resignation, she'd taken the keys from him and trekked across the yard to where the vehicle was parked. Now she was sitting in it, hoping she had some sort of magic mojo the valet didn't, and the car would start.

So far, no luck.

This was an eventuality she'd been avoiding. The Jeep had been a present from her parents for her high school graduation. Even as she got older, there wasn't really any reason to replace the car. It was old and didn't have all the fancy features of newer ones, but it got her from A to B.

Since she found out she was pregnant, she'd been thinking more seriously about getting a new ride. One with doors, perhaps. It seemed as though her old Jeep was making the decision for her.

"Please. Just get me home tonight and I'll promise to sell you to an outdoorsy guy that will fix you up and drive you through all the mud puddles." Kat tried to turn the engine over again and found her attempts to negotiate had fallen on deaf ears. Because her Jeep didn't have ears.

With a whimper, she dropped her head onto the steering wheel in defeat. Why did it have to happen today? And here? Now the family she was trying to impress would have to see her junky old car get towed away from their multi-million-dollar estate. As though she wasn't already having enough trouble fitting in. She and Grandma Ingrid had hit it off, but most of the other people at the party had just regarded her from a distance.

When she went to fix a plate, all the ladies near the buffet had hushed until she was gone. It was quite juvenile for grown-ups, really. Kat wasn't used to being the subject of hot new gossip. And now they could be confident in believing her a gold digger. She didn't even have a functioning car—of course she was after Finn's money.

"Need some help?"

Kat shot to attention and turned to find Sawyer had silently crept up beside her car. "Did you go to ninja school or something?" she asked, pressing her hand to her rapidly beating heart.

"Morgan says I'd make a terrible spy. She insists I couldn't sneak up on her with a marching band going by. I didn't even try to slip out of the house when we were teenagers because I knew I'd get caught. So I'd say you were distracted."

"That's a word for it," she said. Turning away from him, she reached for her purse and rummaged around for her cell phone. She needed to call a wrecker. Most of the other guests were gone by now, so hopefully only the family would still be around when it showed up.

"It's awfully late," Sawyer said. "They're going to charge you extra to drive all the way out here on a weekend after eight. Why don't I give you a ride home? Then you can call someone to get the car in the morning, or on Monday."

Kat turned to him with a sigh. She certainly didn't want to sit out here in the humid summer air and get eaten by mosquitos while she waited. Then again, accepting a ride home from Sawyer seemed equally perilous. "I can call an Uber."

"Don't be silly. I can give you a ride. No one is going to want to come way out here to get you. Besides, I pass near your neighborhood on my way home, anyway."

She regarded him suspiciously for a moment, but when he offered his hand and stood there with an expectant look on his face, she finally gave in. "Okay."

He helped her out and only released her hand when he pointed to his car a couple yards away. "Don't act so put out. Most people would love to be chauffeured around in a brand-new car like mine. It still has the new-car smell."

Kat looked in that direction and spied a silver Audi SUV parked beside a bright yellow Porsche Boxster. She held her breath for a moment to see which one lit up when he pulled out his key fob. The lights on the Audi blinked on and off. She should've known better than to think that Sawyer would drive the flashier car. If she had learned more about him before that night at the aquarium, she would've realized she was with Finn, not Sawyer, when they left for a hotel and got into his bright red Ferrari.

Sawyer opened the passenger door and held it for her until she was inside. She sat patiently waiting as he came around to his side and started the car. It did have the new-car smell. It also looked as though it was fresh from the dealership. No travel mug in the cup holder, no crumbled-up receipts on the floor. It was immaculate.

"How long have you had this car?" she asked as they drove off the property.

"Two months, I think?"

"Oh," Kat said with surprise. "I was thinking more like a few days. This thing looks like it's hardly been driven."

"It's been driven. I just keep it pretty tidy."

"Is your place really tidy, too?"

She watched Sawyer frown at the windshield for a moment before he responded. "Maybe. But I have a cleaning service that comes in twice a week."

That sounded nice. She'd love to have one come in twice a month. Kat shook her head. "I bet they hardly do anything. I bet your underwear drawer is organized like a museum exhibit."

"My underwear is hardly museum quality," Sawyer said with a chuckle. "But I do have them rolled and stood on end as Marie Kondo suggests."

Kat rolled her eyes and relaxed back into the plush leather seat. "You need a little messy in your life."

"How's that?" he asked.

"You just seem very…straightlaced. Maybe you're trying to compensate for your brother or something, but you never seem to make a misstep. You need to loosen up. Even your grandmother agrees."

Sawyer turned to her with a confused arch of his brow. "You were talking about me with my grandmother?"

"Yes. She had a lot of nice things to say about you, actually. I think you're her favorite."

"What makes you say that?"

"Just the way she talks about you. It seems like she really wants you to find someone and settle down. She wants you to find someone who makes you happy, not just someone you think the family will approve of, like your last few girls."

Kat watched Sawyer's knuckles tighten and grow white as he gripped the steering wheel. "I thought this afternoon was about my family getting to know you, not about Grandmother spilling all the family gossip to you."

She shrugged and turned back to the road. "We talked about me a lot, too. And about Finn. About Jade and Morgan's situation. Ingrid really seemed to take a liking to me for some reason. I don't know why."

"Really?"

"What do you mean, really?" Kat turned toward Sawyer as he slowed to a stop in front of her house.

He turned off his engine and looked at her. "My grandmother enjoys the company of interesting people. I don't know why you would think you aren't interesting enough to keep her attention. You're smart, you're easy to talk to, you're an artist. There's a lot of layers to you that I'm sure she would find fascinating. I certainly enjoy talking to you."

Kat noticed he said the last part a little more quietly than the rest. It was a curious admittance from a man who had at one time seemed adamant that she was some kind of crook out to fleece his family. "I enjoy talking to you, too," she admitted.

An awkward silence followed. With any other man in any other situation, Kat would've expected Sawyer to lean in and kiss her good-night. That was the natural progression of a conversation like that. She could sense the statically charged energy inside the car. Even with the air-conditioning on, she could feel the heat of his body nearby and smell the lingering scent of his cologne.

It was enough to make her want to slip off her seat belt and scoot closer to him. Judging by the blood racing hotly through her veins and the tingle that sizzled down her spine when he looked her way, it was clear that Kat wanted him to kiss her. And yet he hesitated. And she understood why.

Their attraction to each other was nothing more than mistaken identity combined with a cruel trick of chemistry. She needed to just thank him, get out of his car and go into her house. She needed to look at her finances and start thinking about buying a new car, not about Sawyer and the way his blazer clung to his broad shoulders. Or the way the deep brown of his eyes reminded her of decadent dark chocolate.

Yes, that was what she needed to do. With a surge of self-control, she reached for the door handle and turned to say goodbye. "Would you like to come in for some coffee or something?" she said, instead of good-night or thanks for the ride.

The words slipped from her lips before she could stop herself. Why would she invite Sawyer into her house? The last time they'd spent any real time alone, they'd ended up kissing, and that was in public at her studio. What would happen late on a Saturday night at her house? With no one there to interrupt or know what was happening inside?

Her belly clenched as she awaited his answer.

"I'd like that."

A surge of excitement and a good dose of worry washed over her. Kat was about to find out exactly what would happen if they were alone again. And deep inside, she couldn't wait.

What are you doing? What are you doing?

Every step Sawyer took up the path to Kat's piazza raised a chorus of doubts in his mind. He followed her inside, knowing full well that he was heading into dangerous territory.

It's just coffee, he told himself, but he knew that was a lie even as the thought entered his mind. If he crossed that threshold into Kat's home, it was like the point of no return. He already ached to kiss her. It had taken everything he had on the ride back not to reach over and cup her bare knee with his hand. He wanted to stroke the smooth skin he'd been eyeing all afternoon.

It was stupid. It was reckless. It was everything Sawyer typically looked upon with disapproval. And yet he couldn't help himself. He felt a bit like Finn, doing what he wanted without thinking about what others thought.

Inside her house, he watched Kat set down her things and kick off her heels with a sigh of relief. "That's the best thing to happen to me all day," she said with a soft smile. "Make yourself at home. I'm going to make some coffee."

He watched her disappear into the kitchen as he happily shrugged out of his blazer and tossed it over the back of a chair. Then he set about checking out more of Kat's place. He had been here before, when he'd delivered the dress from Jade, but he'd been too stressed out to pay much attention to his surroundings then. Now, with her in the other room, he was able to walk around and take in the place Kat called home.

The first thing he noticed was the collection of wood carvings around the living room. He recognized them as similar in style to some of her projects at her studio. There was a tall, narrow carving of a mermaid reaching toward the surface of the water, a couple embracing as the wind twirled her hair around them, and Kat's coffee table was an oval sheet of glass resting on the back of a green sea turtle. She really was a talented artist.

The piece that didn't seem to fit in was a large canvas painting above the sofa. It was a chaotic mash of colors that up close seemed like a mess, but from far away, you could see a little girl in a yellow slicker splashing in a rain puddle. He looked at the signature and recognized the name from Kat's background check. It was by her mother, Astrid Elliott. When he'd first read the name, it had sounded familiar, but now that he saw one of her pieces in front of him, he made the connection. Astrid had been a successful artist when she was alive, with the price of her works skyrocketing after her death. He'd even seen one of her pieces in the museum downtown.

On the fireplace mantel, he saw a framed family portrait that had to have been taken not long before the accident that killed both Astrid and Brent McIntyre, Kat's father. Kat looked like a younger, happier version of the woman he knew, surrounded by the parents who loved her.

He noticed it was the only picture around the house. There was nothing more recent. He supposed that was because she didn't want to have pictures taken of herself alone. It seemed like a depressing thing to do, although the idea had never occurred to him until now. He'd always had more family than he knew what to do with. Lately, he'd gained a sister and two new brothers-in-law. He didn't know what it would be like to be alone in the world the way Kat was.

"How do you take your coffee?" Kat asked, as she came into the room with two mugs on a small tray.

"Black, normally, but it's too late for that. Cream, no sugar, or I'll be up all night."

Kat looked at him curiously for a moment, the curve of her mouth inching upward in an amused expression before she nodded and set the tray down on the coffee table. Thinking over his words in the current context of being alone in her house late at night, he could see why. Coffee or not, he might very well be up all night. *God*, he wanted to be up all night.

He was about to sit down on the sofa when he noticed her fidgeting in her lace dress. "Would you like to change out of your party clothes? You seem uncomfortable."

"Yes," she said with a relieved sigh, as she poured cream into his coffee and then straightened. "This lace has gotten itchier as the night goes on. I just hope I can get ahold of the zipper."

"I can get that for you," Sawyer offered.

Kat's gaze fixed on his for a moment. It seemed as though neither of them took a breath the entire time as she thought over his helpful suggestion and what could come of it. "Okay," she said at last.

Kat swooped her long red hair up off her neck to expose the zipper, and turned her back to him.

Sawyer's hands were almost trembling as he reached out to grasp the tab and hold the fabric taut. He tugged down, separating the teeth and exposing more and more of Kat's bare skin as he went. His fingertips brushed over the clasp of her pale pink bra before they continued down to the curve of her back. The zipper stopped there, just where the top of her panties would be visible. But they weren't.

"Did you go commando to my grandmother's garden party?" Sawyer managed to ask, his mouth suddenly as dry as sand.

Kat chuckled and swept her hair over her shoulder as she turned to him. "I had to. This dress showed panty lines pretty badly and I've never really been a fan of thongs."

The smile faded slowly from her face when she looked him in the eye. He wasn't sure what she saw there, but he was certain every feeling he was trying to hide was visible if she peered hard enough. He was usually good at disguising his feelings, but that was because he rarely had any. Now, standing here with her dress about to slip from her shoulders, he was overwhelmed with feelings like never before.

Without saying a word, Sawyer reached out and caught the neckline of her dress where it rested across her skin. He heard Kat's breath catch in her throat as he pulled at the coral fabric. It slipped off her shoulder, the weight of the dress pulling it from her other shoulder, as well. Kat didn't try to stop it as it slid down her body and pooled at her bare feet.

Sawyer swallowed hard as his gaze raked across Kat's virtually naked body. When she finally did move, it wasn't to grab her dress or cover herself. She reached behind her back and unfastened her bra. In a moment, it fell to the floor with her dress, leaving nothing but the red waves of her hair to cover any of her body from him.

He let out a ragged breath as he studied her pale, creamy skin. He was drawn to her full breasts and the hardened peach nipples that seemed to reach out to him, begging him to touch them. He wanted to. It was wrong, but he wanted to. He was conflicted enough that he was frozen on the spot, unable to leave and unable to pursue her.

Instead, Kat closed the gap between them. She stepped gingerly out of her dress and stopped just short of having her nipples graze the cotton of his dress shirt. "Don't you want to touch me, Sawyer?" she asked.

Hearing her specifically say his name, not his brother's, lit a fire deep inside his belly. This wasn't just a case of mistaken identity. She wanted *him*. In this moment, naked and vulnerable in front of him, she wanted Sawyer to touch her, and he was desperate to give her what she needed.

"More than anything," he admitted, and he meant it. He couldn't remember another woman in his life who had gotten under his skin, or taken over his thoughts, the way Kat had.

"Then touch me. Please. I want you to."

She wanted this. He wanted this. In that moment, Sawyer decided that nothing else mattered. He had to have Kat or he was going to make himself crazy with unfulfilled desire. He would regret not taking the chance, just as he would probably regret sleeping with her, so he might as well do what he wanted to in the heat of the moment.

Reaching out, he cupped one breast in his hand. Kat's head tipped back and her eyes closed as she savored the sensation. Her skin was soft as silk as his thumb traced over it and then teased the taut peak that pressed insistently into his palm.

With his other hand, Sawyer reached around the back of her neck, weaving his fingers through her hair and pulling her mouth up to meet his. She opened herself to him, moaning softly with pleasure as his tongue grazed hers. He drank her in, enjoying the lingering taste of strawberries on her lips from the flavored seltzers she'd sipped all afternoon.

He felt her fingers at his throat and pulled away from her mouth long enough for Kat to tug his tie loose and throw it onto the floor. She unfastened the top button of his shirt, which was always his favorite moment of the day. He supposed it was like Kat kicking off her uncomfortable shoes. He sighed in relief, and was about to dip his head down to taste her breasts when Kat pressed insistently on his chest, forcing him backward until his calves met with the couch behind him.

She pushed him back onto the sofa and crawled onto his lap to sit astride him. Her fingers worked feverishly to unbutton his dress shirt and push the fabric out of her way. Sawyer's hands gripped the flesh of her hips as she dragged her nails through his chest hair to his belly, then unfastened his belt.

Kat rose up on her knees long enough to let him slide his pants down his thighs, then she slowly, deliberately, lowered herself onto him.

Sawyer groaned against her breasts as he wrapped his arms around her and pulled her close to him. He held her still for a moment once she was fully seated, and squeezed his eyes tightly shut. He wanted to savor every moment, every feeling, because this probably wouldn't ever happen again. Soon they would come to their senses and realize how stupid they were, but right now, right this very second, he was going to enjoy every delicious sensation.

After a moment of stillness, Kat ran her fingers through the curls on the top of his head and gripped a fistful. Gently, she pulled back, until Sawyer had no choice but to look into her bewitching green eyes. Then she eased up and sank down on him a second time. Moving slowly at first, Sawyer leaned back and enjoyed the view of his redheaded hellcat taking control. This was the woman who'd slapped him hard across the face at his sister's wedding. The one who had called him daily and tried to track him down to get her way over the artist community. She was feisty. Sexy as hell. Kat was unlike any woman he'd ever been with before.

The slow burn she was building was teetering on the edge of torture. He wanted more and he decided it was time to turn the intensity up a notch. Sawyer reached out and cupped her hips to hold her steady. She braced her arms on his shoulders, letting her breasts sway tantalizingly just out of his mouth's reach. Then he planted his feet firmly on the floor and thrust up into her.

Sawyer watched Kat's expression as he moved hard and fast inside her. Her emotions shifted from surprise to delight, then the tense, almost pained look of a woman on the verge of undoing. He slowed temporarily, reaching between them to allow his fingers to stroke her center. Kat's mouth fell open, her eyes closing as she rocked with him to her climax. And then, once her first cry escaped her throat, he gripped her hips and thrust hard into her again until they were both satisfied and spent.

Kat collapsed against him in exhaustion and he was happy to catch her as she melted into him. She buried her face in his neck, with her hair cascading over his chest and shoulders. He was content to wrap his arms around her and hold her close as their heartbeats and breaths slowed back to normal.

So this is what it was like to do what you wanted to do. Sawyer had to admit it was exhilarating to take a page from his twin's book, damn the consequences. True, he might rot in hell for sleeping with the woman having his brother's child, but he just didn't care. Tonight was worth it.

And he couldn't wait to have her again.

Seven

Kat woke up late. Later than she'd let herself sleep in a long time. Of course, she had been up late with Sawyer. After their encounter on the couch, they'd finally had their cooling coffee, then moved to the bedroom to make love again.

And again.

Now, she was afraid to open her eyes to the light of morning and face reality. As long as she stayed right where she was, she could revel in last night without pondering the consequences.

It had been amazing. She wasn't ashamed to admit it. While Finn and Sawyer might look alike, they were day and night when it came to the bedroom. Finn had the playboy reputation and an adventurous spirit, but she preferred Sawyer's style. He was more serious, but also more thoughtful. She'd never had a man focus so much on her needs in bed. Kat had lost count of how many times she'd come undone under his expert touch. It seemed like anything less would've been a failure on his part.

Things with Finn had been…fine. He was a little wilder than what she was used to. She'd had a good time. But somehow it didn't compare when it came to intimacy, which was what she found she really craved.

It made her wish more than anything that it had really been Sawyer, not Finn, who she'd met that night at the award ceremony. Somehow it seemed like having his baby would be easier. She could envision them actually having a future together where they might be happy. With Finn, she got the feeling she and the baby were just going to be a stone around his neck.

Kat ran her hand across the mattress, and when she found it empty and cold, she pried one eye open. Sawyer was gone. Long gone, by the feel of it.

It was a stark reminder that she wasn't having his child. And she wasn't living some fairy tale.

With a groan, Kat pushed herself up out of bed and clutched the sheets to her chest. She almost felt hungover despite not having a drop to drink. She supposed she was love drunk and still feeling the aftereffects.

"A fine punishment, and duly deserved," she said aloud as she swung her legs out of bed. She really needed to get her priorities in line. There wasn't much sense in sleeping with one twin while wanting to marry the other. At the very least, it didn't help matters. Finn wasn't a model of monogamy, of that she was sure, but she didn't think he'd take kindly to knowing that she and his brother were having sex while she waited for him to return from China.

That was why no one would ever know. Kat would never speak of it. And it certainly wouldn't happen again. It had been an amazing night. One that was hard to regret. But she couldn't let her desires compromise her child's future.

She reached for her floral silk robe from the hook in her closet and wrapped it around herself before stumbling down the stairs to the kitchen. She half expected to see Sawyer sitting there, smugly drinking a cup of coffee, but the house was silent and still.

Which was why the loud beeping of a tow truck outside caught her attention so easily. Realizing that Sawyer must've had her Jeep towed to the house, she slipped into a pair of flip-flops and went out to the piazza to see what was happening.

There, a tow truck was unloading what looked like some kind of luxury SUV into her driveway. The cherry-red vehicle was beautiful, but definitely not hers.

Great. They'd gotten the cars mixed up. Her Jeep was probably getting dropped at some rich guy's yard in Mount Pleasant, where they were about to throw a fit.

With a groan of irritation, Kat tightened the belt on her robe and pushed through the heavy wooden door to flag down the tow truck driver. "Hey!" she shouted, waving her arms at the guy in the cab.

Finally the man noticed her and stopped what he was doing. "Yeah?"

"What are you doing? This isn't my car. You've got the wrong car or the wrong house."

The man turned from the window and picked up a clipboard to read the pages there. "Are you Katherine McIntyre?"

"Yes."

"Then I've got the right house and the right person." He went to hit the lever to continue lowering the SUV off the truck.

"No, this isn't right. This isn't my car. I drive a Jeep. A broken-down, dark green, rusty Jeep Wrangler." She turned to the car halfway in her driveway. She could see now that it was a brand-new Lexus SUV. It wasn't even close to the right car. In her dreams.

"Listen, lady. I don't know anything about an old Jeep. All I know is that I was supposed to bring this vehicle from the dealership to this address and give the keys to you."

"On whose authority?"

The man rolled his eyes. He'd probably never had someone fight so hard against receiving a car. He looked down at the paper again. "Looks like a Mr. Steele had it sent. If you don't want the car, take it up with him. But I've got to deliver it. That's my job."

Before Kat could open her mouth to ask which Mr. Steele had sent it, he flipped the switch again and the cable lowered the SUV the rest of the way to the ground. The man finally climbed down from the cab and busied himself unhooking things and getting everything set up so he could leave. Then he raised the flatbed back into position and walked over to where she was waiting.

"Sign here," he said.

She was too tired to fight with him. She signed the paperwork, which drew an audible sigh of relief from the driver. Then he handed over a pair of key fobs.

"There are worse things than waking up to a new Lexus," he pointed out. "Have a nice day," he added, before crawling back into his cab and disappearing down the street.

Kat looked at the keys in her hand in disbelief, then slowly made her way over to the SUV. It was beautiful, with sporty lines and elegant chrome details. It had to be the latest model, with top-of-the-line trim features. The interior had red-and-black leather seats and a shiny polished wood-and-leather dashboard. It made her old Jeep look like it was made from papier-mâché or Tinkertoys or something.

It was exactly the kind of car she would have chosen for herself if she could've had any car in the whole world. Each detail, from the sunroof to the wheels, was perfect.

But she couldn't accept a gift like this. Not from Finn and certainly not from Sawyer.

Kat reluctantly walked back into her house and hunted down her phone from where she'd left it the night before. There, on her screen, was a text from Sawyer, answering her question at last.

Do you like it?

Kat rolled her eyes and shook her head before texting back. Of course I like it, she responded. But I can't accept it.

Her phone rang precisely five seconds later, with Sawyer's number coming up on the screen. "Come get your car," she answered without saying hello.

"Good morning to you, too," he said in an irritatingly chipper voice. He knew full well how she would react to a gift like that and he seemed to be reveling in it.

"Good morning, Sawyer. Now will you please tell me why there's a brand-new Lexus in my driveway? Where is my Jeep?"

"Your Jeep is at the repair shop. I had it towed there early this morning. The guy took a look at it and said it's on its last legs. The starter has gone out, which is why it won't turn over, but he didn't feel right charging you to fix that because the whole engine would need to be rebuilt before too long, anyway. I can't have you stranded on the side of the road, pregnant and at the mercy of random bystanders."

Kat had been afraid that the news about her Jeep wouldn't be good, but this was even worse than she'd expected. "And so naturally, you bought me a new car instead?"

"Naturally." She could almost hear his smug grin in his voice.

"Sawyer…" Kat said in a stern tone.

"Hear me out," Sawyer argued. "You need a new car."

"That may be true, but it doesn't mean that you need to sweep in and buy one for me. If the Jeep is

DOA, then I'll go get something else. You buying it after last night makes it feel like some sort of thank-you-for-the-sex gift."

Sawyer laughed over the phone line. It was one of the first times she'd ever heard him really, truly laugh. She liked the sound of it and wished she was with him in person to see if his eyes lit up or his dimple was on display. Finally, the laughter faded. "Do you really think I give cars to all the women I sleep with?"

"Well, no…"

"That would be an expensive habit, even for me, Kat. The truth is that yours isn't safe for you to drive and it certainly won't be safe to take my new niece or nephew around town, either. My brother asked me to keep an eye on things until he can get back, and in my opinion, the best thing I could do is get you a safe vehicle to drive."

While Kat was relieved it wasn't a morning-after gift, she still couldn't take something like that from him. Or from anyone. Even from Finn and his team of bribing attorneys, although they'd offered her everything but a car in their settlement package. "I can't accept this, Sawyer."

"That's a shame, since you currently have nothing else to drive. I can tell the mechanic to try and get your Jeep running, but it won't be a quick fix. I hope you don't have anything you need to do the next few days."

Kat sighed. "I actually have a doctor's appointment on Tuesday. Not to mention going to the District to work."

"Well, there's no way your car will be ready that

soon. The guy only took it in today as a favor to me. How about this? Since you need a car to get around, drive the Lexus for a couple of days. I'll see what he can do with your Jeep. If he can get it running, I will take the Lexus off your hands. Maybe I'll give it to Morgan for her birthday."

Kat was more suspicious of this than anything. He'd backed down quicker than she expected. "Are you serious?"

"Absolutely. Red isn't really Morgan's color, but I think she'll like it."

"Why not just return it to the dealership, and I'll get a rental car?"

"I got too good a deal on it. If you don't want it, fine, but someone is getting a new Lexus. There's no sense paying for a rental car, too, when it's sitting there in your driveway."

"Okay," Kat said reluctantly. "Is this why you crept out of my bed at dawn?"

"I hardly crept out at dawn. It was eight thirty and you were out like a light. I hated to wake you up, so I let you sleep."

That made Kat feel a little better, although as she looked down at the key fobs in her hand, she couldn't help but think that Sawyer would get his way where the car was concerned. Where everything was concerned, actually. No matter how much time they spent together, she never seemed to be able to pin him down to talk about the District. There were parties and family members and new cars to distract her, and she was running out of time.

"I'm going to talk to the guy about your Jeep and I'll give you a call back later, okay?"

"All right."

"Oh, and before I forget, do you have plans for the Fourth of July?"

Kat didn't need to look at her calendar to know she didn't. She figured she'd be working at the District, like she always was. They got higher than average foot traffic on holidays. Still, she liked the idea of seeing Sawyer again that soon. "I don't think so."

"Oh, good. Grandmother wanted me to invite you to the family Fourth of July party."

Kat tried to swallow her disappointment that it was Ingrid, not Sawyer, who wanted to see her again. At least she hadn't embarrassed herself too badly with the family if they'd invited her to another gathering. "Another party?" Kat asked. Her toes still hurt from the last one.

"This one is different. Just the immediate family cruising the harbor to watch fireworks from our yacht."

Kat cringed at the way Sawyer could talk about the family yacht as though that's what everyone did on a summer holiday. "I'll think about it," she said.

"I'll tell Grandmother Ingrid you said yes, then."

Before Kat could argue, the call ended and she found herself staring at her phone, dumbfounded. She certainly hadn't intended to get this involved with the Steele family, but now that she was, they were turning into a handful.

It was a nice change of pace from being alone.

* * *

"Come on back, Mr. Steele. Ms. McIntyre is already in the exam room, but the doctor is still with another patient."

Sawyer smiled and nodded to the nurse as she knocked gently on the door and then opened it to let him inside.

"Guess who's here?" the nurse said brightly. "Daddy was able to make the appointment, after all!"

Sawyer saw Kat whip her head around to where he was standing in the doorway. Her jaw clenched, but she didn't bother to argue with the nurse, or have him tossed and cause a scene.

"Great," she said flatly.

Once the nurse slipped back out the door, Kat's smile faded. "What exactly do you think you're doing, crashing my prenatal appointment?"

Sawyer shrugged and settled into the guest chair. "My brother told me to keep an eye on things. I'm sure he would want to be at this appointment if he were here, so I thought I'd pop in and pass any news along to him."

"So you just told them you were the father and they let you in?"

"Yes and no," he admitted. "I was waiting patiently in the lobby for you to finish. They approached and asked if I was the father and if I wanted to come back to see the ultrasound and get the lab results, so I said yes. It's not like they'll ever know me from Finn, anyway."

"I'll know." Kat fidgeted with her uncomfortable-looking paper gown.

"It's a little late to act shy around me," Sawyer said. "I've seen all this, and recently."

"This is different." Kat crossed her arms over her chest and twisted her lips in irritation.

Sawyer sat back in his seat and looked around. He'd never been in a gynecologist's office before. There were big posters on the walls with drawings that reminded him of fifth grade health class, and the exam table had handles coming out the ends like a motorcycle. "What are these?" he asked.

Kat rolled her eyes. "Stirrups."

"Like for a horse?"

"Not exactly, but my feet do go in them. It's for the…exam."

Oh. Yeah, he'd definitely never been in one of these offices before. Or given much thought to what actually happened in them.

He was second-guessing his decision to crash the appointment when a quick rap at the door disrupted their conversation, and a shorter man in a white lab coat rushed in. "Hey, everyone, how's it going today?"

"Hey, Dr. Wheeler."

He shook Kat's hand and turned around to face Sawyer. "Dad? Friend? Moral support?"

"All of the above," he said.

"Okay, great," Dr. Wheeler said without missing a beat. He sat down on his little rolling stool and flipped open the medical file he'd come in with. "So the results on all the tests from your initial appointment look normal. No concerns there. Are you taking your prenatal vitamins?"

"Yes."

"Good. Any problems so far? Nausea? Tenderness? Spotting?" The doctor stood up and guided Kat back onto the table. Sawyer heard her respond, but at that point he checked out. He hadn't fully comprehended what he was walking into today and realized now that he didn't want to see the man behind the curtain, so to speak.

He let his gaze drop to his lap and tried not to think about what that man was doing to Kat. The next thing he knew the lights were dimming in the room and the doctor was spraying gel across Kat's bare stomach.

"We're going to take some pictures and I'm going to try to get a heartbeat on the Doppler. Hopefully we can get a good look at the little guy today."

"It's a boy?" Sawyer asked, perking up from his stupor.

The doctor smiled and shook his head. "We actually haven't talked about that yet. I do have a preliminary result from the NIPT test, if you would like to know. It's 90 percent accurate, but I wouldn't go painting any rooms until after we do the gender confirmation ultrasound at twenty weeks. Maybe we can see something today, but that depends on the baby and how cooperative she or he is feeling."

"I would like to know the test results," Kat said.

"Sure thing." The doctor picked up the folder and flipped to a page filled with lab results numbers. "Well, it looks to me like you guys *should* be expecting a little girl."

Kat brought her hand up to her mouth to stifle a soft

cry. Sawyer wanted to rush to her side and share in the excitement, but it felt like intruding on someone else's moment. It wasn't his baby or his news, despite what he'd told them in the lobby earlier.

"My sisters are going to be thrilled," he said instead, with a reassuring nod to Kat. "And Mom and Grandma Ingrid, too. Once you know for certain you're going to be smothered in a sea of ruffled, pink baby clothes."

Kat laughed and he saw a shimmer of happy tears in her green eyes. He reached out and took her hand, squeezing it gently. He might not be the father, but until Finn got home, he would do what he could to support her through this.

Her gaze met his and she smiled. "Thank you for being here," she said. "I didn't realize I didn't want to be alone for this moment until right now."

He squeezed her hand again and they both turned their attention to the grainy image on the monitor. Dr. Wheeler moved the wand back and forth across her stomach while he searched the darkness for the tiny baby inside.

"Here we go. Hello, precious one."

Sawyer narrowed his gaze at the monitor, trying to make sense of what he was seeing. Then suddenly the profile of the baby came into focus and he felt the emotion of the moment hit him like a punch to his midsection.

He could see every little detail of her face, her little nose and mouth, and her hands balled up in front of her. He could see the curve of her spine and her legs drawn up to her tummy. The beating of her heart was visible, although they couldn't quite hear it over the static.

The doctor hit the keyboard repeatedly, capturing shot after shot of the baby, and then moving the wand to a different location for a new angle. At one point, he pointed out something completely indiscernible and said, "I'd say this is a girl for sure." He typed it on the screen, pointing out some blurry spots, and printed out another image. "You can go ahead and paint."

Then the doctor focused on the tiny fluttering heart on the screen and suddenly the room was filled with the rapid *wub-wub* sound of the baby's heartbeat.

Through it all, Sawyer held Kat's hand, fully enthralled in the moment as though this was his little girl on the screen, whose heartbeat he was hearing for the first time. His brother had screwed up a lot in his life, but Sawyer couldn't help but feel this wasn't just Finn's latest mistake. This might be the first thing Finn had gotten right.

He also felt an incredible sense of jealousy. He had no right to, really. I wasn't as though he'd been pining for a family of his own—far from it, actually. But somehow knowing that a simple twist of fate had put this woman in Finn's path instead of his own bothered him.

Kat. This baby girl. It was supposed to be his. Kat had come to that party looking for him, not Finn. If he hadn't been feeling poorly that night he would've been the one to meet her. Maybe he wouldn't have whisked her off to a hotel the way Finn did, but he couldn't help but think he would've asked her to dinner. And then more. And in time, maybe they would've been sharing this moment together over their child.

Finn hadn't just taken his Jet Ski and played pretend that night. It was as though his twin had stolen his whole future when he put on that name tag.

Eight

"Can I take you to lunch?"

Kat seemed surprised by his offer as they walked out of her doctor's building. "Don't you need to work or something?"

Sawyer frowned. "You sound like my dad. Come on, I'll take you wherever you want to go. Have you started having any weird food cravings yet?"

"I don't know, Sawyer." She seemed uncharacteristically uncomfortable with him. It felt odd to him after the moment they'd just shared. "I probably shouldn't."

Sawyer stopped and shoved his hands into his pockets. "Is something wrong?"

Kat squirmed beneath his gaze, adjusting her purse on her shoulder. His feisty hellcat seemed very out of her element at the moment. "I guess I'm just… I'm just thinking that maybe we shouldn't spend so much time together."

He wasn't sure why, but the words seemed to strike him in a tender spot. Maybe he was reading things wrong, but he thought they were having a good time together. Some could say too good of a time if they took Saturday night into consideration. And he'd bought her an expensive car that would raise eyebrows with his family if they knew about it. But he didn't care about any of that.

He'd done it because it felt like the right thing to do. Finn certainly wasn't going to show up and take care of her the way she deserved to be cared for. He wasn't going to go to doctor's checkups and worry about whether she had a safe vehicle to get around town. Being thousands of miles away was a convenient excuse, but if Finn were in Charleston this very moment, he still wouldn't be standing on this sidewalk beside Kat.

He'd asked Sawyer to handle things while he was gone, and Sawyer had gone over and above the call of duty. But Kat deserved someone who would do that for her. Being the go-between put Sawyer in a position he didn't expect to be in: one where he was starting to have feelings for the last woman and child on Earth that he should. They weren't serious feelings. But it was the closest thing to affection he'd felt for anyone since his breakup with Mira, and Kat's rebuff stung a little more than he expected it to.

"It's just lunch," he said. "I recommend keeping

your clothes on for that, if you're concerned about us crossing the line again."

Kat bit at her lip and tucked a stray strand of auburn hair behind her ear. She had it in a messy bun today, but the breeze had liberated just enough to curve along the edge of her face. It softened the look, in his opinion, but it seemed to be irritating Kat. As did Sawyer's mere presence at the moment.

"Lunch. Just lunch," she finally agreed. "I guess we need to talk, anyway."

Sawyer ignored her ominous addition and instead pointed out a restaurant across the street touting modern Southern fare. The Charleston foodie scene was booming with little spots like this in the last few years. "How do you feel about that place?" he asked.

"That's fine."

They crossed the road together and went inside the restaurant, which was pretty busy considering it was on the late side for lunch. The hostess took them to a booth near the window and they settled in. The waiter brought them glasses of water and a basket of fried corn fritters with a spicy honey dipping sauce, before stepping away to let them look over the menu.

Sawyer decided on a burger with bacon, pimento cheese and a fried green tomato on it. Kat chose a salad with diced fried chicken, candied pecans and dried cranberries.

"Sawyer, before I say anything else, I want to thank you for being there today. It was unexpected, but at the same time, it was nice to have someone to share that moment."

"You're welcome." He got the feeling this was going to be the nicest part of this conversation. She had that worry line between her brows and that was never good.

"That said, I feel like we need to talk about the other night," she said, once the waiter disappeared.

Here it comes, Sawyer thought. He'd insisted on this lunch and now he was about to be dumped by a woman he wasn't even dating. "What about it?" he said, playing coy. He reached for a fritter and shoved it nonchalantly into his mouth. If she wanted to backpedal on everything they'd shared, he certainly wasn't going to act like it was one of the greatest nights of his life and be at a disadvantage with her.

When he stripped the encounter down to the core, it was just sex. Great sex, but only sex. No promises, no emotional entanglements. They shouldn't need to talk about it unless one of them saw it as more than that. It piqued Sawyer's attention that Kat seemed to think it meant something.

"Well, it's just you left so early and then the stuff happened with the car and we just never... I don't know. Never *acknowledged* what we did and that it was probably a mistake that shouldn't ever happen again."

"I didn't really think it was a mistake." He shrugged. "It was fun. I had a good time, didn't you?"

"Yes, of course I did," she said, with a flush coming to her cheeks as she looked away from his gaze and focused on her place setting instead. "I meant that it probably shouldn't have happened, considering what's going on with your brother and me. Or what I hope to happen once he gets back."

Sawyer wanted to tell Kat not to hold her breath where Finn was concerned, but he wasn't sure if that was being helpful or being bitter. If she wanted to try things with Finn, she'd find out soon enough without him telling her.

"It might not have been the smartest thing I ever did, but I don't regret it, Kat. It was what it was. And if it never happens again, that's fine." Even as he said the words he knew they weren't really true, but it was what she needed to hear to feel better, so he'd say them.

Kat's gaze met his again. She studied his face, trying to see into his thoughts or something. She would fail. He wasn't even sure how he felt about all this. He understood her concerns about what was developing between them, even as he fought his own urges to spend as much time with her as he could.

"No one ever needs to know about it," he added. "If you and Finn end up one big, happy family, then great for the two of you. I'm not going to stand up and object at the wedding, if that's what you're thinking."

Now it was Kat who looked a little put out. Perhaps he'd been too aloof about their encounter, but he wasn't sure what else to say. Was she expecting him to slam his fist on the table and demand they be together? For him to tell her all the reasons why he was the better choice? What good would that do? She seemed to want his brother even though they both knew Finn wasn't the ideal candidate for dad and husband.

"Oh, okay," she said after a moment. "Well, then, I guess we just need to put it behind us and there isn't anything more to say about it."

"Very well."

"Speaking of Finn, I heard from him yesterday."

"Oh, really?" Sawyer hadn't spoken to his brother in a while. Finn had been lying low since the news about Kat and the baby had hit the family gossip circuit.

"He says he's coming home next week."

That was news to him. Sawyer had thought he had another couple weeks at least before Finn came back from Beijing. Ideally, he wanted to spend those weeks with Kat in his bed, but since that wasn't going to happen, he supposed it didn't matter when Finn returned.

"That's good to hear," he said, trying not to betray how he really felt. "That means things went well at the new Steele manufacturing facility. There was a bonus for him to open ahead of schedule, as I recall. That should be good for you."

"Why? I don't want any of Finn's money."

"You say that, I know, but you'll end up with something. A trust fund for your daughter, at least?"

Kat reached out anxiously for a corn fritter. "I suppose. He didn't mention anything about work when we spoke. Just that he would be back by next Wednesday afternoon."

"I'm glad to hear it. Then he can be the one here with you instead of me, and I can get back to work. The District closes down in two weeks and I'm going to be up to my neck in blueprints and contractors, getting that place remodeled in my proposed time line. I want it reopened and bustling by the Christmas shopping season. Things went so well in China, maybe I should have Finn handle it," he laughed.

Kat straightened in her seat at the mention of the District, as he'd anticipated. "Yes, I've taken some things home, but I've still got to get all my heavy equipment out. I'll have to hire someone, I suppose, but I've been procrastinating about moving. I guess I was hoping…" Her voice trailed off and she looked at him with her big, optimistic eyes.

"Hoping what? That you'd manage to change my mind and not have to leave?"

They hadn't really lit on this topic since that day at her studio. Other topics, like the baby and getting naked, had taken priority. Sawyer had hoped his argument had been convincing enough to silence her protests, but apparently neither of them had backed down. They'd just been distracted. If Kat was going to give him the cold shoulder and they weren't going to have sex anymore, they might as well return to arguing. That added a little excitement to his day, if nothing else.

"Well, yes," she admitted.

Maybe he had been distracted, but it was possible Kat had been working her side of the argument the whole time. "Is that why you slept with me?" he asked.

The red flush returned to her cheeks. "I would appreciate it if you would stop accusing me of sleeping with you for favors. I told you that wasn't true the first time, after my encounter with Finn, and the answer is the same now. I have not, nor would I ever, use sex as a tool to get my way."

"And yet you admit that you were hoping I would change my mind after the time we've spent together. Was it your stunning argument that you expected to

sway me, or did you think you could take advantage
of our closeness to get me to change my mind? Tell
the truth."

Kat's jaw flexed tightly as she considered her words.
"I had hoped that once you got to know me, you would
understand where I was coming from. Or that you
would be more interested in the plight of the people
you're putting out on the street."

"I'm not putting them out on the street. They don't
live there. And stop trying to turn me into the bad guy,
when you very well could've been manipulating me
this whole time."

"Yes, I'm so devious, spending all my time trying to
seduce my way through the Steele family! And even if
I did sleep with you to save the District, would it have
even worked?"

Sawyer sat back in his chair. If he was honest with
himself, she *had* worn away at his defenses. He had listened to her argument. Sunday morning as he'd lain in
Kat's bed, he'd considered making changes to his plans
just because he thought it might make her smile. But
with Finn coming home, there was no sense in admitting that. Perhaps it was better to put an end to whatever was building between them, once and for all. Kat
was trying to be polite about distancing herself, but he
knew that rarely worked. Anger was like a wrecking
ball to anything they'd built.

"Probably not," he said. "Like I told you, it was fun.
But sex is sex, and business is business. I never mix
the two. It doesn't matter what happened between us
or how one of us might feel about the other. The Dis-

trict closes in two weeks for renovations. No reasoned argument or even a heartfelt declaration of love would change that."

Kat looked at him for a moment and then nodded stoically. "I see." She wadded up the cloth napkin in her lap and tossed it onto the table. "I think I'm going to go."

"We haven't eaten yet."

"The baby and I have lost our appetite." Kat scooped up her purse and got to her feet, then brushed past the confused waiter, who held their food in his hands.

They both watched her dart out the door. Sawyer wasn't surprised. He'd said what he'd said on purpose. Her leaving was the inevitable result, as much as it pained him to see her go. Better now than to go through this while he had to watch her with Finn.

"I'll take the burger," he said to the confused man standing with a plate in each hand. "Box up the salad to go. I'll have it for dinner."

Besides, he thought, knowing Kat, this argument was far from over.

"Nice Lexus."

Kat looked up from the box of tools she was packing up and saw Hilda in the doorway. "Hey there."

"I can't help but notice that your attempts to save the District seem to be backfiring spectacularly. Hot sex, billionaire babies, luxury cars, and yet we're still closing in a few weeks."

If those words had come from anyone else, Kat would've been insulted. But she knew Hilda better than that. "I've screwed it all up," she admitted. "Now every time I try to talk to Sawyer, there's family around who want to chat with me and discuss the baby. Pinning him down on the subject is impossible."

"Well, maybe the protest will make a difference. A little negative news coverage for the Steele family might be just what we need to get Sawyer's attention and keep it."

Protest? Oh, no.

Kat dropped her face into her hand. She'd completely forgotten about the protest *she* had organized outside the Steele corporate offices on July Fourth. It was intended to be the artists' way of reclaiming their independence from the new owner. She'd planned it weeks ago as a last-ditch effort to keep the place open if all her other plans failed. Before the wedding. Before she knew about the baby. Before Sawyer was in her bed.

And well before she'd agreed to go out with the same Steele family to celebrate July Fourth on their yacht.

"You forgot, didn't you?"

Kat turned around to face her dearest friend and shook her head in dismay. "How could I have forgotten? I planned the whole thing."

Hilda wrapped her arm around Kat's shoulder. "You haven't missed it yet. No worries. You've had a lot on your plate, hon. You've got pregnancy brain, so do what I do and put everything in your cell phone. If it isn't in my calendar it isn't happening."

"Right. My phone."

Hilda gave her a squeeze and stepped away. "What is it?"

"I... They've invited me to spend the holiday with them."

The older woman looked at her for a moment and then nodded. "Well, you should go."

"I can't! I'm supposed to be the one fighting to save this place. I can't go out on their yacht while I know you guys are out there sweating to death with picket signs and bullhorns. I would feel so hypocritical. I can't. I just can't."

"You're not the only one fighting for the District. You've been our most vocal member, but there are plenty of others here that need to do their part, too. Let them paint their picket signs and march their afternoon away. Maybe it's even better if you aren't there for that. It could cause you some unnecessary angst with your family."

"But *you're* my family. You're all I've got. All that matters."

"Not anymore. You've got new family now. And they're excited to include you in their lives. That's great. I'm very happy for you. It's what you've always wanted."

"But I don't want a new family. I want you and Zeke and everyone else."

Hilda wrapped her in a supportive hug. It was exactly what she needed in that moment, but it wasn't enough to stop the tears from overflowing down her cheeks and wetting her friend's T-shirt.

"We're not going anywhere, Kitty Kat. Family can

change, but they never really go away. Whether we're here at the District, or it closes and we scatter to the winds, you'll always be able to find us when you need us. I promise."

It was just like Hilda to say that and refuse to let her feel guilty. "You'll always be there for me, but I'm not going to be there for all of you. I ruined everything. I've lost focus."

"You did nothing of the sort. You've put your focus and your priorities where they belong—on your daughter. Tomorrow, you are going to put on a nice dress and a ton of sunscreen and go enjoy the holiday with your new family. We will carry the torch and things will be just fine. No matter what happens."

Kat opened her mouth to argue, but Hilda held up a finger to silence her. "No matter what happens."

Kat took a deep breath and made herself get out of the Lexus at the marina. There still hadn't been any word on her Jeep, which made her think that Sawyer was just humoring her and had no intention of taking back the Lexus. Of course, after the way their lunch had ended the other day, she might step outside some morning and find the Lexus had been towed off to the Steele compound out of pure spite.

Still, for now she had it, and it was allowing her to get around town, which she needed to do. If Finn's attorneys forced some kind of cash settlement on her, the first thing she'd do was pay Sawyer back for the car. She didn't want to feel like she owed him anything, especially after the ugly things he'd said.

She'd just been trying to get a little space to breathe and to think. It was necessary, especially after that moment they'd shared in the doctor's office. Sitting there, holding his hand and looking at the baby together had felt special. It felt right in a way that it shouldn't have. She didn't need those kinds of thoughts and feelings clouding the situation with Finn. Sawyer had reacted with anger, only proving that she was correct. They'd gotten too close and it could jeopardize everything.

Kat hadn't seen or heard from Sawyer since she'd left the restaurant and that was okay with her. She'd even planned on sitting out the holiday invitation in favor of protesting with her fellow artists, but Jade had called her and insisted she come. Morgan and her husband, River, were back from their honeymoon and wanted to meet her. No excuse seemed to stick with Jade, so now Kat was about to spend several hours on a small boat with Sawyer and his family in the middle of the harbor. Space was not an option.

She eyed the boats docked at the marina and her gaze caught the name of the biggest one: *License to Drill*. No doubt that belonged to the tool magnate Steele family. It looked like it had to be nearly two hundred feet in length, towering over the other boats, with four decks reaching to the sky. Maybe she would be able to avoid Sawyer after all.

As she headed that way, she noticed two women standing on the lowest deck. They were like day and night, blond and brunette. As she got closer, she recognized the blonde as Jade. That meant there would be at least one smiling face there to welcome her today and counteract Sawyer's grumpy countenance.

"Kat! You made it!" Jade was looking her direction and waving.

She waved back and walked up the pier to the stairs, where she could come aboard. The two women were there to meet her. "Kat, this is Morgan. She's finally back from her honeymoon."

"Hey, my first honeymoon was such a mess, we decided this one was going to be extra special. I highly recommend Fiji." The dark-haired woman with the golden tan smiled and stuck out her hand. "I'm Morgan Atkinson. I'm still getting used to saying that."

"I'm Kat," she responded, shaking her hand. "I'm sorry if I caused a problem at your wedding."

Morgan waved away her concerns. "It's not a problem. I'm only sad I missed you slapping the daylights out of Sawyer. I know Finn is the one who deserved it, but Sawyer can be a smug little jerk when he wants to be, too."

"Come on," Jade said. "Let's get you settled in and introduced to everyone. I think you're the last to arrive, so we should be departing soon. Morgan's husband, River, is here, and my fiancé, Harley, is around somewhere. Probably hiding from my parents. And Grandma is here, of course. She's excited to get to spend more time with you. We're hoping this time she shares. No one was able to get a word in with you or her at the party Saturday."

"What about Sawyer?" Kat asked, as they climbed a set of stairs to a higher deck.

"He's here. He was chatting up River about construction last I saw them."

That didn't surprise Kat. He probably had drywall and electrical conduits on his brain, with less than two weeks to closing the District.

The women led her through the luxurious interior of the yacht to the elevator. Looking around, Kat had a hard time believing she wasn't in a hotel. There was art on the walls, marble on the floors and polished wood everywhere. Everything was shiny and expensive, with inlaid gold, onyx and mother of pearl, making her feel incredibly out of place and wondering if she still had sawdust in her hair from working at the studio that morning.

They stepped out of the elevator onto one of the higher decks, where the rest of the family was gathered under shade sails around a hot tub and lounging area. Everyone cheered as she made her entrance, and the girls introduced her to the people she hadn't met yet. They mingled and nibbled on canapés while sipping cocktails and enjoying the sea breeze. Kat chose her seltzer and a seat far from Sawyer where she could protect her fair skin from the sun.

The rest of the afternoon was a blur. Once they set sail, the family moved inside, to where a "casual" buffet dinner of shrimp kabobs, baby back ribs, fire-roasted corn and twice-baked potatoes had been set up for them. The family seemed much more at ease without a bunch of guests around. They laughed, sipped their drinks, told Kat embarrassing stories about Finn and pumped her for information about the baby. When she finally told them it was a girl, there were more cheers of excitement.

After a few hours, Kat found herself really enjoying this time with the Steeles. She was having more fun with them than she'd ever expected to. They were remarkably down to earth once you set aside the luxurious surroundings. After eating, some people played cards on the top deck, while others went to a lower lounge to watch the water from shaded sofas. Kat was included in every conversation and game. They didn't look at her with suspicion the way she'd thought they might, nor did anyone pin her in a corner to grill her. Aside from Sawyer generally avoiding her, everyone was friendly and welcoming. Just the way she imagined a family was supposed to be.

She had no idea how things were going to go with Finn when he returned. She had her fingers crossed about that. But if she liked him half as much as she did the rest of this family, they might have a chance. Kat hadn't intended to start a family this way, but it seemed as if her daughter would at least get some decent aunts and uncles out of it.

"You guys need to come outside to the top deck if you're going to watch the fireworks the city is setting off over the harbor. We've got a surprise, too," Morgan said.

Kat had been watching Sawyer and Harley battle each other at chess when they heard the call from above. She was surprised to notice the sun had gone down while they were playing. When she reached the top deck, she noticed the whole boat was lit with pink light.

"Surprise!" Jade and Morgan said, as she stepped out.

"How did you turn the yacht pink?" she asked in amazement.

"All the lights are remote controlled fluorescents and can change to over two hundred thousand color combinations. Tonight, in honor of Baby Girl Steele, it's going to be pink. I don't care if it's the Fourth of July," Morgan declared.

"We've got a few minutes before the fireworks start," Jade said. "Come with us to get some drinks."

Kat followed the girls to the bar, where a gentleman in a polo shirt embroidered with the name of the yacht was waiting to make them a drink. She took her club soda and cranberry juice back with her, enjoying the view from the deck now that the sun had set. Charleston lit up, with the bridge stretching across the waterway and the Yorktown in the distance, was a stunning sight.

The three of them settled in a private area of clustered couches, away from the rest of the crowd on the third deck.

"Okay, so without everyone else around to hear, I'm curious about what's going on with you and Finn," Jade pressed.

Kat placed her drink on the table and settled back in her seat. "Not much, yet. But I'm hopeful for more than what his lawyers offered."

"Was he being cheap?" Morgan asked, an appalled look on her face.

"No, not at all. He was extremely generous, actually. But I guess I'm looking for something different from him. To be honest, what I want is a family for my child. For us both. I grew up with busy parents who were always working, and then they were gone and I was all alone in the world. I want to do this differently. I don't just want money from Finn, I want his time. Real, quality time."

"Do you want to get married?" Jade asked. "It seems like a big leap after a single date, especially for Finn, but I'm sure that's what Dad is going to be pushing for."

"Yes," Kat admitted. "I know it seems silly in this day and age, but I do want to get married to my baby's father. I know I don't love Finn and he doesn't love me, but this is about more than that. It's about creating a supportive and loving environment for the baby to grow up in. Maybe love will come in time. I don't know. I can only hope that Finn will step up and do the right thing, and that everything works out."

"Well, Finn is always surprising people," Morgan said. "I hope for your sake that he takes this seriously and you get everything you're hoping for. Then you can name the baby after her sweet and supportive Aunt Morgan."

Nine

Sawyer didn't pay much attention to the fireworks, the patriotic music or the impressive desserts the yacht's chef brought out when they were over. No, his mind was someplace else, thanks to overhearing Kat's discussion with his sisters.

After she'd walked out on him at lunch the other day, he couldn't decide if he was irritated or grateful. She'd pushed him away and he'd pushed back twice as hard on reflex. Maybe it was for the best, after everything he'd overheard tonight, but he couldn't help but feel like crap since it happened. He wanted to apologize for the ugly things he'd said. He'd almost pulled her aside twice today to do just that. The first time he'd been stopped by a text from Steele security about District protesters outside their corporate offices. Even with

Kat on the boat with him, he knew she was behind it. He'd stewed about it for a while and then went to find her again after his chess game. He found her with his sisters and hesitated. Now that he'd heard what she'd said to Jade and Morgan, he was glad he hadn't spoken to her alone. He needed to butt out of the whole situation.

Kat wanted to marry Finn and live happily ever after with their daughter. She knew the odds were stacked against her, and yet she wanted the best for her baby, and he could tell she wouldn't rest until she had it. Before Finn even knew what hit him, he'd be swept away in a tide of domesticity. He'd own a nice house in a good school district, drive a minivan and be celebrating his fifth wedding anniversary with Kat. Somehow, he did everything wrong and was going to be rewarded with a woman and a life he didn't deserve.

For the third time in recent memory, Sawyer was practically green with jealously of Finn. He hated that feeling.

And so he'd started smothering it with alcohol. Or trying to. The Scotch had unfortunately kicked in right about the time the yacht returned to port and everyone was unloading to go home.

Sawyer ordered a coffee and chugged it so hot he burned his tongue, but he wasn't sure it was going to be enough. He stumbled a bit heading down the stairs, but was lucky enough for Harley to be there and keep him from hitting the deck with his face.

"Whoa, there. Do we need to call you a car, Sawyer?" Harley asked. "I'd give you a ride, but you live the wrong way."

"Shh," Sawyer slurred, and looked around for Trevor and Patricia. "Don't make a fuss about it or my folks will make me ride home with them and stay at the house. I do not want to sober up with our house-keeper's homemade hangover juice."

"Ugh," Morgan groaned. "I think Lena just made us drink that as a punishment for partying as teenag-ers. It doesn't help the hangover at all."

"Well, you can't drive. Can you just sleep over on the boat tonight?"

"I'll take him home. I'm pretty sure it's on my way. Pregnant women are nature's designated drivers, any-way."

Sawyer turned around to see Kat standing nearby. She was the last person he needed to be alone with while his filter was down and his tongue was loose. "You don't have to do that. I'll talk to the captain about crashing here."

"No, you won't. You drove me home when my Jeep wouldn't start. I owe you one. Just promise me you won't throw up in the Lexus. You can't regift a car that smells like puke."

She smiled at her joke and his heart started racing in his chest. Kat had a light sweater pulled over her bare shoulders to protect from the chill of the sea air, but earlier, she'd worn only the strapless navy blue sun-dress. Her hair was pulled back into a high ponytail and it swung back and forth when she walked. He'd wanted to tell her how beautiful she looked today, casual and elegant, but it had seemed like a bad idea. Lately, all his ideas were bad ones.

"I promise," he said instead. Perhaps some time alone would be what he needed to apologize, and then both of them could move on.

Harley and River helped Sawyer walk off the boat, and loaded him into her passenger seat while Morgan put Sawyer's address into the GPS. "Are you sure you can handle him?" Harley asked with concerned eyes.

Kat nodded and climbed into the car beside him. "I'll be fine. I'll just slap him when we get to his place and he'll wake right up."

Harley's and River's laughter was muted by the slamming of the car door. As she started the engine, Sawyer pushed himself up in the seat and put on his seat belt for the ride.

"Thank you for driving me home even though you hate me."

"It's not a problem, and I don't hate you. You might be a jerk sometimes, but I don't want you driving if it isn't safe."

"I'm sorry," he said, after an extended silence.

Kat turned to him for a moment before merging into the traffic and heading to his place. "You're sorry for what?"

"For everything I said to you the other day. I was upset when you said we were over, and I lashed out at you. That wasn't the right thing to do. I know now that you just want what's best for your daughter and that's to be with her father. I shouldn't be angry or try to stand in the way of that. I only want what's best for you and the baby, too."

She seemed stunned by his apology, letting the words sink in before she finally responded. "Thank you, Sawyer. I'm sorry, too. I guess we both could've handled it better. I never should've entertained something with you when I knew what I wanted with Finn. I should've told you."

With the air clear, they drove in silence across the peninsula until they closed in on his place. "You have reached your destination," the GPS announced, disrupting the quiet inside the car as she pulled up in front of his house.

"You can turn into the drive just there." Sawyer pointed and hit a button on his key chain to open the gate to his private driveway.

She turned in and came to a stop, shutting off the engine. "Let's get you inside."

Sawyer looked at her with confusion. "You're coming in?"

Her pointed expression shot down any thoughts he might entertain about her inside his house. "I'm going to help you up the stairs and get you in the house. If you behave, I might make you some coffee and toast."

Sawyer nodded and opened the car door. He was feeling pretty steady on his feet now, but as they moved toward the stairs, he felt less sure. Kat was quick to move to his side. She wrapped his arm around her shoulders and put hers around his waist.

"Grab the rail and help me," she said, so he did.

It took three times fumbling with his keys and dropping them, but they finally made it inside his place. He stumbled in, shrugging out of his blazer and tossing it onto a wingback chair like he did every night. His keys went into a bowl by the door as he flipped on the overhead light.

He paused as Kat gasped, and figured the original rose medallion in the ceiling, along with the restored crystal chandelier, had caught her eye. Instead, when he turned, she was running her hand over the ornately carved wood of the staircase just to their right.

"The woodwork is beautiful."

Sawyer looked around his living room and nodded. "I forget you're a wood carver. You'll find a lot you'll like here. Much of the house had already been redone when I bought it, but thankfully, they left most of the original woodwork intact. The decorator I hired did a good job incorporating the existing historical details into my modern aesthetic."

"I'm surprised you got all those words past your tongue," Kat said with a smile.

"Very funny. The kitchen is this way."

Kat followed him through the living room and into the kitchen at the rear of the house. He'd had it done in all white, with black hardware and dark antique fixtures for a stark, clean look. It seemed to go well with the original white shiplap that ran through the home and the tiny white octagon tiles on the floor.

She strolled through the kitchen, touching the quartz countertop and the faucet before bending over to look at the wood cabinetry of the island. He'd had that piece done by a local carpenter who carved the details by hand. Kat noticed immediately, running her fingers over the scrollwork.

"You don't even cook in here, do you?" she asked, as she stood back up.

He shook his head, making himself dizzy, so he sat on a bar stool on the other side of the kitchen island. "I like things with clean lines, and designs that look tidy. I also like features that will help with resale down the road. This seemed like a good mix, whether I use it or not. And I have used the microwave," he said, pointing out the stainless-steel machine mounted into the side of the island. "And the coffee maker."

Kat nodded thoughtfully. "Well, speaking of coffee makers, you have been a good boy so far. I believe I promised you coffee and toast."

"Coffee is in that jar, and bread is in the pantry over there."

She followed his guidance, moving around the kitchen to prepare a late-night drunk man's snack. A few minutes later, she presented him with a steaming mug of black coffee and a plate with two dry pieces of toast on it.

"It's not haute cuisine, but it's what you need. When you're done, we'll follow it up with a big glass of water and some ibuprofen. You'll wake up feeling like a champ."

"You know a lot about being drunk."

Kat shrugged. "I went to college, same as you. Late-night parties followed by early morning lectures mean you learn how to cope, and quickly. I also lost my parents when I was in school. There are a few weekends

I don't remember after that happened. Water, Advil, toast and coffee are a combination that never fails."

"I think I would've failed the semester if I lost my parents."

"Well, fortunately, I went to an art school. They encouraged me to funnel my pain into my work, and my grades actually improved. Except for chemistry. I got a D in that," she said with a smile.

Sawyer chuckled and finished his requisite meal quickly. As she put his dishes into the sink, he went over to the refrigerator and pulled out two bottles of water. "Here you go," he said, handing her one.

"Thanks. How are you feeling?"

"Better. It all seemed to hit at once tonight. Drinking that late was foolish," he admitted. "But it got you here. I can't complain about that."

Kat set her water on the counter and looked at him with amusement crinkling her eyes. "Did you set all this up to get me to your house?"

"No," he said, with a dismissive shake of his head. "Lately nothing I plan works out as well as I want it to, so I've decided to give that up. Sometimes it's better to just go with the flow and see what happens. It always works for Finn, so why not me?"

She narrowed her gaze at him. "You're not Finn. You're Sawyer."

He shrugged and finished off his water. "Fat lot of good that does me. Finn is the one who reaps all the rewards. He has all the fun, gets all the girls, lives life to the fullest. He always gets what I want," Sawyer said, looking pointedly at Kat.

She dismissed his inebriated tirade, stretching out her hand and gently grasping his wrist. "You may look alike, but the world needs only one Finn. And it needs you to be yourself, because there's only one you."

Sawyer looked down at her hand and followed the line of her arm until he was gazing into her eyes. "Stay with me tonight."

Kat froze for a moment before dropping her hand from his wrist. He could tell by the line between her brows that she was conflicted. She wanted to stay. She wanted him. But she kept putting this fantasy of a future with Finn in front of her own needs and desires.

"Just one night. One last time."

She backed up until she hit the quartz countertop of the island. "You've been drinking. You don't mean it. We both agreed it was a mistake the last time."

He took a step forward and shook his head. "I know exactly what I'm saying, Kat. I'm not that drunk."

"I don't know, Sawyer. I—"

He took another step, but she didn't move away. "Finn will be home soon. And if you get what you want, everything that happened between us will be a deeply buried secret once you move on with your life. I will become your brother-in-law or the baby's uncle Sawyer. Nothing more. And I'll be okay with that, because it's what you want. But give me one last night to keep with me. A night to remember you by."

Sawyer reached out to capture the ever-present strand of auburn hair that fell along her cheek, and pushed it behind her ear. He let his knuckles graze her skin and felt her press into his touch.

* * *

"Please, Kat."

There was something in his voice. In the way he looked at her. Something that told Kat she wasn't going to be able to walk away from him. Not tonight.

She closed her eyes and leaned into the warm fingers brushing against her face. She longed to have those same warm hands on her body and his lips pressed to hers. These last few days, she'd missed Sawyer. Whether he was aggravating her or making love to her, she missed it. And she knew she would miss it for the days and weeks to come.

Why not indulge one last time? Give them both something to remember?

Opening her eyes, she closed the gap between them, cradled his face in her hands and pulled his mouth to hers. The rough stubble of his evening beard prickled against her hands in sharp contrast to her own soft skin.

The moment he realized she wasn't just kissing him, but saying yes to his proposition, the intensity increased tenfold. His arms wrapped around her, pulling her tight against him with the hunger of a man who'd long denied himself sustenance. He pressed her back against the island, his hands roaming across her body just as his tongue explored her mouth.

Kat met his intensity. With everything she had, she wanted him. And if it was the last time, she wanted to remember every moment in his arms.

Her breathing quickened when his lips traveled along her jaw and down her throat. He licked and nibbled at her skin, causing Kat to gasp and writhe as the pleasurable tingles vibrated through her nervous system. Her neck was her weakness and Sawyer instinctively seemed to know it. As her knees softened beneath her from the sensations, he tightened his grip, holding her upright.

And then, when she needed him more than ever, he retreated. She opened her eyes to see him looking down at her with desire blazing in his dark gaze. He seemed pensive, and it scared her. He wasn't changing his mind, was he? Then he took a step back, helping her regain her footing, and reached for her hand. "Come on."

"Where are we going?" she asked.

"I'm taking you upstairs," he said. "If this is the last time we'll be together, I'm going to do it properly, not some quick tumble on the closest hard surface."

She followed him back to the staircase she'd admired earlier, and they went up to the second floor. There, he opened a pair of French doors to the master suite, which took up the majority of that level. In the center of the room was the showpiece—a grand four-poster bed that was carved to look like ivy was wrapped around its massive columns and across the headboard.

Kat couldn't stop herself from walking up to it and touching one of the columns. It was an old piece. Better than her own work, she had to admit. It was beautiful. Perhaps the most beautiful bed she'd ever seen. She had the sudden burning urge to go to her shop and make a headboard at her first opportunity.

"I found this in the attic when I bought the house,"

Sawyer said, as he came up behind her and ran his own hand over the smooth, polished wood. "I had it restored and refinished. I must've known you would be here to see it one day."

Kat turned to face him, looking up at the dark eyes that watched her so carefully. He reached out to brush the hair from her face again and then softly ran his thumb over her bottom lip. Even as he teetered on the edge of being tipsy, he was more thoughtful and loving than any man she'd ever been with.

His attention to detail continued as they moved around to the side of the bed. They slowly removed each other's clothing, caressing and kissing the bare skin as they exposed it. Then he picked her up around the waist and lifted her onto the high mattress. She scooted back as he advanced, covering her body with his until his warm skin chased away the cool conditioned air being circulated by the ceiling fan overhead.

Sawyer propped himself on his elbows, looking down at her. Kat wished she knew what he was thinking, but she was too afraid to ask. Knowing the truth would only make things harder.

He slipped between her thighs, rubbing his hands over the outside of her legs and hips until she nearly purred from the caress. He dipped his head, drawing one of her nipples into his mouth. Sawyer teased it, tugging hard on her flesh until her back arched up off the bed.

Kat dug her heels into the mattress, lifting her hips and seeking him out. He didn't disappoint, moving forward into her without much effort. She was ready for him, welcoming him inside with a hiss of satisfaction.

From there, he took his time. He wanted a night to remember and they would have it. Every inch of her skin was caressed and kissed. Every sound she made he seemed to memorize. When he moved inside her with more urgency, Kat fought to keep her eyes open so she, too, could remember every moment.

Eventually, she lost that battle. Her release exploded inside her just as his mouth clamped down onto hers. He swallowed her cries, taking them into himself for safekeeping and mingling them with his own low groans as he poured himself into her.

It was a leisurely, but emotionally exhausting, love-making session. And when Sawyer collapsed at her side, he was curled up next to her with his hand protectively resting on her belly.

Kat knew it then. If she was being honest with herself, she'd known it before. She'd known it the first night they spent together, but she'd been too stubborn to believe it. It wasn't a part of her plan. It wasn't the way she wanted things to turn out. But that didn't make it any less true.

Kat was in love with Sawyer.

She could tell herself that she wanted to marry Finn, but that was just her own head getting in the way of what her heart wanted. She hardly knew Finn. But what she did know was that there was no way he could compete with Sawyer. His twin had already taken his place in her heart and no matter how hard she tried to push him out, Sawyer was still there.

She closed her eyes tightly and cursed herself. She was an idiot. She'd gone and fallen in love with the wrong Steele twin.

Turning her head, she looked over at him. His eyes were closed, his golden lashes resting on his cheeks. He'd already fallen fast asleep, thanks to the combined sedative effects of good sex and strong whiskey. She wanted to tell him how she felt, but seeing him asleep was enough to give her pause.

Sawyer was a good man. He was as stubborn as she was, for sure, but he had a very strong compass when it came to right and wrong. That he'd given in to his desire for her, even knowing it wasn't right, had to mean something. It meant he cared for her, too, no matter if he knew or understood that himself.

But that moral compass wasn't going anywhere. He'd asked her for one last night and that's all he would take. Once Finn was back in Charleston, he would step aside just as he'd said he would. Even if it hurt him. Even if it broke his heart to do it. And telling him that she loved him wouldn't help. It would only make it harder on both of them. She knew he would put the baby's needs first, just like she had.

And nothing short of a time machine would change the fact that Finn was her baby's father.

Ten

"Nǐ hǎo. Wǒ huíláile!"

Sawyer looked up from his computer and inwardly cringed at the sound of his brother's voice and his massacred attempt at speaking Mandarin as he came down the hallway.

Finn stopped in Sawyer's doorway. He was wearing his usual suit, but instead of a tie, his shirt collar was unbuttoned to show a gold necklace with a jade medallion he'd picked up overseas. "I have returned, twin of mine. Did you miss me?"

"Not particularly," Sawyer said flatly.

Finn smiled and continued down the hall without missing a beat. Sawyer didn't really want to follow, but he wanted to know how things had gone in China, and his father would probably be demanding a full report immediately.

Pushing up from his chair, he went out and followed Finn to the big corner office where Trevor Steele held court. His brother was already in there by the time he reached the assistant's desk.

"Sawyer, come in and shut the door," Trevor said.

Finn was grinning from ear to ear in one of the two guest chairs across from their father. Things must have gone well in Beijing. Or his brother was too busy doing other things to notice that it hadn't.

"The manufacturing plant is complete and operational. I returned home for a few weeks while the staffing team works on hiring from the local area and getting the team trained. I think we will have them punching out hammers and sockets within a month, conservatively."

Both brothers turned to Trevor for his reaction and Sawyer wasn't disappointed.

"Thanks for the update," Trevor retorted, "but I know exactly what's going on over there. Do you really think I'd send you halfway across the world to manage a multi-million-dollar operation and not know what was going on every second of the day?"

Finn's smile faded. "Of course you would keep abreast. You're the president of the company. I just wanted to share the good news with you and Sawyer."

Trevor sat back in his chair and crossed his hands over his chest. "You did fine, son. Better than I expected, really. But it's hard for me to focus on that considering the mess you left behind at home."

"Mess?"

Sawyer's hands curled into fists on the arms of his chair. Completely oblivious as usual. "He's talking about Kat and the baby, you idiot."

"That's not a mess," Finn argued, looking between his father and his brother. "My attorneys have it all handled. I'm going to meet with her this week to negotiate a settlement and get her to sign off. It's fine."

Trevor studied his sons for a moment and then pinched the bridge of his nose. "I don't know how the two of you could look so similar and be so different. You are a damn fool, Finn. It's not fine. You got a stranger pregnant."

"It was an accident! I assure you I did, and always have done, everything in my power to keep that from happening."

"Everything short of keeping it in your pants," Trevor snapped.

While Sawyer did enjoy Finn getting his comeuppance on some level, he was growing uncomfortable being in the room. "Do I really need to be in here for this? I thought we were out-briefing on the new facility."

He started to push up from his chair, but Trevor's sharp gaze caused him to sit back down immediately. "You stay," he said. "You've been the one handling things with Kat while he's been gone. You know her better than anyone."

"I don't see what the problem is," Finn argued. "I plan to take care of Kat and the baby."

"That's not enough. Writing a check and walking

away from your responsibilities is not enough. You've forgotten that I've met this woman. Your mother met her. Your grandmother and sisters have met her. And they like her. *I* like her. She's not your usual weekend delight that you can give a check to and send on her way. She's more your brother's speed, to be honest, but she had the misfortune of meeting the wrong Steele twin. She is smart and kind, and the best damn thing to ever happen to you. She could be the thing that turns your life around. And accident or no accident, she deserves better than what you're offering."

"You don't even know what I'm offering."

"I know what you're *not* offering," their father said sharply. "You know, I sent you to China in the hopes you would grow up. You're almost thirty-four years old and you've been causing problems for the family since you found that pecker between your legs. Now it looks like I'm going to have to make you man up once and for all."

Finn was pressed back so far in his chair, Sawyer thought he might tumble backward. He was smart enough not to say anything else at this point. Even Finn knew when to shut up and just listen.

"That is your child, and you're going to marry its mother. Steeles don't walk away from their mistakes."

"Only when we can't erase them and pretend like they never happened," Finn said.

Sawyer's eyes widened as he looked at his brother in shock. Maybe Finn wasn't as smart as he thought.

"What did you say?" Trevor asked in a biting, sarcastic tone.

"I'm talking about Morgan and how your *guiding hand* completely destroyed her life. You paid off River and just swept her marriage and her baby under the rug, but you can't do that with me, so you're bullying me into doing what you want instead."

Sawyer was afraid to take a breath. He sat still, waiting for the blowback. He'd never heard Finn—or anyone for that matter—speak to their father that way. He could see the anger twitching the muscles in his father's jaw as he considered his words.

"You're right," Trevor said at last, in a cold, calm voice. "I thought at nineteen that Morgan was too young and immature to make her own decisions and I was wrong. But this time, I'm right, and you've just proved you're still too immature to make your own decisions."

Finn didn't have anything to say to that. Neither did Sawyer. What could he say? This was what Kat wanted, although she probably would've preferred it not be a shotgun wedding.

"Tomorrow night, we'll have a nice family dinner to welcome you home. We will invite Kat. And there, in front of everyone, you're going to present her with an engagement ring and ask her to be your wife. Do you understand me?"

Finn swallowed hard and nodded.

"Very good. Now give your travel paperwork and receipts to your assistant to file and go get some rest. You're dismissed." Both brothers stood up, but Trevor's gaze shot to Sawyer. "Not you."

Finn basically ran from the office, leaving Sawyer

behind. He sighed and sat back in the chair, awaiting whatever tongue-lashing he'd earned lately. His father probably knew about him sneaking around with Kat. The man seemed to know everything that happened in this family.

"What am I going to do with him?" Trevor asked with a heavy sigh.

"If you make him marry her, he's going to be miserable. And he'll make everyone else miserable, including Kat."

"I know. But at some point, he needs to take responsibility."

"Let me marry her instead." The words slipped from Sawyer's lips before he'd fully thought them through. He didn't regret them, though.

Trevor snapped his gaze over to his son. "That's a generous offer. Would you care to tell me why you'd like to marry Kat in your brother's place?"

"It's the best solution," Sawyer argued. "Finn doesn't want to do it, but I will, and the problem will be solved. Genetically, legally, it will be my child as much as Finn's. She will look just like me. No one ever needs to know the truth."

His father considered his words for a moment and shook his head. "That's very pragmatic of you. I can always count on you to do what needs to be done, although I'm sure in this case there's more to your motivations than I really want to know. But I can't let you do that."

"Why not?"

"Because this isn't about you. If you want to help,

then I need you to back off and let Finn step up. Let things play out between the two of them. If he proposes and Kat turns him down to choose you instead, let that be *her* choice. If she has any damn sense, she would laugh in his face, but Finn has to make the effort or he never will."

Sawyer sighed. His father was right. This was Kat's decision. They could sit in this office and make all the plans in the world, but in the end, only what she wanted mattered. And as far as Sawyer knew, she wanted Finn. "Is there anything else?"

"Yes. That protest over the holiday. It was all over the news this weekend. That's blowback from your real estate deal, isn't it?"

Sawyer had hoped maybe word hadn't gotten to his father about that yet, but clearly he wasn't that lucky. "Yes."

"It's one thing to try to make money on a property deal, but I'll not have you dragging the family or the company through the mud to do it. Find out a way to make those people happy. Sometimes compromise is key, in business and in romance."

Oddly, this was a little bit of both for Sawyer. But his father was right. There had to be a middle ground that would keep protests off the front pages. The new building could be amazing, but it wouldn't matter if no one was willing to cross a picket line to see it. "Yes, sir."

"One last thing and you can go. Take your brother to the jewelry store. Make sure he picks something nice. Nothing gaudy or cheap. I don't want her turning him down just because he got her the Tuesday cubic zirconia special from Big Eddie on King Street."

Sawyer stood up and nodded. Helping his brother pick out an engagement ring for Kat was one of the last things he wanted to do, but he would to make sure she got something she would love. She deserved that much.

After stepping out into the hall, he headed back toward his office. There, he found Finn sitting on the edge of their assistant's desk, flirting mercilessly as though that wasn't a lawsuit waiting to happen.

"Come on, Finn, we need to go engagement ring shopping so you can propose tomorrow night."

Their assistant, Melody May, sat up at attention and pulled back from Finn. The smile faded from her face and she snatched the travel receipts from his hand without another word.

Finn matched her frown and followed Sawyer into his office. "You really think I should do this? Are you as crazy as Dad?"

"Shut the door," Sawyer said as he leaned against his desk. "And sit down."

"I just got one ass chewing. You don't get to boss me around, too."

"I'm older by two minutes. Now shut the damn door," he barked, pointing to the entrance, "and listen to me."

Finn reluctantly complied and flopped down into the guest chair. "What?"

"A lot has happened while you've been gone. We've all gotten to know Kat very well. Better than you know her. And like Dad said, we like her. The only thing wrong with her is that for some crazy reason, she seems to think that marrying you is the right thing to do. Personally, I think she could do better, but she hasn't asked my opinion."

"What's your point?" Finn said, crossing his arms defiantly over his chest.

Sawyer leaned in to his brother with his stoniest gaze. "My point is that Katherine McIntyre is the single greatest woman to ever walk into your life. She is smart, funny, talented, beautiful…and she's having your child. You don't deserve her in your bed and you don't deserve her as your wife. Not even close. But right now she's there for the taking. And if you let her walk out of your life, you're an even bigger fool than I thought."

"Good evening, Miss McIntyre," Lena said, as she opened the door to the Steele mansion. "Please come in. The family is in the library."

Kat stepped in cautiously and waited for Lena to close the door behind her before she started making her way toward the voices in the east wing of the house.

"Kat!" A woman's voice boomed across the entryway.

She turned to see Morgan rushing over to her from the stairs. "Hey."

Without a word, she grabbed Kat's hand and dragged her away from the library toward the powder room. She tugged her inside and shut the door.

"What is going on?" Kat asked, awkwardly pressed against the pedestal sink.

"Finn is proposing to you at dinner tonight," Morgan blurted in excitement.

Kat's jaw dropped. "Are you serious? I haven't even seen him since he got back from China. We've spoken a handful of times on the phone. Proposing tonight? Really?"

Morgan nodded, a conspiratorial look on her face. "I've seen the ring. Sawyer took him shopping yesterday and it's ah-mazing."

She was stunned. This was just supposed to be a welcome-home dinner with the family. Her chance to see and talk to Finn in person for the first time since the night they'd gotten themselves into this mess. And he was proposing? In the moment, she wasn't sure what to say. Thank goodness Morgan had given her a heads-up or she might've appeared like a very ungrateful recipient when Finn popped the question. After all, this was what she wanted.

Right?

"Anyway, I thought you should know. It ruins the surprise, but personally, I'd rather be prepared. If he does it in front of the whole family, it could be nerve-racking. Plus, I wanted to squeal a little with you about it ahead of time. This is just what you said you wanted the other night on the ship! I'm so happy for you!"

Morgan scooped Kat into a hug and she returned the embrace. Why was her future sister-in-law more excited about this than she was? She pinched her eyes shut and tried to push the image of Sawyer out of her mind. That was over and done. He was stepping aside so Kat could have the family she wanted. It was all coming together.

"Okay, I'd better get back before someone wonders where I've been. See you in there in a minute." Morgan opened the door and dashed out of the bathroom.

Kat took a moment to compose herself. She checked her makeup and smoothed her hair. She wanted to look perfect for the moment. Finn should be proud of his bride, whether he'd intended for this to happen or not. After stepping out of the room, she turned and very nearly collided with Sawyer as he hung his coat in the nearby closet.

"Kat? I didn't know you were here already. Are you hiding in the bathroom?"

"Of course not. I was just putting on some fresh lipstick."

He nodded, trying and failing to look disinterested in her appearance tonight. "Have you seen Finn yet?"

"No. I saw Morgan briefly, but that's it so far."

He nodded again. There was a stiffness about Sawyer tonight. If he took Finn shopping, then he knew what was about to happen. He didn't seem to like the idea very much. Lately, neither did she. It made her want to ask the hard questions while she still had the chance.

"Can I ask you something before we go in there with your family?"

"Sure," he said, pasting on a polite smile.

Kat tried to think of how best to ask the question. "Can you give me any reason why I shouldn't marry Finn?"

She wanted to give him his chance. His moment. Not to do the honorable thing, but to tell the truth about how he felt about her, even if it turned the whole night upside down. Her eyes searched his face, pleading with him to be honest. Marrying Finn had seemed like a good idea until Sawyer showed up in her life. Now, she wasn't sure what she wanted, but knowing if he loved her the way she loved him would help her decide.

"I'm sorry, I can't," he said, looking away. Without making additional eye contact, Sawyer turned and walked across the hall, leaving her there alone and brokenhearted.

The rest of the evening was a bit of a blur, like she was walking through a dream. Kat was distracted and wallowing in her emotional turmoil. They gathered in the library for drinks and mingling before moving into the dining room.

As they migrated down the hall, Finn pulled Kat aside to chat in person at last. It was weird seeing him again after all this time, knowing he was her baby's father, looking so much like the man she loved but not like him at all. Later, as they were eating, she realized she couldn't really remember anything about their conversation. It had mostly been about himself and his work in China. Not once had he asked about her, the pregnancy or the baby. It made the news of his pending return to Beijing in a few weeks a little easier to swallow.

Besides that, it was hard to focus with Sawyer scowling at them. In the library, he'd pretended to be listening to what Grandma Ingrid had to say, but every time Kat glanced in his direction, he'd been looking at her as if he regretted not taking his chance when he had it.

Dinner wasn't much better. She was seated beside Finn, of course, but somehow ended up across from Sawyer. While she tried to engage Finn and River, to her right, in conversation as they ate, she could feel Sawyer's gaze on her.

She wasn't sure how she was going to get through tonight. When the moment came, and Finn got down on one knee, how could she say yes with Sawyer watching? It seemed the thing she'd once hoped for had become an impossible feat.

As Lena cleared the dinner dishes in preparation for dessert, Finn pushed back his chair to make a toast. Kat froze in her seat, finally forcing herself to reach out and raise her glass of sparkling water.

"I'd like to thank everyone for coming tonight and welcoming me home from China. It was an amazing trip and I look forward to returning and continuing to assist in Steele Tools' new venture there. It's such a fast-paced and colorful culture in some aspects, and then so peaceful and quiet in other areas. I was able to find something for each one of you on my trip. The bag of goodies is in the library and I'll hand them out after dessert. But right now, I have one special gift for Kat. I—"

Sawyer abruptly pushed his chair back from the dinner table. "You'll have to excuse me," he said, as he rounded the long table and practically ran into the hall.

Everyone sat in stunned silence for a moment before Finn recovered. "I hope he's feeling okay. Anyway, I wanted to thank all of you for welcoming Kat so warmly into the family while I was gone. I have heard nothing but glowing stories about what a talented and lovely woman she is. And although we haven't known each other for long, I look forward to having the opportunity to know her very well in the upcoming years."

As Finn reached into his suit coat pocket, Kat's heart started pounding in her chest. For a moment, all she could hear was its deep bass rhythm and the rushing of blood in her ears. She thought she might even faint. She closed her eyes, hoping the swimming in her head would pass before she made a fool of herself in front of these lovely people who had welcomed her into their family.

When she opened her eyes, she realized that Finn was down on his knee beside her. He had a small jewelry box in one hand, opened to display one of the most beautiful rings she'd ever seen in her life. The diamond in the center was a large and colorless oval stone, but what really caught her eye was the platinum band itself. The diamond was in a bezel setting with a knife edge designed band. There were three diamonds on each side that tapered in size to a double milgrain design. She could tell the intricate filigree etching had been hand done by an artisan who loved to work with metal and jewelry design as much as she enjoyed working with wood.

"Katherine McIntyre, I know that we are only at the start of our journey together. Tonight I offer you this ring in the hopes that it will be a long, happy one. Will you marry me?"

She didn't know what to say.

It was the moment she'd been waiting for. This might have started off by accident, but Finn was stepping up and helping her achieve her dream of having a real family for her daughter. Mother, wife, father, husband, child, family…it was all coming together. There was only one thing missing from the picture.

Love.

Kat had told herself she didn't need it. What the baby needed was more important. She'd told herself that if Finn would marry her, she would make a good life with him and maybe love would come in time.

The moment was right. The ring was perfect. The proposal was heartfelt and well-spoken. She was surrounded by her new family, who were nearly bursting at the seams, waiting for her to say yes so they could spend the rest of the evening celebrating the new couple. It was everything she'd thought she wanted.

It was just the wrong brother down on one knee.

Eleven

Sawyer could step aside because his father told him to. He could even take his brother shopping to pick out the ring he knew she would love. But he just couldn't sit at that table and watch Finn propose to the woman Sawyer loved.

Realizing that he loved Kat mere seconds before his brother stood up to make his big speech was Sawyer's typical poor timing. Before that, he'd known he cared about Kat and the baby. He liked spending time with her. If marrying her made her feel better about raising her daughter, he was willing to do it, and spare Finn from a fate he saw as worse than death. Sawyer knew he didn't like the idea of his brother with Kat. But until that moment, none of it had added up in his mind to love.

When he realized the truth, it was too much for him to take. He'd been in love before, so he should've realized it sooner. But he was stubborn. He knew Kat was never meant to be his, so he hadn't recognized the signs. How stupid could he be, to fall in love with the woman having his brother's child? Even after he knew she wanted to marry Finn for the child's sake, he couldn't stay away. The whole situation was doomed from their first kiss that day at the District.

So he left. Simple as that. His parents would probably be annoyed. He'd have to explain that he realized he'd forgotten an appointment or something. Left the iron on at home. He certainly couldn't tell them he was in love with Kat and didn't want to watch her get engaged to Finn.

His phone rang several times on his drive home that night, but he didn't answer. He put it on Silent and shoved it into the glove box of his Audi. He didn't want to hear about how it went. He didn't want to see a picture of the blissful couple. He just wanted to go home, drink a beer and reevaluate his damn life.

What he certainly didn't expect was to find his brother sitting in his office the next morning. When he opened the door, Finn was reclining casually on the leather sofa he kept near the window for visits and late afternoon naps.

"Good morning, brother," Finn said in a chipper tone.

Too chipper, to tell the truth. Sawyer looked at him with mistrust, going past the couch to toss his laptop bag onto the desk. "It's too early for you to be up."

"I'm still on Beijing time. I figure since I'm just going back in a few weeks, I shouldn't bother fighting the time difference and the jet lag."

"I figured you were out all night celebrating your pending nuptials."

Finn's brow furrowed in confusion. "Nuptials? You mean you haven't heard?"

Sawyer sighed and leaned against his desk. "Haven't heard what, Finn? It's too early for guessing games."

"You haven't looked at your phone!" Finn got up from the couch and walked over to him. "Hold out your hand," he said.

When Sawyer complied, Finn dropped the ring box into his palm. He opened it, expecting it to be empty, with the ring on Kat's finger, but it was still safely nestled in its velvet bed. "Tell me you didn't chicken out on her!" he said, gripping the ring box in his fist and slamming the lid shut. He would punch Finn in the face right now if he'd changed his mind and broken Kat's heart.

"No way!" Finn said, as he ducked out of arm's reach. "I did my part. Pretty well, too. I didn't want to hear about it from Dad later, so I had a very nice, heartfelt proposal prepared. But she turned me down. Flat."

Sawyer froze for a moment. A part of him was waiting for Finn to say he was joking, but the relieved smile on his face said it all. Kat hadn't accepted his proposal and Finn was thrilled, because there was nothing their father could do about it.

"She said no?"

"She said *no*. With Dad and everyone else there

to witness it. And while I'm relieved… I also have to say that I'm a bit concerned about why she changed her mind."

"Concerned?"

"Yes. Concerned that while I was out of the country, my twin brother may have swooped in and snatched Kat right out from under me."

"What are you talking about?"

"Come on, man. I saw you two looking at each other all evening. I asked you to handle the situation until I got back. I didn't mean sleep with her. What if I'd wanted to marry her? What if I'd really liked the idea of us starting our family together? You would've screwed it all up for everyone."

"Like that would've ever happened. You were only proposing because Dad was making you. And besides that, you never would've been in this situation if you hadn't gone to that party pretending to be me. She went there looking for me, not you. So don't try to act all innocent and put out. If anyone swooped in and stole anything, *you* tried to snatch Kat away from *me*."

"Yeah, well, now you have your shot. I'm off the hook with Dad and she's all yours."

Sawyer narrowed his gaze at his brother with contempt. "No matter what you do, you always seem to get away with it."

"What is that supposed to mean?"

"It means that I've never met someone so reckless, so irresponsible, and yet you never get what's coming to you. You never pay the price for your actions. Somehow you always get off the hook. You don't have to marry the mother of your child. You didn't have to pay when you wrecked Tom's motorcycle. Dad smoothed things over when you got in trouble in school. No matter what happens, you never have to clean up your messes. You always get one of us to handle everything for you, and then you have the audacity to get irritable with me because I happened to fall in love with the girl you're supposed to be with?"

Finn opened his mouth, but stopped short of answering. His angry retort seemed to deflate inside him. He looked at his brother for a moment and shook his head. "Are you serious? You're in love with her?"

Sawyer clenched his jaw in irritation with himself for letting that slip. He and Finn didn't have the kind of relationship many twins had. They didn't share intimate details of their lives. Sawyer didn't want to hear about Finn's shenanigans and Finn was bored by most of what Sawyer did with his time. So this was a big moment for them both. An awkward one, too.

"Yes, I am," he said, turning away and putting the engagement ring box on the edge of his desk.

"And what the hell were you going to do if she accepted my proposal? Mope until the end of time?"

"I'm sure your marriage wouldn't have lasted that long," Sawyer quipped.

"Very funny," Finn said. "I'm being serious."

Sawyer shrugged. He hadn't really thought that far ahead. "Maybe moping. Maybe working myself into a bout of middle-aged hypertension. If she accepted your proposal, maybe I would've asked to take over in Beijing, and disappeared for a while. I thought she wanted to marry you. I wasn't going to interfere, no matter how I felt."

"Why not? You're always interfering in my life when you think I'm doing the wrong thing."

"*Because*…nothing was going to change the reality of the situation, and that was that Kat is having *your* child. Whether I loved her, whether she hated you. That's still *your* baby and I couldn't get in the way of that."

Finn dropped down into the guest chair and considered his brother's confession for a few minutes. "Does she love you?" he asked.

"I don't know." Sawyer followed suit and flopped down into his own desk chair with a heavy sigh. "We never really talked about it."

"But you said that she did want to marry me."

"I thought so. That's what she told Jade and Morgan on the Fourth of July."

"And yet, just a few short days later, she turned me down and made me look like an idiot in front of the whole family. I'd say she did some hard thinking since then. She's got to be in love with you. That's the only reason I could fathom."

"Because there's no way a woman wouldn't want to marry you otherwise?"

"I'm a catch, damn it. And so are you. I say she's in love with you."

Sawyer sat forward and rested his elbows on his knees. "Even if she is…what about your daughter?"

Finn paused and looked at his brother with surprise. His mouth dropped open as he scrambled for words. "She's… Kat's… *We're* having a girl?"

"Oh." Sawyer sat up straight, alarmed at letting that slip. "I didn't realize she hadn't told you yet. I'm sorry. The whole family knows. Morgan turned the yacht pink when we sailed on the Fourth."

Finn shook his head. "We didn't really get to chat about much, with everyone there. A daughter...wow. A daughter is exciting news. Perhaps a little bit of karma for me."

"Perhaps."

"And despite what you might think, I plan to be a part of my daughter's life. I might be a shameless flirt with commitment issues, but I'm not a deadbeat dad. Kat and I can work out the details, but I'll be involved with the baby. As for the mother..." His voice trailed off. "She obviously wants you. She should be with you."

Finn cupped the ring box on the edge of the desk and slid it across the smooth wood to Sawyer, who reached out and caught it before it could fall to the floor. "Take that," Finn said. "Give it to her. Hell, you're the one that picked it out, anyway. You knew what she would like. I'm sure she'd appreciate it a lot more coming from you."

"No, you should return it."

"Nah," Finn said. "There's no way I can walk back in there with a ring that expensive and tell the man at the counter that the woman said no. You take it or I'll stash it in a drawer somewhere and forget about it until some girl staying over finds it hidden away and thinks I'm about to propose. No thanks."

"It was expensive."

"So was that Jet Ski," Finn admitted. "And since I made you give it to me to go to that party for you, like a jerk, why don't we call it an even trade?"

Sawyer couldn't believe his ears. He'd dropped nearly twenty grand on that Jet Ski and yet it didn't come close to the price of Kat's ring. But he realized this was Finn's way of saying he was sorry. His pride wouldn't let him voice the words, not even to Sawyer. But he meant it in his way.

Getting up from his chair, Sawyer walked around the desk and stood in front of his brother with the velvet box in his hand. "You're sure?"

"Take it. Give it to her. Live happily ever after with the mother of my child," Finn said, as he rose to his feet. "Yes, you'll be my daughter's stepdad/uncle and I'll be her dad/uncle, but who cares about labels? We'll all raise our daughter together in whatever weird way makes sense for us, and it's nobody's damn business but ours."

Sawyer looked at Finn with amazement, and for the first time in a long time, felt the urge to give him a hug. He actually couldn't remember the last time he'd hugged his brother. But before he could do so, Finn surprised him and reached out to him instead. He wrapped his arms around Sawyer and patted him firmly on the back.

"Be good to them," he said. Then he turned and walked out of Sawyer's office without another word.

Kat had a million things to do before the District shut down in a few days. She hadn't done a single thing in preparation for the baby. She needed to clean house and buy groceries. So naturally, she was sitting on her piazza drinking tea and reading a book. It was a best-selling self-help title she'd picked up from the library. The author promised to help her identify her own self-sabotaging habits and live her best life.

So far it was stupid. But it was easier to read than think about what kind of disaster her life had turned into lately.

Some people would say things weren't that bad. She'd chosen not to marry a man who was all wrong for her. She supposed that was for the best, even if she did have to turn down Finn in front of his family. Despite that hurdle, her relationship with Finn may have actually become better for the rejection. He'd obviously been pressured to make the proposal and seemed relieved when she turned him down.

They'd had lunch together a few days later and finally got the opportunity to talk without anyone else around. Without interfering fathers and overprotective attorneys, they'd hammered out a plan to co-raise their daughter that made them both happy. Finn agreed to pay for private schools, and would be buying a place closer to Kat, with a bedroom for nights he had custody. Kat hadn't really wanted or needed his money, but would accept the child support payments he insisted on, given that he reduce the monthly amount in favor of setting up a trust fund for the baby that she would get when she turned twenty-one.

It was all very civilized.

And if Kat had heard from Sawyer since he'd walked

out of that family dinner, she might feel better about how it was all turning out. But she hadn't.

Perhaps she had read the whole situation wrong. Sawyer had told her he didn't have any reason why she shouldn't marry Finn. Maybe he'd been telling the truth. Maybe he wanted her only because he knew he couldn't have her. She was a forbidden temptation. And now she was just a single, pregnant lady. Not very tempting at all.

The sound of the doorbell caused Kat to sit up and set the book aside. Glancing out, she noticed a black Rolls Royce parked on the street. She went to the door and opened it, finding none other than Ingrid Steele standing on her stoop.

"Mrs. Steele? I mean, Ingrid?" She corrected herself. "What are you doing here?"

"I'm paying a call on my future granddaughter-in-law," she said. "May I come in?"

Startled, Kat took a step back and welcomed the older woman inside. "Would you like to sit on the piazza or in the house? I'll get us both a glass of tea."

"The piazza and tea sound lovely."

Kat rushed into the house to get some tea and returned to find Ingrid sitting patiently on one of her patio chairs. She handed her the glass and wished she had some kind of cookies or treats in the house to offer. Unfortunately, all she'd bothered to get at the grocery store of late were saltine crackers, cereal and granola bars. She wasn't sure if it was morning sickness carrying into the second trimester or if she was just nauseated by how awful things had become. Either way, chopped-up chocolate chip granola bars on a platter wouldn't quite cut it for the Steele matriarch.

"I didn't expect to see you today," Kat began. "Or for a while, considering how dinner ended the other night."

"Pish posh. You're family now, dear. The other night doesn't change that."

All things considered, Kat appreciated the sentiment. The Steeles weren't the average American family, but they were the closest thing she had. "She will be your great-granddaughter, of course," Kat said, rubbing her belly. It seemed to be growing a bit more every morning of late. "But I'm just...me."

"Well, maybe I'm old and sentimental, but I still think you'll be my granddaughter-in-law someday."

"You know that Finn and I aren't going to marry, right? He never really wanted to marry me. I think he only proposed because Trevor put him up to it."

Ingrid chuckled and shook her head. "Of course Trevor made him do it. But I'm not talking about Finn, dear. I'm talking about you and Sawyer."

Kat looked up from her tea in surprise. As far as she was aware, no one knew about what had happened between her and Sawyer. She forced the mouthful of tea down her throat without choking and asked, "What would make you say that?"

"I may be old, but I'm not blind, dear. There's been something simmering between you two this whole time. I saw that much at my garden party and during the Fourth of July gathering. It didn't matter that you rarely spoke and never touched. You were always stealing glances at each other when the other wasn't looking. I could feel the sexual tension in the air. If you were trying to hide how you feel, you were doing a terrible job, both of you."

Kat didn't bother to argue with her. There was no sense in lying about it now that things with Finn were settled. "Well, I honestly don't know how Sawyer feels about me. He never said anything."

"That doesn't mean much. Men are always stubborn about their feelings, especially in this family. I shouldn't say so, but Sawyer is my favorite grandchild. Even as a baby he was more serious and thoughtful. He would quietly sit in the grass and study a butterfly, while his brother ran through the yard, terrorizing everything in his path. He is my quiet grandchild, but still waters run deep in him. Just because he doesn't say it doesn't mean he doesn't feel it. How did he treat you?"

"When we weren't arguing...like gold."

"That sounds about right. Did you ever tell him how you felt?"

She gave a guilty shake of her head. "No. I was afraid to. And I kept telling myself that I should be with Finn, even though I knew it felt wrong. I thought it was best for the baby."

"What's best for the baby is what will make you happy, dear. Babies don't know anything about DNA or legitimacy. They just want to be surrounded by love and warmth. Don't you think Sawyer could give her that?"

"Absolutely. But he's not here. I haven't seen him since he ran out on dinner that night."

"I'm sure he's sitting at home wrestling with the situation, just like you are. He didn't bolt from the room in the middle of your brother's proposal because he had food poisoning. He couldn't bear to sit there and watch the woman he loved get engaged to someone else. I guarantee it."

"Yes, well, it's been days and I'm sure he's heard how it turned out by now. If he was trying to be a gentleman and let Finn have his chance first, it's done. He hasn't even texted to ask how I am."

Ingrid sipped her tea and then set it aside. "Sawyer is a lot like his grandfather in many ways. Maybe that's why I've always had such a soft spot in my heart for him. They're both perfectionists. Strategists. The two of them would play a single chess match for hours in the library. They didn't like to make a decision or move on a project until everything was just so. That might make them seem like they're slow to act, but once they've made a decision, they're absolutely certain they're making the right choice."

"So he's sitting at home trying to decide if he really wants me?"

"No, no. More than likely, he's plotting and planning how to woo you properly."

Kat wasn't sure she'd ever been wooed. But whatever he was planning—if anything—she wished he would go ahead and do it. She didn't like being in limbo.

"I wish I were as confident as you are," she said. "I asked him if he could tell me a reason why I shouldn't marry Finn, and he said he couldn't."

"Of course he couldn't. He wouldn't interfere if he thought that was what you wanted. It doesn't mean he didn't want to give you a reason. He probably could've named five reasons why you shouldn't marry Finn, without trying very hard. But he didn't believe it was the right thing to do."

"You think so?"

"I've seen my grandchildren grow from headstrong toddlers to corporate leaders and entrepreneurs. I know how they think. And I know," Ingrid said, as she reached out to cup Kat's cheek, "that he cares for you. Just give him time. I have faith that if you want to be a Steele, you will be before too long."

Ingrid looked down at her watch. "Well, dear, this was a lovely visit, but I've got to get going. I have an appointment to see my jeweler." She got up and slipped her purse over her arm.

Kat stood and followed her to the door. "Thank you for stopping by. I feel better about everything."

"I'm glad, dear. I'll be awaiting news."

Kat watched Ingrid go down her walkway and over to where a man was waiting to open the door to the Rolls. Once she'd settled inside, he shut the door and got in to drive her to her jeweler, or wherever her agenda was taking her next.

As the car disappeared around the next block, Kat let the piazza door close and returned to her spot on the sofa. She shoved the book to the other side of the cushions and thought over everything Ingrid had told her.

Perhaps Sawyer *was* sitting in his house, trying to decide on the perfect way to woo her. But she had no guarantees of that, just a confident grandmother. He could just as easily be working on his renovation plans for the District. That was right around the corner, and despite her best efforts, Kat was unable to stop it from happening. She was right back where she'd started, although now she had a baby on the way and a broken heart to complicate things.

That said, Kat wasn't the kind to sit around and wait on a man to decide what he wanted. She had a studio to relocate and a baby to plan for, so she would focus on what she could control. And if he ever showed up with his heart in his hands, maybe she wouldn't stomp on it the way he'd stomped on hers.

Twelve

It was the last day for the District as Kat knew it and loved it. By five today, everyone had to be gone, for renovations to begin. Most of the tenants had already moved out, leaving the old warehouse hollow and empty sounding, when it had once been filled with life and art.

She did love Sawyer, but a part of her would never forgive him for turning this place into some high-end mini-mall for people who liked to be seen as art savvy. Even if he just made repairs and reopened, it wouldn't be the same. Most of the people she knew wouldn't be returning, because they couldn't afford the rent. With each artist who had packed up and gone forever, the District lost a little bit of its soul.

Kat wasn't sure what she was going to do. She was

one of the few who could afford the new rent. She just wasn't certain she wanted to come back. It wouldn't be the same without Hilda and Zeke arguing, or the little chocolate shop owner coming around to test a new recipe on willing volunteers.

Kat's place had an old outbuilding at the head of the driveway that had once been the kitchen. It got so hot in Charleston during the summer that the early homes had been built with the kitchen separate from the rest. Kat's had been converted years later into a storage room when a new kitchen was added to the house, but it wouldn't take much to put her equipment out there. That would be more convenient, especially with the baby, but it wouldn't be the same.

As she opened the door to her studio, even it felt like its soul was gone. All her work and most of her tools were already packed up and gone. The movers had come the day before to take her bigger pieces of equipment and the giant owl that was too heavy for her to move. Today, she was taking a few last items off the walls and closing up shop.

The final thing, the most important thing, was for her to remove the sign above the shop door. The wooden plaque had been one of the first pieces she'd made when her father gifted her with some basic wood-working tools on her sixteenth birthday. The hand-carved sign had a crescent moon and stars etched around the edges, with a textured background that looked like cumulous clouds once she'd applied the dark oak stain and sealant. In the center were the words *Wooden Dreams*.

She had made the sign long before the idea of having her own studio developed. Her father had hung it proudly in the house, where it had stayed until after they'd passed and Kat sold her parents' home. After college, when she'd heard about spaces available at the District, she'd gone down to pick a location and knew exactly where the sign needed to be. It wasn't her best work, but it was one of her favorites, and Wooden Dreams became the name of her shop.

Looking up at it hanging there now, Kat felt the tears start to come.

Just one more item in the list of things she'd lost over the last few weeks. She'd lost her shop, her artist community, her chance at a family and, apparently, she'd lost her heart to a man too honorable to admit how he felt about her. Altogether, it was almost enough to send her back to the dark place she'd lived in after her parents died. Her little girl was the only thing keeping her going. And a little bit of hope. Hope that Sawyer might change his mind.

At least, if Grandma Ingrid was right to begin with. If she was wrong, then Kat had just given away her heart to someone who had no desire to take it. Either way, she hadn't heard a peep from Sawyer. Finn had called to let her know he was heading back to China, and Jade had texted her about setting up a date for a baby shower, but other than that, it was like before the baby, when there were no Steeles in her life.

She had to admit life was simpler then. And lonelier. But she loved her daughter's new family. So at least she had that.

In the empty cavern of the warehouse, the grind of the freight elevator was audible even on the far side where Kat's studio was located. She didn't pay much attention to it, though. It was probably another tenant here to load up their dreams and memories into cardboard boxes.

Instead, Kat unfolded her stepladder to take down her sign. On the second step, she couldn't quite grasp it, so she climbed to the third, which she hated because she felt so unsteady. Thankfully, she was able to hold on to the door frame as she reached up with her other hand to get the sign.

"Whoa," she said aloud, when the unexpected weight of the freed wooden panel threw off her balance. Her center of gravity was all out of whack because of the baby.

"Easy now," someone said, and she felt strong hands at her lower back and hip steadying her.

Kat tucked the sign under her arm and looked around to see who was there. To her surprise, it was Sawyer.

"Hand it to me," he said. "It will make it easier for you to get down."

She reluctantly passed him the sign and climbed down to the wood plank floors. Once she was on firm ground again, she snatched the sign from Sawyer and turned her back on him to return to her shop. While a part of her was happy to see him after all this time, he was the reason she was packing up today, hovering on the verge of tears.

"Kat?" Sawyer called after her in confusion.

"I appreciate your help in keeping me from falling, but why are you here?" she asked. "I haven't heard from you since the dinner party for your brother and then you show up out of the blue. It can't be just to see me or you wouldn't have waited so long. It must be because of the building. Are you here to make sure I don't chain myself to the front doors or something?"

Sawyer appeared contrite. He tucked his hands into his pants pockets and looked down at the ground the way he always did when he was thinking. "I'm sorry, Kat."

She put the sign into the last box she had left in the studio, and then turned around to face him. "Sorry about what? About closing this place down and uprooting everyone and everything I care about? About refusing to tell me how you felt for me, at the critical moment when I had to decide if I wanted to marry your brother? About disappearing off the face of the earth after I turned Finn down, making me wonder if I was crazy or just plain stupid for falling for you?"

He stood there and took every angry word she had to level at him. And when she was done, he reached into his breast coat pocket and pulled out an envelope addressed to her. "I'm sorry for all of it," he said.

Sawyer held out the envelope until Kat reluctantly took it from him. In the corner the address was imprinted for the District Arts Center. But it wasn't her District. This was his, with a fancy new logo to go with the new vision. She tore through the logo as she opened the envelope and pulled out the single-page notice inside.

Her eyes quickly scanned what was written, but she kept having to stop and go back because it didn't make any sense. She couldn't be reading the words she was reading. Starting back at the top, she went through it word by word, hoping this time she could believe what she saw.

It was an official letter from Sawyer's development company about the closure today. It stated that they expected to complete the necessary renovations in three months. At that time, any previous tenants who wanted to return to their studio would be grandfathered in to rent it at their current rate. Any new tenants would pay the higher rates.

Kat's hand began to tremble as she reached the end of the letter, making it hard to read. Especially while her eyes were overflowing with tears. Sawyer was going to fix the place up so it was safe, and let them return. Hilda and Zeke could reopen their studios. They could all do so if they chose to.

It was an incredible compromise and it made her angry that she hadn't thought of that first. But of course, Sawyer the Strategist had.

"Oh no," Sawyer said, whipping a pressed handkerchief from his pocket. "You're crying. I'm sorry. Please don't cry, Kat. I thought you would be happy."

She accepted the hankie, pressing it to her eyes and dabbing the tears from her cheeks. "I am happy. It's just, I don't know, pregnancy hormones combined with everything else. Ignore the tears."

Sawyer reached out to wipe a fresh one from her

cheek with his thumb. "That's hard for me to do. I don't like seeing you cry."

Kat shook her head. "I can't help it. What changed your mind about all this?"

"Once I realized how I felt about you, and that I wanted to be with you, I knew something had to be done about the situation here. You are more important to me than the bottom line. It may take a while to make back my investment in the renovations, but it isn't a rush. I think what I have planned will allow the community here to continue safely, but also bring in more foot traffic. It's a win-win, as long as you're happy." Sawyer reached out to take her hand.

"I'm happy," she said, as he squeezed it gently. "Thank you. On behalf of everyone here, thank you."

"I was just thinking, what would be the greatest gift I could give Kat for an engagement present?"

She froze in place, her hand still in his. She was almost uncertain she'd heard what he'd said, since he continued talking as though he hadn't dropped a bomb in the conversation.

"A ring is traditional, of course, and I have one of those, too, but I really wanted to give you something that would have meaning for you. This place is what brought us together, in a way, so it seemed sort of poetic that it would be what would bring us back together…for as long as we both shall live. I love you, Kat. More than anything."

"You love me?" Kat asked, the letter slipping from her fingers to the ground.

"I do. And I hope that you feel the same way. I

wasn't sure, so I'm taking a gamble here." Sawyer reached into the same pocket, this time pulling out a small velvet box. "Finn gave me the ring he proposed with. I knew you would like it, but it felt wrong to give you the same ring. I was going to buy a different one and then an opportunity came along that I couldn't pass up."

He opened the lid on the box, which looked a great deal older than the one Finn had presented to her. This ring was vintage, she presumed, without even looking at it. Once the box was fully open, Kat gasped at the sight.

The diamond ring was unlike anything she'd seen in the jewelry cases at the mall. It actually looked like a daisy. In the center was a large, round, canary-yellow diamond, surrounded by six smaller diamonds that were at least a third of a karat each. The flower was set in platinum, with leaves and vines engraved into the band. It was unique. Beautiful. And yet oddly familiar.

"This was the ring that my grandfather Edward gave Grandma Ingrid when he proposed. She wore it every day after that, even after he passed away, until a few days ago, when she gave it to me."

That's where she had seen it before. Ingrid had worn it every time she'd seen her. Except the last time, when she'd come by her house. Kat thought back to Ingrid's visit and her next stop, at the jeweler. Perhaps she'd been making plans then, having it cleaned or resized for Sawyer to give her.

"My grandparents were together for nearly sixty

years. I don't know how many I have to offer you, but I will happily give you any that I have left. If you'll have me."

"Will you marry me, Katherine?"

Sawyer dropped to one knee as he said the words and then held his breath. He wasn't certain what the answer was going to be. He'd thought for sure she would accept Finn's proposal, but she didn't. She hadn't said that she loved him, either. She'd just gotten weepy when he said the words, making him nervously talk far more than he'd intended to. But now he'd asked the question, and all he could do was await the answer.

After an extended moment of silence, he was getting more and more nervous.

"Kat?" he asked.

She was looking down at him with tears in her eyes and her hand covering her mouth.

"Are you okay?"

She nodded before wiping at her tears and taking a deep breath. "Sawyer, are you sure you want to marry me?"

He flinched at the question. "I'm absolutely sure. At the moment, I'm concerned about you, though. It doesn't sound like you want to marry me."

"I do," she said quickly, then crouched down until her eyes were level with his. "But what about the baby?"

Sawyer frowned. "What about her?"

Kat swallowed hard and bit her bottom lip. "Are you going to be okay with raising another man's child? Your brother's child at that. It's not the ideal way to start out a relationship, much less a marriage."

"You're pregnant?" Sawyer asked, with mock dismay and surprise.

Kat punched him in the shoulder. "I'm serious. It's a lot to ask of you, to help me raise Finn's baby. You and I both know how he can be. I have no idea how involved he's really going to be in her life. I'm not going to pretend it isn't a big deal."

Sawyer understood her concerns. He'd spent the last week thinking all this through. He made sure every eventuality was thought through, every *t* crossed and every *i* dotted. He no longer had any doubts about what he wanted to do, so he had to make sure the next words he spoke were enough to convince her that it wasn't the issue she believed it to be.

"Kat, I love you. And I love that baby. I have since the first moment I saw her on the screen and heard her heartbeat echo through the examination room. Yes, she's my brother's child. But that's as close as she could possibly be without being my own. As far as I'm concerned, she's as much mine as she is Finn's daughter, and that's how I'm going to treat her.

"I want to be there for every doctor's appointment. I'm going to be there when she's born and I'll fight Finn to hold her first. I want to be there when she takes her first steps and says her first words. That baby is a part of you, and a part of Finn. And as much as he makes me crazy sometimes, you two are the most important people in my life. So that means this baby is going to be an amazing combination of the two of you. She's already the love of my life. The apple of my eye. And I'll love her just as much as I'll love any children that you and I may have together someday."

"Stop now, or I'm going to get jealous," Kat said through her tears.

Sawyer smiled and reached out to caress her cheek. "There's nothing to be jealous about. There's not going to be another woman in South Carolina who is as loved and adored as my wife will be. But first, she's got to accept my proposal." He slipped the ring out of the box and held it up to Kat. "So what do you say? Do you want to marry me and become Mrs. Sawyer Steele?"

Kat looked at him and nodded through her tears. "I do. Yes!" She held out her hand and let him slip the family heirloom onto her finger. "It fits perfectly," she said, before leaning in and giving Sawyer a kiss.

"I know this isn't how you wanted things to turn out, or the family you envisioned when you came looking for Finn that day—" Sawyer began.

"It's not," Kat interrupted. "It's so much better." She kissed him again and he knew that she was right.

Their future together would be perfectly imperfect.

Epilogue

"And with the cutting of this ribbon, I'm happy to declare that the District Art Center is now officially reopened!"

Sawyer gave the nod to Kat and she, along with several of her fellow artisans, used the ridiculously large scissors to cut the ribbon. The audience cheered and the media happily filmed the crowds as they pushed through the front door to see the new and improved District.

Kat was bursting with pride as Sawyer sidled up beside her and wrapped his arm around her ever expanding waist. She was just a week into her third trimester now and she was starting to feel like an overfilled balloon. She couldn't imagine getting bigger and yet she had nearly three months left to go. Beatrice Astrid Steele, or Sweet Bea, as Sawyer referred to her, would be arriving sometime around Christmas. It was the best present she could ever expect.

The renovation of the District was a close second. Sawyer and his team had done amazing work on the building. It was basically a gut job, by necessity, but now there were sound floors covered in ceramic tile, ceilings that weren't on the verge of falling onto anyone's head, electrical and plumbing systems that worked and a new, blessed addition—air-conditioning and insulation. The open space around the warehouse was redone, too, with benches and fountains, trees, and an outdoor amphitheater for musical and theatrical performances. Later tonight, one of the local bands was going to be playing a concert to celebrate the reopening.

Kat and Sawyer followed the crowd inside. Most of the former artisans had returned, but in the unrented studios and newly developed spaces, there were some additions. Not only did they gain new painters, jewelry makers and other crafters, but they got some food vendors, too. A Mediterranean falafel place opened up near the entrance, an artisan Popsicle shop was on the third floor and a cupcake bakery—Kat's favorite stop—was on the ground floor.

There were no commercial chains, something Sawyer had promised her, but there was definitely a nice, upscale feel about the place now. Yes, there were artists at work, but it didn't feel like they were squatters in an abandoned warehouse any longer. It felt like they belonged, and their art was something worth coming to the District to see and, hopefully, to buy.

As they reached Kat's studio, with her Wooden Dreams sign in place, she was surprised to see there were already a few people eyeing her work. She kissed Sawyer on the cheek and went over to chat with her potential new customers.

A few minutes and a sale later, she turned back to find Sawyer on the phone. His face was as white as it had been the day he'd found out she was pregnant with Finn's child. Something was wrong.

She waited on eggshells until he ended the call and then turned to her. "What is it?" she asked.

"There's been an accident. Finn's private jet back from Beijing lost radio contact somewhere near the West Coast. They think the plane went down near Portland, Oregon."

Kat brought her hand to her mouth in shock. "Oh my God. Do they know if anyone survived?"

Sawyer shook his head. "They don't know. Rescue crews are searching for the plane in the woods and out at sea, but without a good idea of where it might've gone down, it might be a while before we know for sure if Finn is dead or alive."

* * * * *

LET'S TALK
Romance

For exclusive extracts, competitions
and special offers, find us online:

JOIN THE
MILLS & BOON
BOOKCLUB

* **FREE** delivery direct to your door

* **EXCLUSIVE** offers every month

* **EXCITING** rewards programme

50% OFF
YOUR FIRST
PARCEL

Join today at
Millsandboon.co.uk/Bookclub

MILLS & BOON

THE HEART OF ROMANCE

A ROMANCE FOR EVERY READER

MODERN

Prepare to be swept off your feet by sophisticated, sexy and seductive heroes, in some of the world's most glamourous and romantic locations, where power and passion collide.

HISTORICAL

Escape with historical heroes from time gone by. Whether your passion is for wicked Regency Rakes, muscled Vikings or rugged Highlanders, awaken the romance of the past.

MEDICAL

Set your pulse racing with dedicated, delectable doctors in the high-pressure world of medicine, where emotions run high and passion, comfort and love are the best medicine.

True Love

Celebrate true love with tender stories of heartfelt romance, from the rush of falling in love to the joy a new baby can bring, and a focus on the emotional heart of a relationship.

Desire

Indulge in secrets and scandal, intense drama and plenty of sizzling hot action with powerful and passionate heroes who have it all: wealth, status, good looks…everything but the right woman.

HEROES

Experience all the excitement of a gripping thriller, with an intense romance at its heart. Resourceful, true-to-life women and strong, fearless men face danger and desire - a killer combination!

To see which titles are coming soon, please visit

millsandboon.co.uk/nextmonth